THE
GIFT
OF
RAIN

THE
GIFT
OF
RAIN

TAN TWAN ENG

WEINSTEIN
BOOKS

Grateful acknowledgement is made for permission to reprint
excerpts from the following printed material:

Two haiku (*Wild Geese* and *Dreaming Heart*) from
On Love and Barley: Haiku of Basho by Matsuo Basho, translated by
Lucien Stryk ©1985 University of Hawaii Press.
Reprinted with permission.

Lines from *The Diving Bell and the Butterfly* by Jean-Dominique Bauby © 1997
Reproduced by permission of Alfred A. Knopf a division of Random House Inc.

To the heirs and estate of Solomon Bloomgarden (1870–1927) the author and
publishers express their gratitude and appreciation for the inclusion of
his poem *Yehoash (An Old Song)*, translated by Marie Syrkin and
last published in *An Anthology of World Poetry*,
ed. Mark van Doren (Cassell & Co. Ltd, 1929)

ISBN: 978-1-60286-074-2

First Paperback Edition
10   9   8   7   6   5   4   3   2   1

For my parents,
En vir Regter AJ Buys wat my geleer het hoe om te lewe.

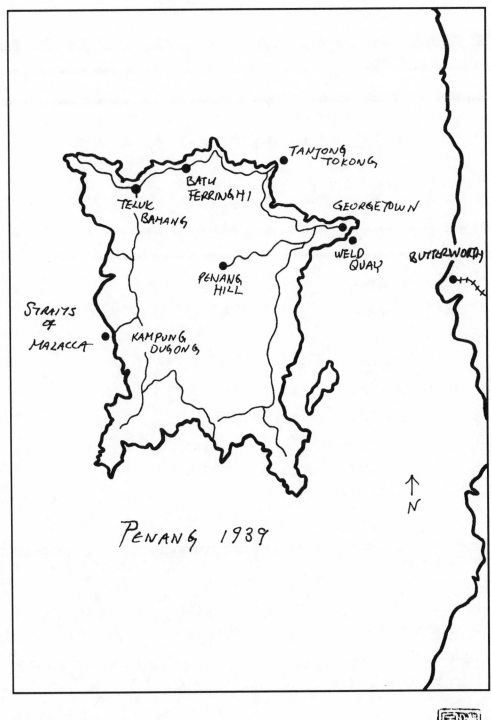

TANJONG
TOKONG

BATU
FERRINGHI

GEORGETOWN

TELUK
BAHANG

WELD
QUAY

BUTTERWORTH

PENANG
HILL

STRAITS
OF
MALACCA

KAMPUNG
DUGONG

↑
N

PENANG 1939

"I am fading away. Slowly but surely. Like the sailor who watches his home shore gradually disappear, I watch my past recede. My old life still burns within me, but more and more of it is reduced to the ashes of memory."

The Diving Bell & the Butterfly, Jean-Dominique Bauby

BOOK ONE

Chapter One

I was born with the gift of rain, an ancient soothsayer in an even more ancient temple once told me.

This was back in a time when I did not believe in fortune-tellers, when the world was not yet filled with wonder and mystery. I cannot recall her appearance now, the woman who read my face and touched the lines on my palms. She said what she was put into this world to say, to those for whom her prophecies were meant, and then, like every one of us, she left.

I know her words had truth in them, for it always seemed to be raining in my youth. There were days of cloudless skies and unforgiving heat, but the one impression that remains now is of rain, falling from a bank of low-floating clouds, smearing the landscape into a Chinese brush painting. Sometimes it rained so often I wondered why the colors around me never faded, were never washed away, leaving the world in moldy hues.

The day I met Michiko Murakami, too, a tender rain had dampened the world. It had been falling for the past week and I knew more would come with the monsoon. Already the usual roads in Penang had begun to flood, the sea turning to a sullen gray.

On this one evening the rain had momentarily lessened to an almost undetectable mist, as though preparing for her arrival. The light was fading and the scent of wet grass wove through the air like threads entwining with the perfume of the flowers, creating an intricate tapestry of fragrance. I was out on the terrace, alone as I had been for many years, on the edge of sleep, dreaming of another life. The door chimes echoed through the house, hesitant, unfamiliar in a place they seldom entered, like a cat placing a tentative paw on a path it does not habitually walk.

I woke up; far away in time I seemed to hear another chiming, and I lay in my chair, confused. For a few moments a deep sense of loss immobilized me. Then I sat up and my glasses, which had been resting on my chest, fell to the tiles. I picked them up slowly, wiped them clean with my shirt, and found the letter which I had been reading lying under the chair. It was an invitation from the Penang Historical Society to mark the fiftieth anniversary of the end of the Second World War. I had never attended any of the society's events but the invitations still came regularly. I folded it and got up to answer the door.

She was a patient woman, or she was very certain that I would be at home. She rang only once. I made my way through the darkened hallways and opened the heavy oak doors. I guessed her to be in her seventies, not much older than I was. She was still beautiful, her clothes simple in the way only the very expensive can be, her hair fine and soft, pulled back into a knot. She had a single small valise, and a long narrow wooden box leaned against her leg.

"Yes?" I asked.

She told me her name, with an expectation that seemed to suggest that I had been waiting for her. Yet it still took me a few seconds to find a mention of her in the vastness of my memory.

I had heard her spoken of only once before, by a wistful voice in a distant time. I tried to think of a reason to turn her away but could find none that was acceptable, for I felt that this woman had, ever since that moment, been set upon a path that would lead her to the door of my home. I took the gloved hand she offered. With its scarce flesh and thin prominent bones it felt like a bird, a sparrow with its wings wrapped around itself.

I nodded, smiled sadly, and led her through the house, pausing to put the lights on as we passed each room. The clouds had brought the night in early and the servants had already gone home. The marble floors were cold, absorbing the chill of the air but not the echo of our footsteps.

We went out to the terrace and into the garden. We passed a collection of marble statues, a few with broken limbs lying on the grass, mold eating away their luminosity like an incurable skin disease. She followed me silently, and we stopped under the casuarina tree that grew on the edge of the small cliff overlooking the sea. The tree, as old as I, gnarled and tired, gave us a small measure of shelter as the wind shook flecks of water from the leaves into our faces.

"He lies across there," I said, pointing to the island. Though less than a mile from the shore, it appeared like a gray smudge on the sea, almost invisible through the light veil of rain. The obligation to a guest, however unsettling her presence, compelled me to ask, "You'll stay for dinner?"

She nodded. Then, in a swift movement that belied her age, she knelt on the wet earth and brought her head to rest on the grass. I left her there, bowing to the grave of her friend. For the moment we both knew silence was sufficient. The things to be said would come later.

It felt strange to cook for two, and I had to remind myself to double the quantities of ingredients. As always—whenever I cook— I left a wake of opened spice bottles, half-cut vegetables, ladles, spoons, and various plates dripping with sauces and oil. Maria, my maid, often complains about the mess I leave. She also nags me to replace the kitchen implements, most of which are of pre-war British manufacture and still going strong, if rather noisily and with great cantankerousness, like the old English mining engineers and planters who sit daily in the bar of the Penang Swimming Club, sleeping off their lunches.

I looked out to the garden through the large kitchen windows. She was standing now beneath the tree, her body unmoving as the wind shook the branches and scattered a shower of glittering drops onto her. Her back had retained its straightness and her shoulders were level, without the disconsolate droop of age. Her skin's suppleness fought against the lines on her face, giving her the look of a determined woman.

She was in the living room when I came through from the kitchen. The room, to which I have never made any changes, was wood-paneled, the plaster ceiling and cornices high and dark. Black marble statues of mythological Roman heroes held torches that only dimly lit up the corners of the room. The chairs were of heavy Burmese teak and covered in cracked leather, their shapes deformed by the generations that had sat on them. My great-grandfather had had them made in Mandalay when he built Istana. A Schumann baby grand piano stood in a corner. I always kept it in perfect tune, although it had not been played for many years.

She was examining a wall of photographs, perhaps hoping to find his face among them. She would be disappointed. I had never had a photograph of Endo-san; among all the photographs we took, there was never one of him, or of us together. His face was painted in my memory.

She pointed to one now. "Aikikai Hombu Dojo?"

My eyes followed her finger. "Yes," I said.

It was a photograph of me, taken at the World Aikido Headquarters, in the Shinjukku district of Tokyo, with Morihei Ueshiba, the founder of aikido. I was dressed in a white cotton *gi*— a training uniform—and *hakama*, the traditional black trousers worn by the Japanese, staring intently at the camera's eye, my hair still dark. Next to my five foot eleven inches, O' Sensei, the Great Teacher, as he was called, looked tiny, childlike, and deceptively vulnerable.

"You still teach?"

I shook my head. "Not anymore," I replied in Japanese.

She named some of the people she knew, all high-ranking masters. I nodded in recognition at each name and for a while we talked of them. Some had died; some, like me, had retired. Yet others, though in their late eighties, continued to train faithfully as they had for almost all of their lives.

She pointed to another photograph. "That must be your father," she said. "You have his face."

The monochrome photograph of my family had been taken by our driver just before the war. We were all standing in front of the portico and the light of the sun and the sea made my father's blue eyes paler, his teeth brighter. His carefully combed white hair seemed like part of the glare of the cloudless sky.

"He was very good-looking," she said.

We were standing around him: Edward, William, and Isabel from his first marriage, and I from his last, each of us carrying his face in one feature or another. There was a timeless quality to our smiles, as though we would always be together, laughing, loving life. I remember the day still, from across the distance of the fleeting years. It was one of the rare moments when I had felt I was part of my family.

"Your sister?" she asked, moving to another photograph. I nodded and looked at Isabel on the balcony outside her room, her rifle in her hand, cheeks sucked in with determination as the lights from below seemed to lift her up. I could almost feel the soft wind that ruffled her skirts.

"Taken at the last party we ever had," I said. "Before the war wrecked everything."

The rain had stopped, and I suggested to Michiko that we have our meal out on the terrace. She insisted on helping me lay the table, and I rolled back the canopy to open the sky to us. We sat beneath a patch of stars, flickering seeds in a furrow in the clouds.

She had a hearty appetite, despite the simplicity of the meal I had made. She was also entertaining; it was almost as though we had known each other all our lives. She took a sip of the tea I had served, looked surprised, and lifted the cup to her nose. I watched her carefully, wondering if she would pass my test.

"Fragrance of the Lonely Tree," she said, correctly identifying the brew which I had specially imported from Japan. "Harvested from tea plantations near my home. One could not obtain it after the war as the terraced fields had been destroyed."

At the end of the meal she held up her wineglass and made a graceful gesture to the island. "To Endo-san," she said softly.

I nodded. "To Endo-san."

"Listen," she said. "Do you hear him?"

I closed my eyes and, yes, I heard him. I heard him breathe. I smiled wanly. "He's always here, Michiko. That's why, wherever I go, I always yearn to return."

She took my hand in hers and again I felt its birdlike fragility. When she spoke her voice was full of sorrow. "My poor friend. How you have suffered."

I pulled my hand away carefully. "We have all suffered, Michiko. Endo-san most of all."

We sat without speaking. The sea sighed each time a wave collapsed on the shore like a long-distance runner at the finishing line. I have always felt a greater affinity with the sea at night. It is magnificent during the day, the waves strong and loud, slamming onto the beach, propelled by the force of the entire ocean behind it. But when night comes that force is spent, and the waves roll to the shore with the detachment of a monk unfurling a scroll.

Then, softly, she began to tell me about her life. She spoke in a rapid, natural mixture of Japanese and English, the two interlacing like colored threads, spinning her tale.

"I am a widow new to my white robes. My husband, Murakami Ozawa, departed earlier this year."

"My condolences," I said, unsure where she was leading me.

"I had been married to Ozawa for fifty-five years. He owned an electronics company, a well-known one. His death made my world, my whole life, suddenly senseless. I was set adrift, and I closed myself up in my home in Tokyo, shutting out the world. I spent my days in the spacious gardens, walking barefoot across the pebble fields, spoiling the neat circles created by Seki, our gardener. He never complained, but only created the patterns again, day after day," she said, a lost look in her eyes.

She could find no strength to pull herself out of her grief, she told me. Outside, the company's board was frantic, for she had been bequeathed the controlling shares by her husband. She shut them all out and took no calls. The servants stirred the silences of her home with fearful whispers.

But the world intruded. "I received a letter from Endo-san," she said, and her movement of looking away from me, as though she had been distracted by the glimmer of dew in the grass, was so unforced that anyone else would have thought it natural.

I was grateful for her kindness, although I managed to absorb her news with greater equanimity than she had given me credit for. "When did he send it?" I asked.

"Over fifty years ago, in the spring of 1945," she said, giving me a smile. "It came out of the past like a ghost. Can you imagine its journey? He had written about his life here, and he had written about you."

I let her fill our glasses. I had visited Japan often enough to know she would feel insulted if I had poured.

"I will tell you how we met," she said after a while, as though she had been mulling over the decision for some time.

"Endo-san worked for his father, who owned a successful trading business. In fact, he was already running the business, traveling around China and to Hong Kong. He spent his evenings teaching in the *aikijutsu* school in our village. As the daughter of a samurai I was expected to be proficient with the sword, and in unarmed combat—*bujutsu*—above all other arts. Unlike my sisters I enjoyed *bujutsu* more than my music and flower-arranging lessons.

"At that time *aikijutsu* was just a fledgling art; it had not evolved into the aikido of today. My father was not impressed with it, but when I saw the class, and the movements, I knew I had found something precious. I think you know what I felt: it was as though my heart, long held in darkness, had turned to catch a glimpse of the warmth and light of the sun."

She laughed softly. "I soon began to treasure the time I spent with Endo-san. My school friends teased me terribly about my feelings for him. But still I dreamed and dreamed, and wrapped myself in clouds of make-believe.

"As the eldest son he was expected to take over the company from his father one day. He was very often away from the country. On his return he brought me gifts, from China, Siam, the islands of the Philippines, and once even a woven headscarf from the mountains of northern India.

"We began to see each other regularly. We would walk along the beach, gazing out to the Miyajima Torii Shrine, and I often met him for tea in the pavilion in the park, feeding the ducks and the obedient lines of ducklings in the lake. I think those were the happiest days I can remember.

"My initial infatuation matured into something deeper and more permanent. My father, who was a magistrate, did not approve of our friendship. Endo-san was of course very much older than me, and his family, although originally of the samurai class, had been relegated to the status of merchants, a very low position on our social order, as you may know. His father had decided to turn the family's various farms and properties into commercial concerns. They were wealthy, but not acceptable to the aristocracy."

I leaned forward, not wishing to miss anything. Endo-san had given me only a cursory description of his childhood and he had never fully revealed his background. During the years when I lived in Japan I had tried to conduct my own inquiries, but without much success, as the documentary records had all been destroyed. But now, hearing it from her, from one who had been there, my curiosity was stirred once again.

She saw my interest and continued.

"The fact that Endo-san's father was a disgraced court official was very much talked about in our village. But that did not bother me at all. In fact, my feelings for him were strengthened and I often said very rude things to his family's detractors.

"My father felt that I was spending too much time with Endo-san, and I was forbidden to see him." She shook her head. "What obedient children we were. There was no question of ignoring my father's commands. I cried every night, for it was a terrible time for me.

"It was also a terrible time for Japan. To survive, we had become a military nation; you are a scholar of Japan, so you know what it was like. Oh, the endless chanting and shouting of war slogans, the violent clashes between the militarists and the pacifists in the streets, the frightening marches and demonstrations—I hated all of them. Even in my deepest dreams I heard them.

"Endo-san's father disagreed with the military and made his opinions widely known. This was seen as acting against the emperor, a crime of treason. His father was sent to prison and the family was ostracized. Endo-san's views reflected his father's, although he was more subtle in expressing them. Still, there were attempts on Endo-san's life, but he remained obdurate. This, I think, was due in part to his *sensei*."

I nodded. Endo-san had studied under O' Sensei Ueshiba, a well-known pacifist who was, paradoxically, one of the greatest Japanese martial artists of all time. I recalled the first time I met O' Sensei. The man was then in his late sixties, suffering from illness, just a few months from death; yet he had thrown me around the training mats until I could not breathe, my head dizzy from the falls, my joints sore where he had locked me.

I told Michiko this and she laughed. "I too was thrown around like a rag doll by him."

She stood up and walked out into the night, then turned back to me and said, "One day, a few months later and after Endo-san had been away for some weeks, I met him again. I was on my way home from the market, and he came up behind me and told me to meet him on the beach, where we had sat so often. I went home, pretended to my mother that I had left something at the market, and then ran all the way to the beach.

"I saw him first. He was facing the sea. The sun looked as if it had leaked its color into the sea, into his face and eyes. When I reached him, he told me he was leaving Japan for a few years.

" 'Where will you go?' I asked him."

" 'I do not know yet. I wish to see the world, and find my answers,' he replied."

" 'Answers to what?' I asked."

"He shook his head. Then he told me he had been having strange dreams, dreams of different lives, different countries. He refused to tell me more.

"I told him I would wait for him, but he said no, that I should live the life that had already been written for me. To attempt to do otherwise would be foolish. We were not meant to be together. My future was not with him.

"I was so angry with him, talking like that. I told him he was *baka*—an idiot. And you know, he only smiled and said that it was true.

"That was the last time I saw him. Later I heard that he had been sent by the government to some place in Asia, some country I had never even heard of—Malaya. It was very puzzling, I thought then, that a man so opposed to Japan's aggressive military policies should have accepted service with the government.

"But as I have said, I never saw him again, even when he came back for a short visit. I could not, however much I longed to. My father had arranged a marriage for me, and I was being taught how to take care of my future husband and run his house. Ozawa, like Endo-san, was involved in his family's company, which was then making electronic equipment for the war."

She paused, and in her face made translucent by memory I saw the girl she had once been and I felt a faint sadness for Endo-san, for what he had thrown aside.

"I have never stopped thinking of him," she said.

I pushed back my chair, feeling tired by the conversation, disturbed by the emotions her arrival had awoken within me.

"May I stay here for the night?" she asked.

I was disinclined to allow another person to unsettle the structure of my life, which had been laid out carefully over the years. I had always appreciated my own company and the few people who had tried to breach my barrier had always been hurt in the process. I looked out to the sea; there was no guidance from Endo-san but that had never stopped me from asking him. It was late and the taxi services in Penang were notoriously bad. Finally I nodded.

She was aware of my reluctance. "I apologize for causing you inconvenience," she said.

I waved her apologies away and stood up, wincing at my stiff joints, hearing the expected pops and cracks in them—the symptoms of age and the lack of training. Old injuries sent their repetitive messages of wear and pain, urging me to surrender, which I always refused to do.

I started to clear away the remains of our meal, stacking the plates into little piles.

"You have no picture of him?" she asked as she helped me carry the plates to the kitchen.

I saw the faintest expression of hope in her eyes, like a weak flaring star, and I shook my head. "No. We never took any," I replied, watching the flare sink into the ocean.

She nodded. "Neither did I. Our village did not have cameras at the time he left Japan. It is so ironic, really—my husband's company now produces some of the most popular cameras in the world."

I led her up the stairs to one of the more serviceable guestrooms. It had been Isabel's room. After the war I had had the bedrooms redecorated, in an attempt to start anew, and sometimes I wondered if I should have bothered. I only see the rooms as they were, hear them as they used to sound, and smell them as if it were still fifty years ago. Someone once asked me if Istana was haunted and I had replied, why yes, of course, naturally so. It is no wonder that I seldom have visitors.

On the landing halfway up the stairs, she stopped, her eyes drawn to the wall where a hole had been gouged out.

"Isabel, my sister. She shot at someone here," I explained. I had never had the scar in the wall covered up.

At the entrance to the room I gave a bow to Michiko and she returned a deeper one. I left her and walked slowly through the house, locking the doors, closing the windows, putting out the lights one by one. Then I made my way to the balcony outside my room. It was the same room I had always had from the moment I was born. I felt a sense of time stretching back, curving beyond sight like the shoreline of an immense bay. How many people in this world can say they have had the same room from birth and, in my case, probably until death?

The high winds had swept the clouds from the sky. It was turning into a crisp, clean night, and the layers and layers of stars above me added an immeasurable depth to the darkness. I thought about the letter Michiko had received from Endo-san. Fifty years! It would have been written four years after the Japanese invaded Malaya, toward the end of the war. The chaotic conditions of countries at war, the paranoia, the seas constantly patrolled by battleships and aircraft, all could have accounted for the letter getting lost. Fifty unimaginable years stretched out like a vast piece of fraying, sun-bleached cloth fluttering in the wind. Had it been that long?

Sometimes it had seemed longer.

Under the ancient light of a thousand stars I made out Endo-san's island, sleeping in the swaying embrace of the waves. I have resisted all offers to buy that fragment of land and have kept it clean and as it was, with his little wooden house beneath the trees, the clearing where we used to practice, the beach where my boat would always touch land.

Memories—they are all the aged have. The young have hopes and dreams, while the old hold the remains of them in their hands and wonder what has happened to their lives. I looked back hard on my life that night, from the moments of my reckless youth, through the painful and tragic years of the war, to the solitary decades after. Yes, I could say that I had lived my life, if not to the full then at least almost to the brim. What more could one ask? Rare is the person whose life overflows. I have lived, I have traveled the world, and now, like a worn-out clock, my life is winding down, the hands slowing, stepping out of the flow of time. If one steps out of time what does one have? Why, the past of course, gradually being worn away by the years as a pebble halted on a riverbed is eroded by the passage of water.

A beam from the lighthouse farther up Moonlight Bay lit up the night. Here it came again, and again, and again. When I was a boy, my father, in the rare moments when he had not been too busy with work, told Isabel and me its history. I could even remember the name of the man who guarded the lighthouse then—Mr. Deepak, whose wife jumped off the lighthouse and hit the rocks below when she found out he had been unfaithful to her. Mr. Deepak was long dead now, yet the lighthouse lived on, a lonely sentinel of the sea still carrying out its archaic duty even in this modern age.

I left the balcony and went into my room and tried to get some sleep. That night, as always, I asked to dream of Endo-san.

The following morning, unlike all the mornings of the past five years, I decided to train again. I found my *gi*, neatly pressed by Maria, in a cupboard. It was my favorite piece, and a slight trace of perspiration, which could never be completely washed away, teased my nose as I unfolded it.

I had converted two rooms on the ground floor of Istana into a *dojo*, a Place of the Way, when I started teaching. The floor was paneled with Japanese pine, polished to a perfect gloss then covered with thick training mats. Fresh lilies were placed daily in a small vase in the *tokonama*, the shrine in a little alcove that also held a portrait of O' Sensei Ueshiba. A wall of mirrors faced a row of high glass doors that opened out to the lawns and beyond them to the sea.

I had limited my class to ten students and had seen them obtain their higher grades, then open their own schools. We had often traveled to seminars and conventions around the world, giving exhibitions and classes, and learning from other masters. My former students used to call me occasionally, trying to tempt me back to that world. But I refused, and told them I had removed myself from the River and the Lake, adopting the Cantonese phrase *"toi chut kong woo,"* used to describe warriors who had voluntarily left their violent world to seek peace.

Sitting in the *seiza* position, buttocks resting on my heels, I began to meditate. It came back to me slowly as I sat there feeling the morning sun warm my face. After twenty minutes I picked up my *bokken*, raised it horizontally in both hands, and bowed to O' Sensei. Then I bowed to the wooden sword and practiced my cuts.

The *bokken* is used in training, when a real *katana* sword is impractical and dangerous. That does not mean it is not an effective weapon. Some swordsmen I have met actually prefer it to the metal blade, and Miyamoto Musashi, the Sword Saint of Japan, was well known for going to duels armed only with two wooden swords against a live *katana*.

My *bokken* was about three and a half feet long, made by a craftsman in Shikoku famous for his skills with cedar. I used to practice five thousand cuts daily, through the top and sides of the opponent's head, cutting through his upper body, splitting him in half, from left shoulder to right hip, the arms moving without thought, cutting so precisely that there was not even a whisper as the wood sliced through the air. This particular morning I lost count when I reached two thousand, but my body knew, and I gave myself to it, seeing nothing, but aware of everything. Light filled my vision; lightness filled my being, embodying the principle that had been absorbed into me:

Stillness in Movement,
Movement in Stillness.

When I had finished I found Michiko facing me in her training uniform. I brought my sword out before me and bowed to it before placing it back on its wooden stand. Wordlessly we practiced with each other, using just our bare hands. Due to my seniority in rank I insisted on being the *nage*, the person defending and throwing. As the attacking *uke*, she had to trust me not to injure her or use excessive force. Endo-san used to tell me that trust between a pair of training partners was the foundation of aikido training, for without it the *uke* would be fearful of creating the attack necessary for perfecting the techniques.

She was extremely proficient, her *ukemi* falls soft and graceful, her hands never seeming to hit the mats in absorbing the force of my throws, but to stroke them gently, like a leaf settling down to the ground before being lifted lightly again by the merest flick of a breeze. She was nowhere near my level, but then very few people are. I was taught by a master and have had the experience of actually using my skills. In turn I became a *Shihan*, a teacher of teachers. Is that not the way of the world?

She expected me to switch roles and allow her to be the *nage*, as was the custom, but I shook my head and she did not protest. By the time we finished we were both soaked in perspiration, our breathing rapid, hearts hammering wildly as we sought to exert control over them.

"You are as good as people have said," she remarked, wiping her face with a towel.

I shook my head. "I used to be better." Long inactivity had eroded my sharpness. But what did I need those skills for now? At seventy-two, who was going to fight me?

She read my thoughts. "Your mind is still very strong," she said. "That is what training is for."

I noticed in the morning light how thin she was but refrained from asking about her health. Aikido trains a person to look and sense beyond the surface and, through the physical contact of training with her, I had felt that she was not well.

We had a light breakfast of porridge and dumplings on the terrace, beneath a bower of bean-vines. Maria came out with a tray of Boh tea. "Maria, this is Madam Michiko. She'll be staying with us for a while."

Michiko raised an eyebrow at me.

"Surely you don't need to stay in a hotel?" I asked, as Maria began complaining about the mess in the kitchen and I waved her away. "Stay here. Go to your hotel and pick up the rest of your things," I went on, enjoying the look of surprise on her face, knowing I had unbalanced her by anticipating her intentions.

I wanted to find out more about her childhood, about the life she had led with Endo-san. She was also good company. It had been a while since I had talked so candidly with another person. "You're most welcome to stay for a few days," I said. "I must ask you this, however: what is it you really want from me?"

"Will you take me to his home? To the little island he wrote about?" she asked.

It was a request I had expected and feared. I leaned back in my rattan chair. It was getting quite warm. Unlike the day before, there was not even a wisp of cloud above us.

"No," I said, finally. "I can't do that." I was not willing to allow anyone else into that part of my life I had shared with Endo-san.

"Then I would like to know what happened to Endo-san," she

said, absorbing my refusal with a greater grace than I had delivered it, echoing the quality of her *ukemi*.

"He is dead. Why do you wish to bring it up? What's the point?"

"He is not dead, here," she tapped her temple softly. She remained silent, and then she continued, "Something else came with the letter he sent."

She went inside the house and returned with a narrow box. Its presence had disturbed me from the moment I first saw it the evening before. I should have recognized the shape and length of it immediately but the wrapping had deceived me. Now I knew instantly what it held and I struggled to keep my composure.

She tore away the cardboard covering, and placed the box on the table. "You may open it."

"I know what it is," I said, my eyes hardening. But I reached out and opened the box and lifted Endo-san's Nagamitsu sword from the bed of cloth on which it had been resting. I had seen him using it so often, but it was the first time in my life that I had ever touched it. It was a simple yet elegant weapon, and the black lacquered scabbard protecting it, so cool and smooth in my hand, was plain, without any form of decoration. It was almost identical to mine, one of a pair forged by the famed swordsmith Nagamitsu in the late sixteenth century.

"It was terribly neglected and rusted when I finally received it. I had a retired swordsmith restore it." She shook her head. "Not many people know how to do it now. It is such a rare work, perhaps Nagamitsu's greatest creation. The swordsmith was quite honored to work on it. He spent seven months polishing, oiling, cleaning. He refused to accept any payment at the end."

She took it from my hands. "Can you recall the last time you saw Endo-san using it?" she asked.

I looked away. "Too well," I whispered, trying to block the sudden rush of memories, as though the sword itself had cut a gash in the dike I had built. "Only too well."

She looked up at me and a hand covered her mouth. "I did not mean to cause you pain. I am truly sorry."

"I'm late for a meeting," I said, getting up from the table. I was stunned to realize that, despite my years of training, I was disoriented. Her visit, our conversation, the appearance of Endo-san's sword—I felt their combined assault upon me. What made it more difficult was that these were not tangible opponents I could throw off. I stood still for a moment, trying to find my balance again.

She faced me. "I am not here to cause you harm. I truly wish to know."

"I'll take you to your hotel," I said, and walked into the house, leaving her holding the sword.

Chapter Two

I drove the black Daimler into Georgetown and dropped her at the Eastern & Oriental Hotel on Northam Road. Traffic was already heavy on the roads and along the streets office workers hurried to work from the food stalls, carrying their breakfasts, packets of *nasi lemak*—coconut rice and sweet curried anchovy paste—wrapped in banana leaves and newspaper. Motorcyclists, the bane of Penang traffic, sped by recklessly as I turned into Beach Street. I let the Sikh doorman park my car and walked up to my office.

Hutton & Sons had occupied the same building for over a century. The company was founded by my great-grandfather, Graham Hutton, still a legend in the East. It was a shadow of its former glory, but still remained a respectable and profitable concern. During the war, a corner of the gray stone building had been torn away by a bomb and the shade of the restored stone could not be matched to the original. It still appeared like a patch of new skin over a wound. As I sat down at my desk, I was aware once again that this company was as much Endo-san's as it was my family's. Had it not been for his influence the business would have been swallowed up by the Japanese. How many times did he shield it from them? He never told me.

I read the various reports, facsimiles and e-mails that had come in during the weekend. The company still traded in the goods it had been founded upon—rubber, tin, agricultural goods grown in Malaysia. We owned a few reputable hotels, prime real estate, and three shopping malls in Kuala Lumpur as well. We operated mines in Australia and South Africa and held extensive interests in shipyards in Japan. Due to my knowledge of the Japanese language and my acceptance of its culture, I was one of the rare few that had foreseen and taken advantage of the spectacular rise of the post-war Japanese economy. Hutton & Sons was still a

17

privately owned company, a fact that I was proud of. There was no one to tell me what to do and no one to answer to.

Even so, my life was regimented: breakfast at home, a pleasurable drive along the coastal road to work, lunch wherever it took my fancy, then back to work in the office until five in the evening. I would go for a swim at the Penang Swimming Club, have a few drinks, and then drive home.

I felt old, and it was not a very pleasant feeling. The world goes by, the young and the hopeful, all head for their future. Where does that leave us? There is the misconception that we have reached our destinations the moment we grow old, but it is not a well-accepted fact that we are still traveling toward those destinations, still beyond our reach even on the day we close our eyes for the final time.

I had ended my classes five years earlier, and had sent my last student to another teacher. My engagements abroad had been pruned considerably and the annual pilgrimages to Japan had ceased. I had also made tentative enquiries as to the sale of the company, and the response had been favorable. I was preparing for my final journey, cutting away all obligations, all moorings, as ready to sail out as a seafarer just waiting for the right wind.

I was surprised at my maudlin feelings, which I thought I had put away years ago. Perhaps it was meeting Michiko, meeting another person who had known Hayato Endo-san. The feelings evoked by the unexpected appearance of Endo-san's *katana* refused to settle, and it was with an effort that I pushed them away and went to work.

When lunchtime came around my mind was already straying and I felt ready to leave my office for the day. I informed Mrs. Loh, my secretary of many years, and she looked at me as though I had been stricken with a sudden illness.

"Are you all right?" she asked.

"I'm fine, Adele."

"You don't look fine to me."

"How do I look then?"

"Something is worrying you. You're thinking of the war again," she said.

After close on five decades with me she knew me well. "You guessed correctly, Adele," I sighed. "I was thinking of the war.

Only the old people remember now. And thank God their memories are so unreliable."

"You did a lot of good. And that, people will always remember. The older folk will tell their children and grandchildren. I would have starved to death if it hadn't been for you."

"You also know a lot of people died because of me."

She could not find a ready reply and I walked out, leaving her to her memories.

I headed out into the sunshine. On the steps of the entrance I paused, watching the funnels of ships sticking out over the rooftops of the buildings. Weld Quay was within walking distance. The godowns would be busy at this time: stevedores unloading cargo—gunnysacks of grains and spices and boxes of fruit—carrying them on their naked shiny backs, as coolies had done two hundred years ago; workers repairing ships, their welding tools flashing sparks of white light, bright as exploding stars.

Every now and then a ship sounded its whistle, a sound so comforting to me whenever I was in my office, for it had never changed in the past fifty years. The briny scent of the sea at low tide, mixed with the smell of the mudflats steaming in the sun, wafted through the air. Crows and gulls hung in the sky like a child's mobile toy over a crib. Sunlight bounced off the buildings— the Standard Chartered Bank, the Hong Kong and Shanghai Bank, India House. A constant flow of vehicles went around the clock tower donated by a local millionaire to commemorate Queen Victoria's Diamond Jubilee, adding to the noise. I have never seen the light of Penang replicated anywhere else in the world—bright, bringing everything into razor-sharp focus, yet at the same time warm and forgiving, making you want to melt into the walls it shines on, into the leaves it gives life to. It is the kind of light that illuminates not only what the eyes see, but also what the heart feels.

This is my home. Even though half of me is English I have never hungered for England. England is a foreign land, cold and gloomy. And the weather is worse. I have lived on this island all my life, and I know I want to die here too.

I started walking, moving through the lunchtime crowds: young clerks laughing with their lovers; office workers talking loudly with one another; students carrying large bags, pushing each other in mock fights; street peddlers ringing bells and shouting their wares. A number of people recognized me and gave me a slight, if uncertain smile, which I returned. I was almost an institution myself.

I decided not to go home yet. I crossed Farquhar Street and entered the cool shaded grounds of St. George's Church. The wind rustled the old angsana trees and made the shadows on the grass waver. I sat on the moss-covered steps of the little domed pavilion in the church grounds as the sounds of the traffic faded away. Birds called, and a jealous crow swooped in and broke up their singing. For a while I was at peace. If I closed my eyes I could have been anywhere on earth, at any time too. Perhaps Avalon, before Arthur was born. That had been one of my favorite stories when I was a child, one of the few English myths I liked, which had seemed almost Oriental in its magic and tragedy.

I opened my eyes reluctantly. Forgetfulness was one luxury I could not buy. I pushed myself up and went out of the churchyard. I started to walk faster, to prepare myself for tonight. I knew what was coming. It would be hard, but finally, after all these years I welcomed it. The opportunity would never come again, I realized. There was no time left. Not in this particular life anyway.

She was already at Istana when I got back from the Club, lying on a deck chair by the pool, her head covered by a large Panama hat. She was staring at Endo-san's island, and there was an undisturbed stillness in the air, as though she had not moved for a long time. A book lay on the table next to her, open flat on the glass surface, waiting to be closed by her again. I watched her from inside the house. She opened her bag, took out a bottle of pills, and swallowed a handful of them.

I could feel the effects of the drinks I had consumed. The Club had been full of the usual crowd—noisy drunken Indian litigators retrying lost cases, and fat Chinese tycoons shouting into their phones to their stockbrokers. There were also the usual ancient British expatriates, leftovers from the war who had stayed on in the country they had come to love. At least they did not try to fight the war with me again today, or castigate me for the role I had played in it.

I asked Maria to leave dinner ready for us, and went for a shower. By the time I came downstairs the servants had gone home and we were all alone. A freshly grilled fillet of stingray marinated with chilli, lime, and spices on a large piece of fresh banana leaf lay on a plate on the table, and Michiko's eyes were drawn to it. Maria always made the best *ikan bakar*—it was the Portuguese blood in her, she always told me. I started to pour a bottle of wine but Michiko stayed my hand. From a rustling package she produced a stout-looking bottle.

"*Sake*," she said.

"Ah. Much better," I replied, handing her two thimble-sized porcelain cups. She warmed the *sake* in the kitchen and poured deftly and we each drank it down in one swallow. The taste . . . I had forgotten the taste. I shook my head. Too many drinks in one day.

This time we were much more at ease with each other, as though we had known each other all our past lives. I liked her laughter: it was light, airy, and yet not frivolous. Unlike many Japanese women I had met, she did not cover her mouth when she laughed, and I knew she truly found what I said amusing. A woman who was not afraid to show her teeth, whether in joy or in fury.

The *sake* went well with the meal, taking the edge off the spicy sauce. The fillet was tender, and our chopsticks separated the flesh easily from the bone. The banana leaf imparted a hint of green, raw flavor, soaking up and lightening the heavy marinade. We finished off with cold sago pudding in coconut milk, sweetened with melted dark palm sugar, which she seemed to enjoy.

"I brought Endo-san's letter," she said, at the end of our meal.

I halted the hand bringing the cup to my mouth.

"You may read it if you wish," she continued, pretending to be oblivious to my reluctance.

I sipped and considered. "Perhaps later."

She agreed, and poured me more *sake*.

We sat out on the terrace again. It was a balmy night, the sea giving off a metallic sheen, the sky starless, an unending sheet of black velvet. I felt a warm glow all over me, and was surprised to discover that the feeling was one of contentment. A fine dinner, excellent *sake*, an attentive listener, the whisper of the sea, a slight breeze blowing, the music of the cicadas—I should feel content. After all, what more could I ask for? I went to the living room, put on a recording and let Joan Sutherland sing into the darkness.

Michiko sighed, a smile around her lips. She stretched out her legs, one after the other, with the daintiness of a stork stepping through a lily pond.

"I was tactless this morning," she began. "I thought you would have been pleased to see his sword again, and to find out that it had not been lost."

I stopped her. "There are so many things you don't know. I cannot blame you."

"What happened to your family, your brothers, your sister?" she asked, filling my cup again. I was only mildly surprised. Obviously she had thoroughly investigated the circumstances before approaching me. Perhaps Endo-san's letter had told her of my family.

"All dead," I told her, seeing their faces float before my eyes like wavering images on the surface of a pool.

Under the faint light of the moon the statues in the garden regained some of their original glory, giving off an unearthly luminescence. "There is a house, further up the road, which has been deserted for years," I said. "Local legend has it that on a night when the moon is at its fullest the marble statues left in the gardens come alive, and for a few hours roam about the grounds. Tonight, I can almost believe that the story is true."

"How sad," she said. "If I were a statue, and came back to life, I would always be looking for what I had lost, for the last thing I had done as a living being. Imagine having to go through your entire existence alternating between stone and flesh, death and life, always attempting to find the memories of your previous lives. I would eventually forget what I was searching for. I would forget what I was trying to remember."

"Or one could just enjoy the moment when one is alive." As soon as I spoke I knew how hypocritical I sounded, how ironic those words were.

Sutherland sang on, flinging her heart out into the night. Verdi's *Caro nome* had been my father's favorite aria, I told Michiko.

"And now it is your favorite," she said.

I nodded. Then I said, "Ask me again, what you wanted to know this morning."

She sipped her *sake*, leaned back in the wicker chair and said, "Tell me about your life. Tell me about the life you and Endo-san led. The joys you experienced and the sorrow that you encountered. I would like to know everything."

The moment I had been waiting for. Fifty years I had waited to tell my tale, as long as the time Endo-san's letter took to reach Michiko. Still I hesitated—like a penitent sinner facing my confessor, unsure if I wanted another person to know my many shames, my failures, my unforgivable sins.

As though to fortify me she took the letter out and placed it on the table between us. Its pages were folded, yellowed like old skin, the faint tattoo of aged ink that had seeped onto the blank side visible to me. Just like me, I thought, looking at the letter. The life I had lived was folded, only a blank page exposed to the world, emptiness wrapped around the days of my life; faint traces of it could be discerned, but only if one looked closely, very closely.

And so, for the first and last time, I gently unfolded my life, exposing what was written, letting the ancient ink be read once again.

Chapter Three

On the day I was born, my father planted a casuarina tree. It was a tradition begun by his grandfather. The lanky sapling was planted in the garden facing the sea and it would grow into a beautiful tree, hard and tall, its cloak of leaves exuding a light fragrance that mingled soothingly with the scent of the sea. It would be the last tree that my father planted in his life.

I was the youngest child of one of the oldest families in Penang. My great-grandfather, Graham Hutton, had been a clerk in the East India Company before sailing out to the East Indies to make his fortune in 1780. He had sailed around the Spice Islands trading in pepper and spices, and came to befriend Captain Francis Light, who was searching for a suitable port. He found it on an island in the Straits of Malacca, on the northwestern side of the Malay Peninsula and within comfortable reach of India. The island was sparsely inhabited, thick with trees, humped with rolling hills, and surrounded by long white stretches of beach. The local Malays named it after the tall areca palm trees—*pinang*—which grew abundantly on it.

Realizing its strategic potential immediately, Captain Light obtained the island from the Sultan of Kedah in return for six thousand Spanish dollars and British protection against usurpers of his throne. The island was named Prince of Wales Island, but eventually came to be known as Penang.

The Malay Peninsula had been partially colonized since the sixteenth century, by first the Portuguese, then the Dutch, and finally the British. The British made the most headway, spreading their influence into almost all the Malay States. The discovery of tin and the suitability of the soil and weather for the planting of rubber trees—both materials of vital importance due to the Industrial Revolution—saw them fomenting internecine wars in their bid to control the States. Sultans were deposed, outcast heirs were put on thrones, money was paid in return for concessions and, when even these failed, the British were not loath to back their preferred factions with arms and might.

Graham Hutton was there when Captain Light loaded his cannon with silver pieces and fired them into the forests: his way of spurring the coolies into clearing the land, my father had told us. The nature of man being such, the ploy had worked. The island grew into a vibrant port, located between the changing of the monsoon winds. It became a place for sailors and traders on the way to China to recuperate, to treasure a few balmy weeks while waiting for the winds to shift.

Graham Hutton prospered, and it was not long after that Hutton & Sons was founded. He was not married at the time, and his optimism in the naming of his company was much commented upon. However, he knew what he wished to accomplish and he let nothing impede him.

Through various underhanded dealings, and his eventual marriage to the daughter of another trading family, my great-grandfather began his legend in the East. The company became known as one of the most profitable trading houses. But the roots of Graham Hutton's dynastic impulses dug in harder; he wanted a symbol to represent his dreams, something to last beyond his own life.

The Hutton mansion was built to perch above a slight cliff and overlooked the meadows of the sea that merged into the plains of the Indian Ocean. Designed by the team of Starke and McNeil and inspired by the works of Andrea Palladio, like many of the houses built at that time, the white stone building was surrounded by a row of Doric columns and dominated by a large curving colonnade crowned with a pediment. Its doors and window frames were made from Burmese teak and my great-grandfather imported stonemasons from Kent, Glaswegian ironmongers, marble from Italy, and coolie labor from India for its construction. There were twenty-five rooms in the house and, true to his ambitions, my great-grandfather, who had made many visits to the courts of the Malay Sultans, named his home Istana, the Malay word for "palace."

Surrounding the main building were expansive lawns; carefully planted trees and flowerbeds lined a straight drive of almost white gravel. The drive rose pleasingly toward the house and, if one stood at the entrance and looked up, the prominent pediment seemed to direct a traveler on a road to the sky. When my father, Noel Hutton, inherited the house, a swimming pool and two tennis courts were constructed. Adjacent to the main house and shielded by a head-high hedge were the garage and the servants' living quarters, both converted from stables when Graham Hutton's passion for race-horses waned. When we were children my brothers and sister and I often dug around the grounds looking for horseshoes, shouting with triumph whenever one of us found one, even though it was crumbling with rust and left that iron-blood smell on our hands which still lingered after persistent scrubbing.

In the normal course of events I would never have inherited all these things. My father had four children and I was the last. I never thought much about the question of Istana's future owner-ship. But I did love the house. Its graceful lines and history touched me strongly and I loved exploring every part of it, some-times even, despite my fear of heights, climbing up to the roof through a door in the attic. I would sit and look out over the land-scape of the roof, like a tickbird on the back of a water buffalo, and feel the house beneath me. I often asked my father to tell me the stories behind the portraits that lined the walls, and the dusty trophies won by people related to me, the inscriptions on them linking me to these long-gone pieces of my flesh and bone.

Much as I loved the house, I had a greater love for the sea—for its ever-changing moods, for the way the sun glittered on its surface, and how it mirrored every temperament of the sky. Even when I was a child the sea whispered to me, whispered and spoke to me in a language I assumed only I understood. It embraced me in its warm currents; it dissolved my rage when I was angry at the world; it chased me as I ran along the shore, curled itself around my shins, tempting me to walk farther and farther out until I became a part of its unending vastness.

I want to remember it all, I told Endo-san once. *I want to remember everything that I have touched and seen and felt, so that it will never be lost and brushed away.* He had laughed, but he had understood.

My mother, Khoo Yu Lian, was my father's second wife. She was Chinese and her father had joined the mass exodus to Malaya from the Hokkien province in China in search of wealth and a chance to survive. Thousands of Chinese came to work in the tin mines, escaping famine, drought, and political upheaval. Her father had managed to become wealthy from his mines in Ipoh, a town two hundred miles away to the south. He had sent his youngest daughter to the Convent School in Light Street in Penang, far away from the coarse coolies he employed.

My father had been a widower when he met my mother. His wife Emma had died giving birth to Isabel, his third child, and I suppose he was also looking for a surrogate mother for his three young children. Yu Lian met my father at a party held by the son of the Chinese consul general, Cheong Fatt Tze, a Mandarin sent from Peking. She was seventeen, and he was thirty-two.

My father scandalized Penang society when he married my mother, but his wealth and influence partly eased the way. She died when I was seven and, except for a few photographs in the house, I have only faint memories of her. I have tried to hold on to those fading recollections, those softening voices and disappearing scents, augmenting them with what I heard from my two brothers and sister and the servants who had known her.

The four of us Hutton children grew up virtually as orphans: after my mother's death my father retreated into his work. He went on frequent trips to the other states to visit his tin mines, his plantations, and his friends. He took the train down the coast to Kuala Lumpur regularly, spending days there while he oversaw the office just behind the court buildings. His only consolation in life, it seemed, was the company, but my brother Edward once told us that he kept a mistress there. At that young age I had no idea what he was talking about, though William and Isabel had giggled. For days afterward I pestered them about it and eventually our *amah* heard me mentioning the word, and warned me, "*Aiyah!* Stop saying that terrible word or I'll beat your backside!"

Our father had instructed that we were to be addressed in the dialect of Hokkien by the Chinese servants, and Malay by the Malay gardener. Like many of the Europeans who considered Malaya their home, he had also insisted that all his children receive their education locally as much as possible. We grew up speaking the local languages, as he had himself. It would bind us to Penang forever.

*

I was not close to my siblings before I met Endo-san, being very much the solitary type. I was not interested in the things that fascinated my schoolmates: sports and spider hunting and fighting crickets for money. And because of my mixed parentage I was never completely accepted by either the Chinese or the English of Penang, each race believing itself to be superior. It had always been so. When I was younger I had tried to explain this to my father, when the boys at school had taunted me. But he had dismissed my words, and said I was being silly and too sensitive. I knew then that I had no choice but to harden myself against the insults and whispered comments, and to find my own place in the scheme of life.

After school I would throw my bag in my room and head for the beach below Istana, climbing down the wooden steps built into the cliff. I spent my afternoons swimming in the sea and reading under the shade of the bowed, rustling coconut trees. I read everything that my father had in his library, even when I did not understand it. When my attention left the pages I would put the book down and catch crabs and dig for clams and crayfish hidden in the sea. The water was warm and clear and the tidal pools were filled with fish and strange marine life. I had a little boat of my own and I was a good sailor.

My brothers and sister were so much older than I that I spent very little time with them. Isabel, who was five when I was born, was closest to me in age, while my brothers William and Edward were older than I by seven and ten years, respectively. William sometimes tried to include me in whatever he was doing but I always thought he did it as a polite afterthought and, as I grew older, I would make excuses not to join him.

Yet, despite my preference for being on my own, there were occasions when I enjoyed my siblings' company. William, who was always trying to impress some girl or other, would organize tennis parties and weekend retreats up into the cooler climate of Penang Hill where, in the olden days before I was born, before the existence of the funicular tram, travelers were borne up in sedan chairs on the shoulders of sweating Chinese coolies. We had a house up on The Hill, which clung on the edge of a sharp drop. It was cold at night up there, a welcome change from the heat of the lowlands, and the lights of Georgetown lay spread out beneath, dimming the stars. Once, Isabel and I became lost in the jungle that covered The Hill after running off the track in search of orchids. She never cried at all and even gave me courage, though I knew she was just as scared as I was. We walked for hours in that green and lush world, until she got us back onto the track again. There were also rounds of parties at Istana where my father entertained, and we were often invited to other parties and receptions, dragon-boat races at the Esplanade, cricket matches, horse races, and any occasion that could justify, even slightly, a reason to dance and drink and laugh. Although I was by necessity included in these invitations, I often felt they were due to the influence my father held more than anything else.

There was a small island owned by my family about a mile out, thick with trees. It was accessible only from the beach that faced out to the open sea. I spent a lot of my afternoons there imagining I was a castaway, alone in the world. I even used to spend nights on it during those periods when my father was away in Kuala Lumpur.

Early in 1939, when I was sixteen, my father leased out the little island and warned us not to set foot on it as it was now occupied. It frustrated me that my personal retreat had been taken from me and for the next few weeks I spied out the activities that went on there. Judging from the supplies being ferried across by workmen in little boats, a small structure was being built. I contemplated sneaking onto the island but my father's caution deterred me. So I gave up on it, and tried not to think anymore about it.

And halfway across the world, countries that seemed to have little to do with us were preparing to go to war.

"May I speak to the master of the house?"

I gave a small start. It was an early dusk in the second week of April and a slight rain was falling, soft as the seeds blown off wild grass by the wind, a deceptively gentle warning of the monsoon season soon to come. The lawns glistened and the casuarina's scent added richness to the smell of the rain. I sat on the terrace beneath an umbrella where I had been reading and staring at the sky, lost in my dreams, looking at the heavy clouds resting on the unbendable horizon. The words, although spoken softly, had jolted me from my thoughts.

I turned and faced him. He was in his late forties, medium built and stocky. His hair was almost silver, cut very short and shining like the wet grass. The face was square and lined, his eyes round and glinting strangely in the twilight. His features were too sharp for a Chinese, and his accent was unknown to me.

"I'm the master's son. What is it about?" I asked, suddenly aware that I was quite alone. The servants were in their quarters behind the house, preparing their evening meals. I made a note to speak to them about allowing a stranger to enter the house without any form of announcement.

"I would like to borrow a boat from you," he answered.

"Who are you?" I asked. Being a Hutton, I often got away with rudeness.

"Hayato Endo. I live there." He pointed to the island, my island.

So that was how he had managed to enter the house. He had come up from the beach.

"My father's not here," I said. The rest of the family was away in London, where they were to join my brother William, who had completed his university studies the year before but had decided to stay on in London with his friends instead of coming home to work. Every five years my father would reluctantly place his manager in charge of the firm and take his children to their home-land for a long visit, a practice many of the English in the colonies viewed as being almost as sacred as a religious pilgrimage. I had elected not to go this time. My father had been annoyed, for he had planned the journey to coincide with the start of my school holidays, and had in fact spoken to the headmaster of my school to allow me to miss the first month of the new term. But I suspected my siblings were relieved: I often felt that explaining a half-Chinese relation to their English friends and distant relations was not attractive to them at all.

"Nevertheless, I require a boat from you," the strange man insisted. "Mine, I am afraid, has been washed away by the tide." He smiled. "It is probably halfway to India by now."

I got up from the wicker chair and asked him to accompany me to our boathouse. But he stood, unmoving, staring out to the sea and the overcast sky. "The sea can break one's heart, *neh?*"

This was the first time I heard someone describe what I felt. I stopped, uncertain what to say. Just a few simple words had encapsulated my feelings for the sea. It *was* heartbreakingly beautiful. We stood silently for a few minutes, joined by a common love. There was no movement except for the rain and the waves. Veins of lightning flared and throbbed behind the wall of clouds, turning the bruised sky pink, and I felt I was being granted glimpses of blood pulsing silently through the ventricles of an immense human heart.

"The sea is the only thing that joins me to my home now," he said, and then looked surprised at having uttered those words.

We walked out into the rain, the grass spongy beneath my bare feet. The boathouse was on the beach, and we climbed down the long flight of wet steps. Once I slipped, and the man's hand shot out and gripped me tightly. I felt the strength of his arm and stopped struggling for balance. I looked at him and said, "I walk these steps every day. I wasn't going to fall."

He appeared amused at my annoyance. I felt the burn where his fingers had clamped onto me and I resisted the urge to rub it. I wondered why he had leased the island.

And then we were on the sand. There was only the roar of the sea and the wind. No other sound existed. Even the birds were gone from the sky. The wind was now stirring up the sea, streaking it white and whipping the unending rain into our faces and hair. At this moment, it was good to be alive.

We hauled out my boat and dragged it down the bay to a spot where it would be easier for him to row across the choppy water. We set it down at the waterline, where the backwash of the waves tugged at it insistently. From this part of the beach I could see only the edge of Istana, like the prow of a great ship rounding a point.

"Thank you for lending me the boat," he said, giving me a slight bow, which I immediately returned without thinking. He looked back to the island and then turned to me. "Come with me. Let me repay your kindness by offering you a meal."

He intrigued me, so I stepped into the boat.

He rowed smoothly, the prow slicing through the rough waves. He headed for the beach facing out to the sea, skillfully avoiding the rocks. Once we neared the island he stopped rowing and let the waves lift us and rush us in. We hit the shore with a shudder.

I stepped out into the water and helped him pull the boat onto the beach. The place did not seem to have changed. I looked around and found the tree where I had so often fallen asleep in the hot afternoons and the rock where I dried my clothes. I touched it as I went by.

We left the beach and walked through a clump of trees until we came to a small clearing. I stopped, taking in the one-storey wooden house with a shaded verandah running around it. "You built this?"

He nodded. "I designed it in the traditional Japanese style. Your father provided me with the workmen."

The lines of the house were clean and simple, blending in beautifully with the surrounding trees. I felt sadness and resentment that the island was now changed by its presence. It was almost as if a large part of my childhood had disappeared without my knowledge, without giving me the time to bid farewell to it.

"Is something wrong?" he asked.

"No," I answered and, after a moment, added, "Your home is beautiful." As I said those words I felt my earlier sadness lifting. If things have to change, if time has to pass, then I was glad he had built this house here.

He went in and lit the lamps, and the sliding doors with their rice paper screens gave off a welcoming glow.

I followed him inside, leaving my shoes outside as he had done. He gave me a towel to dry myself. There was no furniture, only rectangular padded mats around a hearth set into the floor. He lit a brazier, placed a pot over it, and threw in vegetables and prawns. Outside the rain was getting heavier, but I felt warm and protected within the house.

The stew began to boil and steam rose up into the small chimney over the hearth. The smell of it sharpened my hunger. He stirred the pot and, with a wooden ladle, filled two ceramic bowls, handing one to me.

He watched me as I ate. "How old are you?" he asked. I told him.

"And you have not let me know your name," he said.

"Philip," I said.

His eyes looked inward, then stared back into mine. "You are the one who was here before me."

I asked him how he knew.

"You carved your name into one of the rocks here."

"I used to come here every day after school."

He studied me carefully, and from the note in his voice I knew he somehow understood my sense of loss. "You are still welcome to do that."

I was gratified by the invitation. I looked around as we ate. The room was not as bare as I had first thought. A few photographs hung on one wall. There were also two white scrolls that stretched from the ceiling almost to the floor. I could not decipher the writing on them, although I felt strangely soothed by its fluid curves. It was like looking at a flowing river as it twisted and turned on its way to the sea. On the floor between the scrolls a sword rested on a lacquered stand, and there was not a doubt in my mind that he knew how to use it.

A branch hit the side of the house, scraping the roof with its leaves. The rain fell with greater intensity, and from past experience I knew the sea would be choppy and treacherous for my little boat.

"Your family will be worried," he remarked as we went out and sat on the verandah. He unrolled the bamboo blinds to leave the wind and the rain outside like disfavored courtiers. I sipped the hot green tea he had prepared. I took another swallow, liking the taste of it. I had followed his way of sitting, knees folded, feet tucked under the buttocks. My ankles began to burn with pain but I refused to stretch my legs. Even then, at that stage, I wanted to show him I could endure.

I distanced myself from the pain by listening to the layers of sound: through the clatter of rain hitting the roof I could hear the sea, water dripping off leaves, the chink of china as we lifted our cups and placed them down again.

"There's no one to worry," I answered. "My family is in London."

"And yet you are here."

I smiled, without much humor. "I'm the outcast. The half-Chinese child of my father. No, that's unfair," I said, trying to clarify my reasons for not following my family without sounding

33

resentful. How to explain to this stranger the sense of not being connected to anything? It struck me at that moment that, while other children became orphans when their parents died, my future as an orphan had been cast the night my parents met and fell in love. Finally I said, "I just don't like London, that's all. I was there five years ago. It was too cold for me. Have you been there?"

He shook his head. "A dangerous time to be in London."

"People say all those warnings of war are just talk."

"I do not agree. War will break out."

The certainty in his words and a verdict so different from that I had been hearing raised my interest. He was obviously not from these parts. I wondered again who he was and what he was doing in Penang.

I could see one of the calligraphy scrolls through the door. "Where is your home?" I asked.

"A village in Japan," he said, and I heard the longing in his voice. I thought back to his words earlier in the evening when he said the sea was the only thing that linked him to his home and, although I had only just met him, I felt an inexplicable sadness for him, as though in some mysterious way the sadness was mine too.

A streak of lightning slashed across the sky, followed by a crack of thunder. I flinched.

"You should stay here tonight," he said, rising in one fluid motion. I followed him inside, glad to be away from the spectacle of the storm. He went into his room and came out with a rolled-up mattress, placing it near the hearth.

He bowed to me and I was compelled to return it. "*Oyasumi nasai*," he said.

I presumed it meant "good night," for the next moment he had blown out the candles and left me in the darkened room that was lit intermittently by the play of lightning. I unrolled my mattress by the hearth and eventually went to sleep.

I was awakened by a series of short, abrupt screams. For a few seconds I had no idea where I was. I rose from the mattress and slid open the latticed door. The sun was just hauling itself up from the other side of the world. The sky was still covered with clouds pared thin by the winds and there was a palpable sense of freshness in the air; even the waves hitting the shore sounded crisp and clean.

He was in a clearing beneath the trees, his hands gripping the sword I had noticed the night before. It rose up in an arc described by his hands and descended swiftly, soundlessly, followed by his sharp cry. He was clothed in white robes and a pair of black trousers that looked more like a skirt. He looked very alien and very impressive.

He took no notice of me although I knew he was aware of my scrutiny. The air seemed to vibrate as he slashed, stabbed, sliced, and whirled around the clearing. He had placed a circle of thick bamboo trunks around him and now, in one single motion, the sword cut and the sticks of bamboo fell one after the other. The blade was so sharp there was not even the sound of a crack as it sliced them.

The sky was bright when he finished. His clothes were wet and perspiration made his silver hair shine. He beckoned to me to approach.

"Hit me."

I hesitated, looking at him uncertainly, wondering if I had heard correctly.

"Go on. Hit me," he said again in a tone that gave me no choice but to obey.

I launched my fist into his face, using the punch that had stood me in good stead at school whenever I had been called a mongrel half-breed and which had provoked quite a few parental complaints.

I found myself lying on the dew-soaked grass a moment later, my breath knocked out of me. My back felt sore, even though the ground was soft. He pulled me to my feet, his hand firm and strong. There was a look of amusement on his face as he saw my anger. He held up a placatory hand and said, "Come. Let me show you how to do that."

He asked me to hit him again—*slowly*. As my fist was about to connect with his face he deftly stepped aside and came closer to me. His arm rose up and met mine; with a spiraling motion he guided my hand away, gripped my throat from behind, spun my unbalanced body around and brought me to the ground. Then he let me do it to him, and after several attempts I managed to throw him off his feet. I was enthralled.

"What did you feel?" he asked.

"As though everything came together when I threw you," I answered him as best I could. If I had wanted to sound pretentious I could have told him it felt as if the earth and I were spinning in harmony. But he seemed happy and satisfied with my reply.

He continued teaching me until it was almost noon. By then I was feeling quite hungry.

"Do you want to continue learning?" he asked.

I nodded. He told me to come again the following day. As we rowed back to the shore he said, "You must be made aware that the teacher, in accepting a pupil, takes on a heavy responsibility. The pupil, in return, must be prepared to commit himself fully. There can be no uncertainty, no second thoughts. Are you able to give me this?"

I stopped rowing as we approached the beach and considered his warning. The sun was hot, breaking onto the surface of the sea, casting shadows and bracelets of white light onto the seabed, making the tidal patterns of sand undulate like heat mirage. I felt that he was telling me more than what was being said, even though I could not catch a firm grasp of the complete picture. I was certain of one thing though. I wanted what he could offer me, and so I nodded.

I spent the rest of the day thinking about this strange person who had entered my life. The school term had finished for the summer holidays and I was liberated from the monotony of regurgitating Latin verbs and comprehending mathematical formulae. I was in an enviable position: money was hardly a problem as accounts of my purchases were settled monthly by the family firm. The house servants went about their duties and left me alone. We had arrived at an unspoken pact: no negative reports from any one of us to my father. It was an agreement that suited us all.

I would have to be discreet, however, if I wanted to be taught by Endo-san. Most of the servants were Chinese and my friendship with a Japanese could break our pact—the Chinese held no affection for their distant cousins across the seas. My being half Chinese made them assume I was sympathetic to the plight of their families left behind in China—even I knew, from their constant reports, of the atrocities being committed by the Japanese there—but they never knew that I felt no connection with China, or with England. I was a child born between two worlds, belonging to neither. From the very beginning I treated Endo-san not as a Japanese, not as a member of a hated race, but as a man, and that was why we forged an instant bond.

I began my lessons in *aikijutsu* the following morning, entering into a ritual of learning that would continue largely unbroken for nearly three years. I would row across to the island while it was still dark and traces of stars could still be seen hiding behind the veil of the sky. Inevitably Endo-san would already be waiting for me, impatient, his face stern.

We bowed to each other and stretched our limbs. He began with the easiest moves, teaching me to get out of the line of attack smoothly, with the minimum number of movements.

"In a fight, the fewer steps you take, the more effective you will be," he said on my first lesson. He seldom spoke while he taught, his words as economical as the short, sharp movements he advocated.

He also taught me the finer elements of punching and kicking, the vital points to aim for. "To have a strong defense you must know the types of strikes and attacks which exist," he said, as his hands came to my face, my chest, and my groin in a set of three fast, unseen punches. They stopped at my nose; I could see the lines on his knuckles and the faint strands of hair, and smell the light scent of his skin.

"Look down," he said.

His foot had ended at my knee. If he had completed his kick he would have broken it. "Never look at your attacker's fists. Look at his entire body. Then you will know what is coming."

I was taught the fundamental movements during the first four weeks of my training with him. The daily classes would last for three hours. On Sundays Endo-san would demand two sessions from me, one in the morning and another in the evening. He taught me *ukemi*—to fall safely, roll on the ground, and emerge into a firm stance when thrown by him.

His throws were powerful, and initially I balked, fearing injury. I would stiffen my body whenever he attempted to project me into the air.

"You have to loosen up," he said. "You will cause more harm to yourself if you resist the technique. Follow the flow of the energy, do not fight it."

I found it difficult to believe him as his instructions seemed contradictory. He sensed my reluctance and agitation and attempted to reassure me by leading me to a monochrome photograph on the wall in his house. It showed a pair of hands being gripped at the wrists by another set of hands. The palms of the hands that were being held—the passive hands, I thought—were open, seeming to rest on the wrists of the dominant hands. At first I thought the impression created by the two pairs of hands was one of aggression, but to my surprise I found myself soothed by the scene as I studied it.

"I have always felt that this photograph has managed to distill the soul of *aikijutsu*," Endo-san remarked. "There is a physical and spiritual connection with your partner. There is no resistance, but there is trust."

He gripped my hands in the same manner and asked me to extend my arms and lay my palms on his wrists. I felt immediately what he was trying to impart to me. This connective touch, on one level, was the most basic of human interaction, but it seemed also to reach into a higher plane of union that leaped across the physical and I felt I had lost something invaluable when he released my hands.

"In a class, trust is paramount," Endo-san said. "I trust you not to attack me in a manner we have not agreed upon, and you must trust me not to harm you when I neutralize your attack. Without trust we cannot move and nothing can be achieved."

"But I feel I have to surrender completely when you perform a throwing technique on me."

"Precisely. Complete surrender, but not total abandonment of awareness. You must always feel. Feel my technique, feel the direction of the force, how you move through the air and how you are going to meet the ground. Feel, open up, be aware of everything. If anything goes wrong, if my technique is faulty or if I fail you, then at the very least you are in a position to protect yourself and fall safely."

He threw me a few more times and it began to seem easier. I was not so tense and the movements seemed to flow more naturally.

"In return for surrendering to the throw, you are given the gift of flight," he said.

It was true. I quickly came to enjoy the exhilarating sensation of being launched into the air, to float unanchored for a few short seconds before curling my body into a sphere and coming to earth again. And I discovered that the harder I attacked him, the more strongly I directed my force against him, the further he could throw me, and so the longer I could remain in blissful flight. I gave up my fear and at the end of each class requested that he throw me continuously until I was exhausted and could do no more.

There was a canvas bag filled with sand that I had to hit and kick, every day, hundreds of times. He demanded strength and speed, and I worked exhaustively to reach the standards he expected. He was strict and unyielding, but he was passionate about what he was teaching, as though he had once taught before and now missed it greatly. I thoroughly enjoyed the lessons. Our spirits would stretch out the way the light of the sun spreads through the sky. Our breaths came out, through our lungs, throats, soles, skin; we exhaled from our tingling fingertips. We breathed; we lived.

"This is where all power originates—the breath, *kokyu*." He pointed to a spot below his navel. "The *tanden* is the center of your being, the center of the universe. At all times connect it to your opponent's center with your breath and your energy, your *ki*."

His eyes glittered, throbbed with a cosmic energy that seemed to reach into mine. They held me immobile, a hare caught by the stare of the tiger. His hands reached out and smacked my shoulder. "And never, ever look directly into an opponent's eyes. Always remember this."

It is amazing what one can achieve when one has an excellent teacher. Endo-sensei, that was how I called him during our lessons—teacher. I knew he was pleased with me when he realized I was not treating his classes lightly. He never told me, but I soon learned that he showed it in other ways.

One morning, as I was about to return home after a hard and painful lesson, he stopped me and said, "We have not finished." He asked me to follow him into his house. Inside, we knelt on the floor before a low wooden table. He opened a box and removed a brush from inside. He spread out a sheet of rice paper and ground an ink-stick in a square stone mortar that had a slight dip in the center, until a small pool of ink covered the indentation. The grinding released a light trace of incense, unformed words escaping into the air. The ink thickened and, when he was satisfied as to its consistency, he stopped and placed the ink stick on a marble rest.

"The ink, the grinding stone, the writing brush and paper, these were described by the ancient Chinese as the Four Treasures of the Study," he said. He looked closely at the blank sheet of rice paper, as if seeing words that had already been written upon it. He pulled back his sleeve and dipped the brush into the ink, shaped it to a point against the stone and wrote.

It was a series of slashes and curves, his hand pressing the brush into the paper where he required a thick stroke, and lifting it almost off the paper where he wished to leave a light trace. The tip of the brush never once lost a strand of contact with the surface of the paper until it reached the border of the sheet and then the brush was lifted away like a hunting tiger leaping off a rock.

"My name," he said, handing me the brush. His fingers curved around mine as he showed me the way to hold it. "It is like holding a sword, not too tightly, but not too loosely either. By the manner in which a man holds his brush, you will be able to tell how he carries and uses his sword and, ultimately, how he lives his life."

I copied the strokes on the rice paper. "There is an order as to which stroke is placed first, much like the patterns of the ken— the sword," he said. "And, as in aikijutsu where you must never lose the connection with your attacker, so too you must never lose the connection between your brush, your paper, and the center of your being."

I tried a few more times, the brush moving awkwardly, like a wounded bird crawling across a road. He sighed and I could see he was growing impatient.

"Do not write with your mind. Write with your soul. Don't think; the movements must come free from the weight of your thoughts." He folded my effort into a neat square and said, "That is enough. I shall get you your own writing set so you can practice on your own."

He wanted me to learn to speak Japanese, and to read and write the three forms of Japanese writing: *hiragana, katakana, kanji.*

"Why must I learn the language?"

"Because I bothered to learn yours." He looked at me. "And because it will save your life one day."

It was hard work, yet I enjoyed it. Perhaps after years of tedium in a constrictive school I had at last been set free to truly learn.

I spent a lot of time on his island, even when he was at his office at the Japanese consulate. As deputy-consul of the northern region of Malaya, he looked into the affairs of the small Japanese community. As such he was quite free with his time, although on occasions there were receptions and dinners he had to attend. He had declined the accommodations provided by the consulate on their premises, preferring to stay on his own.

The Japanese were not very popular in Asia at that moment, due to their presence in China, I told him.

"Let us not talk of war and events far removed from us," he said stiffly.

I was by now used to his manner of speaking, but I found his reply puzzling. He saw the injured expression on my face and softened his tone. "Your government has been pressuring us to cease our incursions into China, even though England and Japan are not at war, and the whole affair is none of the business of the English. I had to listen to the resident councillor berate me today. As though I had a say in the decisions made in Tokyo. This from a representative of a government that saw fit to turn a nation of healthy Chinese into opium addicts just so it could force the Chinese government to trade with it."

I waved away his apology, for he was correct. The British merchants, backed by their government's gunboats, had twice gone to war to introduce opium into China, shifting the balance of trade and the flow of foreign exchange in their favor. Why talk of events that did not concern us?

I looked at the wall of photographs in his home while he was cooking. He was an avid photographer. There were pictures of Japan, mostly of villages, mountains, and botanical gardens, but not a single one of his family. In fact almost none of the

41

photographs were of people. There was a certain blandness about them, an emptiness which I disliked. They appeared to have been hurriedly taken, as if to serve only as a reminder, and not a memory. There was one taken of high, snow-covered mountains that caught my attention.

"Where's that?" I asked him.

"That is the world's highest mountain, in India."

"And that?" I pointed to what appeared to be the only photograph that he had posed for, and even then he appeared tiny and almost indistinguishable beneath a massive sandstone statue of the Buddha carved into a hillside.

"Bamiyan, in Afghanistan. That is one of three statues of the Buddha. That one I am standing in front of is a hundred and seventy feet tall, carved in the third century. A group of Indian boys took the photograph for me."

"You've traveled much," I said. Photographs of dense forests and deserted beaches, as well as formidable mountains, were pinned to another wall. I recognized the tin mines of Ipoh and the rows of rubber trees that covered much of the west coast of Malaya. Hutton & Sons owned a large number of rubber plantations, and the photographs brought back to me the quiet of the mornings when the estate workers walked back and forth along the lines of rubber trees and made cuttings in the bark of the trees, coaxing trickles of milky sap to fill the cups hanging below the cut sections.

A painting in a little alcove caught my attention. It was a drawing, done in shades of black ink diluted in water, the brush strokes simple and almost casual. It showed a bald man with a heavy beard and an unbroken stroke of paint that implied his robes. His eyes were open wide and I thought they looked lidless. The rest of the painting was empty space. I walked nearer to study it, disturbed by the wide staring eyes and the black eyeballs.

Endo-san, seeing I was transfixed, explained. "That is my copy of a painting by Miyamoto Musashi. The man in the painting is Daruma, a Zen Buddhist monk. Do not touch it," he said sharply, as I raised my fingers to stroke the eyes, as though I could close them for the monk and give him rest.

I knew what a Buddhist was, due to the influence of my mother's sister: Aunt Yu Mei was a firm follower of the Buddha. But what was a *Zen* Buddhist, I asked Endo-san.

42

"A branch of Buddhism very much influenced by Daruma. It teaches its adherents to find Enlightenment by way of meditation and rigorous physical discipline. And before you ask what is Enlightenment, it is a moment of complete clarity, of pure bliss. At that instant everything will be revealed to you. Some take years to achieve this, some months, days perhaps, some never at all. In Japan we call such Enlightenment *satori*. The annals of Zen Buddhism have recorded it happening to young novices, untrained monks and temple sweepers, as well as to learned sages and temple patriarchs." Now his eyes became fleetingly humorous. "It is indiscriminate. When it comes, it comes."

"Are you Enlightened?"

He stopped what he was doing, gave a sad smile and said, "No, I am not. I have never been."

"Why not?"

"That is a question I can never answer. I doubt if even my *sensei* can."

"Will I become Enlightened?" I asked, although at this point I could only understand traces of his words. Still, the asking of the question made me sound serious and intelligent. It seemed to have been an expected query.

"I can only teach you the way, that is all. What you do with it and what it does to you, those are beyond my influence."

Each lesson with him would be concluded by a half-hour session of meditation—*zazen*, sitting Zen. It was to free my mind, to achieve what he termed the "Void." What exasperated him, though, was my inability to master this. It was hard to think of nothing and yet not think at all. Try as I might, I found it elusive. It frustrated me, as I wanted to show him that I could accomplish what appeared to me to be the easiest thing of all. Surely I had done enough of that in school to make me an expert?

"Picture your breath as a long slender string," he said. "Now draw it in when you breathe, draw it deep. Beyond your lungs, right into the spot just below your navel, your *tanden*. Pause, let it swirl around and then imagine it being pulled out again as you exhale. That is all you think about in *zazen*—later, as you progress, you will not even think about that at all. You will not even notice your breath. Later on."

It drove me mad, just sitting there in the Japanese way, my legs tucked under my buttocks. Inevitably my attention would drift away, a deluge of thoughts and images would crash into my mind and I would lose the thread.

But those were magical days, just before the threads that bound the world became unraveled. Europe was going to war, and Japan was setting up its puppet regime in Manchuria as a launching pad into a defenseless China. Dark days were coming. But for the moment the sun still shone on Malaya, on the endless rows of rubber trees, and on the tin mines with their melancholic lunar landscape, where the coarse and tough immigrant Hakka coolies crouched in muddy pools and sieved through tons of earth and water to find some tiny granules of tin ore. There were still parties to attend, weekend trips to Penang Hill, picnics by the beach . . .

Endo-san hit my back with his palm and I hurriedly tried to retrieve my own tangled thread.

I sat facing the sea, the waves rolling to the shore like the ticking of a natural clock. "Look out there," he said, pointing to the horizon. "Do you see the spot where the ocean meets the sky? Sitting here, you think that spot is fixed. Yet as soon as you move, even an inch, that spot moves. That is where you must put your mind, that place where air and water meet."

And then I understood what he wanted and, for the first time, I managed to achieve a state of total awareness, even if for just a few seconds. For that short period of time I was there at the spot, yet I was everywhere too. Spirit expanded, mind unfurling open, heart in flight.

Chapter Four

Captain Francis Light obtained the island of Penang from the Sultan of Kedah, with dreams of turning it into a vital British port. He named it Georgetown, after the King of England. By the time I was born the original settlement had grown into a warren of streets stretching from the Quayside into the fringes of the thick, undisturbed jungle.

Georgetown was divided into sections according to race. The British took the best part, naturally. Hence the waterfront was dominated by Fort Cornwallis and the armed forces' camps. The offices of the East India Company, Hutton & Sons, Empire Trading, the Chartered Bank, and the Hong Kong and Shanghai Bank were all located within the vicinity of Beach Street.

Further in, the town was divided into Chinese, Indian, and Malay quarters. Each had its own characteristics, its own temples, clan associations, guilds, and mosques. The streets, all with English names but for a handful of exceptions, were narrow and hemmed in by shophouses on both sides. The shops at street level sold goods from China, India, England, and the various islands of the Malay Archipelago. Traders and their families lived their entire lives here; it was common for three generations to reside in the same building, and as Endo-san and I walked along Campbell Road we could hear the cries of children, grandparents shouting at their servants, and even the sound of an *erhu* player coaxing mournful wails from his stringed instrument.

And there were the smells, always the smells that remain unchanged even to this day—the scents of spices drying in the sun, sweetmeats roasting on charcoal grills, curries bubbling on fiery stoves, dried salted fish swaying on strings, nutmeg, pickled shrimps—all these swirled and mixed with the scent of the sea, fusing into a pungent concoction that entered us and lodged itself in the memory of our hearts.

I pointed out Armenian Street to him, where immigrants from Armenia had lived and carried on their trades. "That's what I was named after. My middle name, Arminius, although I never use it. My mother chose it. Some people have roads named after them; I have it the other way round," I said, and he laughed.

People stared as we walked through the town. Even in his Western clothes Endo-san looked out of place, his features too refined, too aristocratic for a Chinese. He walked slowly, his back straight, his eyes taking in the surrounding stalls and hawkers.

He surprised me when he took me into a small Japanese community just at the edge of the Chinese quarter, on *Jipun-kay*, Japan Street. It was a busy area and there were camera shops, restaurants, bars, and shops supplying food and provisions. To me there was hardly any difference between *Jipun-kay* and the Chinese quarter: even the signboards looked the same, although I was hardly an expert since I could not read Chinese. However the streets here were very clean. People bowed to Endo-san as they passed.

"There it is," Endo-san said, pointing. "Madam Suzuki's restaurant."

Entering the shop, I found it furnished pleasingly: low wooden tables, shoji screens and framed paintings of scenes of nature. Madam Suzuki, a slim woman with small eyes and lacquered hair, greeted us at the entrance. Endo-san nodded to a few patrons as we made our way to our table.

"I never realized there were so many Japanese in Penang," I said as a young Japanese woman laid our table. I stared at her, watched her quick certain movements. She was much shorter than me, her face painted white, her lips a controlled explosion of red.

"They've been here for years. All attracted to the wealth in this region." He ordered for me, the waitress's voice like the sound of wind chimes as she repeated the orders after him. The food came quickly. Most of the dishes were cold and uncooked, which I found disconcerting. It was also quite bland. I was used to the spicy food of Penang, food that squeezed perspiration out of me like a sodden sponge. I told him this and he smiled.

"I have not grown used to your curries and spices here," he said. "Do you like the tea?"

I took a swallow. It tasted bitter and melancholic, which puzzled me, for how could a beverage capture the essence of emotion?

"I have no explanation for it either," he said, when I asked him. "The Fragrance of the Lonely Tree. It is grown on the hills not far from my home."

"What are you doing in this part of the world?" I was curious. He had never told me much about himself. I had looked up the atlas in the library and thought the islands that collectively formed the nation of Japan made it look like a tilted seahorse swimming against the currents of the ocean.

Endo-san's eyes took on a faraway look and he clasped his hands together on the table. "I grew up near the sea in a beautiful place within sight of Miyajima Island. Do you see that painting of the large structure rising out from the sea?" He pointed to a wall behind me.

I turned to look and nodded.

"That is called a *torii*—a gate to a Shinto temple. It is a famous shrine in Japan. Our village has one that is very similar to that, although I admit it is not as impressive. Each morning the sun comes to rest on it and it burns red and gold, as though the gods had just forged it in their furnace and placed it in the sea to cool."

The unadorned lines and subtle curves of the massive gate looked to me like a Japanese ideogram, as though a word of piety had been transformed into a physical structure, an expression of prayer made real.

He came from a samurai family, he told me, part of an aristocratic dynasty that was dwindling in power. Traders were weakening the power and influence once held by the aristocratic and military classes, and often these families borrowed heavily from these businessmen when the rice crops in their fiefdoms failed. Endo-san's father had displeased the emperor and had moved away from Tokyo to venture into commerce, selling rice and lacquer to the Americans and the Chinese.

"Your father worked for the emperor of Japan?" I asked, impressed.

"Many of the aristocracy do. It is not as important as you think. My father was one of the officials in charge of court protocol," Endo-san said. "He advised Western diplomats on how to address the emperor, the proper clothing to wear, the appropriate gifts to present."

"How did he anger the emperor?"

"The emperor was surrounded by a clique of high-ranking military advisors who wished to expand our territories by taking China. My father thought that would be a grave mistake. Unfortunately he did not keep his views to himself."

His father had ensured that his children would never forget their past and Endo-san had spent his childhood learning the skills of the samurai: hand-to-hand combat, archery, horse riding, swordsmanship, flower arranging, and calligraphy. His father also taught him the skills of trade, marrying the principles of warfare to those of buying and selling. " 'Business is war,' my father used to tell us," Endo-san said as he sipped his tea.

He was born in 1890, into one of the most turbulent periods in Japanese history. Japan was then emerging from *sakoku*, a self-imposed national seclusion under the Tokugawa Shogunate that had lasted for two hundred years.

"*Sakoku*—'chain the land'—meant that Japan had closed her doors to foreigners. People could not travel out of Japan. Some did; those who were caught were sentenced to death. Those who traveled out could never return. The laws made by Shogun Tokugawa Ieyasu were enforced strictly."

He told me that the shogun was the supreme military commander, having more power than the emperor, who was merely a figurehead.

"Due to the shogun's strict laws, this period of seclusion became a golden age for the arts: haiku poetry, kabuki, and Noh plays. But by the nineteenth century Japan was crippled by famine and poverty. We were weak, left behind as the world outside advanced. When the Americans sailed to our shores we had to succumb to their demands to open up the country."

I nodded in agreement. It was the same all over Asia. I myself was the result of such a tale.

"The closed-door policy weakened my country. While the nations of the West conquered and colonized, Japan sat to one side, wishing to participate in world events but hamstrung by its historical seclusion and lack of experience and technical knowledge. We sent our brightest minds to Europe to learn, and the success of the Western nations inspired our own military ambitions." He shook his head slowly.

"And it was the coming of the *gai-jin*—the "outside people"—

48

that made trade so lucrative. By the time of my childhood we were besotted with the West. I was taught to play the works of the great European composers, I studied European and American history and I was given lessons in reading and writing and speaking English. That is why I can talk to you today, in a Japanese shop, in Malaya, thousands of miles from our respective homelands. Strange, is it not?"

"My home is here, never England. England, to me is as strange as—well, as Japan," I said.

Silence fell between us, a comfortable silence, while we considered each other's words. Was it only two months ago that a man came to borrow a boat from me? Today I was having lunch with him, hearing his life story. I felt as though in a dream, a surreal and languid pool in which I floated.

We finished our meal of raw fish and rice wrapped in dried seaweed. It was late when his chauffeur returned us to Istana. As he walked down the steps to the beach he said, "I would like to know more of Penang. Will you show me around?"

"Yes," I said, pleased that he had asked me.

That was how I became his guide, taking him around the island. He wanted to look at temples first, and I knew immediately which one to show him.

Endo-san was fascinated by the Temple of Azure Cloud, where hundreds of pit vipers took up residence, coiled around incense holders and the eaves and crossbeams of the roof, inhaling the smoke of incense lit by worshippers.

He bought a packet of joss sticks from a monk and placed them in the large bronze urn after whispering a prayer. Plates of eggs had been left on the tables as offerings for the snakes. I stood around, uncertain. Religion had never played a large part in my life. My mother had been a lapsed Buddhist, but I attended the weekly service at St. George's Church with my family. This temple, with its intricate writings and large wooden plaques— their lacquer chipped and faded—felt strange to me. The various gods and goddesses housed in different altars stared at me from beneath half-closed eyes as I walked past.

A bell tolled, and through the smoke I heard the chanting of monks. A cobra uncurled itself from a pillar and slithered across the uneven tiles, swaying to the drone. Its tongue stabbed out to taste the air, its scales shining like a thousand trapped souls. A passing monk picked it up and slung it over the back of a chair. He asked me to touch it. I stroked its dry, cool skin. Like the snakes, I felt myself being slowly drugged by the smoke and the chanting, which vibrated through my body to be absorbed by my blood and bones.

"A fortune-teller," Endo-san said, pointing to a massive old woman cooling herself with a rattan fan. "Let us see what she can tell us."

I sat before her as she examined my hand. Her skin had the same texture as the cobra's. She studied my face and looked as though she were trying very hard to recall where she had seen me. "You have been here before?" she asked.

I shook my head.

She stroked the writings on my palm and asked for my date and precise time of birth. She spoke in Hokkien: "You were born with the gift of rain. Your life will be abundant with wealth and success. But life will test you greatly. Remember—the rain also brings the flood."

Her vague pronouncements made me pull my hands away from her, but she was not offended. She looked at Endo-san and her eyes became dreamy, as though trying to remember a person she had once known. She returned her gaze to me, her eyes coming back into sharp focus, and said, "You and your friend have a past together, in a different time. And you have a greater journey to make. After this life."

Puzzled, I translated her words for Endo-san, who could only speak a few phrases of the local dialect. He looked momentarily sad, and said softly, "So the words never change, wherever I go."

I waited for him to tell me what he meant, but he remained silent and thoughtful.

"What does my friend's palm show?" I asked the fortune-teller. She crossed her arms over her chest and refused to touch Endo-san. "He's a *Jipunakui*—a Japanese ghost. I do not read their futures. Beware of him."

I was embarrassed at the way she had dismissed Endo-san and wanted to soften her harsh words before I conveyed them to him. "She isn't feeling well, she says can't do any more readings today,"

I said. But he saw the struggle in my expression and shook his head, touching me on the arm to let me know nothing had escaped him.

I paid her and we walked out of the dim, timeless space of the temple into the sun, leaving the reverberations of the place behind, our bodies slowly tightening, coming to stillness again. Everything seemed to move faster outside, even the shadows cast by the sun.

"What did you mean, when you said the words never change?" I asked, as he bought me a glass of cold coconut juice from a roadside hawker.

"I have seen many fortune-tellers, of all sorts. Some have read my face, some my palms. Others went into a trance and asked the spirits for guidance. And always they came back with similar words. That old one back there did not even have to touch me to do the same," he said, starting to walk back to where his chauffeur was waiting for us.

"What did they tell you?" I asked, catching up with him.

He stopped, and turned to face me. I felt compelled to look at him directly. "They told me that we had known each other a long, long time ago. That we will know each other in the times to come."

I found what he was saying, coupled with the fortune-teller's strange pronouncements, quite incomprehensible, and told him so.

"You are a follower of Christ," he said. "You would not be aware of the Wheel of Becoming in which the Buddhists believe."

I shook my head. Seeing my ignorance, he went on, "What happens after you die?"

I answered that easily. "You go to heaven—if you're good."

"But what happened before you lived? Where were you then?"

That simple question caused me to stop walking and think. It could not have been heaven. Otherwise, what was the point of leaving it and going back there again? Finally, I said, "I don't know."

"You had another life. After the end of that life you were reborn to this life. And so it will go on and on until you have redressed all your weaknesses, all your mistakes."

"And what will happen then?"

"Perhaps after a thousand lifetimes, you will reach Nirvana."

"Where is that?"

"Not where, but what. It is a state of enlightenment. Free from pain and suffering and desires, free from time."

"Like heaven," I said.

He turned to look at me and twitched his eyebrows. "Perhaps."

"So the Christian way is shorter. You only have to die once."

He laughed. "Oh, definitely."

I thought no more of the fortune-teller's words. Endo-san's explanations made no sense to me and so I did not dwell on them. My training intensified. Apart from the hand-to-hand combat, he now made me practice with a wooden staff. The weapon came up to my shoulders when it was planted on the ground and he wielded it with great dexterity. In his hands the stiffness of the wood seemed to transform into fluid flexibility.

"Once you have mastered the rudimentary movements of the staff, you will learn how to use a sword. In some instances the staff will be more deadly than the sword," he said. "A sword has only one cutting edge but a staff—*jo*—has two ends to strike. And the entire *jo* is a cutting edge."

He swung the staff, his hands moving up and down the shaft smoothly. "As with all the principles of *aikijutsu*, you do not meet the force of the strike head-on. You parry, you step to the side to avoid the blow, you redirect the force and unbalance your opponent. It is the same with the *ken*, the sword."

I heard the seriousness in his voice as he continued, "These principles apply to your daily life as well. Never meet a person's anger directly. Deflect, distract him, even agree with him. Unbalance his mind, and you can lead him anywhere you want."

The *jo* shot out from his hand and I stepped neatly aside without thought. Putting an *atemi* punch into his ribs I got him tilted off his feet. Merging my subsequent movement into his tilt I threw him to the ground, disarming him of the staff. He landed gracefully and curled his body into an *ukemi* forward roll, to come up again on his feet. When he turned around I was pointing the tip of the *jo* at the softest part of his neck.

We stood there, facing each other, our breaths barely discernible. Only the whisper of gentle waves and the rustle of leaves could be heard.

*

From that moment on we went all out. He still held back, but not by much. As for me, I gave it my all, and in return I received punches, kicks, and bruises from him. I was thankful my family was not around to see me hobbling up from the beach, rubbing my body, putting camphor balm on my bruises. He had warned me that in all fights one had to expect to get hit. The point was to minimize such occurrences.

I trained on my own too, making the effort to get into the daily habit of waking up earlier than my usual time. Long before it was fashionable to go running purely for health reasons I was already doing it, running along the beach, sometimes ten miles a day. I lost whatever fat I had, replacing it with a strange combination of a runner's body and the muscular frame of an *aikijutsu-ka*. I also worked on my swordsmanship, doing hundreds of cuts daily, increasing my speed until my sword came slashing down in a blur. All these activities made me eat voraciously and Ah Jin, our cook, started complaining that I was losing weight in spite of her good cooking.

These were the foundations of a regimen that would go on until I was old—the foundations that made me one of the most respected teachers in the world after the war. The only respite I had was when Endo-san had to attend to his own business. And what that was I never asked. It would not have been polite.

Chapter Five

The most rewarding way to see the place one lives in is to show it to a friend. I had taken the beauty of Penang Island for granted for a long while now and it was only through acting as Endo-san's guide that I learned to love my home again with an intensity that surprised and pleased me.

After the experience with the fortune-teller in the snake temple I made an extra effort to ensure that we avoided the temples whenever we explored the streets of Georgetown. There was never a shortage of places to show him and, in order to impress him with anecdotes and little known facts, I learned more about my home by asking the servants at Istana and reading the books in my father's library.

One evening we stopped outside St. George's Church, drawn by the voices of the choir in practice. We stepped inside and sat at the last pew. When I was younger, I whispered to him, I used to sing with the choir.

He silenced me and closed his eyes as the voices surrounded us, and I sat and listened again to the traditional English hymns that had formed the music of my boyhood. I had given up singing when my voice changed, four years ago, but it comforted me that the tunes and the order of service remained the same.

Afterward, when we were walking within the church grounds, Endo-san said, "That was a very stirring selection."

"Maybe now you can begin to understand why the English feel they have to colonize half the world."

He saw I was only half serious. "What were those last few lines?" he asked. "I heard mention of a sword."

I could still remember the verses I had sung so often: "*I will not cease from mental fight; Nor shall my sword sleep in my hand . . .*"

He nodded and repeated those lines. "I cannot agree. The sword must always remain the last option."

"It's just a song," I said.

"But a song, as you have noted, powerful enough to drive a nation."

"We use swords in training," I pointed out.

"What am I teaching you?"

"To fight," I said.

"No. That is the last thing I am teaching you. What I wish to show you is how *not* to fight. You must never, ever use what has been taught to you, unless your life is in danger. And even then, if you can avoid it, so much the better."

He made me promise him that I would always remember that.

It rained heavily for the next few days and I could not show him around the town. But when the skies cleared again I took him exploring through the quay and the godowns on the waterfront. We walked out to the end of the wooden jetty and stood looking out to the Malayan mainland.

"What is that place?" He pointed to a collection of buildings on the Butterworth shore where two ships were in drydock, lifted high out of the water, their rusted hulls looking as if they had been smeared with galangal powder.

"The second largest shipyard in the country after Singapore," I said. "The navy uses it for their repairs as well."

Endo-san studied the shipyard for a while. Then he turned back to look at the range of hills behind us. "I wanted to ask you what that hill is called, that one with the houses on it."

I knew even without looking what he was referring to. "Penang Hill. The highest point on the island. Those houses you see are government houses and holiday homes. We have a house up there too."

"Will you take me there?" he asked.

"I was planning to," I replied.

We hiked up Penang Hill in the early dawn at the end of the week. His chauffeur dropped us at the foot of The Hill, two miles out of Georgetown, near the Botanical Gardens, and we walked for ten minutes into the forest. It had rained the night before and the path was slippery, the dead leaves turning to mulch beneath our boots. The branches soaked us as we pushed them away. "It's here somewhere," I said, using my walking stick to lever myself up a muddy slope.

"Well, I have never heard of it," Endo-san replied.

"That's because you've never traveled with the locals." I slipped, and his hand held me firmly, pulling me to a standing position.

"Careful."

"There it is," I said. "Moon Gate."

Once it must have been as bone-white as the full moon on a cloudless night. Now the wall with the empty circle in it was stained with moss and fungi. Bird droppings, smeared by the strokes of the rain and dried by the heat, streaked its sides. It stood alone at the edge of the jungle, just a square slab of plastered bricks painted white, three steps leading to the round gateway set in the center.

We went through it, and started the climb up Penang Hill.

"How high is it?" Endo-san asked.

"A little over two thousand feet. It'll take about three hours to reach the top. Nothing like the world's highest mountain."

We could have taken the funicular railway, which had been in operation since 1923, but Endo-san had refused. He wanted to feel the climb, he said. We would take the funicular on our way down.

Within an hour I was soaking wet. My bag felt heavy and despite my daily training my breathing became labored. "Come, keep moving," Endo-san said, hitting my bare calves with his stick. He moved in front of me and set the pace. Rainwater streamed down the path to soak our boots. My hands were muddy from gripping wet branches and pushing myself up from the ground. Roots, many as thick as my wrists, reached out from the earth and made our progress difficult.

We stopped at a wooden tea shack at the halfway point, greeting the other early-morning hikers.

"Look at them," Endo-san said. "They do not look as tired as you. And some of them are not young anymore."

"These are people who climb The Hill every morning. I'm quite certain they're already used to it," I replied, a touch defensively.

Endo-san took out his camera and photographed me sitting on a wooden bench as I drank a steaming cup of tea. Around me birds in bamboo cages brought up by the hikers twittered and hopped on their perches, sensing the approach of dawn.

"Let us go on, you have rested enough," Endo-san said.

We resumed our climb. The sun spread through the canopy of leaves and warmed the air. Tendrils of steam curled up from the ground, as though someone had lit joss sticks and stuck them into the watered earth. Monkeys whooped as they crossed from branch to branch, showering us with heavy droplets of water and damp twigs. Occasionally we caught sight of them, big brown furry creatures that disappeared quickly into the trees, leaving only the trembling leaves to betray their passage.

Just before noon we reached the summit, emerging from a lane behind the Bellevue Hotel. The air was cool at this height and the wind was blowing in banks of mist. We bought crushed sugarcane juice from a hawker and I drank it hurriedly, as though afraid it would disappear. We went past the hotel and went down a narrow road. There were no cars up here, just bicycles and a few army trucks.

"The Hill is always crowded with *ang-mohs*," I said.

He looked puzzled.

"Red Hairs," I explained. The phrase was used to describe the Europeans, many of whom were avoiding the worst of the hot season in Georgetown by coming up to The Hill. Endo-san laughed.

We turned left at a stone fountain set in a circle of flowering plants and entered the gates to Istana Kechil, the Small Palace. I took out the key and opened the front door. There was no one inside. My father came to shoot snipe, birds from Siberia which chose to winter here, and he never allowed anyone to use the house, even when we were not staying there. It had been a long time since we last visited.

The house was musty and cold with the silence of desertion. We opened the windows and doors and went out into the garden, where the bougainvillaea and hibiscus trees were in full bloom, moving in the wind.

Endo-san climbed onto the low wall of granite blocks that bounded our property to prevent people from falling into the ravine below. It was turning out to be a clear day and all of Georgetown lay spread out beneath us. We could even see across the channel to the mountains of Kedah. Turned into shades of blue by the distance, they lay beneath a layer of clouds. Surrounding the mountains were flatlands, cut up into quilted squares of rice fields. Narrow threads of white stitched the smooth surface of the sea: ferries carrying cargo to the mainland; steamships heading for Kuala Lumpur, Singapore, India, and the world beyond; navy boats patrolling for pirates from Sumatra and the Straits of Sunda.

He set up his tripod and began to take photographs: east, west, all directions, shifting his camera with precision, as though he had marked out a grid on the ground. The camera clicked and clicked, like a gecko in mating season.

I remembered the photographs in his house and wondered why he was never shown in them. Was it because he had always been traveling on his own? "Let me take some pictures for you, so you can be in them as well," I offered.

He declined. "My face would only spoil the pictures."

From experience, I knew the night would be cold on The Hill, so we had come prepared. We walked to the Bellevue Hotel for dinner in our black dinner jackets. The headwaiter seated us on the verandah, giving us a view of the lights of the town below, which flowed inland like a tide of white phosphorescence from the water's edge at Weld Quay. The seas enclosing Penang were unseen in the darkness, and only granules of light indicated where the boats were.

Endo-san said with an appreciative tone, "Thank you, for bringing me up here. That sight is worth the climb, is it not?"

"Yes it is, Endo-san," I said, knowing somehow that this would be a night I would always remember.

He narrowed his eyes when he studied the vines in the trellises above us. Something among them made a slight movement. "Are those snakes I see, curled around the vines?"

"Pit vipers," I said. "One of the hotel's claims to fame. There's no need to worry—no one's ever been bitten here. You can hardly see them, they're so well camouflaged."

"But you know they are lying in wait just above, ready to fall on you."

"I ignore them, as does everyone eating here."

"The great human capacity for choosing not to see," he said.

"It makes life easier," I said.

The waiter placed a stove and a pot on our table. On a large plate were some eggs, lettuces, chicken, fish balls, and noodles. As the pot boiled we started to throw everything on the plate into the pot.

"What is this called?" he asked. "Looks like our *shabu shabu*."

"Steam Boat. Perfect for a night like this."

"When is your family returning from London?" he asked, as he placed a cooked egg on my dish.

"Near the end of the year." I burned my tongue as I bit into the egg.

"Tell me about them."

I thought for a while. One takes one's family so much for granted, I never really thought about describing mine to anyone. I took a sip of tea to cool my tongue and said, "My father's forty-nine years old. He has gray—almost white—hair, but a lot of women think he's very good-looking. He keeps fit by swimming and sailing. He works extremely hard. He used to spend more time with us, but after my mother died . . . That's what Isabel tells me. I was too young then . . ." I shrugged, unsure how to explain my father's detachment from his children after my mother's death.

"Yes, I met him, when I signed the lease for the island."

"I have two brothers. Edward's twenty-six and William is twenty-three. They're very much like my father, I think. Edward read law—like my father, he's a qualified barrister but he's chosen to work in the family business. William left university last year and my father wants him to work for the family as well."

"As all fathers do," Endo-san said.

"Edward—well, I'm not close to Edward. He's cold, and we seldom talk. Isabel is twenty-one, and I think she is stronger than my two brothers in many ways. At least she always gets her way. She wasn't very pleased with me when I told her I would prefer to stay at home than go with them to London."

"And you, where do you fit in?"

I shrugged my shoulders. "The half-Chinese, youngest child in an English family? I don't think I fit in anywhere at all."

Endo-san remained silent, and suddenly I found myself saying all the things I was never able to say to my father. "What makes it worse is that I go to the same school my brothers attended. Many of my teachers used to teach them and everyone knows who my brothers are. But instead of making me feel closer to them, it has only widened the differences between us."

"You are not what everyone expected," Endo-san said softly. "And young people are often oblivious to the hurt they can cause."

"Yes," I replied, feeling relieved that he had not belittled my circumstances, but had in fact understood them so thoroughly.

I wrapped my hands around a cup of tea to keep warm. There was only a small crowd tonight, mostly senior British Army officers in their uniforms and with their wives. I recognized some of them. Their voices were loud, happy, and carefree. I pointed them out to Endo-san, and he studied them, almost as if placing them in his mind. A six-piece band started to play and a few of the men led their women onto the dance floor.

"A popular place with the army," he remarked.

"Oh yes. They maintain a small garrison here. Like a lookout point. It makes sense because from here they can see the whole island and the surrounding seas."

"All the way to India," he said.

"Yes, all the way there. Perhaps even all the way to Japan."

He laughed. "Then I shall come up here more often."

We woke up early and greeted the sun as it rose over the rim of the sea. We left the house and climbed down a track to the edge of the cliff, where we sat on a cold, narrow ledge, and began *zazen*. In the vegetable farms below us I heard the roosters crowing. Mongrel dogs barked and wooden gates slammed. Mist wreathed the valleys in thick patches, like frost on moss-covered boulders.

I gripped the edge and felt faint from fear. It was only six inches wide and there was a sixty-foot drop to the tops of the trees below. In my mind the drop lengthened to abysmal depths and I wanted to open my eyes. I imagined the ledge giving way, heard it crumble as the stones broke beneath our weight. To the west, clouds sailed in with the rain and I thought the wind would blow us off. I held on harder and wished the exercise were over and complete. My eyes could not help but drop down to the pointed tops of the trees, spears waiting eagerly in a pit.

"Let go," he said. "You will not fall."

"What if I do?"

"I will catch you."

I glanced up to find him looking at me, not a smile on his mouth, just a nod, and then he closed his eyes again. I thought about his words, words uttered softly, without any faltering, words that would mark a change in my life.

At that moment, I knew I would trust him completely, whatever the consequences to me. I closed my eyes and loosened my fingers and the euphoria of release rushed through me. The sun came out from the clouds and joined us like an old acquaintance. Soon my eyelids burned red beneath as the light filled the world. I no longer felt I was on the cold hard ledge but as if I were floating high above the land, close to the heat of the sun, whose light I could see inside my head, illuminating an expanse that seemed wider than the universe.

After a light breakfast, we went out onto the lawn. We bowed and he kicked me, aiming for my kidneys. I was not fast enough— I was staring at his eyes, at his hands, still thinking of the ledge and his words to me. The pain flared like red ink splashed on paper and I dropped to my knees. I saw his other leg start to move and knew it would go for my head. I rolled along my back and came up standing. The kick missed me and for that split-second he was mine. I lifted his leg, using its upward swing, and kicked the inside of his shin. He grunted and I pushed him off balance, onto the grass. He rolled up onto his feet and sent another kick to my side. I jammed it by moving into it, stopping it from extending fully, but I went right into his fist. It slammed into my cheek and I saw white. I fell backward, and blacked out for long seconds.

"You are improving. But you are still looking at my hands, my feet, and my eyes," he said. He pulled me up and examined my eyes and my cheeks, his fingers stroking my face. "Nothing serious," he said.

"How can I not look at them?"

"You must get rid of your fear. Your eyes dart from my hands to my legs because you are afraid, unsure of yourself. Let go of your worry about getting hit and it will not happen."

I shook my head to clear the fog and to understand what he said.

"Get up. We shall do it again."

I sighed, stood up and went into a fighting stance again.

By the time the lesson ended the storm clouds had come in low, scraping the tops of the range of hills like a dragon's underbelly moving over rocks. We stood by the wall to watch them.

"I always like your clouds here," Endo-san said. "They fly so low."

"On days like these, when the clouds are thick, heaven seems closer, and I almost feel I can touch it."

He looked at me, hearing the wistful tone of my words. "You can touch heaven any time you wish. Let me show you."

He called it *tenchi-nage*, the heaven-earth throw. He gripped both my arms forcefully and asked me to separate them, to raise one arm into the sky, as though to reach into the heart of heaven itself. I lowered my other hand as if to connect with the center of the earth. I felt the weakening of his attack immediately. His strength was divided, torn between the earth and the sky. I entered into his sphere of balance and threw him off his feet easily.

"Now you will always remember me as the man who taught you to touch heaven," he said.

He was looking for a house for the consulate, for the staff to use on their leave. I brought him to a mock-Tudor house that had been built on the northern face of the hill. It had an all-round view from the Indian Ocean to the misty distances of the Malay Peninsula. "It's always been let out to holiday-makers," I said. "The owner's an American silk merchant from Bangkok."

He studied it and took a few photographs. "We shall see if it suits the consul's preferences. But I am certain Hiroshi-san will not find fault with it. Does it have a telephone?"

"Yes. It's one of the few houses up here that has a telephone line."

He folded his tripod and packed his camera, and we started walking back to Istana Kechil. The path wound past the gates and entrances to other homes, all owned by the British. We were at the very top, for even here a hierarchical system was imposed—the local Chinese and Malay people could only own properties on the lower levels, all looking up to the big *ang-moh lau*—Mansions of the Red Hair. A question occurred to me as we walked.

"Why does Japan have a consular office in Penang?" I asked.

"It has a few such offices in Malaya. There is one in Kuala Lumpur and one in Singapore. We have some trade with this part of the world. As I have told you, after so many centuries of seclusion, Japan now wants to a play a part in the destiny of the world."

On the way down in the funicular, which moved so silently I felt we were on a leaf floating down the hill, he asked, "Have you been to Kuala Lumpur?"

"I have. Now and then my father takes us there for a weekend. We have an office there. Most of the trading companies made Kuala Lumpur their headquarters, but he refused to move ours there."

"Well, I agree with him. Your island is much nicer than Kuala Lumpur. I intend to make a short visit there in a few days' time. Again, I need someone familiar with it. Would you like to join me?"

I did not hesitate at all. "I'd like that very much," I replied.

Chapter Six

Uncle Lim, our family chauffeur, came out from the garage when I returned. He looked at me, narrowing his already small eyes. "You've been spending time with that Japanese devil. Better not let your father know."

We spoke in Hokkien, the dialect brought over from the Hokkien province of southern China. The majority of the Chinese immigrants in Penang had been born there before sailing to Malaya in search of work.

"Yes, Uncle Lim," I replied—we always addressed our older servants in respectful terms. "But he'll only find out if you tell."

"I need to send the car to the workshop. I don't know how long the repairs will take. I won't be able to drive you around for some time."

I shook my head. "It doesn't matter. I'm going to Kuala Lumpur with Endo-san next week."

"That man cannot be trusted," he said.

"You dislike all Japanese, Uncle Lim."

"I have good reason to. Day-by-day they're advancing deeper into China. Now they've started bombing the towns." He shook his head. "I've asked my daughter to join me here. She should be arriving in Penang in a month's time."

I heard the anger in his voice, and stopped needling him. Uncle Lim had two wives, who had both left the Hokkien province to work in the silk factories owned by the British in Canton. Every two years he would request leave to return home. That was the one day when my father would drive him to the pier and help him load the bags and presents onto the liner. Despite my father's offer to pay for a cabin, Uncle Lim invariably booked a berth deep inside the ship. "The money can be used for better things," he would say, showing the thriftiness that the Hokkien people prided themselves in but which I often considered to border on miserliness.

"Is your family safe?" I found it hard to accept that Endo-san's people were capable of carrying out such attacks, but from the look on Uncle Lim's face I realized I was wrong.

He nodded, but said, "They're running, leaving for the south. I told them to come here, but they refused. I couldn't order them—that's the problem when women start working in factories, eh? But at least my daughter still listens to me."

"I'll ask one of the girls to prepare a room for her here," I said, knowing my father would have said the same. I wanted to say something more, but at that moment I felt as though I was being spun around in one of Endo-san's *aikijutsu* movements, not knowing where I stood. I could not abandon what I had begun with Endo-san, for my classes with him had become a way of life for me and the knowledge he was imparting to me was too precious to be surrendered. Endo-san was not responsible for what was happening in a land far away, I told myself. So I kept silent and thought that the offer of a room for Uncle Lim's daughter would be sufficient on my part.

Uncle Lim shook his head. "She'll stay with my cousin in Balik Pulau. They'll have a place for her."

I looked at him as he walked away. I knew he was only in his early fifties but I now saw that he was growing old. The other servants were afraid of his temper, but he had never shown it to any of us. My *amah* told me that when my mother first entered Istana as its new mistress she had often wandered into the kitchen, much to the disapproval of the servants there. It was their domain, and she had interrupted their way of running the place. What was more, she was a Chinese woman who had married a European. There had been much unhappiness until Uncle Lim requested my mother to leave the servants alone and stay out of the kitchen. Only he had been brave enough to do so.

Uncle Lim stopped and turned around. "Your eldest aunt rang today. She would like you to pay her a visit as soon as you return."

I made a face. Ever since my mother's death, Aunt Yu Mei had thought she had a duty to watch over me.

"What does she want?" I asked.

"It's almost the end of Cheng Beng, have you forgotten?" he

chided me, referring to the Clear and Brilliant Festival, when families gather to tidy the graves of their parents and ancestors, and place offerings of food and paper money.

"I haven't forgotten," I said, although I had.

It was only just starting to occur to me what a strange place I had grown up in—a Malayan country ruled by the British, with strong Chinese, Indian, and Siamese influences. Within the island I could move from world to world merely by crossing a street. From Bangkok Lane I could walk to Burmah Road and Moulmein Road, down Armenian Street, then to the Indian areas of Chowrasta Market; from there I could enter the Malay quarters around Kapitan Kling Mosque, then to the Chinese sections of Kimberley Road, Chulia Lane, and Campbell Street. One could easily lose one's identity and acquire another just by going for a stroll.

Uncle Lim drove me to Aunt Yu Mei's home before taking the car to the workshop. I watched as he backed into the short driveway and drove off. He had been worried about his daughter and I felt sorry for him, but I knew his dislike of Endo-san, just because he was a Japanese, was wrong. If not, then he should have had nothing to do with my father either, for even I knew of the suffering the British trading houses had caused in China.

Aunt Yu Mei lived in Bangkok Lane, behind the Siamese Wat Chaiya Mangkalaram Temple, where my mother's ashes were kept. Bangkok Lane had two rows of townhouses, the shaded porches reaching almost to the road's edge. Many of the houses' wooden blinds were rolled up, looking like huge sausage rolls hanging beneath the eaves. The houses were all built close together and groups of children played in the road. Cats sunned themselves on the balustrades, twisting their tails and licking their paws. They stopped when I neared them and eyed me with suspicion.

I rang the bell and called out through the wooden shutters, "Aunt Mei!" I heard her on her wooden clogs as she came to the door. It opened and she led me inside. In the front hall, the smell of incense came from an altar on which a bronze figurine of the Buddha sat looking down, eyes half closed, a single palm almost touching the ground to ask the Earth to be his witness.

66

Aunt Yu Mei had never told me her precise age, although I guessed she was about forty and running to that certain plumpness so common in Chinese women. She was the assistant headmistress at the Light Street Convent, the oldest girls' school in the country. She had even, as a very young woman, taught English to my mother's class there. Isabel, too, had been a pupil at that school and had told me that my aunt was strict, but well loved.

My aunt bore scarcely any resemblance to my mother, though she often liked to state that they were identical. Her hair was pulled tight into a shiny bun and a pair of glasses was constantly held between her fingers. As she talked, she would wave them in the air to punctuate her points. She led me to a chair, where she pushed aside a stack of examination papers she had been correcting.

"Did you do well this term?" she asked.

"Reasonably, I think. I wouldn't know yet."

"I hope you've done better than you did last term," she said.

I made vague movements in the air with my hands, feeling uncomfortable with her questions about my academic life. I was at best an average student and she was always trying to change that.

"Did you buy the oranges like I told you to?" she asked.

I lifted the basket I had brought. She glanced at it and nodded in approval. "Your grandfather was wrong when he said you would forget your roots."

I did not know what to reply. In truth I was only doing this to humor her. Every year, at the Festival of Cheng Beng, she would request that I pay my respects to my mother at the temple. My father never objected to her insistence that I light the joss sticks and pray to my mother. In fact, I often felt that he had a high regard for Aunt Mei. Despite her modern education, despite crossing worlds, she was still a woman of tradition—my grandfather had seen to that. Yet she was as strong-willed as he was and had been the only one from my mother's family who had dared to attend her wedding to an *ang-moh*.

We walked to the temple near her house. The crowd was thin, as it was still a few days before the actual festival. We entered the grounds of the temple and walked past the stone statues of snarling, serpentine dragons and mythical birdmen, all painted in brilliant hues of turquoise, red, blue, and green.

The temple was constructed in 1845 by the Siamese community on an extensive piece of property granted by Queen Victoria. Built in the traditions of Siamese architecture, it was trimmed generously in gold and maroon. Stone reliefs of the Buddha decorated the walls in a repeating motif. We walked past two guardian dragons on long concrete plinths, their bodies curling like waves, and left our shoes by the entrance, where a sign in English warned: "Beware of Shoe Thiefs!" Aunt Yu Mei was disgusted at the misspelling.

We entered the temple, our feet bare on the cold marble floors which were patterned with pink lotus flowers. It was like stepping on an infinite series of blossoms. Aunt Yu Mei put her hands together and prayed before the figure of the reclining Buddha inside. The statue was over a hundred feet long from the top of his head, past his flowing robes, to his bare feet and shiny nails. The Buddha lay resting on his side, one hand supporting his head, the other following the curve of his body, his eyes half asleep and half awake, completely aware. It was the same look Endo-san had whenever he was meditating. Small gold reliefs of the Buddha, replicated on the walls, reached up to the roof of the temple. An artisan high up on bamboo scaffolding was patiently outlining them in red paint with a dainty calligraphy brush.

I thought again of the day I had visited the snake temple with Endo-san. How strange religion is. I was used to the austerity of the Anglican Church, and to me temples and their rituals—thick with incense smoke and smells and bright with color, and with their enigmatic words and vague pronouncements—belonged to a disquieting, unfamiliar world.

Aunt Yu Mei nudged me to pray to the reclining Buddha, so I clasped my palms together and tried to appear prayerful. I followed her around the Buddha's couch to the columbarium behind and started searching for my mother's urn. The whole wall looked like a massive honeycomb, every hole housing a porcelain urn. I identified my mother's by her photograph, and placed the oranges on the low table beneath it. Aunt Yu Mei lit the joss sticks and the red candles and placed them in a vase. She closed her eyes and her lips started moving rapidly. Up near the ceiling, a pair of swallows chased each other around the head of the Buddha, their breathless cries loud and resonant. The giant reclining Buddha did not flicker an eyelid.

I held the joss sticks in my hands and tried to picture my mother, tried to gather my scattered memories of her. Pieces of them floated by, fraying and tattered. Every year it became harder and harder. It was like trying to recapture in a bottle the perfume with which the ancient Greeks drenched the feathers of doves, setting them free to flutter around their homes, scenting the air with every beat of their fragrant wings.

Perhaps Aunt Yu Mei knew this; perhaps that was why she insisted I accompany her every year.

The sharpest memory I still held of my mother was of the period during her illness when I was seven. She and my father had been visiting the tin mines in Sungai Lembing, a one-street town located in a central state of Malaya. She had accompanied him in his search for a rare butterfly, and when they returned home she started to show the symptoms of malaria. There were no complications and she should have recovered, but who is to question such things? My father turned one of the rooms into a sanatorium, appointed a nurse to look after her, and had the doctors visit our home twice a day. During that time only Aunt Yu Mei visited. My grandfather stayed away.

She slept most of the time, even when I was brought in to see her. The smell of her room—of the frangipani flowers she so loved that were placed there by my father daily—made me nauseous. I would make excuses to avoid going in there, especially when the fever seized and shook her. I spent more time on the beach, hidden away so no one could find me. When she died the servants had to search the beach to take me home.

I could only stand in silence when my father saw me after the servants finally brought me to her room. He walked around the bed and even then I did not feel his arms around me. I saw only my mother, eyes closed, skin pulled taut, her famous cheekbones now unnaturally high and sharp.

As though to compensate for the horror of the previous weeks, the funeral was beautiful. It was a Buddhist ceremony, though the local Anglican priest had protested strongly. It was a puzzle to me why he had done so—my mother had never been a Christian. All of us attended the ceremony, much to the priest's disapproval.

On the day of the funeral, three monks came to Istana. I stood by a window and watched them as they entered the driveway. They walked across the lawn—the grass so young and new it gave off an unnatural luminescence—past the stone fountain that my mother had loved so much and through the doorway with the cross hanging above the lintel. The monks' saffron robes seemed to catch fire in the sun, so that they looked like flames blowing into our home. The monks led the ceremony that went on through the night until dawn. They rang their bells and chanted from a tattered book, circling the coffin, leading the spirit to its destination, ensuring it would not lose its way.

William tried to comfort me, but I pushed him away. Isabel cried softly. She had found a replacement mother in mine after her own mother's death, and now had lost another one. Edward stood in a corner, solemn but unaffected; he had not been close to my mother. My father reached for my hand. He tried to smile but was overcome by sorrow. I pulled my hand away and he did not even feel it. I was suddenly sorry for my fears and disgust of the past weeks, sorry I could not see or touch my mother again. She was gone.

In the weeks after the funeral my father spent more time with his children—especially me—and Isabel and William tried to include me in outings with their friends. But some children never feel at home in the family they were born to, and I was one of such. I found more solace in the unnameable openness of the sea, on the little beach on the island that Endo-san would one day make his home.

The thin, childlike cries of the swallows brought me back to the Wat Chaiya Mangkalaram Temple. I inserted the joss sticks into the ashes in the vase, making sure all three sticks were straight and would not lean to one side. Aunt Mei was very particular about such matters.

We tidied up the table and packed our little basket. The fruit would be left for the monks. A few worshippers glanced at me as we walked out. As we passed a wall of murals, each panel a scene from the life of the Buddha, Aunt Mei said, "Your grandfather would like to see you."

She was aware of the effect of her words. We both stopped at the same time and studied a panel. The paint had faded and in some places had peeled, leaving behind a musty picture of an Indian prince beneath a tree, one hand stretched out into a void.

"After all this time?" I asked.

"He just wants to talk to you."

"Did you have anything to do with it?" I asked.

"Of course I did," she said, her glasses waving in her hand, and I realized I was being impertinent: she had been trying to persuade my grandfather to meet me since the day I was born. "Will you go and see him?"

I looked at her eager eyes, at her plump face, and knew I owed it to her to do so. I took her hand in mine—it felt so soft and warm—and said, "I'll have to think about it. I really don't know now."

"When will you know?" she asked, making sure I would not elude her.

"When I come back from Kuala Lumpur. I'm leaving next week."

"You are going to K.L.?"

"Yes," I replied, wondering if the sharper tone I had heard in her voice was imagined.

She looked at me. "I'll inform your grandfather."

Endo-san was solemn when we bowed and concluded the class. "Come with me," he said. We entered his house and he ordered me to sit and wait. He went into the back and came out with a long narrow box.

"This is for you," he said, lifting it up with both hands and bending to touch his forehead to it.

I received it in the same manner and placed it on the *tatami* mat. I undid the dark gray ribbon that bound it and opened the box. Inside, a *katana* rested on a bed of silk.

"It looks expensive," I said. "And it seems to be identical to the one you use."

"It is a companion piece to mine."

"You're giving a Nagamitsu sword to me?" I asked, my eyes widening. He had told me that his sword was unique, and much sought after by collectors because it had been specially commissioned.

Although it was customary for Japanese swords to be made in pairs, one sword was always made much shorter than the other for close-quarter fighting. What made Endo-san's swords so highly prized and so unusual, I now realized, was that both were of the same length.

He nodded. "The swordsmith was Nagamitsu Yasuji, a member of the great Nagamitsu family which had been forging swords since the thirteenth century. This pair was made in 1890, after the Haitori Edict of 1877 prohibited the wearing of swords."

I lifted my sword, surprised at its perfect balance. I opened it a notch and he stopped me. "That is enough. You must never pull out your sword completely without the intention of using it. Otherwise it will always thirst for blood."

The two swords, he explained, were mounted in the *buke-zukuri* style, which was the most basic and practical. The scabbard—*saya*—was a dark brown, almost black lacquer, and the hilt was wrapped in a deep gray braid which felt rough and yet gave a comfortable grip.

"There is only one way to tell the difference between the two," he said. "Look." He pointed to a *kanji* character engraved on the blade near the guard. "*Kumo.* That is the name of your sword. It means *cloud.*"

"And what is your sword's name?" I asked.

"*Hikari,*" he said. "*Illumination.* But '*kari*' can also be read to mean '*wild goose.*'"

I was overwhelmed by his gift. "This is too valuable to be given to me," I protested even though I wanted it.

"I would rather give it to you, to be used in your lessons, than have it hidden away," Endo-san said. "I am quite certain that Nagamitsu-san did not intend his work to be kept inside a cupboard. But remember, it must never be used casually. It is always the last resort."

I bowed to him. "Thank you, *sensei.* But what can I give you in return?"

"That is your problem, to be solved by you alone."

I sat thinking and then said, "I'll be back in a little while." I ran to the beach and rowed back to Istana. I did not even bother to tie up the boat, but went up the steps into the house and headed into the library. I went to the shelves, searching for a particular book of poems. I found it, found the page, and rowed back to Endo-san's island. He had already brewed tea in my short absence.

He lifted one eyebrow when I knelt before him and opened the book to the marked page and began to read:

In the blossom-land Japan
Somewhere thus an old song ran.

Said a warrior to a smith
"Hammer me a sword forthwith.
Make the blade
Light as the wind on water laid.
Make it long
As the wheat at harvest song.
Supple, swift
As a snake, without rift,
Full of lightnings, thousand-eyed!
Smooth as silken cloth and thin
As the web that spiders spin.
And merciless as pain, and cold."

"On the hilt, what shall be told?"

"On the sword's hilt, my good man,"
Said the warrior of Japan,
"Trace for me
A running lake, a flock of sheep
And one who sings her child to sleep."

He placed his cup on the *tatami* and I closed the book. "Who wrote that?" he asked, so softly.

"Solomon Bloomgarden. It's a Hebrew poem. My father read it to us once, long before we knew what a warrior of Japan was."

He sat so quietly for such a long time that I was afraid my gift had been inadequate or—worse—that I had somehow given offense. Then he blinked and smiled, although I could still see a faint shade of sorrow in his eyes.

"It is a good poem, a beautiful poem," he said. "Your appreciation of it makes me glad, for it means you are starting to understand the lessons I am trying to teach you. Please write it down for me and I shall consider my gift of your *katana* to have been returned in full. *Domo arigato gozaimasu.* Thank you."

Chapter Seven

Michiko closed the anthology of poetry. "It is a heartfelt poem," she said. She touched the dusty cover of the book at almost the exact same spot Endo-san had done, on the day I read the poem to him.

"I wrote out a copy for him, just as he asked and he always carried it with him even after he had it lodged in his memory," I said. "I once asked him why. And he said he was afraid of forgetting where he came from."

There was no reason to show her the book—I could still recite the poem from memory—but somehow it made what I had been telling her all the more real. "There were times when I wondered if it had really all happened or whether everything was a dream, like the Chinese philosopher's dream of the butterflies," I said.

"'You the butterfly—I, Chuang Tzu's dreaming heart,'" she quoted Matsuo Basho's haiku. "Does the philosopher dream of the butterfly, or is he merely the butterfly's dream?"

I placed the book back on the shelf and led her out of the library. "It's late."

"I am not ready for sleep yet. Are you?" she asked.

I was not. But I felt, for the moment, unable to go on telling her about my youth. I looked out of a window into the dark night and made a sudden decision. "I want to show you something. We'll have to walk some distance. Are you up to it?"

She nodded, her eyes sharing the infectious excitement in my voice. I went to my study and took two flashlights from a cupboard. I shook them to check that the batteries were still working and handed one to her. We walked down the wooden steps onto the beach, choosing a path high above the tide line. Hundreds of translucent crabs scuttled away at the vibrations of our footsteps, parting before us like a curtain of glass beads. There was sufficient light to render the flashlights unnecessary, so we did not switch them on.

"Do you still have your Nagamitsu sword?" she asked.

"Yes, I do."

"I never realized the one sent to me was one of a pair," she said. "Even the swordsmith who restored it never knew."

"The Chinese consider it a great taboo to present a friend with a knife or a sword, as it would sever the ties of friendship and bring unhappiness," I said. "I've always wondered whether Endo-san knew that."

I walked faster, uncertain if I had made the right decision in choosing to reveal my whole life to her. I reassured myself that I could stop at any moment I wished, any moment at all.

I could have walked in total darkness, so often had I done this, and somehow she knew it, for she followed me without hesitation. There was only the thinnest slice of moon wedged into the sky between the clouds, which was perfect for what I had in mind.

The beach narrowed. Ahead, we could make out the dark clumps of boulders blocking our way and hear the waves against them. An estuary lay beyond these rocks, but to get there I had to guide her away from the beach into the windswept trees that edged the beach.

The walk became harder as the ground inclined upward and I switched on the flashlight so that she would not trip over tree roots. The smell of the sea was soon layered with the sharper, almost chemical, scent of fresh water as we followed a track that would bring us to the river. Crickets stitched their regimented notes into the air. The wind was cold, and the leaves in the trees rubbed together as though to keep warm.

The river itself was quiet but for the gargling of frogs. Then an owl skimmed soundlessly over the water and there was a sudden petrified silence as the frogs felt it pass.

The path went downhill again. We caught the scent of a frangipani tree and came to it a few moments later. Next to the tree was a wooden shack which leaned dangerously into the river. Inside was a sampan and, with Michiko's help, I managed to set it in the water, where it bobbed, eager to get going.

"Whose boat is this?" she asked as I helped her in.

I shrugged. "I put it here for anyone to use. But no one ever comes here."

I pushed us off and immediately the flow of the river caught the boat. As we drifted downstream I heard her soft but labored breathing and worried that the walk had been too much for her.

"Are you all right?" I asked.

"I'm fine," she said.

I dipped the oars into the water and slowed our progress. "Close your eyes," I said. I switched off the flashlight and studied the movement of the clouds. The wind was pushing them across the weak moon, gradually filtering out its light from the sky, turning the night completely dark.

When we had drifted to the right place, further down the river, I whispered softly, "Now—open your eyes."

She drew in her breath. A light layer of mist rose up from the surface of the river and, in the trees, shining as though the stars had fallen to earth, tens of thousands of fireflies were sending out their silent mating signals. We were caught in a frenzy of fragmented light. I heard Michiko let out a sigh and felt her hand reach for mine. I moved it away and gently spun the boat in a circle, keeping it in the same spot as beneath us the river ran to the sea.

I wet my fingers and sat unmoving, trying to discern a pattern in the fireflies' random flight, the stillness within movement which, Endo-san said, all living things possess. I reached out and plucked one from the air, sticking it to my dampened finger, and offered it to Michiko.

She took it carefully. The insect lay in the bed of her palm, its wet wings adhering to her skin. Its light seemed to pulsate with the beat of her heart and cast a faint glow onto her face, reflecting in her eyes.

There were tears when she lifted her face to me. "How did you know?" she asked.

"Endo-san once told me he used to go to the river outside his home and watch the fireflies. He often went with a friend, and tonight I had the strongest feeling you were the friend he had spoken of so fondly."

She blew gently onto her palm, drying the firefly. It flew off into the flurry of blinking lights that swirled around us. "I have not seen such a large number of *hotaru* for a long time," she said. "I returned to the river near my home a few years after the war, but the fireflies had all disappeared, as though blown away by a terrible storm."

I paddled us to the edge of the river and let the boat nudge into the bank beneath a canopy of branches heavy with droplets of light. I leaned back into the boat and said, "My father told me about this place. I never knew about it until then."

She remained quiet for a while and I wondered if she had drifted off into sleep. The boat creaked as it flexed to accommodate the flow of the river. It was so peaceful, just sitting there in the darkness surrounded by a blizzard of fairy sparks, even as the fireflies were communicating with one another without making a sound.

I felt myself nodding off, but then she spoke. "You must know the tale of the shepherd boy in China who was too poor to buy candles for his studies at night."

"I've heard of it," I replied. "He filled a white cloth bag with fireflies and used the light they gave off to study at night, didn't he?"

"Yes. It was Endo-san who told me about it. He had heard it on his travels to Canton."

"I heard it from my mother when I was very young. She also told us that the shepherd always released them the following morning, and would catch different ones at night," I said, trying to remember. "She was full of interesting stories like that. She knew many of the folktales of China, but she loved most those that involved insects and birds and butterflies. Especially butterflies."

"Why butterflies?" Michiko asked.

"My father collected them. He had cases of them, all carefully mounted. In fact, that is why they were in that town where she caught malaria; they were on an expedition to find—" I waved my hand carelessly, "I can't even remember what it's called now— some rare specimen for his collection. The name will come back to me."

"I did not see any butterfly collection in your house," she said. "What happened to it?"

I said nothing and she was too considerate to ask again. After a short silence she said, "When you sat so still, trying to catch a firefly for me, you reminded me so much of Endo-san. He could sit as unmoving and immovable as the statue of the Buddha in Kamakura. That was how he appeared, on the day his father, Aritaki-san, was placed on the *shirasu* before my own father, who adjudged him guilty of treason against the Emperor."

I knew of the procedure she was referring to. In Japan, in the years before the Second World War, an accused person was required to kneel before a magistrate in a sand-covered square enclosure known as *shirasu*—the "white sand"—where judgement was given. I had been told of overzealous magistrates who also carried out executions on this pristine white patch, because the sand absorbed the spillage of blood so easily and could be quickly replaced with new, unblemished sand.

"I was not completely honest when I told you that I ceased my relationship with Endo-san upon my father's orders," Michiko said. "In fact I disobeyed him. He was so enraged that he ordered an official investigation into the anti-government comments and statements made by Endo-san's father. It was not difficult to bring charges against him after that."

She leaned forward, rocking the boat. "In Japan, to destroy a person, you only have to discredit his blood-kin. So you see, in my selfish way, I played a part in the downfall of Endo-san's family."

I did not know how to respond. What balm would my words, uttered half a century too late, be to her anyway?

"And Endo-san sat, so immobile, for so long, a statue planted on the white sand after the proceedings were over and his father was taken away," she continued. "He never spoke to me again, except for that last time, to tell me he was leaving."

I touched her hand with the softness of a firefly alighting on her skin. Then I picked up the oars and took us out into the middle of the river and let it carry us slowly to the sea. We floated down-stream through trees thick with burning fireflies, until they faded away and we were once again in the dark, guided only by the strengthening smell of the sea and the faint light of the moon.

It felt unsettling to have another person living in the house and I wondered if I had been too hasty in extending an invitation to her. And yet it felt good, somehow. She was an unobtrusive guest. I had never spoken to anyone of my own experiences in the war and, to my surprise I realized that she was the first person who had ever asked me to describe them, who wanted to know about them from me instead of hearing wildly differing fragments from various people and drawing their own conclusions. No one else had ever considered raising their questions directly with me.

This last realization left me shaken. Was it because I had all this time been silently transmitting signals that could not be detected or deciphered by others, and thus could never elicit the response I wanted? Even the fireflies, however voiceless they were, still managed to send out their messages and have them responded to.

A hand touched my arm, and I blinked and pulled in my thoughts—a fisherman hauling in his drifting nets from the sea. Michiko's face was tense with concern. "I called you twice, but you never answered."

"I was very far away," I said. It was so effortless to admit this to her.

"It happens more often the older we get, does it not?" she said. "Maria wants you to know lunch is ready. She is not going to wait."

As we left my room she said, "I have not thanked you for taking me to the river last night. The sight of the fireflies brought back so many memories."

"I'm sorry if they brought you pain as well," I said. "That wasn't my intention."

She shook her head. "I've learned to live with that. Who can look back and truly say all his memories are happy ones? To have memories, happy or sorrowful, is a blessing, for it shows we have lived our lives without reservation. Do you not agree?"

She did not wait for my reply but turned and went down the stairs. I was suddenly aware that I had not been as silent all these years as I had thought. The sole reason Michiko had heard was because of Endo-san's letter to her. He had heard, he had known. And in sending her to me he had responded.

Chapter Eight

Endo-san's chauffeur dropped us at Weld Quay, in Georgetown harbor. The visit to Kuala Lumpur had been postponed for more than a month due to his work commitments and by now I was quite impatient to get going. We pushed our way through Chinese and Tamil dock coolies as they ran about, shouting and pushing carts of smoked rubber sheets, tin ingots, and bags of cloves and peppercorns. Rickshaws clattered past, their wheels bouncing on the uneven roads. I felt the sense of excitement of one about to rush headlong into an adventure and an unrestrained smile spread over my face. Endo-san saw it, and his eyes danced in reply.

He had chartered a small steamer from a Dutchman and we waited at the end of the pier for a boat to carry us to where the *Peranakan* lay. The small, almost flat-bottomed sampan, rowed by a Malay boy, smelled of dried fish and rotting wood. The steamer lay angled on its side, waiting for the tide to lift it out of its rest. It was small compared to the others we saw moving out to sea. A few planks of a different shade had been hammered over the cabin and the deck had a faded canvas awning to keep the sun out. Two wooden chairs were placed under it. A small banner of smoke hung above the blackened funnel.

As we climbed aboard, the sun seemed to make up its mind and rose rapidly. The light spread like golden powder flung by some sweeping hand. I looked back at the harbor. The shore was lined with godowns and braced with a line of stilts and walkways. Tiny figures ran on them, some in white vests, others bare to the waist. The Tamils wore white headcloths and their voices sounded like the cries of the gulls now flying above us. Beyond the harbor, the low humps of the island appeared like moss-pelted boulders, and the tiny homes embedded in the side of Penang Hill glinted bright as dewdrops.

The sea around us lightened, changing from the thick murki-

81

ness of early dawn to a clear emerald. Shoals of tiny fish, so translucent that they left no shadows on the sand bed, darted away at our movements. A few jellyfish floated in the water, their tentacles flowing behind the unseen currents like a girl's hair in the wind.

The Dutchman met us on deck, his face burned to a wooden brown, his eyes the color of the sea, only clearer, brighter. When he took off his cap his bald scalp had the hardness and glossiness of a nut. He appeared to be in his fifties and looked quite strong, an impression heightened by a big hard stomach that seemed to come between us as we spoke.

"Good to see you again, Mr. Endo," he said.

Endo-san introduced me to Captain Albertus van Dobbelsteen.

The captain looked at me closely when Endo-san mentioned my name. "Hutton, from the company?" he asked.

"That's correct," I replied, looking at Endo-san and wondering what the Dutchman's story was.

The Malay boy hauled our bags aboard and tied the sampan to the steamer. The wooden boards creaked as we moved under the canvas. Endo-san sat down but I leaned over the railing, loving the wind and the flecks of water that sprayed me as the steamer gave a shudder and came to life. Like a fist, a cloud of thick black smoke punched out of the funnel and then opened into the wind, followed by a steady, gray stream that trailed behind us.

I put on a straw hat and smiled idiotically to Endo-san. I could not help it; the feeling of excitement, of something new, sang in my blood and made my head light.

"I take it you have never been on board one of these before?"

"No, never in my life." In all my previous journeys to Kuala Lumpur with my father we had traveled by rail: across mist-covered limestone hills, through dark green forests.

"Then you are going to enjoy these few days. We won't be rushing, because there will be a stop I would like to make."

I waved a hand to indicate my indifference. The distance from Penang to Port Swettenham, where we would have to disembark to enter Kuala Lumpur, was about five hundred miles. We would be tracing the coastline, keeping within sight of it for most of the journey.

"The captain doesn't seem to like me," I said, tipping my head toward the cabin.

"Albertus? He used to sail for your father's company up and down the Yangtze River in China until he was sacked a year ago."

"What happened?"

"There were complaints—he could not keep his hands off the crew. Also, he happened to be drunk most of the time. Don't worry, he is sober now. And when he is, he is one of the best steamer captains there is. These Yangtze sailors are the best."

I looked back at the cabin, wondering if my father had personally dismissed the captain. Noel Hutton could be hard and unrelenting when it came to doing the best for his business. From company gossip I knew which misdemeanor would have been the deciding factor: he would never tolerate a drunken ship's captain. For a moment I felt sorry for Captain Albertus but he appeared to be doing well for himself.

We had a late breakfast, cooked by the Malay boy—coconut rice and a sweet and spicy anchovy paste, with a perfectly fried egg on top—*nasi lemak*, I told Endo-san. Captain Albertus joined us, drinking coffee from a chipped enamel mug. He handed us a small jar and said, "Put this on when the sun gets higher."

I opened it and took a sniff. "Coconut cream."

"And some herbs and oil. My own concoction. Helps to avoid sunburn," Captain Albertus replied.

The cream was soon put to use as the heat baked us. The sun was alone: the clouds had deserted the skies. We were on the most famous straits in the world, making the same journey seafarers had been making for hundreds of years, the Chinese, the Arabs, the Portuguese, the Spanish, Dutch, and British. And before them, who knows?

I sat next to Endo-san and gave a contented sigh. He looked up from his book and said, "Happy?"

I nodded and then began to tell him of my visit to Aunt Mei. He put aside his book and leaned back. "Tell me about your mother."

I told him what I could remember, treading water in the shallows of my memory. "Now my grandfather, whom I've never seen, and who cut off my mother from her family when she married my father, wants to see me."

"Then you should see him. Family is the most important thing you will ever have."

"You really think I should see my grandfather?"

"*Hai.* You may even find that you like him," he said, and returned to his book.

I thought of the grandfather I had never met, and wondered what he wanted from me. I examined my feelings for him and found I felt barely anything, except a glimmer of obstinate dislike that seemed to originate more from a sense of rejection than anything else.

Halfway through our journey the chord of the engines changed. It was three in the afternoon and I had fallen asleep on deck. I woke up as I felt the slight turn in direction. I shaded my eyes and looked around me.

We were approaching the coastal mangrove swamps. The shoreline came closer, the waves making an effervescent line of white on the rocks. There was no beach in sight, just an endless row of mangrove trees, their roots exposed as the tide started to withdraw, leaving them slick and glistening and arthritic. The water around us lost its turquoise color, tainted by the rusty leaching of the roots, like leftover tea. Birds chased their reflections on the water and flew in and out of the jungle rising above the trees.

The engines stopped and I could suddenly hear the silence of the swamp, threaded through with birdcalls and the drilling of insects. The lap of water against the roots sounded dispirited. As we swayed in the backwash of the waves the Malay boy dropped the anchor. Through a break in the mangroves a landing platform jutted out, and on it a mongrel dog stood barking at us, hopping left and right in that futile and idiotic way that only dogs have.

"Where are we?" I asked Endo-san when he climbed out from the cabin.

"Just twenty miles south of Pangkor Island. I did not wake you up as we passed it; you were sleeping so deeply. We are getting off here, at Kampung Pangkor."

"What are we doing here?"

"Visiting a friend."

The Malay boy loaded the sampan with boxes taken from the cargo hold. We climbed down a rope ladder into the sampan and Captain Albertus brought us to the jetty. Endo-san held a long box which I had helped carry onto the steamer. It had felt strangely heavy but I had refrained from asking about its contents.

By the time we reached the jetty a small crowd had gathered. They were Malays, dark-skinned and wide-eyed, who stared at us, chattering loudly.

A small Japanese man appeared through the crowd, bowing to Endo-san once we had climbed onto the platform. They walked away, talking in Japanese. I followed at a distance, hearing Captain Albertus shout to the villagers to take care with the boxes. Behind the mangrove swamp, the village appeared busy. The narrow lanes were muddy and slippery. Chickens ran around the little plots of vegetables fronting the small wooden shacks built on stilts. A wide estuary curved around the village and, on its banks, tied to poles, was a line of fishing boats with clumps of nets hanging on their sides like fuzzy growths of fungus.

We followed the small Japanese to the provision store he owned. He closed the door and pushed away some salted fish lying on a counter. The store was heavy with the smell of old onions and chillies and mice. He lit a pipe, saw the look of annoyance on Endo-san's face and hastily put it away.

"Kanazawa-san," Endo-san introduced him to me.

"*Konichiwa*, Kanazawa-san," I greeted him and bowed. The man looked surprised, but returned my greeting politely.

Endo-san opened the box and picked out a rifle. The smell of gun oil and powder charged the stuffy air and I felt my stomach churn.

Endo-san led me along a fern-covered path and for the first time in my life I entered the real jungle of Malaya. Beetles crawled up tree trunks, their crab-like pincers rasping on the bark. Butterflies, some bigger than my palm, soared away as we rustled the bushes. Behind us lay the village, but I knew I was lost. We had been walking for half an hour, climbing over fallen trees and crossing a riverbed strewn with smooth round rocks. We came to a clearing and he unslung the rifle. He took a small box containing bullets from his pocket, and loaded it.

"Why do I have to learn how to shoot?" I asked. Isabel was a champion marksman at the Penang Shooting Club, but I had never been keen on the sport.

"As your *sensei*, my duties are not confined to the *dojo*." He swept his hand around, indicating the forests, the columns of trees soaring to the emerald canopy above. "This, the whole world, is your *dojo*."

He handed me the rifle and using a knife cut a small circle in a tree. It seemed too far away. "Utilize the principles of *aikijutsu*. Focus, extend your thought, your *ki*. Breathe, and relax."

I stared at him, uncertain. For the first time since we met I felt unwilling to follow his instructions. He saw my hesitation and showed me the movement, which he made so fluid and assured. His eye went to the sight, his body into a side stance. I heard him exhale and then the sound of the shot. A small burst of splintered bark exploded and the echo of the shot set a thousand flapping wings in flight.

"Follow what I have just demonstrated," he said. There was no possibility that I could disobey the tone of his voice.

I took the rifle again and repeated his movements with as much accuracy as I could achieve. The gun was heavy and the first shot arced high into the leaves as I stumbled backward.

"Extend your hand, keep the extension and the kick will not unsettle you."

My ears rang and I steadied myself. Little by little I managed to get it right, although by that time the tree had been mutilated. Sap ran down the trunk like blood from a severed artery and shreds of wood lay scattered around its roots.

We stopped when my hands were trembling from the shooting and my shoulders felt sore. "I'm not expected to use this, am I?"

"No," he replied. "But it may be useful to know how to. My grandfather taught my father to shoot when the Americans came to my country. It was virtually impossible to obtain these foreign weapons, but my grandfather did. I was taught, using similar weapons, by my father."

"What does Kanazawa-san require the rifles for?" I asked, when he allowed me a moment's rest. I was trying a different tack to get him to answer my question. Lead the mind, and the rest will follow, Endo-san had instructed me so many times. Learning to use a rifle in the jungle was quite different from the bantering atmosphere at the Penang Shooting Club where Isabel practiced. The whole journey, which had begun on an enjoyable note, now seemed filled with an uncertainty. Perhaps it was being in the heart of this untamed land where anything could happen. I had swum too far out from shore, lured on by something beyond my confined life, and suddenly I wanted only to head for home.

It would never cease to be a cause of wonder that Endo-san could sense my every mood and uncover my uncertainties. He took the rifle from me and said, "Knowing how to shoot does not mean you have to use it. In fact, I would prefer that you never use it. I have never used a weapon against anyone, least of all something as unrefined as a firearm. If you are strong here," he touched my head gently, "no one will be able to force you to resort to it."

He sat down on the root of a fig tree. "Do you understand?"

"Resistance," I said. "To strengthen my mind, there must be resistance, something hard enough to fight against."

Endo-san nodded. "Kanazawa-san runs the local provision store, as you have seen. Now and again he has requests for special items. He takes care of the few Japanese rubber buyers working in this area. Pirates have been attacking his village. He has to have some means of protection."

"Pirates?" I asked. "Where from?"

He shrugged. "Sumatra, or Java. The villagers' fishing has been affected because they fear going out to sea."

"Why is Kanazawa-san here, in this part of the country?"

Endo-san did not reply. He stood up and bowed. "We will end our lesson here. It is getting dark. I think we should get back to the village."

As he led us out of the jungle, I realized that, although I had tried to lead his thoughts to where I wanted them, he had without effort lifted me off the ground and spun me around in more circles. A part of me wondered at what he did not say, but another part of me was once again made aware that I had been chosen by a remarkable teacher, and that fact was of greater importance to me.

We were put up at Kanazawa's house and his wife fussed over Endo-san and me during dinner, pouring us cups of tea and *sake*.

I met some of the Japanese rubber buyers. They were all quite young, all of them could speak the Malay language, and each had an indefinable toughness in him. I would not be able to identify this quality of theirs until I began training with some of the consulate's staff, and only then it would come to me that the rubber buyers I had met had the air of well-trained soldiers.

They talked of a recent attack by the pirates. "These new weapons will be very useful to us," one said. "Now we can get rid of them all."

"We've already killed quite a few," another said, lifting his *sake* cup. They all laughed, but the mood turned somber as more *sake* was consumed.

"Where are you from, Endo-san?" a rubber buyer asked.

Endo-san said, "The village of Toriijima, Toshi-san."

"A most beautiful place. I once saw the shrine at sunrise," Toshi said. "I wish I could see it again. Don't you miss your home?"

Toshi looked around the table. The question was directed to no one in particular, but the rubber buyers looked to Endo-san.

"I do. We all miss our homes. I am certain you miss your family and the women who are waiting for your return," Endo-san said and I heard a low note of sadness in his words. "But we have our duty. If we fail in our duty, we fail our country, and our family." He looked firmly at me as he said this, as though hoping that, some day, I would understand.

Endo-san spent the next morning conferring with Kanazawa and I was left to wander along the river, keeping my eyes on the banks for crocodiles hiding among the mangroves. I was reminded of the Malay folktale of the cunning mouse deer which, while drinking by a river, has its leg captured in the jaws of a crocodile. It escapes being eaten by deceiving the predator into believing that the captured leg is only the root of a mangrove tree.

Storks stood unmoving in the rusted shallows, watching me. The strength of the wind seemed able to only rustle the fringe of the jungles, leaving the deeper interior unruffled.

The storks heard the planes before I did. There was a frantic beating of wings as two Buffalo planes from the Royal Australian Air Force flew low over the hills and along the estuary. The storks opened their wings and rose above the river into the trees as the planes headed out to the sea, the sun shining on their cockpits. A crocodile I had missed thrashed into the river to burrow into the mud.

I saw Endo-san emerge from Kanazawa's store and went to meet him. "Get ready to leave," he said. "And we have a new passenger."

Two of the Japanese men I had met the night before at Kanazawa-san's home led a man from a wooden shack, his hands bound with rope, and brought him to the jetty.

"But he is a Japanese," I said.

"That makes his crime more serious."

I waited for Endo-san to explain. "Yasuaki was caught stealing from Kanazawa-san's shop. He had been doing it for some weeks," Endo-san said.

"Why did he do that?"

"He was making preparations to run away, to abandon his duty. He was appointed to purchase rubber for his country. But instead he spent his time with the local women, and fell in love with one of them. The theft of food and supplies was to enable him to run off with this woman."

"And for that he is to be punished?" I asked.

"You have absorbed your lessons well, but you have yet to comprehend how important the concept of duty is," Endo-san said.

"Duty even above love?" I asked, thinking of his words the night before at the dinner table: *If we fail in our duty, we fail our country, and our family.* The Japanese people held duty in high esteem, I had learned, but to see it impose its unbending burden on the most timeless of human needs made me question the value of it.

He heard the tone of my voice, and softened the harshness of his words. "It has always been so in our way of life. One cannot escape it."

"What's going to happen to him?"

"That will depend on the authorities in Kuala Lumpur. He will probably be sent back to Japan."

"Will he see the woman again?"

Endo-san shook his head and climbed into the sampan.

We passed a few fishing boats, which had dared to brave the dangers of the pirates, returning home after a night's work. The men on board seemed to recognize the *Peranakan,* giving short bursts from their horns and calling out to Captain Albertus. When we neared Port Swettenham a shoal of flying fish shot out from the sea and soared alongside us before dropping back into the water. I stood on the stern, waiting for them to appear again, to lose their ties to the sea and, for a few moments, to find a new identity as they took their breath not from water but from wind.

Yasuaki, the Japanese rubber buyer who had placed love before his duty, watched me. Endo-san had asked me to untie his ropes and now he leaned against the stern and said, "I feel sorry for you."

"Why?" I asked, shading my eyes against the light, hoping to see more of the flying fish.

"Nothing good will come from your association with us," he said.

I turned away from the sea and studied him with greater attention. I placed him around Edward's age, maybe older. Until now he had remained silent, perhaps thinking of the woman he had been separated from.

"What was her name?" I asked.

"You are the first person who has asked me her name. But what does her name matter?" Nevertheless, he looked pleased that I had asked.

"I would like to know," I said.

He studied me for a moment. "Her name is Aslina."

"Was she a girl from the village?"

He shook his head. "Her father ran the canteen at the airfield near the village. You would have seen the planes when they flew past. They do it every day."

I had found a map and studied it in Kanazawa's shop. The village we had spent the night in was an hour from Ipoh. The map showed an air force landing strip only half an hour east of the village, marked in red by the Japanese shopkeeper.

"Was she worth disobeying your duty?" I asked.

"I could not be placed in a position where I would have to harm her, or her people," he replied.

"Harm her? How?" I asked, but he had turned back to the flying fish, an expression of longing on his face.

"You must really love her," I said, feeling suddenly sad. I had never felt such an emotion. Isabel often went on at length about it, although we teased her. I had always thought love was a thing only young girls fretted about, but here was a seemingly intelligent man who had experienced it, and who now was paying dearly for it—his reputation ruined, the girl he loved lost to him.

"Have you ever met someone who is so close to you, so right, that nothing else matters? Somebody who, without being told, knows each and every aspect of you?"

I looked at him, uncertain of what he was trying to tell me.

"Well, that is how I feel with Aslina. And duty?" His voice turned bitter. "Duty is a concept created by emperors and generals to deceive us into performing their will. Be wary when duty speaks, for it often masks the voice of others. Others who do not have your interests at heart."

I was about to ask him more, but Endo-san came over to me and said, "Get your things together. We will be reaching Port Swettenham very soon."

Chapter Nine

We arrived in Port Swettenham late in the afternoon. I watched as Yasuaki was led away by the staff of the Japanese Embassy. I raised my hand in a small wave but he never returned it.

A car with a Japanese driver took us into Kuala Lumpur. We entered the town an hour later, and I recalled the last time I had been here. It was almost ten months before, when we celebrated my father's forty-ninth birthday in the Spotted Dog Club just in front of the cricket padang in the center of the town. The ground was busy now, the cricketers running between the shadows cast by the court buildings across the road. I heard the *thock* of the ball hitting the bat and then cheers as the batsmen ran. It was a typical afternoon in the biggest town in Malaya: the English would leave their sweltering offices, go to the Spotted Dog to have a gin and tonic, play some cricket, and then return home for a bath before coming back to the club for dinner and some dancing. It was a good life, a rich life filled with ease and enjoyment.

The Japanese Embassy was a converted bungalow on a hill just behind Carcosa, once the official home of the Resident General of the Federated Malay States. The road leading up to it was cool and shady, the old angsana trees littering the way with leaves and pods and twigs that crackled under our tires. The sentry at the gates saluted us through.

A youth in military uniform brought our bags to our rooms. The fan was switched on immediately. Then we went out onto the verandah where we were served glasses of iced tea.

The Embassy looked down a wooded slope thick with flame-of-the-forest trees. I stood drinking my tea and thought about the concept of duty, which had troubled me during the entire drive. It was so confusing and, it seemed to me at that moment, so pointless. Where was the freedom of choice that each of us had been born with?

Endo-san had told me at the beginning of my lessons how strong the duty of teaching was, once undertaken. It was never offered freely or haphazardly. A prospective student had to provide letters of recommendation in order to convince a *sensei* to accept him. Teaching could never be accepted without all its burdens and obligations and I had come to understand this eventually. Yet in my mind I heard Yasuaki's words, warning me about duty and generals and emperors. A moment of unease made me finish my drink in a single swallow.

"We must pay our respects to Saotome Akasaki-san, the ambassador to Malaya," Endo-san said, beckoning to me to follow him downstairs.

Although the bungalow was built in the typical Anglo-Indian style, with wide wooden verandas and large airy ceilings, it had been decorated strictly by a Japanese hand. The rooms were partitioned by paper shoji screens, scrolls of calligraphy hung at well-lit positions and a faint smell of incense cleansed the air as we passed. Stark, skeletal flower arrangements stood on low tables. "These are Saotome-san's personal arrangements," Endo-san said. "His *ikebana* has won prizes in Tokyo."

Another youth in uniform slid open a door and we placed our cotton slippers outside before entering. The room was bare, save for a photograph of a sullen-looking man. Endo-san knelt on the straw mats and bowed to it. I did not, but I presumed the portrait to be that of Hirohito, the emperor of Japan. We sat with our buttocks on our heels and waited for Saotome-san to join us. He entered and there was a flurry of bows before we were at last comfortable, sitting in front of a low wooden table.

The ambassador was a distinguished, almost haughty-looking man, except when he smiled. Then he looked merely handsome and ordinary. In his dark *hakama* and black and gray *yukata* robe patterned with silver chrysanthemum blossoms he appeared much older than Endo-san, although his movements were just as graceful.

"Is this your student I have heard about?" he asked in English, smiling at me. His voice was like rice paper, thin and brittle. I could picture him as somebody's grandfather.

"*Hai*, Saotome-san," Endo-san replied, indicating for me to serve the hot *sake*.

"How is his progress?"

"Very good. He has made tremendous advances, physically and mentally."

Endo-san had never once expressly commented on my studies. Now, to hear it before the ambassador was pleasurable. It added to the warm glow left by the *sake*.

They switched to Japanese immediately, the older man looking intently at me to see if I could follow. His accent was slightly rougher than Endo-san's but, after a few sentences, I sailed with the flow of their conversation.

We were served dinner, which came on little porcelain plates, each with just one or two pieces of food. I enjoyed the marinated eel, the sweetened chicken and the little rolls of raw fish wrapped in rice and seaweed. The two Japanese men ate daintily, examining their food in the chopsticks, commenting on the taste and color and texture, almost as though they were making an artistic acquisition. I was famished and had to restrain myself from eating too much, too fast.

"How is the situation in Penang?" Saotome asked, placing his chopsticks on an ivory rest.

"Quiet and peaceful. Our people are contented and there are no distressing matters," Endo-san replied. "We have found a suitable house on Penang Hill to lease for our staff and their families. I will show you some photographs later. Apart from that, I have almost unlimited free time and we have been traveling around the island."

Saotome-san smiled. "Ah, such splendid days, hm?" he said in English. I stopped eating, knowing it was a direct reference to me. Suddenly the old man did not seem so benign. I felt like a mouse before a tiger.

"You seem to know a lot about me," I said, disregarding all the lessons I had learned and confronting him directly.

"We make a point of knowing our friends," Saotome said. "I hear your father is the head of the largest trading company in Malaya?"

"Not the largest—that would be Empire Trading."

"We have some businessmen interested in Malaya. Would your father consider collaborating with them? To be partners with these people? They are keen to obtain a share in your father's company."

I thought of what he wanted to know. Deep down, I suspected our future could depend on the answer I gave. I said carefully, "I think he would be willing to listen—after all, he has nothing against your countrymen—but I can't speak for my father. You'll have to ask him yourself."

Saotome leaned back and said, "Oh. I suppose we would have to." He picked up another piece of fish. "Would you consider working for us, once you have finished your studies? I understand you have only another year to go."

I gave Endo-san a questioning look. "In what capacity?" I asked.

"As an interpreter, a person to liaise with the Europeans and the Malayan people. A goodwill officer, you might say." Saotome saw my uncertainty. "You do not have to reply now. The work will be interesting I can assure you."

I promised Saotome that I would consider his offer, and he smiled and said, "Now, would you like to have more of that eel? I saw you were quite, quite hungry."

The shoji door opened and a soldier knelt and bowed to Saotome. Next to him was a young Chinese girl in a robe, her hair tied into two lacquered balls.

No words crossed the space between us and the kneeling figures until Saotome said, "Lift her face to me."

The soldier put his fingers under the girl's chin and brought it up.

"Open her robes."

The same hand dropped from the girl's chin and pulled her robes open to one side, revealing a single breast, uncertain of its shape yet, still breaking into womanhood.

Saotome studied her and gave a smile, tiny as a cut. His throat pulsed and his tongue touched briefly the corner of his lips, an artist's brush adding the final perfecting stroke.

I found the eel did not taste so sweet now.

For the next few days I was left alone. Endo-san had to attend various meetings with Saotome and I wandered about the streets. I was disappointed, for I had hoped to show him the town and my father's office. I walked through the commercial center on my own, marveling at the new shops and the crowds of people. Like Penang, the town was segregated into different sections by race. I had to struggle to remember my rusty Cantonese in order to speak to the Chinese here. Unlike the Hokkien Chinese of Penang, almost all of them were immigrants from the province of Kwang-tung, attracted by the tales of wealth and success brought back to China by those of their countrymen fortunate enough to grow rich in the dangerous and soul-sapping tin mines around Kuala Lumpur and the Kinta Valley, where Ipoh was situated.

I sat in a tearoom and thought again about my grandfather. I wondered what sort of a man he was to cut my mother off so completely. What was so wrong with marrying someone outside your own people? Why was the world so concerned with such matters?

The owner of the tearoom came for my order, asking in English what I wanted. I saw the expected look of surprise and barely concealed disgust when I answered in Cantonese. That was my burden—I looked too foreign for the Chinese, and too Oriental for the Europeans. I was not the only one—there was a whole society of so-called Eurasians in Malaya—but even then I felt I would not belong among them. I felt as Endo-san and the Japanese people here must feel: they were hated by the locals as well as by the British and Americans, for their exploits in China were now becoming daily topics of debate from the street peddlers to the Europeans drinking their ice-cold gin in the Spotted Dog. Yet I had seen another side of them—I had seen the fragile beauty of their way of life, their appreciation of the sorrowful, transient aspects of nature, of life itself. Surely such sensitivities should count?

I thought back to the conversation with Saotome. There had been a hidden layer of meaning, I was sure. Did the Japanese wish to set up a company to compete against ours or did they intend to make my father an offer of purchase? I knew we would never sell. In his own way, my father was as Oriental in his thinking as the people of Penang. The company was to be held only by the family. Graham Hutton would not have allowed its sale. The only way the Japanese could obtain Hutton and Sons was to take it by force and there was no way that would be condoned by the British.

At the railway station I telephoned Aunt Mei. The platforms were busy, the early morning sun gilding the onion-shaped domes on their tall minarets, finding its way through the gaps in the Moorish cupolas and arches. The station was one of the loveliest buildings I had ever seen. Endo-san sat on a bench, reading a file from Saotome. A shaft of sunlight spilling through a roof window made him seem to glow.

I told Aunt Mei that I would get off at the station in Ipoh, and I obtained the address of my grandfather from her. "Please let him know I'll visit him, Aunt Mei."

"Yes, yes, of course I will tell him that. I am glad you wish to."

"I want to tell him he was wrong to have treated my mother so badly. There was good in their marriage."

There was a short silence and then she said, "There were indeed a lot of good things. You are one of them."

Endo-san waved to me and I hung up the phone after thanking her, and we boarded the train.

The journey was pleasant, the scenery a rushing blur of greenery broken by clumps of little villages near the tracks. Whenever we slowed down at these villages a cluster of naked children ran alongside the train and we pulled down our windows to buy food and drinks from them. I pointed out water buffalo lying in muddy rice fields and once we had to stop as an elephant and her calf crossed the tracks. Near the town of Ipoh the train went across a vast lake, its surface smooth and reflective, so that for the ten minutes required to cross it I felt we were skimming across a pool of mercury. Herons flew alongside us and rose over the carriages, circling to land at the reed-covered edges of the lake. When I saw the gray-white limestone cliffs of Ipoh grow nearer I said, "I'll have to get off soon."

"Will you be all right?" Endo-san asked.

"I think so. It shouldn't be too hard, seeing someone who has never meant anything in my life before."

"You must not be bitter, or judge him before you get to know him," he said.

"I don't know if I'll get to know him," I said. The thought of establishing a connection, an understanding between my grandfather and myself, did not appeal to me and I was starting to regret my decision to see him. We would have nothing in common to bind us.

97

"Do not turn back now," Endo-san said. "I have no doubt in my mind at all that it will be your grandfather who will make sure you get to know him. And I am certain the means he will use to achieve this will be quite unusual."

"You've met him, haven't you?" I asked, making a guess.

"I have," he said. When I remained silent he became curious. "You are not going to ask me when and why?"

"I'm sure you had good reasons," I replied. I thought back to that day on the ledge up on Penang Hill when I decided to trust him completely. I told him that now, and a shade of sorrow darkened his eyes.

"*Sumimasen*. I am sorry," he said, after a while.

I was about to ask him what he was apologizing for when the train slowed down and we entered Ipoh station. I tidied the table in the compartment and threw away the little packets of food.

"You have to go," he said, pulling my bag from the overhead rack. He opened his wallet. "Do you have enough money?"

"Yes," I smiled, touched by his concern. "My grandfather is one of the wealthiest men in Malaya, you know."

"Take some money anyway. I will see you in Penang. Come to the island when you return home."

"I will." I gave him a quick hug and got down on to the platform. I turned and waved to him once and then walked out of the station.

Chapter Ten

I was not surprised to find a car waiting for me. The old Indian driver leaning against it straightened when he saw me come out into the sunshine. "Mr. Hutton?"

I gave him a quick nod.

"Your grandfather's house is not far away," he said as he opened the door for me.

I had never been to Ipoh. My father had never brought us here, even though we owned mines in the Kinta Valley surrounding the town. Ipoh was originally just a little tin-mining village, fought over by the warring princes of the Perak Sultanate until the British intervened to prevent the succession of wars from spilling out into their neighboring protectorates. Chinese coolies were soon imported to work the mines, and by their ingenuity and hard work the village grew into a sizeable if charmless town with its own railway station, schools, courts, and wealthy residential districts. Ipoh was well known for the caves in the limestone cliffs that surrounded it. Many of them had been used by hermits and sages seeking to meditate in seclusion from the world. After they died or disappeared, temples were built in these caves to deify them.

The town was hot and dusty, almost bare of trees, and the limestone cliffs reflected the glare and heat of the sun. We left the streets of the town and turned into Tambun Road. The mansions along this road were owned by the Chinese mining tycoons, most of whom had begun as shirtless coolies in the mines. When they had made their fortunes they built their houses in the European style, so for a while I felt as though I were back in Northam Road in Penang.

The car entered the driveway of a house that could have been anywhere in Penang, with its standard woodwork, its central portico and pediment. What set it apart was its color. The entire house had been given a coat of light yellow, the sort of color no European would ever use to paint his walls.

When I stepped down I saw Aunt Mei under the porch. "What're you doing here?" I asked.

"It is only three hours from Penang," she replied. "I have come to visit my father."

Despite feeling slightly annoyed with her manipulations, I was glad to see a familiar face. The house was oppressive. Marble lions reared up on pedestals on each side of the doors, which were made of thick wooden horizontal poles set in a sliding frame, and appeared to me like the bars of a cell. It was dark within, but the flowery patterns on the marble floors glowed softly. Large portraits of mandarins with braided queues and sitting on slender, simple chairs hung on the walls. A staircase curled down in the middle of the hall. Doors opened into formal sitting rooms on both sides.

Aunt Mei led me to a sitting room that had only four rosewood chairs, two on each side, against the walls. An old triptych hung on the last empty wall, showing connected scenes from a mandarin's household. The triptych faced an open courtyard, sunken in the middle, with four large jade-colored jars placed at its corners. A solitary miniaturized tree stood on a wooden stand in the center.

A maidservant served us Iron Goddess of Mercy tea as we waited. The house was still, except for the cries of birds and the flutter of swallows' wings in the eaves. Far away I heard the sound of water falling over rocks which lightened the atmosphere and seemed to cool the house. There came a movement outside the room and we stood up expectantly.

He entered the room alone, dressed in his mandarin robes. Khoo Wu An was a large stocky man, the robes barely hiding the muscles in his arms, which had once spent eighteen hours a day hauling water and sand from the mines, or so my aunt had said. She had also told me he was sixty years old, but to me, on that day, he was a formidable man, whatever his age.

Meeting for the first time, we studied each other with careful curiosity. He had soft white hair and wide intelligent eyes which blinked rapidly behind his rimless glasses. I was aware of a deep quietness and Aunt Mei's reined-in natural buoyancy. He indicated a chair. "Please sit down," he said in English and in a deep rolling voice that was confident and firm. I hid my surprise and returned to my seat. He had a brusqueness to his manner which was softened by his warm and open smile.

"How was your journey?" he asked.

"Uneventful," I said, hoping he would not catch the touch of irony in my voice.

He poured more tea for me. Then he took out a small piece of jade, a slender pin like a blade of grass, which hung on a thin silver chain around his neck and dipped it briefly into his cup. He looked at it and then inserted the pin back beneath his collar. It was a movement so natural, the result of years of habit, that he and Aunt Mei seemed unaware of it.

He now looked at me without reserve, his graying eyebrows trying to meet, perhaps hoping to find traces of himself in my features. A typical old Chinese man, I thought. But I was mistaken.

"You are very much like your mother," he said.

"People always say I resemble my father."

"Then they do not know what they are looking for," he said firmly.

"And what should one look for then?" I asked.

"Something beyond what the face presents, something obvious and yet intangible. Like breath on a cold night, perhaps."

He stood up when I had finished my tea, and said, "We are experiencing a dry spell in Ipoh. You must be hot and tired. Go and have a rest and cool yourself. We will talk more tonight."

He smiled at me again and watched as Aunt Mei took my arm and led me upstairs.

From the manner in which Aunt Mei led me to my room, I knew. We went up the stairs and walked along a corridor. Its emptiness was filled by small half-moon tables placed against the unadorned walls, upon which rested vases and figurines of three old men which, Aunt Mei later told me, were the Taoist trinity of Prosperity, Happiness, and Longevity.

She opened the door and waited for me to enter. The room was furnished in the European style, and a four-poster bed stood in the middle, the mosquito netting piled high above. There was a dressing table by the windows and in the corner a Balinese teak *almari*, a squat heavy cupboard that overwhelmed the porcelain washbasin beside it. Aunt Mei was about to speak, but I held up my hand and said, "My mother's room."

The wooden floorboards creaked as I walked across to the window. High wooden shutters opened out to a narrow balcony, which curled over a garden hidden from the world outside by walls pressed with creepers. In the center of the garden was a fountain, and with a feeling of something shifting I knew I had seen it before, perhaps in the other life Endo-san believed in. I studied it with greater attention and saw it was similar to the one that was in Istana.

My grandfather was correct. The weather was dry and hot and I stepped back with relief into the room. I opened the *almari*, but it was empty.

"Everything was removed after she married your father. Her clothes were given away, her books donated to the Ipoh Library. Everything," Aunt Mei said. "When I came back one day I found this room as empty as you see it now. I was furious with your grandfather."

"What did my mother say when you told her?" I asked.

"She never said anything. But your father asked me to describe the fountain you see outside to him, how it looked, even how the water sounded. He told me to be as detailed as I could, and then he built another one so that she would have something from her home, from her youth."

We sat on the bed, listening to the water running in the fountain, to the birds that so loved it in this heat. "Would you like to sleep here?" Aunt Mei asked.

"Yes," I said. "I would."

I slept well: the sound of the fountain rested me. When I woke the afternoon sun had come in through the slats of the shutters, striping the wooden floorboards. They were burning hot when I walked across them. The fan on the ceiling spun slowly, reflecting fragments of sunlight. Birds whistled and chirped outside and the strong smell of frangipani came in from the garden and sought refuge in the room. I looked at my watch; Endo-san would have already arrived at Penang, I thought.

A maidservant knocked on the door and informed me that my grandfather was waiting for me. I washed my face in the basin and went down to confront him. I had decided that I would express to him my disappointment at how my mother had been treated. I would let him know that my father had been a good husband to her. Then I would tell him that I saw no point in our meeting again and that I would leave the next day. I had not even unpacked, which should make my departure easier and quicker.

"You look much rested," he said. "Did the room agree with you?"

"It did. The sound of the water and the smell of the flowers were very soothing."

I wondered if he had been behind the choice of room I had been given. He led me out to the garden, pointing out the various flowers to me, their fragrance unabashed and heady. I looked, but could not find a frangipani tree.

When we approached the fountain, he asked, "Is it very similar?"

Before, I would not have felt the faint, controlled timber of emotion in his voice. But Endo-san's lessons had taught me that there is often movement in stillness, and stillness in movement. And so it was that I felt it clearly within me, the hidden mixture of regret, sorrow, and hope. I kept my face as carefully controlled as my grandfather's voice had been, so as not to embarrass him.

I circled the fountain that my mother had loved so much, crouching to examine the carvings of birds and trees that ran around its wall and the plump angel that stood poised with a jug in the center. Dragonflies, looking like long, thin red chillies, hovered above the water's surface. I watched them for a moment and a memory returned to me of how upset my mother had been when William and I snared the dragonflies in the fountain in Istana when we were younger.

I was six then and William was thirteen. He had shown me how to tie threads to the bodies of the dragonflies we had caught. I had thought then that my mother's displeasure was disproportionate to our harmless act. Now I knew why we had saddened her and silently I said to my mother, "*I'm sorry,*" and hoped she could hear me.

I blinked, nodded to my grandfather and said, "Yes, the fountain at home is very similar. It even sounds the same."

He sat down on the rim of the fountain and looked at his feet.

When he looked up again I saw the expression on his face softened by the truth of his words. "That is good," he said. "I am glad."

Dinner was a simple, almost monastic meal. He fussed over me and placed food in my bowl with his chopsticks. We had watched dusk cloak the garden in a golden light with no more words spoken. I reminded myself to tell him I would leave the next day, but I found my resolve to be weaker than before.

The maidservants cleared away our meal and brought out a tray bearing dainty little teacups and a teapot. He opened his fan with a flick of his wrist and waved it at Aunt Mei. "Please leave us," he said.

She looked ready to refuse but my grandfather said, "Go, Eldest Daughter," and she could only comply. She rose from her chair and left us, trailing an air of annoyance behind her like a thwarted feline. My grandfather looked amused, his eyes blinking rapidly. He lifted the lid of his cup and sniffed at the steam. Again he took out the small pin and wet it in his tea. He caught me staring and I took the opportunity to ask him, "Why do you keep doing that? Does the pin alter the flavor of the tea?"

"It warns me of the presence of poison."

"But you didn't use it to test your food when we were having dinner," I said, feeling pleased that I had caught him in an inconsistency.

"I do it merely out of habit now, and only when I drink. It is almost as though the pin *does* change the taste of my tea, a taste that I have grown used to."

He held the pin up so I could examine it. It was slightly over an inch long, and the color of the jade was faint, almost like sunlight seen through a delicate leaf.

"Does it really work?" I asked.

He gave me a reflective, almost dreamy smile. After a little while he said, "Yes, once, long ago, it did."

"How did you get the pin?"

"Let us start at the beginning. I know everything about you, but you know nothing of me. I do not think that is quite fair, do you?" he asked.

"How do you know everything about me?" I asked

He waved his hand in the air, as if to say that it did not matter.

I recognized that movement for I too had the same mannerism. It felt uncanny to meet a man who had some of my own habitual gestures. "Let me tell you about myself, about this strange, cruel man, this man with an iron soul who is your grandfather. Go on, drink your tea. It is good Black Dragon tea and I will not poison you."

Like Aunt Mei I felt compelled to obey him. For the moment the past days disappeared as he began to speak and soon I was caught up in his tale.

"Most people think I am a crude, uneducated coolie who found my fortune in the mines. No, do not save me face and deny that that is what you thought as well. I was thirty years old when I arrived in Penang, part of an endless wave of people fleeing the chaos in China. I was different from them, though, for in my bags I had a small fortune in gold ingots, taken from the Imperial Treasury in the final days of the Ching Dynasty. Are you aware of the Ching Dynasty?"

I told him that Uncle Lim used to tell me stories about China, about its many dynasties and its Imperial House. I had found them fascinating at first, but as I grew older the stories seemed to stagnate and I became tired of them.

"It was the last dynasty of China," I said. "After that the Republicans led by Dr. Sun Yat Sen toppled the monarchy." He seemed impressed that I knew my facts. "Is that why you left China?" I asked.

"I left a long time before the monarchy became as dust in the Gobi desert. Even at that time, the intelligent ones could see that an age was nearing its end. Something new would come in and sweep it all away, everything we knew and had lived for."

He took another sip of tea. "Do I look old to you? No? You are very diplomatic. No matter how I look, I *feel* old. And yet how can I feel old, I sometimes ask myself. I, who have escaped history. For if one escapes history, does not one then escape time?"

"No one can escape history," I said.

"You are wrong," he said. "I often think of one who has been written out of history. I see his face, eternally young as it was on the day we first met in a courtyard of the Forbidden City. This was in 1906—it seems like a lifetime ago. These days everybody knows that Pu Yi was the last emperor of China, having ascended the Dragon Throne at the age of three. But no one knows of the one before him. No one—except me."

"How did you come to know about him, if he was 'written out of history'?" I could not help asking.

"I was his tutor," he replied, enjoying the skeptical look on my face. His eyes peered at me over the top of his spectacles and he gave me a crooked grin. "It might surprise you to learn that I was once a respected scholar of classical Chinese philosophy and, at the age of twenty-seven, one of the youngest members on the Imperial Board of Examinations.

"My achievements brought me into the most exalted circles of all, when I was appointed to teach the emperor's heir, Wen Zu."

"His son?"

"No, not his son. Wracked by perpetual illnesses, the emperor was childless, his spirit weakened by too much wine and countless courtesans. The real ruler of China at this time—as I expect you know—was the Dowager Empress Tzu Xsi, and it was she who had recently selected Wen Zu, the son of a distant cousin, as the successor to the throne.

"I was apprehensive at having been chosen as Wen Zu's tutor. It would mean leaving my wife and my two daughters. Your mother, Yu Lian, was just beginning to take her first steps." He smiled wistfully at me before continuing. "Your aunt, Yu Mei, would have been about seven years old."

"But it was a great honor for you," I said.

"True. My father, a Manchu Bannerman, was extremely proud of my appointment, but my mother cried, fearing for my life. There have always been stories of people entering the Forbidden City and never coming out again. On the night before I was to leave for the palace, she entered my room and, from her hair plucked a hairpin made of jade which she had obtained from her Buddhist abbot. She pressed it into my hand, and told me that it would keep me safe from harm. And then she hugged me tightly, something she had not done since I was ten.

"At dawn my father and I rode through the streets of the city. A few night watchmen were still going about, their lanterns swaying as they patrolled their areas, singing out their words of warning into the chilly air. Suddenly the warren of streets fell away and we sped across an empty, silent field of stone. I could hear nothing but the breathing of our horses, their hoofs clattering on the stones, and strangely, my own heartbeat. Behind us a touch of the sun lightened the sky. The hulk of the palace rose up before us, silent and dark. I could barely make out its countless upturned eaves, its many layers of roofs.

"Then the sun hit the palace and my breath was stopped short. All its intricate details could be seen, every curve, every window, every golden tile on the roofs. The celestial pairings of dragons and phoenixes twined around the columns, writhed up and down, frozen forever in their passionate chase.

"We came to a high, white wall, planted intermittently at the top with banners fluttering gently in the morning wind. At the main gate the guards lifted their gloved palms to stop us. The wooden doors opened almost as if on the silent command of those within. We rode through a narrow tunnel and then out into the strengthening sunlight. We dismounted at a guardhouse. From now on we walked.

"Like two small insects we crossed the immense courtyard, past two lines of helmeted guards. We walked up a flight of marble steps which seemed to go ever on up into the sky. At the top we were greeted by a strange-looking man. I sensed that he was old, but his skin was pale and flawless. My father advanced, said a few deferential words to him and then returned to me.

"He said, 'You will follow Master Chow into the palace. From now on you are under the protection of the Imperial House.' My father's voice then hardened. 'You are also under your obligations as a member of the House. You must forget all your mother's nonsense. You have the court's permission to visit your family once a month and I shall come to see you whenever it is permissible.'

"I nodded, trying to hide my fears from him. He held my shoulder and it was the closest my father had come to expressing his love for me.

"Master Chow, I learned later, was a eunuch. He was the first I had ever seen, though I had heard many stories about them. He had the slender limbs and soft skin of one gelded at an early age. He also had the corpulence of one who had grown used to a life of abundance in the palace.

"We walked through dark, empty hallways but we were never alone. I could hear whispers and sense hidden movements all around us. Columns rose up into the darkness of the unseen ceilings and doorways opened to more dim corridors. Footfalls floated, soft and silent as the disturbances of dust. I suddenly felt what my mother had feared. There was so much sorrow trapped within these walls.

"My small room was lavishly furnished, quite unlike my own at home. I put down my bundle of belongings and thanked Master Chow. Even then, I knew instinctively that one should not cross this ageless being.

"He nodded to me and informed me that Wen Zu would be waiting to meet me at breakfast, in the Pavilion of Willows.

"I changed into fresh clothes and let the sun and the sounds of laughter guide me to the Inner Courtyard where the pavilion was situated. Surrounded by willow trees, the courtyard was actually a series of large interconnected carp ponds, humped with many graceful stone bridges. In the center, like an exotic flower, was the pavilion. That was where I met the young man who was to be my student and eventually my friend."

"What did he look like?" I asked.

My grandfather's eyes softened. "He wasn't remarkable-looking at all. He was just a youth—two years younger than yourself, maybe. His face had not yet been hardened by the realities of his life. The eyes were guarded but lively and curious. 'So you are the one sent to be my tutor,' he said.

"He wasn't emperor yet, so I was quite informal with him. 'Yes, and to help you with your studies.'

"He made a face. 'I dislike studying. When I am emperor I shall stop studying.'

"I said that I disagreed with him and he said, quick to have the final word, 'That is why you were sent.'

"We had a hurried breakfast. I was hungry after the morning's ride. It was quiet, except for the songs of birds and the busy clicking of our chopsticks against our bowls. Already the day was late. I told him that he was to have his first lesson that day, copying out the *Analects* of Confucius. Because of the presence of the Western powers in the International Settlement in Shanghai I would also teach him English, which I had learned from foreign missionaries.

"I quickly came to understand the structure of power within the hermetic atmosphere of the palace and of our places within it. This was an important process, the way young animals in the wild learn about their environment and its hazards, for it was a matter of life and death. Friends were lost and enemies made on chance remarks and the interpretation of words."

"Did you ever meet the emperor?" I asked.

"Not at first," my grandfather shook his head. "The emperor was almost never seen. Master Chow headed the ranks of the eunuchs who controlled the palace. The various wives and concubines of the emperor had negligible presence, since they had not done their duty by giving him a male heir. I came to feel sorry for Wen Zu, for his position was dependent solely upon the failure of these women. My place in the whole complex scheme was wound tightly with Wen Zu's.

"Over and above all was the presence of Tzu Xsi, the Dowager Empress. She was known fearfully as 'the Old One.' Her influence weighed down the air of the palace, making it seem corrupt, sweet-rotten, malevolent, and cloying, like the opium she used. All eyes were her eyes, all ears, hers. She seemed to know of all things occurring in the palace. But I would not be summoned to her until almost five months had gone by. It was easy to be overlooked in the vastness of the palace, or so I thought foolishly.

"Although I was reasonably strict with Wen Zu, my loneliness and his life of isolation gave rise to a strengthening friendship between us. My ability as a martial artist impressed Wen Zu as well. Each morning, before the palace awoke, I would complete a series of fighting forms in an unused garden. He caught me in the middle of my exercises one day and insisted that I teach him the movements."

"How did a scholar like yourself acquire such skills?" I asked.

"How? I was sent to the Shaolin Temple in the mist-covered Kaolin Mountains for apprenticeship when I was six. It was a final attempt to improve my health. Would you believe I was once a sickly child?" My grandfather tapped his chest with his fist. "Nobody knew what was wrong with me. Gods were implored and mediums consulted, to no avail. My mother spent hours boiling pots of strange herbs and exotic meats in the hopes that I would recover. One day a wandering monk was literally dragged off the street to be consulted. Within a month, after letters of introduction had been sent by my mother and a reply received, I was taken on the journey south to the temple."

"It seems like a drastic measure," I said.

The old man nodded. "To send a boy with minimal chances of surviving into adulthood to those monks with their relentless and punishing training? My mother did it to save me."

"Did she accompany you?"

My grandfather shook his head. "I was placed under the care of the chief of a trade caravan. I can only recall bits and fragments of those weeks of endless traveling over deep, barren gorges and bamboo forests bristling with bandits. But I remember my arrival at the temple. The main building was simple and old, located in the middle of the shady and extensive temple grounds. What drew my eye, however, were the mountains surrounding the temple, rising into the clouds. I could make out small stone steps clawing up the steep, pine-covered mountain, and, even more amazing, the small darting figures of bald-headed monks carrying buckets of water on those steps."

"It was part of the monks' training," I said, making a guess.

"As I was soon to discover—yes," my grandfather said. "My illness and my weak physical state were not tolerated. My head was shorn clean immediately and within a day I was out before dawn, two wooden pails hanging over a pole slung over my shoulder. I joined a stream of novices running up the mountain to obtain fresh water from a waterfall, one of many hundreds of ants scurrying up and down the slippery steps. I slipped and fell many times. I bloodied my knees and banged my head, and I cried every night. Although not cruel, my fellow monks did not go out of their way to pamper me.

"The routine was endless. After filling up the stone reservoirs, we would sweep the training halls of the temple, clean the altars, remove the burnt incense sticks from the censers, and place fresh flowers and fruit before the deities. Then, with relief, we would all gather in the dining hall and have our breakfast of hot gruel and tea, which never varied, not once in my six years there.

"There were also lessons in the teachings of the Buddha and the endless chanting of sutras, which I disliked. But I enjoyed the martial training of the Shaolin Temple, which would never have existed had it not been for one man."

"Who was he?" I asked, and he smiled at my impatience.

"In my first week I was brought to a cave hidden in the mountains. Tendrils of mist blurred the tops and ravines as we climbed higher and higher. I watched as below us a hawk floated and then sank into the mist.

"We went deep into the cave until we came to a wall, at the place where the temple's most famous priest had meditated for ten years. I explained to Wen Zu how Bodhidharmo was an Indian monk who had traveled all across China. Arriving at the temple he found that the monks were weak and soft, often falling asleep while meditating. He incorporated a training regimen in order to harden their bodies and minds. This was the foundation both of the strength and of the eventual fall of the temple, years after the Indian monk had already left them.

" 'Why?' Wen Zu, the future emperor, asked me.

"The monks became the best fighters in the country. Notwithstanding the fact that they had no interest in politics, the emperor became fearful of their skills and sought to exterminate them. But the temple was too well-fortified for the emperor's soldiers. It took a corrupt monk to disclose a secret way into the temple and all of the monks and novices were slaughtered in the battle which followed. But five senior monks escaped and in time became known as the Five Ancestors, bearers of the temple's knowledge."

"What happened to Bodhidharmo?" I interrupted my grandfather.

"Wen Zu asked me the same question," he said. "He was fascinated by the monk. No one knew, I told him. After ten years of continuous meditation, sitting in that cave, facing the wall, he went as he came, like a hawk returning to the mists.

"I told Wen Zu how I had once sat down at the same spot, in the same position the monk must have done and stared at the empty wall. There is a story that Bodhidharmo had become enraged when he fell asleep while meditating and so to defeat sleep he had sliced his eyelids off so that they would never betray him by closing. He remained aware, vigilant, even in the deepest pools of meditation. In the dark, in his cave, I heard the trickling of a mountain stream, the tiny cries of bats, and felt the cold wind cut into the cave.

"Wen Zu grimaced with unease when I told him this. He liked his sleep, and he was wary of any unnecessary pain. I too could not fathom the total dedication shown by the temple's most instrumental monk.

"However, the story of Bodhidharmo continued to haunt Wen Zu, and he asked the eunuchs to obtain for him books about the monk. This was a mistake, though we were unaware of it. For it soon traveled to the Old One's ears that I was opening Wen Zu's eyes to the world, a world of which she did not want him to have any inkling.

"'Records of this monk appear throughout China,' Wen Zu informed me, after reading extensively from piles of books and journals obtained at great expense. 'He went as far as Japan, where his teachings merged with local beliefs and rituals.'

"I was amused by the authority in his voice. 'What are you doing?' I asked, pointing to his books.

"'Reading,' he said.

"'No. You are studying,' I replied, and he had the grace to laugh. 'You have succeeded where others have failed,' he said."

"What about your family? Didn't you miss them?" I asked when he paused and I refilled his cup of tea.

"Oh, very much. Once a month I obtained permission to return to my family. It pained me that your mother and Aunt Mei were growing up so quickly in my absence and I wondered if my appointment as royal tutor was such an honor after all. My father, as promised, visited me whenever he could, always bringing a dish my mother had cooked or a piece of clothing she had made. He looked older, and I became aware of the changes happening to the world outside. The Western powers were tearing up China and the emperor was helpless, the country weakened. You know there is a saying of Confucius: '*When the Son of Heaven is weak, the nation is weak.*' A simple but penetrating truth, don't you think? My father's visits always left me despondent; when he left, the palace seemed bigger, more empty, the silences louder.

"Time felt like smoke in an airless room in the palace, seeming not to move at all, but to hang suspended. One morning I was taken by Master Chow to the Hall of Ten Thousand for an audience with the Dowager Empress Tzu Xsi. As we neared the hall we seemed to rise and float on the scent of opium. Surrounded by her retinue of tittering eunuchs and handmaidens dressed in riotous colors, she examined me with her squinting, intense eyes.

"Even then she was old, old as the huge tortoise on a golden chain next to her, which she kept as a pet and as talisman. The creature's shell had been completely covered by tattoos of intricate lines and sacred words. On a brazier a pot of soup was being warmed. The slow, struggling movements of a frog being simmered alive caught my eye. I could smell the aroma of its cooking flesh and wondered how I would feel if I were being slowly boiled to death.

"She gauged my potential to stand in her path. Our eyes met and I held them steadily, but I dropped them after a second and she was satisfied. She inhaled on a pipe held out to her. Her fingers were clawlike, the nails grown so long they had curled like wires and had to be sheathed in gold. She beckoned to me with one elaborate finger and I leaned forward.

" 'Make sure the Heir to the Throne learns his lessons. You are here also to open his eyes to the world,' she whispered, her voice thick as the smoke that curled out from her barely opened mouth. 'Open his eyes, but not too much.'

"I could only nod and drop to my knees in obeisance, hating myself for disgracing my mother's people by my actions."

" 'Your mother's people'?" I did not want to interrupt him again, but there were so many questions I had to ask in order to clarify matters before I got tangled up in his tale.

"My mother came from a long line of revolutionaries who wished to overthrow the government, most of whom had gone underground to avoid persecution and death. She was a Han, and historians consider them the true people of China. They had fought against all outlanders who had invaded and conquered China, including the Manchu people who founded the Ching Dynasty in 1644. My father was a Manchu, and I always wondered how much my mother had loved my father to cross to his side. However, she made certain I never forgot her history, and even as a child I was told of the exploits and the greatness of her people. Now, in the center of the hall, facing this crone who was the leader of the enemies of my mother and her blood, I had to humble myself."

"But you were the tutor to the future emperor," I said.

"It was an unspoken view within the ranks of the older eunuchs that Wen Zu's future as emperor was not looked upon with favor by the Old One. He was too distantly connected to her and therefore her influence upon him would be minimal once the emperor was gone. Wen Zu was merely a temporary measure; there were persistent rumors that the Old One had more than one other candidate in mind and, in time, an heir closer to her would be announced. After I met the Old One, I began to fear for Wen Zu's life and for mine as well. I kept these fears hidden. It was a tumultuous time: the country was still recovering in the aftermath of the Boxer Rebellion in 1900."

I had read somewhere that the rebellion had been sparked off by riots and attacks on foreign missionaries and local Christian converts by members of the Righteous and Harmonious Fists. These were people dispossessed by drought, famine, and earthquakes. They blamed these calamities on the stranglehold the Western powers were exerting on China. The harmony of the country had been knocked out of kilter by the presence of these hated foreign devils, and the Boxers' aim was to expel them from the country.

"I've always wondered why they were called 'Boxers,'" I said. "It paints a strange picture of people running around in boxing gloves."

"The name was given to them by European historians. They believed that spiritual incantations and martial-arts training would render them impervious to blades and swords, invincible against the foreigners' 'fire-spears.'"

"Thousands of them must have died," I said.

He nodded. "The foreigners—which included the Japanese—retaliated decisively. They sacked, looted, and burned the Summer Palace, and the dowager empress and the emperor were forced to abandon Peking and escape to Xian, the ancient capital eight hundred miles to the west. I knew all this because my father had been part of the emperor's escorts when they fled Peking.

"Peace was eventually made with the foreign devils, and China surrendered more territories and lost more face.

"One evening, Wen Zu led me to one of the many silent, massive halls. Palace officials named it the Hall of Repentance. A silk fan hung from a wooden beam in the middle of the empty hall. It was spread open and was twenty feet wide. I looked up at the white silk, pleated with the thin ivory bones of the fan. Vertical lines of writing in black ink covered the fan. I picked out the names easily: Nanjing, Tientsin, Hong Kong, Amoy—so many of them. These were the ports and cities relinquished under the terms of the Unequal Treaties, as a consequence of wars fought and lost by China against the West. The words on the fan seemed to us like the reprimands of our forebears, as if asking us, 'How could you have allowed this to happen?'

"Perhaps aware of his tenuous position as the future emperor of China, Wen Zu would regularly make proclamations that he hoped the God of Heaven could hear and so help him secure his fate. 'When I am emperor you will stay on as my friend and advisor,' he often said. 'Many changes will have to be made to make our country strong again. We have to show the West our capabilities.'

"He was only restating the old ideas that had swept the palace a few years earlier before the Boxer Rebellion, when the emperor had been petitioned by a group of reformers who wanted to restore the empire based on a vague reinterpretation of Confucian writings and to modernize it along Western ideals."

"The emperor would have turned them away."

"On the contrary, the emperor gave his support and issued a series of edicts proclaiming the reforms that would take place. But the reformation movement failed and the emperor, disillusioned, fell back into his old habits of indolence and self-indulgence.

"I thought we would hear no more of reforms and modernization, but I was wrong. In the spring of 1908, in my second year in the palace, the movement was revived. Once again the emperor was roused out of his stupor, eager to reclaim his dignity. For a while he was intoxicated, not by wine or opium, but by the thought of himself being recorded as the savior of the dynasty, especially in light of the grave humiliation suffered in the aftermath of the Boxer Rebellion. Against the dowager empress's wishes he initiated his reforms once more.

"Given power by the emperor's proclamations, these new

reformers rampaged through Shanghai, Canton, and Peking. They destroyed the factories and all the stocks of opium owned by the Western trading houses.

"My father, on one of his visits, warned me not to get involved. I passed on his warning to Wen Zu, who did not heed me. He took to visiting the Hall of Repentance regularly, reciting the names of the lost ports and ceded territories like a sutra. 'Those ports will once more belong to China,' Wen Zu said, his eyes shining as they saw the future as envisioned by the reformers. 'We will own the country again.' He made his views well known in the palace. Like many young men he liked to shock, but I was certain he was quite sincere in his beliefs. However, sincerity was sometimes not a virtue in the palace."

"How did you endure for so long in the palace? It must've been stifling," I said.

"We often escaped to the city outside for an hour or so. We walked the streets I had known all my life, past the tea houses and the brothels with fancy names like Tower of Dizzy Stars and the Inn of Cosmic Pleasure. Heavily painted women stood on the balconies and waved their scented handkerchiefs, calling out to the people below, promising them exquisite, heavenly pleasures. The streets were crowded with beggars, performers, and hawkers, and the air was plaited with the smells of roasting meat, boiling sweets, fried tofu, dirt, and refuse. Refugees from the north lay dazed on the streets, victims of drought and war. I heard so many languages in the streets: there were voices from Mongolia, from the Gobi Desert, and from the outer hems of the empire. Arguments were carried on in various dialects of the provinces; all were different-colored threads sewn into the tapestry that was the Middle Kingdom. This truly was the center of the world. We had invented the compass, and I found it fitting that we were placed right in its heart.

"It was not unusual to come across opium addicts lying on the roads, eyes glazed, uncaring, even as the reformers kicked and shouted at them. Opium dens were torn down and foreign-owned opium factories and warehouses were set alight, sending clouds of sweet smoke into the sky, so thick, so potent and unending I thought the gods in their homes above us would become intoxicated with the fumes. Maybe they did, for the country suffered catastrophes and disasters. I knew many impoverished addicts congregated at such burnings, sucking in the air, hoping to extract every ounce of their drug from such wanton waste. I worried about the Old One's reactions, for the reformers were surely eroding her influence, opening her to greater danger from the Westerners, who were enraged by the destruction of their properties. It was also well-known that the Old One's clawed fingers clutched many such enterprises.

"On one of these trips we saw a eunuch carrying a wooden box into the shop of a dealer in antiquities. The owner examined the contents of the box, appeared spellbound, and seemed willing enough to part with a large number of gold taels.

"We knew then that what we were witnessing was one of the many methods the eunuchs used to enrich themselves. Theft of palace treasures was one of the unsavory practices the emperor, in a fit of reformatory success, then decided to stamp out.

"We watched as the palace accounts were scrutinized. The eunuchs panicked and many escaped into the night, taking with them containers holding their most precious possessions—their preserved organs. They knew they could not enter Heaven if they were not complete.

"To save themselves some took to accusing their fellow eunuchs of theft. Most distressing was the number of suicides. It became quite common for a serving maid to scream with horror when she opened a door to find a pair of legs dangling before her eyes, the body swinging from the beams. What frightened me more were the rumors that some of these suicides were murders ordered by the Old One.

"And then we heard the rumor that the dowager empress had secretly selected another heir, an infant barely weaned from his mother. The factions that had once backed Wen Zu shifted, like the bits of glass in the mirrored tube which an English tutor had once shown me, creating new configurations of power and leaving Wen Zu to stand on his own. The appointment had not been announced and I tried to calm Wen Zu's anger and fears. It was a direct insult to him to have to cede to an infant, and I knew then that Wen Zu had become inessential, and even inconvenient, to have around.

"Although most of the eunuchs were too clever to infuriate Wen Zu—for who knew how the winds of Heaven would blow tomorrow?—they were politically wise enough to know of his precarious position. But the younger ones got along well with us, in particular Tsiao Li, a slender beautiful youth who, I knew, loved Wen Zu. He was the one who warned me."

"What did he warn you about?" I nudged him on gently when it seemed to me he had become lost in his thoughts.

"Strange how I can still remember it so clearly," he said in a soft voice. I leaned closer to him, not wishing to miss anything. "It was a hot summer's day, the carp ponds so still the dragonflies seemed mesmerized by their own reflections on the water. As I walked along the paths circling the ponds, waiting for Wen Zu to join me in a game of elephant chess, Tsiao Li came with a message from Wen Zu.

"The young eunuch was unusually formal. 'His Highness regrets to inform you that he has been summoned by the emperor to discuss the reforms and is therefore unable to join you.'

"I made a face. 'Must you talk in that terrible way? Can't you talk like a normal person?' I was too annoyed and too hot to pay attention to him, expecting him to reply with one of his usual witty barbs.

" 'You must eat properly and take care of your health. And His Highness's also. Once one's health has been broken it cannot be reformed.'

"The unusual use of the last word he had spoken and the note of fear in his voice made me stop fanning myself. I met his eyes and was chilled. Suddenly the summer heat did not bother me any more.

" 'Yes,' I replied with difficulty in the same stilted form. 'As must you.'

"I looked behind him. A few courtiers stood on a bridge, gazing into the pond. 'It is not only food I must fear but also the dagger beneath the honeyed tongue,' the young eunuch said.

"He turned, and walked away quickly. I stared at the plate of fruit before me. That was the last time I spoke to him, for two days later he was fished out from an old well, water dripping from his mouth, eyes wide open.

" 'You are mad,' Wen Zu said when I told him of the conversation with the eunuch. 'Nobody would dare!' he said. Silence fell. We both knew there was only one person in the palace who would dare.

"I took out the jade hairpin my mother had given me. It had been presented to her by her abbot who had once taught at the Shaolin monastery and it was said that it had come from one of the Five Ancestors who had used it to test their food for poison, the existence of which would turn the jade a darker green.

"Wen Zu nodded when I told him this. Unlike me, he believed it completely. Perhaps by that time he was also frightened for his life. I remembered one of the many strange sayings I had to memorize in my English lessons, something about a drowning man clutching at a straw. We were now dying youths clutching at a hairpin.

" 'Put it into this.' Wen Zu pointed to the pot of snake's tongue grass tea, a cooling infusion perfect for a hot summer's day. I poured some into a small cup and wet my pin with it. We held our breaths as the pin came out of the tea.

" 'Does it look darker?' he asked.

"I studied it closely. 'I don't know. I think it does. I think they will poison us in small doses.'

"He masked his rising fear behind his annoyance. 'Can you not tell at all?'

" 'I don't conduct tests for poisons every day,' I said.

"He snorted and walked away. If there had been poison, the amount would be tiny, I reassured myself. I resolved to test every dish we ate with the pin. But first there was one person we had to warn.

"I had seen the emperor once from some distance away, in the early days of my arrival. Now, as we entered his chambers, I wondered if the person before us was the same man. He appeared to have regained his health: the pallor so common to opium smokers was gone, although he still coughed violently. His skin, once stretched taut and dry, now had the elasticity of his relative youth. We touched our heads to the ground and shuffled to him on our knees."

"It couldn't have been easy to get to see the emperor," I said.

"The audience with him had been possible only because of Wen Zu's brashness; breaching countless rules of etiquette and bureaucracy, he had simply gone to the emperor's quarters and asked for an immediate response. Outside, dusk had fallen. Occasionally, by a trick of the wind I seemed to hear the night-watchman cry out the hour, his voice mournful as a wounded hound.

"The emperor listened to our carefully worded warning. He frowned at us but in his sad eyes I saw that he was aware of the turn in the tide. I was afraid for him. Through his recent edicts he had wielded his power with delight. Such power had been denied to him for a long while. I wondered for how much longer would he be allowed to exercise it before it was taken away again, this time perhaps for good.

" 'You have brought unsubstantiated accusations against persons you do not want to name. What do you expect me to do?' he said finally.

"I kept silent, but from the manner in which Wen Zu lifted his head I knew the words he was going to say. Looking back, perhaps if I had stopped him, things would have turned out differently. I suppose, as his tutor, I had failed him.

" 'If my words have been obscure, forgive me. What I wish to state is that we suspect we are being poisoned by the dowager empress. We further suspect that you are also being fed doses of poison.'

"The emperor stood up and came to us, lifting Wen Zu to his feet. 'Thank you for warning me,' he said. 'Now it is time for you to go to sleep.'

"He already knew his fate, we saw. And consequently, ours had also been revealed. He led us out and at the door he said, 'Let what you have discovered be good advice: never let your children become dangerous to you.' His eyes looked up to the moon, his laugh knowing and bitter. 'That was also the dowager empress's advice, years ago.'

"I did not sleep well that night. I held on to the pin tightly and whispered a prayer to my mother's gods for protection.

"A month later the emperor fell ill. Doctors from the International Settlement visited him, but found nothing wrong. To cure him the Old One ordered that opium be administered to him. And it seemed to me that on the day the order was carried out I could scent and taste the pervasive sweet odor in every room in the palace. The reformation movement, its head cut off, fell to pieces. Those members who could not flee in time were assassinated.

"It was time for a new emperor to ascend the Dragon Throne and Wen Zu knew with certainty that it would not be him. One night the pin came out black from a bowl of soup and he let out a moan. I threw away our food, as I had done for weeks, and thought of my plans to escape. I refused to be killed here, my body thrown into some abandoned well. I had to get my family to a safe hiding place. 'You must come with me,' I urged Wen Zu again. He stared, fascinated, at the pin.

" 'Where will we go? Where in the vastness of China can we hide from her? We have no money, no friends. Her power is limitless. She will hunt us down.'

" 'My mother has friends. They will shelter us, and guide us to a safe place.'

" 'Your mother's friends? They are revolutionaries and criminals, and they would happily see me die, or worse, they would just capture me and send me back to the Old One out of spite.'

" 'No. You're my friend, and that is enough.' I held his shoulders firmly, but he looked away and said, 'Tell me about your famous monks again.'

" 'This is no time to seek refuge in fairy stories. We must act now! Tonight!'

" 'I am so afraid. She will find us down wherever we hide.' He laughed shortly. 'She'll even come after us when we are dead. We'd have to stay vigilant forever. Even after death.'

"When he turned his gaze away from the pin I saw his eyes were just as dark. They were filled with a terrible fear and, worse, something I could not identify.

" 'We'll leave tonight,' he said, after a long pause.

"I closed my eyes in relief. He had seen the sense of my arguments.

"I started to pack a small bundle of clothes in my room. At the Hour of the Rooster everything fell quiet. Suddenly even the moon seemed loud. I stopped moving and waited. A moment later I heard a small wail, keening, drifting over courtyard after courtyard, like a crow flying from tree to tree, sending out the awful news.

"The emperor was dead. I continued my packing and then panic jolted me. I snatched up my bundle and moved silently across the corridors, avoiding the spectral figures carrying lanterns. Everyone was moving, going somewhere. The wailing was unrelenting, as though it wanted to penetrate the very edges of the empire. I ran through the hallways until I saw the familiar lights in Wen Zu's room. It was empty. I spun around, fear making me dizzy. I found his note on the table. I read it, folded it away and made my way to the Hall of Repentance where the massive silk fan hung.

"It was dark, but a small candle gave some light. I heard no sound except for the constant wailing, blowing like a desert wind. I entered the hall, crossing over the wooden threshold, the floorboards creaking. The silk fan lay half folded on the floor like a giant crane shot down from the sky by an archer, its spine cracked, its wings broken.

"Wen Zu sat on a wooden chair, his back to me, facing his handiwork. From the blood on the floor I knew he was dead. On the table his left arm stretched out, his hand holding a long narrow knife. I stepped around the spreading pool of blood—thinking how appalled he would be by the mess—and faced him.

"He had cut his own throat. His robes stuck to him in a bloody paste. And he had cut his eyelids off before he killed himself. His brows and cheeks were crusted with blood, and his eyes stared ahead, eternally aware, vigilant even beyond death against the woman he feared so much.

"I knelt before him, and bowed to him who was, for the briefest moment, between Kuang Hsu's death and his own, the Emperor of China, the Son of Heaven."

Here my grandfather stopped and I realized it had become painful for him to continue. I was torn between consoling him and urging him on. The house had become silent and the courtyard, lit by the moon, had the desolate air of an abandoned stage. He got up from his chair and stretched himself.

"Did the dowager empress order the death of the emperor?" I felt a heavy sadness for Wen Zu's death and for my grandfather's loss.

He shrugged. "No one would ever know, for she died the day after Kuang Hsu's death. I knew that the factions which had wanted Wen Zu dead would also want to cut off all the loose ends. My life was still in danger. I ran.

"I became one of the hysterical figures that crowded the night in that palace. I sent a message to my family and my father made arrangements for my wife and daughters to join me. I invoked my mother's name whenever possible and we were given safe passage to Hong Kong. As I hurried up to the boat, the driver of the cart that had carried us to the harbor said, 'Don't worry. Your parents will be moved to Hong Kong also. You'll see them soon.'

"I waited for three years but they never came. Eventually we sailed to Malaya, hoping to evade whatever people they sent after us. In that time the three-year-old distant relation of the dowager empress was named emperor, and China collapsed. Do you know the phrase from the foreign devils' God Book?—'*Woe to you, O Land, when your king is a child, and your princes feast in the morning!*'

"The monarchy disappeared forever and Sun Yat Sen's Republicans prayed before the tombs of the old Han Chinese emperors, informing them that, at long last, foreign invaders—white or yellow—no longer ruled China. It was only then that I finally felt safe. By that time Malaya had become my home—even your grandmother grew to love it here.

"Aunt Mei said she died not long after she came to Malaya," I said.

"Giving birth to my third child, a boy," my grandfather said. "He was too weak, and did not live long."

He let out a heavy breath, and I knew we had come to the end. "All records and traces of Wen Zu disappeared. He never existed in history except to me and to those few who remembered him. Many of them will be gone now. Perhaps only I am now aware that once there was an emperor by that name and that once, strangely enough, I was his friend." My grandfather stopped, his eyes looking far, far back in time. "I have never told anyone of him. Not even my wife or my children. But the lessons I learned in the palace have stayed with me."

I sat as unmoving as the miniature tree in the courtyard. Somewhere in the house some jasmine incense had been lit and I breathed in its light, discreet scent.

The wily old man, I thought. I saw too late that he had used the magical jade pin to lead my mind, taking it to wherever he had wanted me to go. Despite Endo-san's lessons, I had fallen into the trap my grandfather had laid for me. But I could not help liking him. I had come to Ipoh expecting accusations and acrimony to be thrown from both sides. I had planned never to see him again after this meeting but the afternoon by the fountain, and now this strange tale, had made him human, a man with a history, not the caricature of a controlling, narrow-minded man. I realized I could not be indifferent to him now, especially when he made it clear that I was the only one to whom he had ever divulged his past.

He would never come out and ask for forgiveness for casting my mother away, and to ask him to do so would be futile. The offering of this strange fragment of his past was a request for understanding and absolution.

He reached out and took my hand. "I have told you this long-winded, winding tale because I want you to know your history also. I want you to know that you have a long tradition behind you, so that you do not have to chase after a tradition that is not yours."

He meant Endo-san, that was obvious. Once again I wondered who was reporting my activities to him. "But I want to," I said, looking him firmly in the eye. Who was he to tell me what to do?

"You must wonder why I was so against your mother marrying your father. What a terrible, bigoted, and vindictive old man, you must have thought. And I did not even bother to attend her funeral."

"It had crossed my mind," I said.

"I went to her, in the temple. I saw your father in the crematorium, placing your mother's bones and ashes in the urn. I asked her for forgiveness. But of course it was too late then.

"When she set her heart on marrying your father I tried my best to prevent it. I had been warned that she could not marry him."

"Warned? By whom?"

"A fortune-teller at the snake temple in Penang."

I held my breath and a feeling of unreality came over me as the memory of the day I had spent with Endo-san at the temple uncoiled itself inside me.

"Because of her warnings I tried to stop the marriage and, when I failed, I allowed my anger to dictate my words."

"What was the warning?" I asked.

My grandfather lowered his eyes and placed his hands on his lap. "The fortune-teller said that both families would be brought to ruin through a child of Yu Lian—"

"That could mean anyone. If my mother had married someone else—"

"—through a child of mingled blood of Yu Lian, who would eventually betray them," he went on.

"Betray them? To whom?"

"You know who. The Japanese. They are already making plans to invade Malaya. You are extremely close to one of their highest officials."

"He is merely my teacher," I protested. "The Japanese would be foolish to start a war with the British in Malaya. Endo-san's a diplomatic official, not an army officer."

"Next to a parent, a teacher is the most powerful person in one's life."

"Is this why, after all these years, you finally decided to speak to me: to warn me of some fortune-teller's words—words which already caused my mother so much pain?"

He shook his head. "I am not asking you to do anything against your own wishes or reason. I have learned over the years that life has to take its own path. Look at Wen Zu and me. Even with all the warnings we had, still our lives followed the pathway that had been written down. Nothing could have changed it." He sighed, and walked to the edge of the courtyard, raising his head to look at the sky, now covered with clouds.

He turned to me and said, "It's late. Go to bed. I'll show you my garden tomorrow. People in Ipoh say it is one of the worst in town, but I disagree!"

Aunt Mei was quivering with barely controlled curiosity the following morning, eager to discover what he had told me. "We talked about his family and my mother," I said. "We're getting along well."

"I know you two are getting along well," she replied, almost tartly. "He doesn't usually spend so much time with anyone without getting irritable."

I thought about her life. My father once told me her husband

Henry had been killed in a riot between the Malays and the Chinese. Tensions between these two races erupted occasionally in violence and blood; Henry had been on his way to fetch her from the school where she taught when his Austin was surrounded by an angry mob. They turned it over and set it aflame. She had lived her life alone since then.

She led me to the Hall of Ancestors, where the tablets of the dead were placed, small wooden boards carved with the details of those gone by. They sat on a descending altar, shaped like the steps of an amphitheater, watching us play out our lives. The burned-out ends of joss sticks poked like twigs from a large brass urn on a low rosewood table. Three evenly spaced oil lamps shed their light on plates of offerings—mandarin oranges, apples, and buns.

"Why are these tablets here?" I asked. "They don't contain the ashes of the dead, do they?"

She lit some joss sticks and gave three to me. "These are memorial tablets of the dead of our family. Here we keep their memory alive. We pray that they will watch over us, and keep us safe." She pointed to a red tablet, carved with golden strokes. "That one there is your mother's. And the one just above it is your Uncle Henry's."

"Thank you for arranging this meeting," I said softly, speaking into the rising smoke. I meant the words for Aunt Mei and she smiled. But she said, "They can hear you, and I am sure they too accept your thanks."

I ended up staying with my grandfather for a week and he took great delight in showing me around the town.

One evening we walked past an open-air stage that had been erected in the town square. Some sort of performance was about to commence and we joined the crowd in front of a row of the largest joss sticks I had ever seen—each one approximately seven feet high and with the thickness of a telephone pole—their tips glowing with the redness of fresh magma and giving off clouds of incense smoke. Although rows of seats were provided, the crowd seemed to prefer to stand, and not a single chair was used.

"What's going on?" I asked my grandfather. "Are we not allowed to sit on these chairs?"

He shook his head, his eyebrows almost meeting in reproach at my ignorance. "The Festival of the Hungry Ghosts begins today. Once a year, for a month, the gates of the underworld are opened to allow the spirits to roam the earth. They are eager to revel in human pleasures again, even if vicariously. Most are benign, but some are angry and malevolent. We take special care not to offend these spirits, so we offer prayers and food, and traders and shopkeepers sponsor these public performances to appease them so that their business affairs are not disturbed." He pointed to the rows of vacant chairs. "Those are for the unseen guests. No one is allowed to sit there."

The curtain opened to the audience's applause. It was a Chinese opera and the actors were heavily made-up, their faces painted white and then rouged artfully. Their costumes were flamboyant, in bright shades of red, their headgear heavy and elaborate. The music from the orchestra was raucous, and the actors enacted stylized fights through a variety of acrobatic movements. I tried to enjoy the elaborate backward somersaults and exaggerated sword-fighting but the idea of being surrounded by spirits, voracious for all the sensations of human experience that they could never tangibly savor again, filled me with unease. I studied the faces in the crowd, wondering who was revenant, and who was real.

The day before I was to return home, my grandfather dismissed his chauffeur and drove us out of town to the limestone hills. Close up, the hills did not seem as bare as I had thought. Shrubs and trees clung to them like mold and, in certain parts, the vegetation was thick and smooth as a bear's pelt. Half an hour's drive out of the town, the sky darkened as it prepared to rain.

"I was hiking though the grounds around this hill," my grandfather said, "when I saw that clump on top—there, do you see it? The one that looks like a cat's head. I managed to get past the trees and the undergrowth and there I found a cave. The entrance was so well hidden that I would not have found it if the bats had not started to fly out to hunt their evening meal. I suppose it brought back the memories of my youth spent at the monastery and the caves that surrounded it. Inside the cave I found inscriptions of what I thought were Buddhist sutras on the wall, and I thought immediately of Bodhidharmo. Who knows, perhaps he came all the way here? These hills were so popular with the hermits in those ancient ages. I made up my mind to buy the hill and to build a temple here. You can see it now," he pointed.

We came over a rise and stopped to rest. The temple had been built into the rock. It was small and simple compared to the larger ones strewn around these hills. It looked deserted and unused.

"Is there anyone still living in it?" I asked.

"The monks have since left to join the bigger monasteries. But I still come here occasionally. You will see why."

As we climbed higher up the slope the temple became otherworldly. I could scarcely believe that it had been built by human hands. It was quiet around us, so quiet that even the cloud thickening above seemed like an intrusion.

The walls of the doorway had faded to the color of the rocks around them. There was no door, just an open entrance edged with grass and creepers. A seed had fallen into a crack in the wall and had sprouted into a sturdy little guava tree, its branches reaching across the entrance. We moved it aside and went into the bare, tiny hall. Beetles scuttled away, their legs rasping on the floor like the sound of prayer beads rapidly manipulated by a monk. I heard the echo of faded chanting. In spite of its peaceful emptiness the temple seemed inhabited by a presence.

"Come," my grandfather said.

We entered a passageway, its walls smooth from the gentle trickle of rainwater seeping through. The tunnel curved upward, and once I tripped over the uneven floor. A circular glow of light drew us on until we emerged into sunlight. I blinked my eyes and turned around in wonder. The tunnel opened into a clearing set within the circle of hills. My grandfather saw my face and grinned. There was no way out except by the tunnel through which we had come. The walls surrounding the clearing rose up straight, jagged, and slippery. Only the tenacious roots of trees and little bushes made it all the way to the top. The sky above was just a hole, the clouds drizzling us with the lightest of rain, as the earth and grass released their imprisoned scents.

He took my arm and I followed him to an overhang, and under it I saw the writings that had so transfixed him. They surged across the uneven rock face, from top to bottom, unimpeded by the bumps and striations and hollows of the surface, graced with a fluidity and energy that made it seem as if they had been written with a brush dipped in fire.

I traced the writing with my fingertip and, to this day, I know those words were part of an ancient magic, created by an ancient wisdom, for I felt them as my finger touched them. *I felt them within me.*

He watched as my finger traveled the writing all the way to the last flourish, and when I looked at its tip I saw it glowed a light red. I felt a slight heat, and smelt a faint burning scent.

"What do they say?" I asked.

My grandfather shrugged. "I do not know. But do you think that matters? They have spoken to you, have they not?"

I could only agree with him.

He looked to the sky. "It is good that the rain has come. I used to come here whenever it rained and sit under those words and watch the water run down the side of the rocks. You have brought the rain, and for this I thank you."

I understood he meant more than that. He was grateful I had come to visit him and that I seemed to understand him better now.

He took off his shirt, and I saw his muscles were hard, unrelenting to encroaching age. "I was told you have had some lessons. I would be very much obliged if you show me some of them."

I brushed droplets of rain from my brows, bowed to him and readied myself.

He was fast—faster than Endo-san. His fists pushed me back and I could do nothing except block them, feeling the pain shoot up my arms as I did so. His arms were rock hard. I slid a low kick to his shins and he grimaced, and for a few seconds his hands stopped moving. I moved my hands into his circle and let him grasp them, opening me for a quick, spiraling *kote-gaeshi* wrist-lock on him.

As I tipped his balance I aimed a sharp punch into his side. It was like hitting a slab of granite and did not affect him in any way at all. He broke my lock, regained his balance and swung a kick at my head. I blocked it with my arms and the force of contact sent me stumbling. I went into a forward fall to escape his attacks, knowing he would break my arms soon if I kept meeting his strikes directly.

The ground was growing slippery yet his feet were rooted

firmly to it as he used only his hands. Twice I kicked him in his kidneys, which only brought a hardening of his face and a grim smile. I intercepted one of his fists and pulled him forward and executed my favorite move, *iriminage*, the entering throw. I brought my arm up under his chin, lifting his head high up, but he felt my intention and countered it by turning around and coming up behind me. And then he had his arms around my neck in a chokehold, his knee in my back, and the unreplenished air in my lungs dissipated quickly into my blood as he tightened his hold.

He let me go, and I sucked in the cool wet air, my head drumming madly. He pulled me up from my knees and beat the wet grass off my legs. He picked up his shirt and put it on again. The rain and the perspiration on his chest stained the cloth dark immediately.

He glanced at his watch. "You lasted six minutes. Quite acceptable. A lot of people could not get past four minutes with me. I can see that you have an excellent teacher."

He went through my mistakes, correcting them. "You were too loose here, and that is why I could escape from your locks. That last one would have been deadly if you had held me close to you. However, you left a gap, and it was easy for me to walk around you.

"As for your punches and kicks, I am sorry to tell you that against a man who had been trained as I was as a boy, they were useless. But then you would not meet many of us now. We are relics from another time."

He was silent, then he said, "You have been taught to kill. I sensed it in the way you fought." He shook his head, and I wanted to tell him he was wrong, that Endo-san had often repeated the warning he had given me outside St. George's Church, that I was never to resort to using what he had taught me to kill. Yet at that moment I realized my grandfather was correct.

My grandfather and Aunt Mei saw me off at the railway station in the morning. "I am glad you came," he said. "We have been estranged for too long. I hope you will think kindly of me, when you think of me at all." He took my hands, examining the bruises he had inflicted on me in the past days. "I hope your Mr. Endo will be more gentle with you than I have been. Since the lost emperor, I have never taught anyone in my life."

I stood near the train, feeling the sadness of a farewell to a new-found friend. "You've given me much food for thought, Grandfather; what are a few bruises compared to that? Will you visit me in Penang?"

He was moved by my invitation. "We shall see what the world has in store for me, but yes, I would like to see you in Penang. Perhaps you will also indulge me and take me to your mother's resting place, where we will face her, and tell her what a foolish man I have been."

"I think it would make her very happy to see both of us together," I said. "There is one thing that's been bothering me. Where did you plant your frangipani trees?"

Grandfather and Aunt Mei looked at each other. "We took out the tree near the fountain years ago, when it withered," he said. "We never planted another one. Your mother loved the scent of its flowers."

I thought of the scent I had caught on my first day here, the scent that had seemed always discreetly present during the days I had stayed in my grandfather's home. The old man looked at me keenly; a knowing and almost mischievous smile lifted the corners of his lips and reached into his eyes. And I knew something magical had happened to me.

I climbed into the carriage, standing at the doorway as the train pulled out of the station. They stood waving to me until the train went around a bend. I went to my seat and closed my eyes, and thought about the emperor who had been written out of history.

Chapter Eleven

When I saw the low hills of Penang as the ferry approached the harbor, I realized that I had missed my home deeply. I felt that I was returning as a different person. I had set out on a disturbing journey down the coast to Kuala Lumpur and had met my grandfather, who had shown me a facet of my heritage of which I had never been aware.

The moment I saw Uncle Lim I knew who my grandfather's source of information had been. He did not look at all surprised when the rickshaw man left me at Istana.

"You can tell my grandfather I came home safely," I said.

He gave an embarrassed smile and carried my bag to my room. In the kitchen a girl was stirring a pot of soup. She looked up shyly. "This is my daughter, Ming," Uncle Lim said, when he came in. "She doesn't speak much English, so you'll have to speak Hokkien to her."

She was a slim, boyish-looking girl, hair cut badly, her eyes slanted upward, black and rich as the dates she was now adding into the pot. "Can I offer you some soup?" she asked.

"That would be nice." I sat down at the kitchen table, telling Uncle Lim to join me. "How long have you been spying for my grandfather?" I said, hiding my amusement.

"Did it go well between the Old One and you?" he asked as Ming ladled the soup into our bowls.

"I should have met him a long time ago." I tried to think when Uncle Lim had joined our household, but failed. It had definitely been before I was born. I waited for him to answer my question and when at last he saw that I was not to be distracted, he told me.

"I came just after your mother married your father. I was already working in Penang. Your grandfather told me to come and work for Mr. Hutton. I couldn't refuse; I owed your grandfather a debt. You won't tell your father?"

"You keep quiet about what I have been up to and I'll do the same for you," I replied.

Ming brought the bowls of soup to the table. "How are things in China?" I was curious to know. Somehow that country did not seem as remote to me as it once did, and I realized that this was because of my grandfather's sharing of his own past with me.

Uncle Lim sighed. "Very bad," he said.

"We heard terrible reports from the towns taken over by the Japanese. Nanjing was the worst," Ming said, and closed her eyes.

"What happened there?" I asked. After taking over Manchuria and setting up a puppet government in 1931, the Japanese were vigilant in finding reasons to invade the rest of China. And this they had done, on 7 July 1937, when Chinese and Japanese troops clashed on the Marco Polo Bridge near Peking. The Japanese now controlled most of the northeastern territories of China.

Ming told me of the most recent events, and at first I did not believe her. Although foreign journalists had been prevented by the Imperial Japanese Army from sending dispatches out to the world, news of their savagery had been carried by fleeing refugees and foreign missionaries. Even so, I steadfastly refused to believe that any human race could be so barbaric, so bestial. She saw the look on my face, and said, "I don't care whether you believe me or not. You'll find out for yourself, when the Japanese come here."

Looking back, it was strange that everyone, every Chinese, every Malay and Indian, knew with complete certainty that the Japanese would eventually invade Malaya. The Chinese feared that the Japanese would extend their massacre of the people of Nanjing into Malaya, while the Malay and Indian communities hoped that the Japanese would free them from colonial rule. The majority of the English scoffed at the notion that Malaya would be attacked, feeling secure behind the naval batteries of Singapore. I was torn between two beliefs, like everything in my life. I knew the Japanese were not as incompetent as they had been painted by government officials. But neither were they strong or foolish enough to engage in war with the British Empire.

As they talked, I saw the strong lines of love between father and daughter, even though Uncle Lim had hardly seen his daughter while she was growing up in their village. I watched Uncle Lim laugh when she described the village headman and his antics; it was the first time that I could recall him laughing like a person, like a father, like a man. I felt out of place, a stranger to this bond, and quietly I left them.

Ming stayed for a few more days, and then one morning she was gone. Uncle Lim had taken her to a village in Balik Pulau, the Back of the Island, where he had relatives. For several days afterward he appeared more cheerful, and even promised to teach me Chinese boxing.

Endo-san had disappeared. His home was empty when I went across to his island. I slid open the doors and felt the silence. A box of photographs lay on the floor. He had been pinning them to his wall before he left. I studied them, especially the one taken of me at the tea shack on Penang Hill. I looked so different then, I thought, my childish face so unlike the one I saw in the mirror now. The other photographs were tedious shots of coastlines and forests and little towns. I stopped going through them after they all began to look the same. He had pinned a map of Malaya on another wall, and I saw the red lines he had traced of our journey, as well as other places he intended to visit. He apparently had no interest at all in going to Singapore, for it looked clean, unmarked by any notes or lines. On a shelf I found his note: *Gone to the East Coast. Keep training.*

I realized how much I had missed him during my visit to my grandfather. He had become a defining feature in my life. I missed spending my mornings with him, watching him, listening to him, anticipating his moods, his whims. I longed for the way the sun fired up his silver hair, the way his teeth glinted behind his smile, his wry humor, and the hidden sadness within him. Yet there was so much that I did not know. I made up my mind to question him more about his life when he returned.

The new term began and I was grateful that Endo-san was not around, as I was kept busy with schoolwork and with having to fulfill the social obligations normally attended to by my father. Although my family was absent from Penang, invitations still arrived almost daily. As the sole member of the Hutton family in Penang my father expected me to represent him when he was away.

One afternoon, after finishing my homework, I went to his study to go through the correspondence that had started to grow like mushrooms on his heavy oak desk. I opened two letters from Isabel, telling me of their wonderful time in London. I read them first, as I knew they would be imprinted with her enthusiasm and excitement. She wrote that they missed me and would be returning soon. The rest of the mail was social, and I put it in the wastepaper basket in short order after writing to regretfully decline the invitations. I had some discretion in choosing which to respond to, but when the Crosses called, one had to go. It was like getting an invitation from the dowager empress of China herself, I thought, as fragments of my grandfather's story surfaced in my memory.

The Cross family was similar to ours in many ways. They too had been in Penang right from the beginning and their company, Empire Trading, was legendary throughout Asia, spoken of in the same tone of admiration and envy as Jardine Matheson of Hong Kong. The patriarch of the family was Henry Cross, who was my father's contemporary. They were good friends, as close as anyone could be in this competitive island. Both had been at Oxford before coming home to run their family businesses.

I read the card from Henry Cross, inviting us to his son George's fifteenth birthday. I let out a soft groan, thinking of the awful evening that I would have to endure. But it would be an unforgivable insult to Henry Cross's face if I turned it down.

After generations spent in the East, many of the British had come to understand the concept of "face," which could be simplified to mean nothing more than mutual respect. To the Chinese, however, it held a deeper meaning than that: if Henry Cross came to my father's parties (which he invariably did) then my father gained considerable face. If my father helped out a servant financially without appearing to do so, he would have saved the servant face and, strangely, would not have lost face before his staff. It was a labyrinthine process of transaction and relationship. It had to be absorbed like mother's milk, otherwise it would only confuse one. I had given much face to my grandfather by visiting him. And he had reciprocated by accepting me and telling me his tale and showing me his cave in the hills.

I knew George Cross only by sight. He was a year younger than I, although his brother Ronald was my age. We attended different schools, and there was always that flavor of competition between St. Xavier's and the Penang Free School.

On the evening of the party I sighed as I changed into something presentable and waited in the portico for Uncle Lim to bring the Daimler round. The night was humid, the crickets were busy, and the wind through the windows felt good. It was too pleasurable a Friday evening to be spent at a party.

The Cross mansion was on Northam Road, which was better known as Millionaires' Row. The locals called it Ang-Mo Lor— the Road of the Red-Hair. The house made the adjacent consular offices of Thailand—which, despite the country's official change of name in May, was still referred to as Siam by the people of Penang—appear tiny, almost like its garage. We entered the ornate black and gold wrought-iron gates which hung from marble posts as imposing as monuments to well-loved heroes, and drove up the winding gravel drive. The house, all white, lay bathed in lights. It was built in the Italianate style, dominated by a pair of flanking pillars. I could hear the Jerry Maxwell Band playing a selection of jazz tunes, laughter on the air, the clink of glasses. Behind the house, the sea separated the island from mainland Malaya and I tasted the tide on my tongue.

There were the usual speculative glances when I entered—*here comes the half-caste*, I thought wryly. I was received by Henry Cross, who looked very robust and tall, graying at the temples, almost bald on top. He gave me a warm handshake; I always got on well with him.

"When's your father coming back? Or is he enjoying London too much?"

"They'll be home soon."

"They won't recognize you when they do. You seem to have grown up a lot. What are you going to do when you leave school? Not long now, is it?"

"I don't know," I shrugged. "I'll think about it when the time comes."

George shook my hand, as I wished him a happy birthday and gave him his present. I asked after Ronald.

"He's showing some of his friends around the grounds," George replied.

I turned and looked at the guests. As always, all the important people were present—the resident councillor and his wife, representatives from the various banks and from the German, Siamese, Danish, American, and Russian consulates. The local Chinese and Malay tycoons moved among them, as well as a scattering of Malay princes in golden yellow, the royal color that only they could wear. I saw a famous author from England, whose books I had enjoyed. I moved toward him, but was intercepted by Ronald. By his side I recognized his friend Yeap Chee Kon, the son of the president of the Chinese Chamber of Commerce, whom we all referred to as Towkay Yeap.

"Well, well. You certainly look different," Ronald remarked.

"Try cooking for yourself and this is what happens," I answered, smiling.

Ronald introduced me to his friend. Penang was a small island, and I knew people called him Kon, which I now did. He looked at me with a curiosity I found disconcerting. He radiated a sense of confidence for someone so youthful. He was a head shorter than me, although he seemed more muscular, which heightened the air of toughness about him. His eyes, narrow and dark, conveyed a forceful intelligence, and I had the feeling that he was accustomed to having his opinions proved correct. He was wearing white; I was later to discover that he almost never wore any other color. His handshake was strong, and the way he examined me made me dislike him. I stared straight back, unafraid.

Ronald saw someone he wanted to talk to. Kon looked over his shoulder at me as he followed Ronald. I heard my name being called and turned to see Alfred Scott beckoning to me. Mr. Scott was the manager my father had appointed to oversee Hutton & Sons while he was away in London. He had worked for us ever since I could remember and he was the only person my father was willing to relinquish the firm to whenever he had to be away. Even so, I knew he expected daily reports to be sent by telegram, whatever the cost.

"I received a message from your father today," he said. "They're leaving tomorrow. You're to meet them when the ship docks. I'll get you the date of their arrival. Can't remember it at the moment."

"Growing old, Mr. Scott?" All of us called him that, even my father. Scott was in his fifties and had never married. Although my father had often tried to bring him closer to our family, the manager had always kept to himself, preferring to spend his free time on the rubber plantations.

"I also had a telephone call from a Mr. Saotome. He said he knows you. You seem to have impressed him." He looked hard at me. "He wanted to know if we'd accept a Japanese partner, or if we were willing to do business with them." Mr. Scott shook his head in disbelief.

Saotome's persistent interest in our company worried me. I never knew what Saotome had done to the girl offered to him, and Endo-san had only grunted when I asked.

"What did you tell him?" I asked Mr. Scott.

"I told him what was was laid down by your great-grandfather: that unless his surname was Hutton no outsider would be allowed in."

I winced at his blunt reply and he barked his distinctive laugh, causing the people around us to look indulgently amused. His eyes followed a slim Malay waiter and then he lowered his voice and said, "I don't trust this Saotome fellow. He was very insistent that we change our minds."

"Have you told my father?"

He shook his head. "It's not all that important. I can let him know when he comes home. I've enough to report to him as it is."

I agreed with his decision and told him so. He finished his drink and said he had to go home. "Hate these parties," he said.

The Japanese consul, Shigeru Hiroshi, saw me and came over. He was a thin, sickly looking man in his fifties, ill suited to the climate. His head was shaven bald, like many of the Japanese I had seen. He was too small for his dinner jacket, his shiny scalp matching the gleam of his lapels. "You must be Endo-san's *deshi*, his pupil. He has described you well."

I bowed and asked him where Endo-san was. For a quick moment he hesitated, then said, "He is in Kuala Lumpur."

"Again? After his recent visit?" I knew he was lying, for I recalled Endo-san's note to me. Hiroshi did not reply but instead asked me about my lessons. I was accustomed to their way of avoiding any truths they did not wish to reveal, and so I gave him face and did not ask him further questions about Endo-san.

The conversation turned inevitably to the presence of the Japanese in China and he began to tire me with his description of Japanese superiority. "We have the best army in Asia now. They are disciplined, highly trained, and civilized," he said, loudly enough for a few circles of guests around us to hear.

"Oh, but what about Nanking?" I asked, using the English name for Nanjing. Decades later most Japanese would deny all knowledge of the appalling things that were done there but, as my question cut across the conversations around us and people turned to look, I knew Hiroshi was fully aware of the events that had taken place. He flinched and I could see his mouth tightening like a bowstring being stretched. "Were the Japanese troops there 'disciplined, highly trained, and civilized?'" I persisted.

He finally moved. He swallowed his drink and then said, "Yes, of course they were. Why would they not have been?"

There were loud snorts around us, especially from the Chinese, and he flushed with anger.

I left him and as the party went on into the night I ended up on the beach, walking slowly away from the noise. I could see some lights along the waterline of Province Wellesley across the channel, glimmering like the stars overhead. The moon was out, reflected in the dark oily water. The lanterns of fishing trawlers out at sea swayed drunkenly.

I saw a ghostly white figure ahead of me and wondered who it was that had also found the crowd unappealing. As I approached the figure turned around and I could only keep moving; to walk back would have been too obvious.

"You should be careful of the consul. He doesn't like being made a fool of," Kon said.

"How would you know?" I answered, his superior tone raising my irritation. I moved closer to him, which was a mistake.

The punch seemed to shoot out from nowhere. I avoided it, but I knew it was very close, and threw one in return. It was intercepted and my wrist would have been broken had I not countered and spun him around. We broke away from each other, grinning.

"You're very good," Kon said.

"So are you," I replied.

We circled warily. My heart pounded and I cleared my mind, placing it somewhere over the horizon. I had no inkling of the level of his skill, but the way he had almost caught me off-guard indicated an ability that could overwhelm mine. Subtly I changed my stance and opened myself to an attack, giving him a bigger target.

He launched his strike, left-right punches to my head. I swept them away and entered his space. Using the power of my hips I spun and effortlessly threw him onto the sand. My foot aimed for his face, but this time he was ready and it was deflected. I had overextended myself; there was no other choice but to heave my body into his. I slammed into him and we tumbled on the wet sand. I hit him and for just a second his hold on me weakened enough for me to grapple his wrist and twist it into a bone-breaking lock. He tried to move but it was excruciating for him. His struggles heightened the intense pain. I increased the pressure.

"Enough?" I asked

"Yes."

I let him go, backing away, keeping my eyes on him in case he attacked again. In actual fact the levels of our skills were similar, but my mind, due to Endo-san's strict training, was the stronger. The moment Kon launched his attack he had already lost. I was content to wait, forever if need be; he had been too eager to start the fight.

He stood up; the look in his eyes told me his curiosity had been satisfied, his suspicions confirmed. He faced me and without the need for words we both bowed. I did not try to hide my sense of disbelief. We were both students of *aikijutsu*, the art of harmonizing forces.

Endo-san had often told me about his teacher, Morihei Ueshiba, after our classes had ended. Ueshiba was a gentle-looking man with piercing eyes and a quick temper, quick to flare, quicker to dissipate. His name and tales of his prowess were already spread widely across Japan and he was acknowledged as one of the greatest martial artists of all time, even by teachers of other disciplines. Born in the 1880s, he had revolutionized the concept of the warrior arts. The secret behind his power, Ueshiba often told his students, was based on love, love for everyone, for the universe, even for the one who was about to kill you. For love was a power of the universe, and with the universe behind you, who could defeat you?

I had often thought his message was similar to Christ's emphasis on love. Originally *aikijutsu* was hard-edged, brutal. Ueshiba would eventually smooth the edges by rounding out the techniques, making them completely circular. The movement of the circle was the source of all his techniques. However, it remained extremely effective. The techniques I had learned from Endo-san were still rooted in the old-style *aikijutsu*, for Endo-san had left Japan when Ueshiba was still discovering the concepts that would ultimately ensure him immortality. From Kon's movements I could see clearly that his *sensei*'s style differed slightly from Endo-san's; it was softer and rounder. Though I was unaware of it then, I was witnessing and experiencing the evolution of an art.

"Where did you learn all that?" I asked. As the son of a well-known Chinese businessman, I did not expect him to be so proficient in Japanese fighting techniques.

"From my *sensei*," he said. To my astonishment, he spoke to me in Japanese and I wondered if I had had too much to drink. He stood up, brushing sand off his clothes and tucking his shirt into his trousers, always fastidious about his appearance.

"Well, who is he?" I wanted more answers from him.

"Tanaka-san," he said, enjoying my impatience. "He'd like to see you."

I agreed to meet Kon at his home at dawn the following day and visit his teacher. I wanted to meet his *sensei*, and I was certain that Endo-san would be pleased to know of the presence of another man who was adept in *aikijutsu*.

We sat above the reach of the incoming tide and talked of other things for a while. Kon suddenly said, "My father and I went to your mother's funeral. I can still remember parts of it, although I was very young then."

I could not recall seeing him there. So many people had turned up, not to mourn but because of my father's position. "That was a long time ago," I said.

He too had lost his mother at an early age, Kon told me. I sensed the carefully hidden hurt in him, the feeling of having been abandoned, and to my surprise it felt very similar to mine.

"I'm sorry," I said. "I know how you must feel."

"Coming from you I know at least that's the truth."

I was uncertain how to respond to his remark. I saw a smile surface and then sink back into his solemn face, and a short burst of laughter came out from me. His face lost its control and he shook gently with increasing mirth.

We talked for a long time on the beach that night; although we did not know it then, it would be the start of a strong friendship.

It was only when Uncle Lim was driving me home that I realized Kon had not asked me a single question, that he had seemed to know all about me and perhaps even about Endo-san.

Chapter Twelve

The following morning, Kon and I cycled to Tanjung Tokong, the Cape of the Temple, to pay a visit to his *sensei*. We went along a deserted stretch of beach past the Ocean Pearl Temple. The Cape was a fishing village, the community completely of Hakka bloodline, and the temple was the site of worship of Tua Pek Kong, a pilgrim who had settled in Penang even before Francis Light. Like so many pilgrims, he had been deified after his death.

We cycled along a narrow lane bordered by tall wild-grass, and then onto a sandy path that went downhill. I would not have found the place if I had been on my own.

At the bottom of the path we came to a wooden bungalow with a veranda running around it and a thatched attap roof that sat on it like a straw hat. A pair of coconut trees stood bent over it at one side, their leaves giving sound to the wind. Squirrels scampered on the sparse lawn, running up the trees, chattering busily, when we approached.

Hideki Tanaka waited at the top of the steps, his face impassive though not unfriendly. Like Endo-san's, his hair was cropped short and gray, but he had a larger, thicker figure.

"I've been waiting for you," he said in Japanese.

I nodded my head and bowed deeply.

We sat on the veranda facing the sea. The tide was low, and flocks of gulls and birds hopped on the exposed beach, their beaks piercing the sand for food. The empty beach stretched as far as the eye could travel, the seabed as black and rich as newly ploughed fields. Pools of water were trapped between the bumpy sand ridges created by the receding tide, and I wondered where all the sea had gone.

"Sometimes I feel I could walk all the way across to the mainland, across this sea that has opened before us," Tanaka said, following my gaze. "Walk all the way home."

143

"Like Moses," I answered.

He looked puzzled, as though I had named a friend he had forgotten, then his face cleared. "Ah, yes. The prophet who parted the Red Sea. A charming story." He instructed Kon to make us tea.

I felt peaceful sitting with him, yet underlying his tranquil mood was a strong sense of loneliness. I recognized it as I had sensed the same in Endo-san. How strange to find two such similar Japanese on this island.

Kon came out with hot green tea and for a while we sipped in silence, taking in each other, gazing out over the earth left behind by the vanished sea.

"Kon told me about you last night, how you fought him to the ground. He was very displeased by that." Tanaka laughed. "Very few people have ever defeated him. That is why I told him, practice *zazen*, practice it every day. The power of the mind will always overcome the strength and weakness of the body."

"Do you know my *sensei*?" I asked.

He nodded. "Endo Hayato-san. From one of the well-known families near Toriijima."

"You don't have a high regard for him?" I ventured.

"We studied under the same teacher, Ueshiba-sensei."

I waited for him to explain; his reply had been typical of the sort Endo-san gave me whenever he did not wish me to pursue a matter. I looked directly at Tanaka, letting him know that I had not been fooled by his evasion. Tanaka gave a smile but did not elaborate.

I sighed inwardly, and asked, "What was Ueshiba-*sensei* like?"

"The gentlest, kindest person I've ever known. But also terribly hot-tempered. The greatest *budoka*—martial artist—Japan has ever produced. Endo-san was one of his best pupils. As was I."

"How did the two of you end up here, on this island?"

"I don't know. Fate? Endo-san left Ueshiba-sensei a few months before I did. There was some disagreement between them. I didn't know he was here until a few months after I arrived. By that time I had settled in and bought this house. I had traveled all over Asia, and strangely seemed to find an affinity with this island. So I stayed." He sighed. "To attempt to find some peace."

"Strange," I said. "That was what Endo-san said to me too. To find peace."

"You must understand, Japan is undergoing a social upheaval. There's a lot of hatred and ambition there, a bad combination. The Militarists and the Imperialists are agitating for war. Some of us don't believe in war, and thus we are considered traitors and outcasts.

"I was ordered to teach the army recruits. To teach *aikijutsu* in order for people to be able to kill and murder. *Aikijutsu*, the very concept of which is based on love and harmony! I could not do so and neither could my *sensei*. To avoid further orders from the government he moved to Hokkaido Island, cut himself off from the world and started a farm there. I chose to leave Japan."

I was certain there was more to this story than he was revealing, but I respected his intentions not to tell me more. He sent Kon inside to boil more water.

"Do you have great affection for Endo-san?" he asked, pouring me another cup of tea. I felt a growing sense of well-being, sitting under the shade of the veranda, listening to the birds and the leaves, feeling the breeze on my body.

I considered his question. "Yes. Yes, I do admire him. I also have strong feelings for him. Not a day goes by that I do not wonder what he is doing, where he is at that moment. He makes me happy to be alive . . ." I said, my voice trailing off, unable to put what I felt into words.

"That's good. I think, in the end, it's your love for him which will save him."

"Save him? From what?"

He merely gave a smile and I knew I would not obtain any more from him on that subject. Once again I resolved to ask Endo-san about his life before he left Japan.

Tanaka attempted to hit me then, his fist light and blurred like a tiercel swooping down to capture its prey. I avoided it by shifting my seated body to one side. When he pulled back to withdraw his hand my arm stuck to his, following it back to him, turning it into an attack on him. He turned his torso and overextended me until I was off-balance. I pushed myself to a crouch and shot out a side-kick at him, which I knew immediately was a mistake. He swept it easily aside and slammed me facedown onto the wooden floor. All this while he was still seated in the *seiza* position, his face devoid of expression.

"Your *suwariwaza*—sitting techniques—are still relatively weak. You must practice them more often. If you are strong even while sitting in this uncomfortable position, then think how much stronger you will be when you are upright, *neh*?"

He hauled me up while I tried to cool my flaring temper. I realized he had a point. I turned and bowed to him, my forehead touching the ground. "I appreciate your guidance," I said. "Would you consider teaching me?"

He shook his head. "It would be against all ethics to teach you while you are still the pupil of another *sensei*. However," he looked up as Kon came to stand at the doorway, "there's no rule against the two of you learning from each other. I'm of the opinion that the two of you will benefit greatly from being friends."

Kon smiled and I knew we were both thinking of our shared laughter the night before. I had found a similar soul.

Tanaka became serious, his voice almost insistent. "Endo-san has trained you well. Now it is up to you to find out why he has done so."

I was growing worried about Endo-san's absence when I found a note from him, telling me he had returned. Something in me leaped like a fish in clear water and a lightness danced within me as I rowed to his island. I approached the thicket of trees with eagerness and called out his name as I neared the house.

He looked dark and sunburned, and his hair shone brighter in contrast. "Welcome home, *sensei*," I greeted him, and I knew he was happy to see me. He invited me into his house, and we sat in front of the hearth.

"Have you been keeping well?" he asked.

"Yes, Endo-san," I said. I had been disturbed by my conversation with Tanaka and I wondered now if I should tell Endo-san about it. I hesitated. Then I decided that I did not want to keep anything from him, so I described my meeting with Kon's *sensei*. He did not appear unduly surprised, but when I asked if he would like to visit Tanaka, his voice lost its warmth.

"I do not wish to meet him."

"But why? We're practicing the same art, both are styles of *bujutsu*—in fact both of you learned from the same man."

His voice turned cold and I felt I had gone too far in pushing him. "Be satisfied that both styles work equally well. Be aware that ultimately it is not a question of styles of the same art, or even of different arts; it is rather a question of the person. You cannot say, as an example, that Chinese martial arts defeated Japanese methods yesterday. How can one art defeat another? Can you state that painting 'was defeated' by flower arranging? It is only the person who can vanquish another.

"However, if you feel you have anything much to lose by not learning under Tanaka-san, I would be happy to let you go. You are aware that it has never been acceptable to have two *sensei* for the same thing?"

I flinched at his curt words; they were like chips of ricocheting granite piercing me. "No, no, *sensei*. I'm sorry I gave you the wrong impression. The thought of leaving your tutelage has never occurred to me."

He softened his tone, and that was the closest to an apology I would get from him. "You found the boy Kon formidable, yes?"

I nodded.

"Yet you managed to control him. Why?"

I told him what I thought that night after I had met Kon, when I analyzed our encounter—that my mind was stronger and calmer than his. It was what Tanaka had told me as well.

Endo-san gave a rare, radiant smile. "I see I have not wasted my time with you. Yes, the mind. Once you control the mind, the body becomes helpless. At a higher level, *bujutsu* is fought by the mind. Remember that. Now you understand my insistence on you practicing meditation. Your mind will save you when your body cannot. I am pleased that you train so much on your own. I value the amount of hard work you have put into yourself. You have realized entirely on your own that if you yourself do not put in the work required—for any endeavor!—who else will do it for you?"

His words touched me. In all my years my father had never spoken to me this way; no one ever had. Sitting in the *seiza* position, I bowed deeply, my forehead touching the ground, the lowest anyone could reach, yet I never felt higher in all my life.

One question remained to me. "If a higher level of *bujutsu* involves fighting with the mind, what then is the very highest level?"

He closed his eyes for a while, seeing things he would never show me. "That," he said, "would be never to fight at all."

Chapter Thirteen

The situation in Europe was worsening. Hitler had launched his Panzer divisions into Poland, starting the tear that would soon rip the fabric of Europe into rags. I was on Endo-san's island one evening when he called me into the house. He had tuned in to the BBC Overseas Service and I heard Neville Chamberlain's voice, given a tone of hollowness by the distance and static, declare that Britain was now at war with Germany.

"Will your family be safe?" Endo-san asked.

Alfred Scott's secretary had given me details of my family's voyage home a few days after the party at Henry Cross's house. "They left Southampton two weeks ago," I answered.

"The sea lanes will be patrolled by German submarines," he said.

I checked the date on his calendar. "They should be halfway home now, well away from Europe." I tried not to show my concern, but the journey was so long, the distances over unprotected waters so vast. I felt guilty, for they should have been home two months ago, but because I had chosen not to go with them, my father had decided to extend their stay in London, since I would not be missing my new term at school. I reminded myself that I would call Scott to see if he had heard anything further from my father.

We continued to listen to the news. It was all so far away that I did not think it would affect our lives here at all. The news that came seemed like a serialized story, to be heard or read over breakfast and then forgotten until the next, more terrible, instalment arrived the following morning.

In spite of the resumption of the school term, Endo-san had intensified my training after he returned from his travels, almost as if he had to conform to some unwritten schedule. He agreed to conduct his lessons later in the evening to accommodate me, but then proceeded to push me to near fury, and there was no one I could talk to except Kon.

Once I became Kon's friend I grew aware of the stories surrounding his father, Towkay Yeap. They had been floating in the air for a while, but I had never given much attention to them. Uncle Lim, especially, delighted in gossiping about the alleged leader of the Red Banner Society.

"You're like one of the kitchen servants, going on and on like that," I said to him one day, but still bursting with curiosity to discover more.

I learned that the Red Banner Society was a triad, a Chinese criminal gang, led by someone they called a Dragon Head. Many of the early migrants from China were members of these organizations, bringing with them the traditions and practices of their triads and, for a payment, helping subsequent fellow migrants stand on their own feet in a new country. The Perak Wars of Malaya of the 1880s had been backed by opposing triads, each out to carve a bigger territory for itself. They earned their revenue from protection fees paid by members, from prostitution and illegal gambling. Many ran their own opium dens and smuggled in the drug as well.

"Are you a member of any?" I asked Uncle Lim, and he glared at me, offended that I could ask so personal a question.

"Don't make Towkay Yeap angry," he warned me instead. "Some say his power is greater than that of the governor of Singapore."

"Is my grandfather in these triads? He is, isn't he? Is that why you are so loyal to him?"

But Uncle Lim said he had to search for some parts for the car, and refused to say anything more

In the little spaces of free time when Endo-san was busy, I became a regular visitor to Kon's home. The house was in the wealthy Georgetown Chinese area that divided into Pitt Street, Light Street, and China Street. It was located two houses away from La Maison Bleu, the former home of Cheong Fatt Tze, who had been Chinese consul general to Singapore in the service of the Manchu government. His funeral, in 1916, my father once told me, was the

largest Penang had seen; even the Dutch and the English govern-
ments had ordered flags to be flown at half-mast across their
colonies. "That house is where I met your mother, in 1922," he
said to me. "Cheong Fatt Tze's eldest son continued his father's
tradition of holding his famous parties. And there, one evening, I
saw your mother dancing. I walked up to her and she smiled at
me, and without a word she left her poor partner standing alone,
and danced only with me for the rest of the evening."

I watched him smile as he saw my mother again. "Do you
know what she did when her heel broke?" he said. "She took off
her shoes and threw them into a corner, which created a minor
furor among the other women. And then she said, 'Are you not
going to act like a gentleman and take off your shoes as well?'"

"What did you do?" I asked.

"Took off my shoes and danced with her all night until it was
time to go home," he replied, his eyes bright with memory.

La Maison Bleu, the Manchu's house, got its name because its
walls had been dyed with indigo obtained from India, and that
made it easy for me to find Kon's home just down the road.

I knocked on the wide wooden doors. A whitewashed wall ran
around the property so that I could not see inside. A moment later
an old man pushed the doors open with difficulty and I stepped
over the low threshold. The doors closed behind me and the
sounds of the streets were immediately silenced.

The house was built in the Chinese style, the edges of the roof
pinched upwards. The terra-cotta tiles on the roof were thick with
aged mold, the pigeons picking their way jauntily over them. I
saw Kon come out on to the balcony on the second floor. I waved
to him and he disappeared back inside.

He met me at the front entrance and led me into the main hall.
A large wooden screen, carved with a thousand detailed figures
and leafed in gold, barred all outsiders from the house within.
Red lanterns hung from the crossbeams of the ceiling and square
wooden pedestals inlaid with mother-of-pearl supported vases
and jade figurines. The clay tiles felt cold under my bare feet when
I removed my shoes. I began to cool down from the heat outside.

Towkay Yeap, Kon's father, came out from behind the screen
and shook my hand. With his thin, bony face and dark, intelligent

eyes, he had the appearance of a scholar from Confucian times. I had heard rumors that, like many of the wealthy older Chinese, he was a habitual frequenter of the opium dens in town. Indulgence in the drug often caused the flesh to melt away from the face and stretch the skin tight, and looking at his face now I could almost believe the stories.

He inquired after my father, and said they had some dealings together. "One of the rare few English *Tuan Besars* who would openly do business with us," he said, honoring him with the title of "Big Boss," the term given by the Malays to great men. "I was at your parents' wedding."

He seemed genial enough, and I wondered if he would be capable of ordering the deaths of his enemies. I shivered when I felt he knew what I was thinking. To unsettle me further he said, "Please convey my regards to your grandfather in Ipoh."

I was discovering how small my world was as Towkay Yeap gave me a fathomless smile before he turned away into his study.

"This is a lovely house," I said to Kon as we went up a wrought-iron spiral staircase in the cobbled courtyard. I heard the female voices of his household, the *amahs* chattering in the kitchen, the sound of a steel cleaver on a wooden chopping block as lunch was prepared, and I caught the smell of glutinous rice steaming when a soft wind blew through the house. A dog barked at my presence and a male voice scolded it. *"Diamlah!"*

"My father bought this place from Cheong Fatt Tze, who had it built for one of his lesser wives. It's very much smaller than La Maison Bleu."

"How many wives did he have?"

"Eight official ones."

"Lucky number," I said.

"For us Chinese, yes. This house has only ten rooms, but Cheong's had thirty-eight. Apart from that the features and decorations are almost identical. Built by the same team of craftsmen."

I had thought my room was bad enough, but there were even more books in Kon's. Unlike mine, his books, in addition to those written in English, included volumes in Chinese.

"Sorry about the mess. I have a large collection of books on Chinese history and art," he said. "Since I began my studies with Tanaka-san I have also begun collecting books on Japanese culture." Kon moved a pile of books from a chair and asked me to sit. Large windows and a door opened to the balcony let in the light. I heard the cries of a hawker and the *tok tok* sound as he knocked on his wooden clappers while pedaling his pushcart past the house, selling wonton noodles.

"How did you meet Tanaka-san?"

"At the Flame-Watching Ceremony at the Ocean Pearl Temple near his house." Kon saw my blank expression and explained, "On the fourteenth night of the Chinese New Year, my father, as one of the trustees of the temple, performs a ceremony. Some embers of holy paper are placed in an urn and fanned until they catch fire. The temple monks then read the flames and predict the New Year's fortune. People often wait outside the temple to hear the monks' proclamation. I was there that night when a fight broke out. I saw Tanaka-san quell it, and I made my way to him, and asked him to teach me."

"So you began learning under him after that night?"

Kon shook his head. "He refused me at first. But I found out where he lived and waited outside his home every day after school until dark. This went on for a few weeks until he relented. And you?"

"I had it easier than you. Endo-san came to my house to borrow a boat and after that offered to teach me."

"He must have seen something in you," Kon said, "some quality you have."

I felt uncomfortable with the subject. I had often wondered why Endo-san had decided to make me his pupil. Had it all been merely an accident that he leased our island and then made himself such a large part of my life?

"Do you think my meeting him, and our meeting—all of it— was by chance?" I asked.

Kon touched one of his books. "It depends on who you ask. Some people would view it as a consequence of choices made in our previous lives."

"Endo-san once talked about the Buddha's Wheel of Life. I don't believe it. Surely we are not fated to continually pay for the same mistakes?"

And then Kon said something to me that made me wonder if each life that began was as pure as some would wish to believe.

"The problem is," he said, "some mistakes can be so great, so grievous, that we end up paying for them again and again, until eventually all our lives forget why we began paying in the first place. If you're able to remember, then you must make the greatest effort to put things right, now, before you forget again."

He stood up and said, "Enough talking. Let's go and practice. I'd like you to show me some of the things you've learned."

We left his room of the many books and unsettling words and went downstairs to his training room. But I never forgot those words he said and they would return to me again, through Endo-san's voice.

"You must pay attention. Everything we do here is life and death," Endo-san said, his exasperation making him brusque.

Lately our tempers had been swimming just below the surface, ready to leap out of the water like a marlin taking the bait. I bit back a reply, cursing him inwardly, cursing myself. Now, in my lessons with him, the taint of uncertainty and distraction often hung in the air. He often seemed preoccupied, his eyes distant and his thoughts far away in time. Sometimes I caught him staring at me, but I felt he was in another time. Then he would come back from where his thoughts had been drifting and turn away from me, making me feel as if I had done something wrong. As a result, my mind was everywhere but in the present and I lost my concentration, which only made him angrier.

At the level in which we were training, my lack of awareness was dangerous. In an unanticipated move, Endo-san flipped me over him in a wrist-lock throw. I was not fast enough to follow the direction of the movement to protect myself, and a sharp pain tore into my sprained wrist.

Endo-san knew even without being told that I was injured. He fetched a box containing his medicinal supplies from the house.

He dipped his finger into a jar of herbal ointment and rubbed it into my hand, his movements rough and hurried. I winced but soon the sprain began to heat up as the ointment seeped into my skin.

"It will heal in a few days," he snapped, and went back into the house to prepare dinner. I changed into dry clothing and followed him. It was only after I sat down that I realized my injured hand was incapable of working the pair of chopsticks. I placed them heavily on the table, and the saucers and soy sauce container rattled. His eyes met mine, and he moved in closer to me. He deftly picked up a sliver of salmon and held my chin with his hand as he placed it into my mouth. I chewed it slowly, my eyes never leaving his. He laid his chopsticks neatly on the table and took a drink of tea.

There was only the sound of the pot bubbling over the hearth. He was so close to me that each breath he expelled, I took, and every breath that I surrendered, he possessed. I waited for him to continue, to quiet the sudden turmoil within me. As I heard his breathing I knew the next step would be dependent on me, and so, putting my feet firmly on the path I would take, I leaned forward and received another offering from his hand.

That moment notched the beginning of our relationship, our real relationship. We had passed beyond the boundaries that encircled the pupil and the master. From that moment, he began to treat me more as an equal, although I sensed that he held back as though he did not want to repeat a mistake made in his earlier life.

Chapter Fourteen

The day of my family's arrival home came sooner than I had expected. One morning I woke up and knew the house would again be full of sounds and laughter, that there would be parties and dances and tennis luncheons.

I waited at the gates to the pier at Weld Quay, beside the black Daimler that Uncle Lim had polished to a high sheen. I munched on a piece of banana fritter, watching the P&O liner enter the harbor, bringing my family back to Penang. They had been away for six months, including the eight weeks required for the voyages there and back. I had enjoyed being on my own and I hoped their return would not encroach on the routine to which I had grown accustomed.

The noise of the docks surrounded me—stevedores and coolies hailing each other, street peddlers hawking their wares, people greeting their friends, dogs barking, little children running around as their frantic grandparents shouted for them to stop. Above us gulls wheeled and cried and occasionally the horn of a ship sounded as it approached the pier. For a few moments I wished Endo-san was next to me.

I was worried by the number of Australian soldiers milling around the quay. They were all very young, their faces red from the heat, patches of perspiration darkening their olive green uniforms. What disturbed me more was the look of purpose on their faces; they knew they had a reason to be here and I wondered if the rest of us were to share in that knowledge. The governor of Singapore had assured those of us in Malaya that the presence of the soldiers should not be a cause for alarm, that the War Office was only concerned with protecting the supply of rubber and tin. Looking around me, I wondered if he had been entirely truthful.

Uncle Lim returned from the harbor office. "The ship's docking now," he informed me. I had a healthy respect for him; he was tough as a boxful of nails and had taught me more than a fair share of dirty street-fighting tricks. But he was soft-spoken and gentle too. "Your father wouldn't like you to spend so much time with the Japanese," he said, as though to remind me again.

"We'll just have to make sure he doesn't find out, won't we?" I said. "Anyway, he's a very good teacher," I continued when Lim started rubbing his elbow, at the spot where I had hit him and immobilized him the night before.

He saw my smug smile. "You were lucky last night. I was a bit drunk."

I gave an exaggerated snort. "I'm quite willing to allow you a rematch whenever you're sober."

He shook his head and said, "That Japanese has been a good teacher to you, I have to admit."

I saw my sister Isabel first as she ran—as ever, despite the many times our *amah* had scolded her for doing so—out from among the disembarking crowd, her hair streaming behind her. At twenty-one years of age she was becoming very beautiful, with a strong hint of our father's features. We were the two who most resembled him; Edward and William took after their mother. She ran into my arms and Uncle Lim stood to one side discreetly, assuming once again the role of the quiet driver.

"You look so different!" she said, catching her breath easily. "We've missed you."

I could not lie to her, so I did not say I had missed her too. She let me go and turned to look for the others. "Oh look, there's Father. He's sent the boys to collect our luggage."

Noel Hutton, my father, strode out from the shade of the quay and into the sun, jamming his hat onto his head, looking every inch the quintessential Englishman. He was just an inch below six feet, well proportioned, but with a slight paunch from his soft life. I have to say he was very handsome, his eyes a clear marble blue, his jaw firm, ears sticking out slightly in an endearing way. His hair was already an unblemished gray.

He looked for his favorite car first, running a quick examining eye over it, checking to see if it had been damaged in his absence. He saw me and for a second he looked puzzled, his brows tilting down toward his nose. Then he smiled and shook my hand, and

I smelled his familiar scent. Years later, after the war, I found in his room a sealed bottle of the Burberry's after-shave he had used and twisted it open. The smell of it, so sudden, so unexpected, made me drop the bottle. It fell to the floor and the contents spilled out, darkening the floorboards. And, for a moment, I thought my father was with me again.

"Have you been keeping out of trouble?" he asked me, glancing at Uncle Lim, who nodded slightly.

"Of course I have," I said. It was my turn to look quickly at Uncle Lim.

He put his arm around my shoulders and I knew without question he loved me. So why couldn't I give him the same amount of love? Was this flaw in me due to the bitterness I still felt about my mother's death, which had left me feeling like a foundling on the family's doorstep?

He let go of me and shook Uncle Lim's hand. "Welcome home, sir." Uncle Lim spoke only in English with my father, even though he knew he could speak his Hokkien dialect almost fluently.

Edward and William came out with their baggage, following the porter they had found. They too were astounded at the change in my appearance. I had not seen William for three years yet he still looked the same to me, his smile hinting at new and as yet unperpetrated mischief, his movements energetic and quick.

"Been starving yourself I see," William said. He shook my hand then punched me on my shoulder but this time, unlike previously, I avoided it easily and caught his hand. I turned his palm into his wrist, locking his joints and forcing him to bend his knees.

"Hey, let go, that hurts!" he said.

I released him. "Where did you learn how to do that?" he asked.

"It looks as if our little brother has learned to fight back," Isabel said. "Good for him." She reached over and kissed me quickly on the cheek.

In the car all they could talk of was the war in Europe. "We were lucky we got out when we did. Hitler's U-boats are sinking too many of our ships," my father said to me. "We're in for some tough times ahead."

"Britain will need more raw materials for her factories," I

predicted. The view in Penang among the merchants was that the war in Europe would lift Malaya's economy out of the slump it had fallen into. The prices of tin and rubber and iron ore would soar.

"That's obvious, but shipping them there would be a problem," Edward pointed out.

"We'll be all right here," William said. "Far away from the war." He said this with some bitterness, and I realized he had been reluctant to return to Penang. He had always made it clear that he had no desire to join the family company. Only my father's direct command had been strong enough to ensure that he made the eight-thousand-mile voyage home with them.

Noel's lips pressed together as he looked out of the window. "You know I'd prefer you to work in the company for a year or two before you enlist. And that was the promise you made to me, before you left. At least learn where all the money comes from that you've been throwing away on your friends in London."

William was stung, and before he could reply I rushed in to fill the silence. "The *Straits Times* was vehement and condemnatory about the sneak attack on the naval base at Scapa Flow."

"Bloody Germans," Edward said. "Over seven hundred lives were lost. British lives," he added, as though those had a greater value.

"And the Japanese in China," my father said, turning back to us. "They're tearing the country apart. How's your family, Lim?"

Uncle Lim's eyes looked at us in the rearview mirror. "They seem safe, sir. My daughter is already here."

"Good. You should send for your wives as well. I do think they'll be safer here. Nothing will happen to them in Penang. Malaya's one of the safest places to be at the moment."

I thought again of Ming's stories. In the last few weeks Uncle Lim had never failed to give me the latest news of Japanese cruelty he had read from the more strident local Chinese newspapers. I wanted to tell him to stop, but a part of me craved to hear it.

"You don't think they'll invade Malaya?" Isabel asked no one in particular.

My father, looking out into the distance, said, "I think they'll try. And they'll fail. Singapore's armed to the teeth to fight anyone. They have thirty-inch guns pointing out to sea. Destroyers are cruising the oceans watching out for any foolish

Japanese ship that tries to slip in, and as you can see there are soldiers everywhere, even here in Penang. We'll be safe."

His opinion was the prevalent view among the Europeans in Malaya. His confidence assured us and we left the subject and talked of their trip. "Now," my father said. "You know what I missed most in London? Would anyone mind if we stopped at Rajoo's *mee rebus* stall?"

The tense atmosphere in the car was immediately lightened. Isabel and Edward laughed and agreed to let him indulge in his favorite Indian noodles at the only roadside stall he would eat at.

Life returned to normal during the remaining months of that year. It was my last term at school and I made conscientious preparations for the final examinations for my school certificate. Endo-san reduced the frequency of my lessons to allow me time to study. I did very well, getting high marks in Latin, mathematics, and English. Most of my family members were astonished, but not Endo-san. He knew what I could achieve when I set my mind to it. After all, it was he who had trained me to do so.

My father was a great reader and proud of his library. In his luggage he had, as usual, brought back a large collection of books from London. The affairs of the company had kept him from unpacking them immediately on his return and I knew he was eager to get down to the task. After breakfast, one weekend in December, he said, "You've got lots of time now. Come and help me with my books."

He knew I would enjoy helping him, for we always wore a similar look of contentment on our faces as we went around the library, putting the right book in the right place on the shelves, discussing them as we did so, arguing about the merits and flaws of each.

The library was in the western corner of the house, away from the rooms where we dined or received visitors. Despite its size, it was a quiet and comfortable place. The windows were open. Outside, the sun was giving off that light that was only present in Penang—bright, warm, alive, stirring up the colors in the sea. A breeze gently shook the casuarina tree as a few sparrows danced in its branches, their wings fluttering frantically.

A mahogany desk was placed near the windows and my father often sat there when he had work to do. The shelves reached all the way to the ceiling, but one wall had been set aside to exhibit his collection of butterflies and *keris* blades.

The butterflies were mounted and neatly labeled in glass-fronted wooden cases, neat rows of *papilionidae*, their desiccated wings still rich with color, destined never to fly again. My father had been an enthusiastic lepidopterist, traveling all over Malaya to add to his collection, until my mother became ill while accompanying him on one of his trips to the rainforests. He had been hoping to find Rajah Brooke's Birdwing, a rare species first discovered by Alfred Russell Wallace in 1855.

He had indeed found it on that trip, and now it was mounted in its own box, a large beautiful creature, almost seven inches across its opened black wings, which were decorated with a row of luminous green tooth-shaped patterns. These days he usually walked past it without even looking at it or at any of the other cases. He had also stopped collecting butterflies since that trip, directing his interest instead to the acquisition of traditional Javanese and Malay blades. He already had eight of them in his collection.

He stopped before these curved daggers now, each blade, usually with seven waves, looking like a frozen snake. The *keris* were short, about the length of a man's arm from the elbow to the fingers. The hilt of the particular *keris* he was examining was a mythological animal carved from ivory and decorated with diamonds.

He had bought this particular *keris* just before leaving for London, from the deposed sultan of a Malay state who had fallen on hard times. The sultan had warned him of the magical elements of a *keris*—each dagger housed a spirit that would protect the owner from misfortune, in return for regular sacrificial offerings of food and drink. But because it was being passed to a European, the sultan had assured him that the soul of the *keris* had been removed by a *bomoh*, a Malay warlock, and no such rituals would be required of him.

Noel lifted the *keris* off its mounting, the expression of reverence on his face similar to the one on Endo-san's whenever he examined his own Nagamitsu sword. Now that I had my own sword I could appreciate my father's fascination. I took it from his hands, testing its craftsmanship with a few stabs and slashes. It was exquisitely made, the combination of iron, nickel, and steel making the blade itself dark and oily looking. Whorls resulting from the process of forging and folding the blade caught the light, looking like smoke rising to the tip of the blade when I held it up.

"You look as though you know how to use it," he said.

I shrugged and returned the *keris* to him.

"I did some research into it at the British Museum," he said. "The old sultan wasn't lying. This was forged for a king at the time of the Majapahit Empire, five hundred years ago," he said. He placed it back on the wall and shook his head. "Among the creations of our modern world, what do you think will still exist and have historical and aesthetic value five hundred years from now?"

"I don't know," I said. "I've never really thought about it."

"You should, with your interest in history," he said. "I grant that it's not an easy question to answer so early in the morning."

He went to an open crate and said, "This is for you."

I took the heavy book from his hands. I had first read of H. G. Wells's *The Outline of History* a year ago in the *Straits Times* and since then had been requesting a copy from the bookstores of Kuala Lumpur and Singapore, with no success.

"How did you know—?" I began. I had never told him about the book.

He enjoyed the look of surprise on my face. "I *am* your father, you know," he said, the blitheness in his voice almost concealing the emotions contained within his simple declaration. But I sensed it, and modified my reply accordingly to let him know I had understood, and to avoid a loss of face on his side. We each knew what the other had meant, and that was enough.

"Thank you," I said. "Can I read it now?"

"Not a chance. You're going to help me shelve these first," he said.

We spent the morning cataloguing his recent purchases, with me making mock sneering remarks at some of them and my father putting up halfhearted defenses. One of the maids came in to dust, but when she saw us laughing and chattering she quietly left us.

"Did you visit the temple with your aunt?" he asked.

"Yes, I did."

"Good. I asked her to make certain you went." I could see that he was gratified that I had obeyed my aunt. "Your results were excellent. I wish William had done as well as you have."

"I did the best I could," I said, a hot flash of embarrassed pride making me stammer slightly. He did not give praise easily.

"Which university would you like to go to? With your results, you could have your pick of them."

"I really haven't given it any thought," I said. "But there's still time."

He nodded thoughtfully. "You'd have to wait until next October anyway, and at the moment it's too dangerous to send you away."

One of the few drawbacks of going to a local school was that our academic terms were arranged differently from those in England and I would have to wait until the beginning of the next English school year to further my education. And who knew how long the war in Europe would last?

At that moment I was satisfied with this state of affairs, for I did not wish to halt my lessons with Endo-san. Ours was a relationship that could not be put aside carelessly, as he had warned me, and I knew I was obliged to keep my side of the bargain. And there was still so much I wished to learn from him.

"I don't want you wasting your time as William's been doing," my father warned me. "Have you thought of what you want to do in the meantime?"

"I'd like to work in the company for a while," I said. "Join Edward and William. I want to know a lot more about our family."

The idea had been turned over in my head and considered for some time. It had also been strengthened by seeing how much importance my father placed on William's presence in the company. The awareness of my heritage had been awakened by the visit to my grandfather, and from the unconcealed happiness on my father's face I knew I had made the proper choice.

"That's wonderful," he said. "We'll find something for you."

Just before noon he said, "Well, that's done. Let's have a drink."

"I've something to tell you," I said, making a quick decision. I sat down and told him about my lessons with Endo-san: he had insisted that I tell my father. It was one of the very few times my father lost his temper with me. The earlier warmth was now swept away by his anger.

"He's a bloody Japanese!" he said, his voice rising.

"To whom you leased the island," I replied, sending my mind out to where the sea and sky merged, maintaining my center. Before I had met Endo-san I would have shouted back at my father.

"You know what they're doing in China. What does he want with you?"

"To teach me his culture, and some self-defense abilities."

"You don't need that sort of skill. And I don't trust him."

"I do."

He let out a sigh. "I know I haven't been a good father. You're running wild."

I shook my head. "I haven't been running wild. Look at me. I'm fitter than I've ever been. My mind's sharper, clearer. Look at me closely."

He sat down and looked into my eyes. I wanted to turn away, for there was so much despair in his own. "When you were born your mother made me promise that I would never control you the way she had been controlled by her father. But seeing how you associate with a Japanese makes me wonder if I should have."

"If you cared for her, then keep the promise you made," I said, latching on to the small opening he had exposed and using it to my advantage. "The war isn't going to be fought here. Nothing is going to happen. You've said so yourself." In my head I heard Endo-san's voice: *Redirect your opponent's momentum back into himself.*

My father remained silent, unsure of what to say, and I knew I had once again got my own way. "I met my grandfather," I told him. *Lead the mind*, Endo-san had said. Now my father looked at me with greater interest, his thoughts for the moment taken where I wanted them to go.

"How is the Old One?" he asked.

"He's still very strong," I said. "I think we liked each other, and I've invited him to Penang. He seems sorry for the past, and for how he treated Mother."

"I did love your mother, you know," he said. "People thought I had gone native, the way so many do. But they didn't understand what she and I felt for each other."

"I know," I said, trying to hold on to the fragile connection that had, unexpectedly, grown between us. He never spoke much to me about my mother and I could hear him struggle as he tried to tell me more. He returned his glance from the mounted butterflies but he was not quick enough to hide the look of pain in his eyes, as though he had unwittingly cut himself with one of his *keris*.

"There was so much to overcome. I thought I could do it. But she knew, even from the start, how difficult it would be. Yet still she married me. Her father had his servants move her belongings out of the house the day she told him the date of our wedding. She never saw him again," he said. I willed him to continue.

"The local Europeans treated her badly, and she was never welcome among her own people. But she was so strong, so indomitable, and I drew my strength from her when she was alive. She wanted to prove everyone wrong."

His voice softened. "I never showed you the river near our house, did I?"

"I think I know where it is," I said. It was not one of my habitual solitary haunts though. I preferred the sea. My father now disclosed to me what a special place it was, what I had never known.

"It was our secret hideaway, the quiet place we escaped to when things became too much for us," he said. "We always went at dusk, guided by the scent of the frangipani tree she planted there. We would row downstream, and she would lie in my arms, and we would wait in our boat for the fireflies to appear in the trees along the riverbank. There were thousands of them, lighting the darkness for us, showing us the way."

I saw a picture of them in my mind, two totally mismatched lovers trying to find their place in the world, surrounded by a protective barrier of light.

"A few weeks after we were married, I came home late one night. The house was dark. I ran inside, convinced something terrible had happened."

"What *had* happened?" I asked. As far back as I could recall there had always been a light on at Istana at night and it was hard to imagine its massive structure indefinable against the night sky.

"She was waiting for me, a candle in her hand. She put a finger to her lips and led me upstairs to our room. At the doorway she blew out the candle and pushed the door open. I couldn't believe what I saw," he said, his voice dipping into a whisper.

"She had let the mosquito netting drop over the bed, covering it completely. And in the darkness, between the creases of the net were hundreds of fireflies she had collected from the river."

He stopped, feeling awkward, but he saw the look of understanding and curiosity in my face, and after a short silence he said, "We spent the night beneath a shower of light. That was the night you were conceived."

I leaned back into my seat and let out a long stream of breath, trying to hide from him the tears that, like the tide slipping unnoticed into a rock pool, had seeped into my eyes. But when I looked up at him I saw that the eyes which I had inherited were shining as well.

"She caught all the fireflies the following morning and put them into jars and returned them to the river," he said, his voice strained, but a forlorn smile that indicated he deeply missed my mother and her quirks appeared on his face.

"I often think how hard it is for you; you always pull away, try to make yourself not a part of us. But you're a Hutton too. You can never escape that fact. Do you know how much we have all missed you?" my father said.

He ruffled my hair, which I had not let him do for a long time. He got up and walked away, leaving me in the library, surrounded by all his books. I walked along the shelves, looking at the titles: Herodotus's *The Histories*, Plato's *Symposium*, Maugham's collected short stories. All the great books were here, ranging from literature to history and philosophy. I opened the book he had given me but found I could not read the print on the pages. His gentle words had unsettled me and told me I had hurt him all these years. He had always been an intensely private man and it had taken a great amount of surrender from him to let me know the details of my conception. Like the best of fathers he had endured my callousness with dignity and silence, and I could only sit down, close the book, and think of ways to make it up to him.

Chapter Fifteen

I paused in my tale; Michiko was staring out into a sky lit by a pale moon. It was past midnight and it had been over a week since I had answered the door and let her into my house. We had settled into an unstated routine, with me telling her more and more of my history every night after our meal had been consumed.

I took a sip of tea, watching her. She was quite beautiful, in the way only Japanese women can be—demure on the outside, yet with veins of steel within.

"Our boat ride down the river . . ." she whispered. "To think that your parents once were there too, and that we saw the same sights as they did. It makes me feel as though the lights from the *hotaru* we witnessed were the same ones your parents had lain under, almost like the light of the stars which has been shining for millions of years, illuminating everything on its voyage, and which has only just now reached us."

I had never thought of it before, but her observation made me feel that we had indeed been in the presence of the same source of radiance that had once brought comfort to my parents, and which a few nights ago also worked its wonder and imparted a similar, if weakened, sense of solace to me.

"Would you like to rest?" I asked softly.

She closed her eyes. When she opened them there was a liquid glitter in them. "I would like to hear more, but not tonight. I am tired." I helped her to her feet and led her to her bedroom.

Although I thought I would not require much sleep, I woke up late the following morning. Michiko was already on the terrace when I went outside.

"Did you sleep well?" I asked, pouring her a cup of tea.

She shook her head, wincing as she stretched herself. I thought she had grown thinner since the day she came, and that worried me.

"The pills don't work anymore, do they?"

The cup rattled in the saucer as she took it from my hand and she set her mouth. "I despise them, but some days the pain is so complete I have no alternative. Not even *zazen* helps."

"You've seen all the doctors?"

"All the doctors and experts money and influence can summon," she replied. "How did you find out? No one knows."

"Your weight loss, the pills you take when you think no one can see. Your journey here to Penang. Little things," I said. I wondered at the role I was now playing, that of a teller of tales to an old and ailing woman, taking her through one part of my past after another.

"Do not worry, I can last until you come to the end."

"I'll try to leave out more things," I attempted a weak joke, but she shook her head.

"No, please do not do that. I wish to hear all of it. Promise me that," she said, and I did.

I got up and said, "I'll see you this evening?"

"Yes, I look forward to that." She too rose, and we bowed.

"I was wondering . . ." she said.

"Yes?" I stopped at the door and turned back to face her.

"I would like to see some of the other places you took Endo-san to in Penang. Do not worry, I will not insist on going to his little island. I see now it still hurts, after all this time."

I agreed to her request. I had gone back to many of those places in the days after the war, when in the silences of my life I missed him. I had gone hoping the places would still retain an echo of his presence, and of his passage, but I had only met with emptiness. The echoes were louder in my head, confined within the universe of my mind.

Sitting behind my desk on Beach Street I wondered if, by telling Michiko about Endo-san, I could let the echoes in my mind expand beyond the boundaries of my memory, so that their strength would finally weaken and fade forever into silence. A part of me wished dearly for that, for him to finally leave me. But the part that would always love him balked at the possibility of such an irreplaceable loss. My grandfather's words came to me so loudly that I turned involuntarily to look behind me, as though he were standing there. *Next to a parent, a teacher is the most powerful person in one's life.* And Endo-san had been more than my parent, much more than my teacher.

"Mr. Hutton?" Adele asked.

I left the voice of my grandfather and returned to the present. "What is it?"

"Miss Penelope Cheah is here to see you. The reporter as well."

"Oh yes, send Miss Cheah in first, please."

After the war, I had frequently found myself driving past houses abandoned by their owners, many of whom had died in the war, either in the camps, or at sea when their fleeing ships had been sunk by the Japanese fighter planes. When peace returned, many of these properties were bought by companies that tore them down to build modern shops. A sense of loss overflowed within me each time another house, surely the only one of its kind in the world, was destroyed and turned to unwanted rubble.

"Well, why don't you buy them?" Adele had said when I came into the office one morning, complaining bitterly of another demolition I had seen.

"And do what with them?"

She shrugged her shoulders. "Restore them. Open them to the public or turn them into exclusive hotels."

I stared at her until she became uncomfortable. "Forget it. It was a silly thought," she said.

"No, it wasn't. It's a wonderful idea," I said.

So I established the Hutton Heritage Trust and over the years I saved countless buildings from disappearing, from the shop-houses of Georgetown to the mansions along Northam Road. Many were restored using craftsmen from China and England. I tried to obtain materials as close to the originals as I could, some-times even traveling all over the hinterland of China to look for the proper tiles or to seek out a craftsman who had been trained in the ancient ways. Some people collect stamps; I collected old houses.

Three years ago Towkay Yeap's home, the house that the Manchu consul had built for one of his eight wives, came under the hammer. I never knew what happened to Kon's father. Towkay Yeap seemed to have vanished after the war and his house became dilapidated, standing vacant until an Englishman tried to turn it into an art gallery. When the Englishman died the banks had moved in and I had to put in the highest bid ever recorded in Penang for a house. "I made many enemies at the auction," I told Adele. "But I got it!"

I searched for an architect to organize the project for Towkay Yeap's house, for the design of the property was one that my usual team was quite unused to. After reading an interview with Penelope Cheah in an architectural magazine I had contacted her and invited her to my office. She was small, Chinese, and in her thirties, her eyes bright and sharp, her mind, like her hands, full of rolled-up plans ready to be opened and made real.

She showed me what she had done for her own ancestral home in Leith Street, which had been similar to Towkay Yeap's, and I liked it.

She and I had traveled to Stoke-on-Trent to search for floor tiles, to MacFarlane & Co.'s foundry in Glasgow to find an iron-monger who could replicate the original wrought-iron grilles, and even to the Hokkien province in southern China to hire a master craftsman to repair and recreate the broken roof tiles.

I had only one principle: every item had to be the original or as close to it as possible in this disposable age. For I always recalled my father's question to me in the library when he had returned home from London, the one that I could not answer at that time: "What, among the creations of our modern world, do you think will still exist and have historical and aesthetic value five hundred years from now?"

Some days I shake my head when I think how many architects and consultants have resigned while working for the Trust. But Penelope Cheah, in addition to her architectural qualifications, had a love for the old colonial buildings of Penang. We shared that love, and it sustained her whenever I was impatient, demanding, and unreasonable.

Adele now showed her into my office, and her smile was as usual cheerful and indefatigable. She alone had lasted longer than any of the other architects.

"How's progress?" I asked.

"It's almost complete. And it'll be the best restoration ever undertaken by the Trust. There's talk that UNESCO may give us the top award for heritage conservation."

"That's wonderful. It'll also be the last restoration I'll ever do."

"I don't understand."

"I'm growing old, and tired. I wanted to stop a long time ago, but this one—this one has special memories."

"You've done so much to conserve the history of this island. It would be a terrible shame to stop," she said.

"Lately I've been wondering, how much can one hold on to history?" I said. "I've been trying to stop time from going forward and perhaps that's misguided and foolish."

"Do you remember the first few times we went inside the house after you bought it?" she asked, her attempt to pull me away from my melancholic mood obvious.

"Yes. It was awful," I answered, humoring her and touched by her concern.

A week after the paperwork for the sale was completed I went and stood outside the wooden gates of Towkay Yeap's home. It was as though the years had never come and gone. The light was the same and, as I reached out my hand to touch the square wooden knob, I heard the cries of a hawker and the *tok tok* sound as he knocked on wooden clappers while pedaling his pushcart past the house, selling wonton noodles. The hawker went past me and his sounds faded away.

I went into the garden and, although I had seen many derelict homes, its neglected—no, *abused*—state shocked me. The roof was half gone and pieces of tile, broken into shards like the eggshells of a mythical bird, littered the bare, sandy lawn. The rosewood doors had been removed, used as firewood by squatters, and the Art Deco stained-glass windows were shattered.

It was worse inside. Where the beautiful gold-leafed screen had not been axed, smoke from the squatters' cooking fires had destroyed it. The fittings were all gone and only nubs of them remained embedded in the walls, buds doomed never to bloom.

I shook my head now as I recalled that day. Penelope smiled in shared memory. "It looks different now," she said, unable to subdue the pride in her voice.

"I'd like to show it to a friend of mine. When can you have it ready?"

"End of this week?"

"That's a good time," I said. Adele came in and reminded me

of my interview with a journalist from the local newspaper. I had
been reluctant to grant it, but the editor had been interested in
doing an article on the Hutton Heritage Trust.

"Don't go yet," I said to Penelope. "You're part of this as well."

The journalist was a young and courteous Chinese man and we
talked for a while of the preservation of history and the collective
memory of the island. But I realized he had another reason for the
interview as its direction changed.

"This year is the fiftieth anniversary of the end of the Japanese
Occupation," he said, looking uncomfortable. "How would you
justify the role you played in the Occupation?"

"That's all in the past," I said.

"Is it? Among some people you are known as a war criminal
who somehow managed to escape justice. Is that perception true?"

Penelope protested. "That has nothing to do with the Trust."

I silenced her with a look. I rode on my anger for a while,
knowing how formidable I could appear when I wanted to, and
then let it burn away. "How old are you?"

He had been expecting an attack from me, and he looked wary.
"Thirty-four."

"Then you weren't there. You didn't know. And it never
affected you directly. Get your facts right first."

"The problem, Mr. Hutton, is that in your case there are just
too many facts. All of them conflicting."

"Therein lies the truth you seek," I said, seeing him appear even
more confused. I stood up. "You must leave, now. Please."

At the door the young journalist stopped. "I'm sorry, sir. I was
instructed by my editor to ask those questions."

I sympathized with him. The editor, a woman my age, had
suffered immensely under the Japanese during those years and she
had always hated my role in the war. She had accused me of
standing by and watching when her grandfather was attacked and
murdered, while I was requisitioning a piano from their home.

The journalist held out his hand. "My father's bedridden now
and his end is near. But when he heard I was going to meet you,
he begged me to convey his gratitude to you for saving his life and
my mother's from the Japanese death squads."

"What were their names?"

He told me, but I said, "I don't remember them. I'm sorry." I took his hand in mine, as though trying to establish through him a link to his parents.

"It doesn't matter. There were so many. And you were wrong. I was directly affected. If it hadn't been for you, I wouldn't be here talking to you today."

I gripped his hand harder. "Who's to know what might have been? But tell your editor—tell her that if I were a war criminal, as you have said, then I never escaped. I've been here, all my life. I never ran."

I returned to Istana late in the evening. I entered the kitchen and found Michiko bent over the sink, her hands clamped to its edge, the veins in her wrists screaming to escape her skin. I dropped my briefcase on the floor and held her as she tried to bring her coughing under control. The white porcelain sink was speckled with blood, as were the sides of her mouth. Her face was white and she looked like a demented kabuki actor, lips smeared with vermilion paint.

I sat her down and wiped the blood from her face, and then I gave her a glass of water. She did not drink it, but placed it on the table. Silently I washed the sink before Maria saw it; Maria, like so many of us who grew up during the Japanese Occupation, hated the sight of blood.

"You were there, when they dropped the bomb," I said.

"Yes," she whispered, breathing hard.

I gave her the pills she needed. "Already I can feel these losing the fight. They will let me down soon," she said.

"Drink the water. It'll make you feel better."

"Thank you, Philip-san," she said, her voice weak.

We went out to what had by now become our place, on the terrace, where for a few hours each night I could distract her from her own pain by revealing mine. Although I had been uncertain initially, I found that these moments spent with Michiko had not been as difficult as I had feared. It was painful, yes, but in recalling the days of my childhood for her and the events that had compelled me to take the steps from boy to man, I felt myself throwing off the ballast of age, rising and breaking free from the lashings of time, so that I could look down, look back, and marvel at the path my life had taken.

We had shared something special that night at the river; I felt as though the fireflies had brought their illumination into a part of my life that had always been kept submerged in the dark. The journalist's questions that day had been far from impertinent. Perhaps I could have tried harder to explain, to recount what I had experienced in the war. But the pain had been too vivid, the feeling of guilt too overpowering. And there was pride as well. My English and Chinese upbringing had ensured—*commanded*—that I keep my feelings in check so as not to cause awkwardness and embarrassment and bring shame to myself and my family's reputation. I found it ironic that the two streams of my blood, from opposing points of the compass, had flowed into an unlikely confluence that drowned my ability to express my feelings.

Now, to be able to divulge it all to an unacquainted woman who had arrived unexpectedly at my home gave me a feeling of release, of having made it to dry land again. The sensation was, admittedly, also tempered by apprehension.

What had made me overcome my fear was the awareness that Michiko was not weighed down by the history of my island home and its people and their presumed knowledge of my life. I knew then that I would push myself to reveal everything to her, however difficult it would become. There would often be times during the hours we spent together when I would be tempted to change the truth, to soften it and make myself stand in a better light. But what would be the point of that, at our age?

Michiko had appeared unannounced, but she was not a stranger. She had known Endo-san, and perhaps in my story she could still recognize why, after all this time, he remained alive in our thoughts.

Chapter Sixteen

I started working at Hutton & Sons in the beginning of 1940, following my father around and learning the business. For the first time in my life I truly came to know him. He was a tough and sharp negotiator, but flexible in his approach where it mattered: he was at ease with the unwritten customs and rules of the Malay traders and he was adept at conducting business with the Chinese. He knew when to push them and when, for the sake of face, to let them win, thereby ensuring a bigger victory for all parties involved.

I had to curtail my visits to Endo-san because my father expected me to follow his hours. He placed me in my own office, a small room for which nobody had found any use. The staff called me *Tuan Kechil*, the Little Boss, and the Sikh guard saluted us each morning as we passed through the glass and wooden doors of the entrance.

It was a strange moment for me when I first stepped inside the building. When I was young I had sometimes visited my father in his office to play at his desk, but it was different now. That first day I felt I was being connected with a tradition; I felt I was taking my place among those who had come to Penang a century ago. The checkered black and white marble floor of the lobby, the slowly revolving fans, the large round pillars, and the quiet broken only by the sound of typewriters and telephones all affected me, and I could comprehend why my father had made this his sanctuary.

He voiced the emotions I was experiencing when he said, "You can feel time here, can't you?"

"Yes," I replied. He reached out and made an abrupt adjustment to my collar, straightening my tie. "Well, come on. Let's go and make more money today," he said.

"Spoken like a true Chinese," I remarked, and he grinned.

I learned in great detail about the range of trade in which we had our fingers. We owned three million hectares of rubber plantations across Malaya, four tin mines in Perak and Selangor, sawmills, pepper plantations, a steamer line, orchards, and other properties. My father seemed to be continually on the telephone, and Mrs. Teoh, his efficient Chinese secretary, was on her feet the entire day, running between the various rooms searching for files. I assisted by reading the reports and then summarizing them for Mr. Scott and my father, and checking the paperwork that was required for our exports, which all went to England.

Occasionally I would be sent to the godowns on Weld Quay to check on the coolies or to supervise the unloading of goods. These godowns—rows of large stores and warehouses fronting the harbor—were dark and hot, most of them piled high to their corrugated tin roofs with sacks of pepper and chillies, cloves, cinnamon sticks, or star anise. These I found tolerable, but I hated entering those that stored sheets of smoked rubber. The stench would adhere to my clothing and hair. I would return from these visits with my shirt clinging to my body and my tie undone, to gulp down the pot of tea Mrs. Teoh always made for me.

I soon had to visit the harbor daily, for the Malayan Communist Party was talking the Indian coolies into laying down their sweat-towels and going on a nationwide strike.

One morning my father called me into his room. The manager, Mr. Chin, had telephoned him minutes earlier in near panic, his voice so loud I could hear him through the receiver. "The bloody Reds are causing trouble again. What should I do?"

"I thought the government had banned the Party?" I asked my father.

"That wouldn't stop them harassing our workers," he said, as he put on his jacket and we prepared to visit the godowns.

A crowd was already forming when we crossed Beach Street to get to the harbor. My father let out a curse. "Bastards!" he said. An Indian man stood on a wooden crate, shouting anti-British slogans. He saw us and raised his voice, "Here come the people who oppress you, work you like slaves and pay you wages that wouldn't even feed a dog!"

A group of Chinese men stood next to him, dressed neatly and saying nothing. "They're from the MCP," my father whispered to me. Some of our workers had already crossed the line, shouting along with the speaker, but when they saw Noel Hutton their voices lowered and faded away. In the silence the Indian's voice sounded even more strident. He shook his fist. "Why are you afraid? Why are you shaking like weaklings?"

My father walked to the center of the crowd, which opened for him. "Anyone who wants to go with these troublemakers is free to do so," he said in Malay, which the workers used. "Just don't come in to work tomorrow." He repeated his words in Hokkien and turned in a circle, looking into the eyes of each worker. "Those who have decided to throw in their lot with this monkey, get off my property now. Your names will be circulated and I will make sure no one else hires you." There was an angry wail from the workers.

A Chinese coolie picked up one of the curved iron crowbars the workers used to lift gunnysacks from wooden pallets. He came in at a run. My father stood, unafraid. I was about to move and push him away but as the coolie swung his crowbar my father jabbed a punch into his face, breaking his nose with a crack. The coolie fell to his knees, his hands covering his shattered nose and the crowbar clattered to the ground. Shouts erupted from the workers as they surged and moved to help the fallen coolie.

Another dockworker came in swinging a chain, moving deliberately around my father.

"Let me handle this," I said to him, expecting him to tell me to keep quiet and stand aside.

To my surprise he said, "He's yours," and retreated.

I moved closer and the workers started chanting, their bodies moving in time to their voices. The coolie was a muscular, broad-shouldered man, strengthened by his brutal work, still wearing a vestige of the pigtail they had cut off years ago when the Manchu had been driven from the Dragon Throne in China. I had seen such men lift and carry a hundred pounds of rice on their shoulders, all the while swearing and laughing and singing the bawdy folk songs of their villages.

He started to swing the chain faster and I kept my patience, waiting for the right moment. I refused to make the first move, for he could have snapped the chain like a well-used whip and taken one side of my face off.

He flicked his wrist and the tip of the chain shot out, but I angled my body and avoided it easily. He pulled it back into the swinging movement, which became faster still, the chain singing as it made an infinite figure of eight in the air. The coolie raised his hand back to slash me and I stepped in and extended my hands into his backward swing, putting him off balance. My hands coiled up his arms and caught the chain and, as he stumbled, I wrapped his wrists in a lock. Everyone heard the crunch as I broke the bones of his wrist. The coolie let out an agonized scream and went down on one knee, clutching his hand like a shot animal. I spun around on my heel in a tight circle and kicked him across the jaw. The crack as it shattered was louder than the sound of his wrist breaking.

The workers and the MCP members stared in shock, but not for long. They ran off into the side streets and back lanes surrounding the warehouses when the police arrived.

My father came to me and held my shoulders. "Are you all right?"

"Yes," I said. I had felt completely calm when the attack was taking place and was now disconcerted to find that I was shaking. A muscle in my calf began to twitch in a reaction to what had occurred. I took a few deep breaths, pulling them into the depths of my stomach and soon felt myself regaining a certainty about the world. It was the first time in my life that I had injured another man, and I felt guilty but also elated.

It was difficult to take in the image of my father breaking the coolie's nose. I suppose children never expect to see their parents punch someone, much less break a nose. And I could say the same of him, that he never expected to see a son of his do what I had done. There was a stillness in his eyes as he contemplated me. "Mr. Endo's teachings?" he asked.

I nodded and he shook his head.

"What was all that?" I asked him in return, my hands moving in a boxer's jab.

"Oh, that?" he said. "Oxford Boxing Cuppers, 1911: I fought at welterweight for Trinity." I laughed as the tension of the fight broke over me. I gave him a hurried embrace, surprising both of us.

*

I was disconcerted at how quickly the months passed as 1940 wound its way to a close and a new year began. Despite the worsening war in Europe and China, we were kept busy. There was so much to learn at the office and my father was a hard taskmaster, often keeping very long hours, to which he expected me to adhere as well. Although he seemed to have accepted my lessons with Endo-san, I could still see the quick grimace of aggravation on his face if I had to leave the office before he had finished with me for the day.

Endo-san too was suddenly overwhelmed with work; his absences from Penang increased and it was difficult for us to keep to a schedule of lessons, so he was often greatly displeased when I was even slightly late.

I knew Noel was using the excuse of work to make me miss my classes and one afternoon I went into his office and sat down in front of him.

"You always seem to make me work late on the evenings I attend Endo-san's class," I said.

He was not unwilling to admit it. "I would prefer that you spend less time there. I've had comments made to me about the company you keep."

"Whose comments?"

"People in town. Our associates." He meant the members of the Chinese business community, with whom we had long-standing and extensive dealings.

"And what did you tell them?"

"That it was really none of their business," he said.

Despite my anger with him, I was touched by his loyalty to me. "Is my friendship with a Japanese affecting the company?" I asked, softening my tone.

"Not at the moment," he said. "But eventually you'll have to choose between continuing your instruction with Mr. Endo and protecting our company's face."

"It's not a choice I can make," I said. "I promised him that I would learn as much as he can teach me, and as you have so often taught us, I can't go back on my word." I stood up. "I have to go. I have a class to attend."

"It's not just our company I'm worried about," he said. "I've no wish to see you caught between two opposing sides and suffer in the process."

I was already at the door of his office, but I stopped. "I'll find a way to keep everything in balance," I said, sounding more assured than I felt.

William, despite his initial reluctance to work in the family company, had settled into a dependable routine that satisfied our father. I knew he still chafed at having to capitulate to our father's wishes but he kept his dissatisfaction well concealed.

In any case, he had discovered a new passion. One Sunday afternoon when it was raining too hard for me to visit Endo-san he brought a small box into my room and placed it on my bed. He opened it and lifted out a camera.

"Look at this," he said. "I ordered it from Singapore and it's finally here." I took the Leica from him and examined it. Endo-san's camera was an earlier but similar model. William was tearing the box apart.

"What's wrong?" I asked.

"There's no instruction booklet!"

He shook the box in frustration and I said, "Look at you, like one of the monkeys at the Botanical Gardens trying to tear open a packet of food." He looked miserable and I felt sorry for him. My father's words in the library more than a year before, when I was helping him unpack his books—*You always pull away, try to make yourself not a part of us*—suddenly jarred me again.

"Here," I said. "I know how to use it." He was doubtful, but as I showed him he soon found out that I was almost an expert. I was bound to be, after watching and helping Endo-san for so long.

"You're good at this," he allowed himself to admit.

"I must have learned something from all those times you made me help you with your toys and projects," I said.

"Which you invariably slipped out of," William replied. "You always preferred to spend time on your own on the beach."

I understood what he did not say. William was fascinated by anything mechanical or complex. He would always show some new gadget of his to me, hoping I would share his enthusiasm. I never did, and the thought now came to me that it was not the objects in which he had tried to interest me but in the fostering of a stronger link between us. I wanted to tell him this, to let him know that I now understood; but the years of isolating myself had made me unable to breach the barricades I had erected. I felt like a prisoner, able to see far from my confines but unable to reach out beyond them.

And would William be able to sympathize with my situation anyway? He had been certain of his position in life, from the moment of his birth. He had never had to fight his classmates for his identity, never had to catch the glimpse of superiority in the eyes of the people around him, from the servants to our father's friends and associates. He had never had to feel like an impostor in his own home.

I found that I was staring at William, who looked uncomfortable. I wanted to speak, to let him know his efforts had not gone unappreciated. But I could not at that time disclose to him how much Endo-san had transformed me through his lessons, which I knew were partially responsible for this growing insight into my relationship with my family. I felt William would not understand the sense of certainty my *sensei* had created in me. In strengthening my body Endo-san was also, as he had promised, fortifying my mind. It was a process that offered me the ability to bridge the conflicting elements of my life and to create a balance.

William went to the window. "The sky's clearing. Come on, let's go and see if this thing works. If you haven't buggered it up for me."

We spent the rest of the afternoon in the garden. The camera worked much better than Endo-san's. As he took his photographs, William said he was happy I was working with our father as it meant that we could now go for lunch together in town. Edward was often away in Pahang or Selangor, or down in Kuala Lumpur. With the war in Europe, the demand for rubber and tin had risen and every one of us, including Isabel, was kept busy filling orders and organizing transport and shipment for our goods.

"It's getting too dark, and I think I felt a drop of rain," I said an hour later. We had finished his entire stock of film but at least William was now familiar with his camera. We walked up the driveway and, as we passed the fountain, I stopped and I told him about my visit to my grandfather.

"Remember that time when we—"

"Caught those dragonflies? Yes," William said. "What a vile pair of brats we were."

"I now know why my mother punished us so severely."

He listened to my explanation and sighed. "I'm sorry," he said.

"So am I," I said. "But it's too late now."

He hooked an arm around my shoulders and squeezed. For a moment I was a young boy again and he was the big brother who always got us into trouble, the one who always made our father ask, "What mischief have you two been up to now?"

I held up my palm and caught the start of another shower. "Your camera's getting wet. Let's go inside."

Although we worked in the same building, William and I rarely saw each other during the course of the day. He suggested we make a habit of going for lunch together at the Chinese restaurant around the corner from our office. Invariably he paid. "I'm earning more than the peanuts Father pays you. No, don't argue with me. I went through the same process." And invariably I would order the restaurant's famous banana pancakes. "You keep eating the same rubbish every day," William complained.

We normally met at the restaurant just before lunch, to obtain a good table. One afternoon he was late, and I sat in the restaurant as the crowds started coming in. When he finally arrived I asked, "What kept you?"

He sat down and I could see he was excited about something. "You'll have to find some way to tell the old man that I've enlisted in the navy."

I knew William was still unhappy about his return from London, even though it was over a year ago now, and I had tried to make things easier for him at the office by absorbing most of the more mundane tasks normally assigned to him. Still, to hear his news disappointed me. I would miss him if he had to leave Penang.

"He'll be bloody livid! Why me?" I asked.

"Well, because you're the youngest and therefore I order you to, and er, also . . .well, because he has a soft spot for you."

"It's not me he has a soft spot for. That honor goes to Isabel," I replied. "In fact, why don't you ask—"

"*We* don't think so," William shot back. Clearly he had already

182

discussed this with Isabel. "Anyway, I don't think he'll go *completely* up the wall. I won't be sent to England. It's just the navy here. You know . . . in Singapore. In case the Japanese go mad and attack us. And I said I'd work here for a year, and I have. So I've kept my promise."

He swept one hand around the restaurant. Despite its greasy tiled floors, dirt-edged ceiling fans, and churlish waiters, it still served the best food in town. "Haven't you noticed? There are only old people here now. All the young men've left to fight in the war."

"Well, tell him yourself then. I suggest you just do it straight to his face and not waffle around. He hates that."

"At least be there when I tell him."

Although I already felt a sense of loss, I could not prevent a small grin from appearing. Here was a man courageous enough to go off to war, yet who was still afraid of his father. Seeing his pleading look, I agreed to William's request.

"Really?" William asked. "You will?"

"Yes, yes. I will. Now let's bugger off. We've all got work to do."

That evening, as I watched my father walk in the garden feeding his carp, I thought of his life, how lonely he must have been after both of his wives died. I wondered whether a mistress who could fill the gap in his bed could also fill the void in his heart. For his sake I hoped she could. Since our conversation in the library, I knew now without a doubt that he had loved my mother, and that they had found, for a fleeting moment, their own place in the world.

I called out to William, "I think now's a good time to tell him."

We went out into the dusk. Somewhere down the road the Hardwickes' gardener was burning the leaves he had raked during the day and the smell of the smoke tinged the light with sweetness and sorrow. The gravel path sounded like ice being crunched as we walked past the fountain and the row of palm trees. I looked at the fountain and compared it again to the one in my grandfather's garden. I hoped it had given my mother at least some solace.

I turned back to look at the house, comforted by its presence behind me. It loomed like a protective ancestor. I could feel its physical reach and, at a deeper level, its connection to me. I wondered then if William could feel it too, as we waved to our father.

A saffron haze covered everything as the sun set and the trees and the grass looked as if they had been dusted with powdered gold. The rows of lilies lining the driveway gave off a tender perfume. My father threw away the remaining pieces of bread into the pond, brushed his hands against each other and said, "What mischief have you two been up to now?"

So William told him, in a stuttering voice which gained assurance, a trickle growing into a stream, a stream into a river. I watched our father's face as the river reached the sea. Anger changed to sadness and then sailed out to acceptance. He shook his head slowly, but William knew he was safe now.

"I suppose we all have to do what feels right," he said, as he put his arms around us and we walked up to the house, now warm and lit up from within, glowing like a Chinese paper lantern, and suddenly appearing just as fragile.

As we entered he stopped us and said, "How about a party? It's been such a long time since we had one. We'll make it a going-away party for William. Something extravagant and irresponsible, for we may never see such days again."

Something in his voice made me aware that he was beginning to see the signs, that the war would come to Malaya, that all the old ways would be washed away forever.

"All of you are growing up so quickly," he went on, looking from me to William, and then to Isabel, who had come out to tell us that dinner would be ready soon. "So, who wants to help me arrange it?"

"I will," I replied, as William said at the same time, looking and pointing at me, "He will." I saw our father's smile of pleasure that I was at last a part of my family.

I saw less of Endo-san, who seemed to be traveling more often. Whenever he returned he would make my training harder, but soon he was away too much, and so he arranged for me to train at the Japanese consulate with the consul's bodyguards.

The consulate was some distance away from home, in the quiet suburb of Jesselton Heights, bordering the Penang Turf Club. I cycled there and the sentry waved me in, and I took the precaution not to meet Hiroshi, parking my bicycle behind a grove of mango trees. The *dojo* was in a separate building, away from the consulate and near the kitchen. As I approached, the smell of food made me hungry, but once I entered the *dojo* my appetite fled at the first sight of my training partners.

They looked tough and grim, and I soon discovered that they were a brutal bunch. All of them were from the military. From that first day, from the moment I bowed to them, I took a lot of punishment. I had to change my style and resort to fighting with my head, aiming for their pressure points as Kon had shown me, instead of punching them in their chests or faces. This effectively put me on an almost equal standing with them, although a few of them, from Okinawa Island, were extremely lethal in karate—the way of the empty hand. When Okinawa was subjugated by Japan a few centuries ago, the use of weapons was banned by the ruling Japanese, so the peasants had resorted to training using tradi-tional farming implements like rice-flails and sickles. Their main weapons of choice were their hands, which were hard and callused from years of training. Getting hit by one of those hands was no laughing matter. I tumbled across the wooden floor when Goro, my principal sparring partner, broke through my defenses and drove his fist into my ribs. For a few seconds I was winded, my chest burning as pain spread through it like a toxic chemical. I knew I had to get up. In my head I heard Endo-san say, "One does not have the luxury of lying on the floor."

Goro laughed. "A Chinese. Worse, a half-breed!" he said and walked away to train with his friends. I pulled myself up and sat on one of the benches. I bent over and tried to bottle up my nausea, so as not to shame myself further and, worse, shame Endo-san. Goro was a member of the consulate staff, though I was uncertain what his actual position was. He was a few years over thirty and there was a certain coarseness to his face that I disliked and distrusted. He was a true devotee of karate, and looked down on other forms of fighting.

On the island later that evening, Endo-san rubbed his camphor ointment on my chest. "You will meet all kinds of people. Some are good; some will be like Goro-san. You have to be prepared."

I no longer asked what I had to be prepared for: I suppose, deep within me, I already knew the answer.

I watched him as he moved around preparing our evening meal. I thought of that day when he had walked from the sea into my life and transformed it completely. We had grown closer in that time, settling into a warm routine, although we were still extremely careful not to be seen in public together. Anti-Japanese feelings were running high, continually kept on a flame by the Aid China Campaign. There were, however, always social and commercial occasions when we were thrown together. Then we would make polite conversation that was loaded with guarded references to our life. We developed our own language to the extent we could ostensibly talk about the dock workers' demands while actually referring to a class the night before.

There was more gray in his hair, and he looked fatigued. I thought back to the evenings I had spent with him and the things we had talked about. He had opened my mind, and set it ablaze with his. I thanked him for the ointment. "I like this smell," I said.

"Do not grow accustomed to it," he said. He put away the bottle and came back to sit with me by the hearth. "What is it?"

I wanted to ask him about the heavy presence of the military at the consulate. It came on top of all the other things that had been worrying me. Those rubber purchasers I had met in Kampong Pangkor—what were they really involved in? I recalled the questions Endo-san had often asked me and saw in my mind the boxes of photographs he had taken. I wondered about his frequent trips around the country. What was he actually doing?

But how did one ask? And—which made me more fearful— what would be the answers and their effect on my association with him?

He repeated his question and yet I knew my own queries and doubts would never be voiced. Even then, perhaps, I knew but I chose to ignore, to push away. Such was the strength of my bond to him that I needed and wanted no explanation for my acceptance. Even then I already loved him, although I did not realize it, never having loved before.

"Do you remember you told me how beautiful the sea looked, that first time we met?" I said softly. Through the *shoji* doors we could see a fragment of the night sky through a gap in the trees. It was crowded with stars. Far away the surf raced along the sand, hissing as it melted into the beach.

He smiled but his voice was subdued. "I remember. I saw your eyes soften. It was like seeing stone turning to honey."

Thoughts floated by like intoxicated butterflies: of taking care of him, preparing his meals, spending the rest of my life learning under his guidance; thoughts which would always remain thoughts, never becoming real, when even to acknowledge him in public was fraught with risks. So many things most people take for granted.

"What are you thinking about?" he asked, as he yawned.

And I said, with not a small trace of sadness at the way of the world, "Butterflies."

Chapter Seventeen

I increased the frequency of my visits to Kon's home. I had never been close to the other boys at school and it was only with Kon that, for the first time in my life, I was made aware of the possibility of such a friendship.

I learned a lot from Kon. We spent evenings breaking down our techniques and trying out new ones. I found Tanaka-san's *aiki-jutsu* much gentler than Endo-san's, the movements much more circular than those I had been taught. Kon, in turn, found my near-linear motions effective and fast, so we found an equilibrium, a harmony between the circle and the line. I told him about my classes with the consulate staff and he said, "That's nothing. You should try some of the illegal matches that take place every month."

"What're they?"

"The triads run a match every fortnight in one of the godowns in the harbor. Anyone may enter for a fee. There are no rules, no restrictions whatsoever. You can be eighteen, or younger or older, male, female, it does not matter."

"Have you ever fought in them?"

"Yes, once. When Tanaka-*sensei* found out he was very angry and even threatened to stop teaching me. I stopped going immediately and on his insistence gave the money I'd won to a temple."

"We do so much just to please our teachers," I said, and I could see he understood.

We dried our bodies and changed out of our soaked training *gi*. The question came out of me before I could reconsider or reframe it—"Have you ever killed anyone?"

He folded his clothes into a neat bundle, creasing them firmly with his palm. "No, I have not," he said. "To ask that question, I think you must have."

"No, but I injured a man." The admission came out quickly,

before it could be taken back and hidden away deep within me. I told him what had happened, the steps I had taken to protect my father and myself. "I'm worried now that these things will come easier to me."

"You shouldn't have done that. The MCP members are vicious. You'd better warn your father to be alert."

"You think they'll retaliate?"

He shook his head for he had no answer but I felt better for having talked to him. "Come to the party," I said. "Bring your father and Tanaka-san."

"I will," he said. "But come with me. I have something to show you."

I saw the excited look on his face and followed him down the wrought-iron spiral stairs into the courtyard, sending the pigeons flying up to the eaves. We went outside to the garage at the back of the house. He opened the doors and the light caught the silver of the car hidden inside.

"I can't believe it," I said, staring with wonder at the MG. "Your father's?"

"No. Mine. A present for my birthday. Like it?"

"You lucky sod," I said. I stroked the warm metal of its low, sleek body. He opened the top and jumped inside. He started the engine and the walls of the garage suddenly seemed too flimsy, as though they were unable to contain the low rumbling noise.

"Want to go for a drive?"

We took it slow within the streets of Georgetown, aware that we were the center of attraction and loving it. Once we were on the coastal road he opened up the throttle, hurling us around the narrow curves while scarcely slowing down. The hard rock face of the cliffs rushed by on one side while, on the other, a terrifying drop into the rocky seas kept him alert. A municipal bus passed us on the opposite side as Kon overtook an army lorry and we just managed to squeeze back onto our side, almost scraping the rockface. The troops in the lorry cheered us and I turned and waved to them. We left them behind and went our way in the speckling sunlight that waited above the weave of the trees.

The road was heavily shaded and it seemed that sometimes we traveled within a cool, damp tunnel that smelled of earth and mulch. Through the gaps in the leaves, the sea shone blue and warm in the light, and tiny sailboats from the Penang Swimming Club appeared like colored thumbtacks on a sheet of brilliant baize.

Kon drove well and the MG hugged the road, sticky as a caterpillar on a branch. We drove all the way until the road finished, past the beaches of Tanjung Bungah and Batu Ferringhi—I barely saw Istana before it dropped behind us. He turned onto a dirt road to the Bay of Reflected Light at the northeasternmost tip of the island, scattering the chickens in a Malay village. He drove on until the tires started to sink into sand and then he stopped.

I let out a breath. "That was . . ." I shook my head and laughed.

We got out of the car and sat on the beach, watching the green, glowing waves, feeling the adrenaline that had intoxicated our blood seep away. Fishing boats were beached on the sand and we heard the cries of the cormorants tied to the boats. The fishermen often put them on leashes to catch fish, supplementing their harvest from the nets.

Kon's face was gleeful, young, and so filled with life. Now, when I am old and with so much having happened to us, that is how I recall him, on that day when we broke all traffic rules, when we sat at the end of the world, watching the sea where the Straits of Malacca meet the Indian Ocean.

"You know about my father, of course," Kon said, without preamble.

I wondered what he wanted me to say and, not knowing, decided to speak the truth. "I've heard—well—rumors and stories."

"Have you heard of the triads?"

"Uncle Lim has told me about them. But I'd like to hear it from you."

He took in a long breath then said, "The triads are a strange product of history. The name comes from their use of a triangular diagram signifying the relationship of Heaven, Earth, and Man. They were formed originally as resistance to Mongol rule over China. There are heavy influences of Buddhism—in fact most of the founding members were Buddhist monks. But the details of these are now lost in time. My father is of the view that the triads as we know them stem from the start of the Ching dynasty. When the Manchu people conquered China in the seventeenth century, they attempted to wipe out all forms of resistance . . ." Kon explained that through the centuries, a more criminal element had crept into the makeup of the triads. The mass migration of the Chinese helped spread their influence and power beyond China. Triad members communicated and recognized fellow members in public by means of elaborate hand signals.

He stopped and I struggled to understand what he had said. It sounded confusing, a secret brotherhood, like the Freemasons of which my father often joked about Mr. Scott being a member.

The British had outlawed all forms of secret societies as a way to curb the triads. It was useless of course. The triads were a law unto themselves; nobody could control them except their Dragon Heads, the leaders of the societies.

"Is your father a Dragon Head?" I asked Kon, crossing over the boundary of friendship. But Kon was already on the other side of it, waiting for me.

"He's the head of the Red Banner Society."

I knew I had heard that name before and not just from Uncle Lim. I searched my memory and recalled that the newspapers had, at one time, written a detailed story about the violence and unrest created by warring societies out to enlarge their territories. The Red Banner Society had made a name for itself as being a well-organized, ruthless group. Its roots lay in the Hokkien province of China, from where so many of the Chinese in Penang came. It was said to be one of the strongest societies.

"When my father steps down, I'll be the new Dragon Head. I hope this won't affect our friendship," Kon said, and I heard the way he tried to hide his worry, that I would not be his friend anymore.

I was touched, and I said to reassure him, "It won't; you have my word."

He looked relieved but then swiftly hid his emotions, and I suddenly saw how isolated he was, how the reputation of his father had resulted in him having very few friends. Like me he had decided to be satisfied with his own company. I saw so much of myself in him, especially the hardness within us that had been the result of our decision to walk alone and so protect ourselves from being hurt.

"Let me show you something," he said. He laced the fingers of both hands into a pattern, thumbs facing forward, the smallest

191

fingers pointing down. "This is the sign that will lead you to my father. The market in Pulau Tikus is controlled by us, and anyone you show it to will have to obey."

I practiced creating the sign. "Why are you telling me this?"

"If you ever need help, make this sign and you will be given assistance."

"I don't think I'll ever need it," I said.

"Learn it. You never know," he said.

I knew that, through this offering, an unspoken vow of friendship and even of brotherhood had been sworn between us. It did not have to be voiced, which only made it stronger.

"Come on," he said. "Let's go into town for dinner. Here," he threw the keys at me. "Your turn."

Georgetown after dark was a different world, and the place Kon took me to was something I had never encountered at night before. We parked the car and walked into Bishop Street. The five-foot passageways outside the shops were crowded with hawkers cooking under the light of hurricane lamps. I had been warned against walking into this area of town at night but with Kon beside me I felt safe.

"Ah, the White Tiger; you honor us tonight." The porridge seller greeted him with good humor, asking after his father. He wiped the oily table with a face towel slung around his meaty shoulder and we sat down on wooden benches along the passageway. A fat man in a singlet dipped strips of dough into a cauldron of bubbling oil and, when they turned a golden brown, picked them up with a pair of chopsticks a foot long. This *yew-char-kway* would be dipped into our fish porridge, which would be garnished with shallots, spring onions, a few drops of sesame oil and slivers of ginger.

"Why did he call you that?" I asked.

Kon shrugged, and pointed to his shirt. "Maybe because I like wearing white."

"And the Tiger?"

He looked put out at my question, and I held out my palms. "I can guess. I don't wish to know."

"Eat your food," he said.

"Why is that woman smiling at us?" I asked. A young Chinese woman in a red *cheongsam* waved her handkerchief to catch my attention. She stood outlined in a doorframe, the light behind her making her look older.

Kon turned to look. "She's a whore, and she wants you in her bed."

"Oh, I thought she was just an old friend of yours."

The food came, and we ate hungrily. The *yew-char-kway* was crunchy and steaming hot and tasted wonderful soaked in porridge. "I'll have another bowl of porridge," I shouted to the hawker. Trishaw pullers came and parked their trishaws by the road, and then sat around us, and suddenly the atmosphere was noisy and filled with their friendly curses.

"You should sit like them," Kon said.

"What? How?" I studied the men, noting that they pulled one leg onto the bench when they sat, and kept one knee protruding over the table like the peak of a hill as they shoveled food into their mouths.

"Maybe at the next Resident Councillor's Ball," I said.

We both stood up at the same time as a commotion came from the brothel. A rough male voice rose over the noise of the tables. "Get out! Out!" The swinging doors clapped open and a middle-aged Englishman tumbled out onto the passageway and crashed into a pillar. He rolled around as a Chinese youth came out and kicked his head.

"Enough of that!" Kon said and blocked another kick. The Chinese pulled back his hand and clenched his fists, but then he recognized Kon.

"Master Kon, I apologize. But this *ang-moh* was making a nuisance of himself."

"Leave him to me," Kon said. The man obeyed him without another word, and went back inside. The trishaw pullers around us went back to their food.

Kon led the drunken Englishman to our table and gave him a cup of tea. "Are you all right?"

"Yes, yes. Pretty girls . . . Oh yes, we'll have a good time . . ." the man mumbled. Kon forced the tea into him and after a moment he seemed to sober up. "I think you saved me there. But who the hell are you?"

"Two friends out having dinner," I said.

"Can you take me back to my hotel?"

I shouted for our bill and the Englishman eyed me with a calculating look.

In the car he told us his name was Martin Edgecumbe. "What were you doing in that part of town?" I asked.

"You seem to speak the local dialect well for a European," he said, ignoring my question.

"My mother was Chinese," I said.

I told him my name, and he narrowed his eyes. "Noel Hutton's son?"

"That's correct."

"And you?" He looked to Kon, who told him his name.

"Are you going to say you know whose son he is?" I said with a touch of sarcasm.

"Towkay Yeap's son," Edgecumbe said.

"I think it's our turn to ask—just who the hell are *you*?" I said.

"Take me to the E & O," Edgecumbe said, once again ignoring me.

As befitting the grandeur of the legendary Eastern & Oriental Hotel, Balwant Singh, the Sikh hall porter, seemed unperturbed when we supported Edgecumbe, his nose bleeding, upstairs to his room.

Kon cracked some ice, wrapped it in a towel and gave it to Edgecumbe. The room was luxurious and a balcony opened out to the swimming pool and the sea below. The night wind blew from shore to sea, streaming through the coconut fronds. The surf glowed white where it edged the beach and the moon, full and round, appeared so close and hard.

"What other languages do you two speak?" Edgecumbe asked as he patted his nose with the packed ice. Kon, shaking his head at such feeble attempts, snatched the ice and pressed it hard into Edgecumbe's nose. He shouted in pain. "Bloody hell! Let go!"

"Stop struggling; this will make the bleeding stop."

I turned away to save him face, suppressing my laughter. He asked the question again and I said, "I speak Hokkien, English, Malay, some Cantonese, but none of the Indian dialects. My friend here speaks all the languages I speak, as well as Mandarin."

"And both of us speak and write Japanese," Kon added.

I wondered why I had left that out. Perhaps deep down I felt it was a shameful admission, not a wise thing to reveal. But I also knew that I had become so close to Endo-san that I hardly thought of his nationality now and, when we conversed, I was not aware that we spoke Japanese or English or a mixture of the two, but only that we spoke and understood each other so well. Hearing Kon state that I was fluent in Japanese sounded surprising even to myself.

"That's unusual," Edgecumbe said. "Then perhaps fate decided we were to meet tonight."

Kon and I looked at each other, wondering what the man meant.

"You wouldn't have heard of Force 136," Edgecumbe went on, "so let me tell you what it's all about. I must warn you that this is all classified and once you leave this room you are prohibited from discussing it with anyone else. Is that clear?"

I wanted to leave the room. I wanted no knowledge of what he was going to tell us, but Kon said, "Yes, we understand."

"It's a unit formed by the British military. We're quite aware that the Japanese *may* intend to invade Malaya, although the Foreign Office doesn't think it probable. We haven't been sitting on our backsides, however. We've begun recruiting selected people to form groups of 'stay-behind parties' to counter the Japanese, *should* they declare war on us."

"An organized resistance campaign," I said, seeing the picture with immediate clarity, marveling at the audacity of the plan, at the same time feeling a sense of betrayal. So the British government already suspected that an attack would come, that Malaya would fall, and still they maintained daily that it would not, that the guns of Singapore would repel any such attempt.

"We're looking for people who can speak Malay, Tamil, English, and any of the local Chinese dialects," Edgecumbe continued.

"And then what?" Kon asked. His fascination with the plan made me want to take him away from Edgecumbe. I saw now that there was one big difference between Kon and me—he was idealistic and I was not. To me, Edgecumbe was no different from the *mandurs*, those eighteenth-century recruiting agents who had gone from village to village in India, enticing as many people as they could to sail to Malaya as coolies.

"Groups will be placed in the jungles to team up with the

villagers and the jungle tribes. They'll gather information about the enemy, probably even carry out sabotage against the Japanese," Edgecumbe explained.

"And you'd like to recruit us?" Kon asked.

"I think you two would be perfect for it. You have the linguistic advantage. Christ, you two can even speak Japanese! We'd provide you with training, you know, elementary hand-to-hand fighting, nothing too complicated for you two youngsters. Some instructions in firearms as well and basic jungle survival skills."

I did not like where the conversation was leading. I stood up and said to Kon, "It's been a long day and I'm exhausted. How about heading home?"

"We'll let you know, Mr. Edgecumbe," Kon said, and the man wrote down his telephone number and gave it to Kon.

"Don't think too long. There isn't much time," Edgecumbe said and, to me at that moment, he sounded very, very sober.

Chapter Eighteen

Kon was quiet during the drive and when I got out of the car at Istana I said, "What did you make of that chap Edgecumbe?"

He turned off the engine. "He sounded genuine. I might consider his offer. You?"

"I don't know, really. Obviously I can't discuss this with Endo-san. I'll have to think it over."

Edgecumbe's proposal troubled me. The fact that he already had volunteers meant that there were rational people in Malaya who thought that war was highly probable.

"Let me know," Kon said and started the engine.

"I will. Remember to come to the party," I called out as he drove away. I saw him wave and waited under the portico until the lights of his vehicle had faded away.

Much as I needed to, I did not have the opportunity to talk again with Kon about Edgecumbe. Isabel and I were kept busy preparing for the party and, when I could snatch a quick moment, I was always told that Kon was not at home or that he was with his friend, Ronald Cross.

I let myself be diverted from morbid contemplation of the future. We made trips to the Cold Storage Company and Whiteaway Laidlaw & Co., making gleeful, almost manic purchases of crates of champagne and *pâté de foie gras*, telephoning Robinson's in Singapore to deliver fresh Australian strawberries, making sure the house was cleaned and every surface dusted.

Due to the amount of work to be done we asked Uncle Lim if Ming would like to help out for extra money. She came a day later and I was happy to see that her stay in the village had removed her customary look of worry and fear. She was betrothed to a fisherman and seemed happy with the prospect.

Isabel gave me the name of a person she wanted to invite. "Put this one on the list," she said, handing me a piece of paper.

"Peter MacAllister," I said, eyeing her. "Who's he? From your shooting club?"

"None of your business. Just put his name down."

"All right, but you know damn well that the old man won't approve of any man you bring," I said. "He's never liked any of your boyfriends."

"Peter's not 'any man' and Father will approve," she said.

"So who's Peter?"

"He's a barrister in K.L.," she said. "He's forty-seven."

"Oh dear," I mocked her. "In that case we *must* put his name down."

"I'm really glad we're doing this," Isabel said as we came out of Pritchards, where she had been choosing linen for the tables. I had taken the morning off in order to help her.

"Yes, it's been a long while since our last big party," I agreed.

"I also meant this," she circled a hand in the air between us. "Spending time together."

"It's enjoyable," I said. "I have better things to do, though." I put on a disdainful and bored look but could not sustain it for long, and we both laughed.

It was an hour before lunchtime, and we decided to have drinks at the Eastern & Oriental Hotel. I looked around when we entered, wondering if Edgecumbe was still staying there. It had been almost a week since we had left him holding his ice pack in his room. I had a strong desire to discuss his offer with Isabel but Edgecumbe's warning had been unequivocal.

She chose a table on the veranda, by the sea. The wooden blinds had been pulled up, and the breeze and the sun on our skins felt like a balm concocted from wind and light.

The E & O Hotel was owned by the Sarkies brothers, two Armenians who also ran the Raffles Hotel in Singapore. It was proud of its guest list, which had included Noël Coward and Somerset Maugham.

"He visited us once," Isabel said. "You remember?"

"Who?" I said, distracted by the menu and thoughts of Edgecumbe.

"Somerset Maugham, silly. You weren't listening. Father had a small dinner party for him and I was so disappointed when he never wrote about us. Probably found us too boring for words. You were quite young then."

"I agree. We're the most boring family in town!"

We watched a group of children swimming in the sea under the attentive eyes of their *amahs*, who were dressed in their customary black and white *samfoo* and sat beneath large umbrellas. The children's joyful laughter carried on the wind and I found it was infectious.

"You should always look like that," Isabel said.

I turned away from the sea. "What should I always look like?"

"Exactly like that," she said. "You seem more happy recently. I don't know how to describe it, but you feel more like a part of us."

"I was always a part of all of you," I replied, suddenly feeling reticent.

"No, you kept a certain distance. I suppose it was a bit hard, after Auntie Lian's death," she said, referring to my mother.

My parents had married in 1922 when Isabel was just four years old, and my mother had taken care of William and Isabel until her death in 1930. Edward had never warmed toward my mother but Isabel had once told me that Yu Lian had been more of a mother to her and William than to me because they at least had been old enough to remember her.

"I've got only fragments of her in my memory," I said.

She shook her head and blinked. "I don't even have fragments of my real mother. All those photographs and portraits of her in the house are as strange to me as they must be to you. I think that's preferable—at least I can't miss what I don't remember."

I heard the unexpected brittleness of her voice and thought for a moment about what she had said. It shook me that she sounded so bitter. I saw her then as she truly was, confused by her own inexplicable anger, trying to drown it by being Isabel: perpetually laughing, constantly seeking out the next exciting thing to do, always striving to be the center of attention.

I shook my head. "It feels just as bad. There'll always be a void inside, whatever the form of our losses, whatever the deficit of our memories."

She rolled her glass of wine between her hands, like a potter giving shape to his creation. "Perhaps you're right. Memory is a tricky thing. When I said I have no memory of my mother, I meant I don't remember her here," she touched her forehead, "and yet—" her hands returned to shaping her glass.

"And yet you feel her here," I said, my hand resting on the spot above my heart.

I stopped her moving hands and held them tight, feeling the hardness of the wineglass beneath, almost on the point of cracking. "That's not memory, Isabel," I said. "That's love."

She blinked her eyes again, and ran a finger across them, hiding her tears. We had revealed more about ourselves in those few moments than we had in recent years. Was this part of the process of growing up, that we finally noticed the people closest to us in a different, clearer light?

She looked up and said, "That sounds very mature, coming from you."

I ignored her attempt at flippancy. She leaned forward and said in a softer voice, "So is this great insight what your Japanese teacher has shown you?"

"I suppose Father's told you about him," I said.

"Philip, you've always had a secretive nature. William and I picked up bits of it from here and there. Who is he?"

With the exception of my father, I had kept my association with Endo-san away from my family. We had always led our own lives and so it was easy to maintain my regular classes with Endo-san without drawing attention to them. What I had discovered with Endo-san was precious to me and I was reluctant to discuss it, fearing that the power, the purity of it, would be diluted if I did so.

"He rents the island from us. He's built a little cottage on it, and I met him when you were all away," I said to Isabel, keeping to the bare facts.

"You know it's dangerous to be friends with the Japs," she said.

I was annoyed that the mood between us had changed. It was obvious that she was repeating someone else's opinion and probably using the very same words. "Who taught you to say that? 'Peter'?" I said.

She had the good grace to lower her eyes and give a light blush. "Peter's well connected and he's been hearing things," she said.

"What sort of things?"

"That the Japs will attack Malaya. That they've already had spies here for years. In towns and little communities all along the coastline, situated near strategic military locations. They're disguised as traders and shopkeepers, rubber buyers, and fishermen. I just hope your Japanese friend isn't one of them."

"No, I'm quite certain that my 'Japanese friend' isn't 'one of them.' All those things you've heard are merely rumors. It's almost lunchtime. Are you going to order something to eat or not?"

I was in my little cubicle when my father came out from his office. "How are preparations for the party coming along?"

I shuffled the box of invitation cards I had collected from the printers. "Just about to fill in the guests' names."

"Send an invitation to Mr. Endo and one to the Japanese consul," he said. "I've decided to invite some of the other Japanese in Penang as well."

It was a nice gesture from him but I asked, "Is that wise? We're also inviting quite a number of the Chinese towkays." I gave him a list of the names of the local tycoons. The Imperial Japanese Army had taken Canton only the week before and even Ming was unusually silent, wondering about her mother, though Isabel had tried to calm her fears, telling Ming that her mother was probably safe out in the countryside. The Chinese community in Penang, as well as members of the Aid China Campaign, had marched and demonstrated against the Japanese in Malaya, demanding that they be deported. The resident councillor had accepted a petition from the Chinese Chamber of Commerce, headed by Kon's father, with a similar request. Much to the Chamber's anger the resident councillor had refused to forward its petition to the governor in Singapore. The editor of a local newspaper had obtained the petition and published its entire contents and the names of the petitioners. The Chamber was now publicly known to have been ineffective. This was a great loss of face by the Chinese.

My father smiled in a way that I did not much like. "They're your friends, so it'll be up to you to keep the peace."

I put the cards down, wondering how I was going to do that.

"Oh, by the way," he said as he was about to enter his office, "don't forget to invite your grandfather and Aunt Mei."

The party was to be held on the last Saturday of October 1941. As my father had predicted, it would be one of the last great parties of the year. It started well, with William arriving home from his naval training two days before the event. He did not tell us he was coming and walked into the house, into the dining room, as we were having dinner. My father raised his glass to William, and Isabel gave a delighted scream.

William was still in his uniform and we made him turn around and show us. I noticed a spark of envy in Edward's eyes and saw also that our father had caught it.

"I've been assigned to a warship in Singapore," William said. "HMS *Prince of Wales* no less, sinker of the *Bismarck* and the pride of the navy. She'll be my new home for the next few months."

We made denigrating remarks about his cropped hair and sunburned face.

"What's more," he said, looking at me, "we've also been trained in hand-to-hand combat—I could take you on any day, little brother."

We jeered at him and Isabel said, "Oh, shut up, William!"

"So, how are the preparations for my party coming along?"

I threw a chunk of bread at him. Isabel laughed and followed suit, and then Edward and our father joined in, pelting William with our bread rolls. "Who said the party's for you?" I said.

"Well then, I suppose I'd better be going back to Singapore, hadn't I? All right, all right, no more bread rolls please. That's all we ever eat anyway. I'm sick of them."

He sat down at his usual place and ate hungrily, accompanied by our rude comments about the table manners of sailors. As the night matured we pushed our plates aside and, helped by the wine, the heat and fire and spark of our conversation grew warm and mellow. I saw a look of contentment settle on my father. His face softened, and the blue glow of his beautiful eyes lost their hardness. I looked at all of us, from one to the other, each reflecting our father's feelings. I looked inside myself and was pleased to find that I too was content and happy. My father looked across the table at me and nodded softly. We both knew that, after years of walking my own path, distancing myself, I had finally returned to my family. It was a homecoming for William. It was a homecoming for me.

Chapter Nineteen

Invitations to the party had been sent to all the right people: the British ruling class of Penang, which meant the resident councillor and his wife, high-ranking civil servants, military and naval officers; a few playwrights and musicians; the editors of the various newspapers; and the people who really ran the island—Chinese tycoons, Malay aristocrats, and British *Tuan Besars*. And then there were the Japanese whom I had invited. It was truly a gathering of friend and foe.

Isabel was nervous as we went about the house making the final arrangements. Her hands shook as she polished the glasses and I had to take them from her. "What's this, the Penang Shooting Club's five-time champion with her hands shaking? How could you ever aim at anything like that?"

"Oh, shut up!" she said.

I laughed as she went upstairs to her room, but I envied her, having found someone who meant so much to her, whom she could introduce to our father and to the people at the party. I took my afternoon swim and went over all the arrangements, trying to think of anything that I had overlooked. I was worried about Endo-san's presence, wondering how I would act. I had had to invite Shigeru Hiroshi and I was certain he had never forgiven me for making him lose face at Henry Cross's party. Then there was Kon; his father, Towkay Yeap; Kon's *sensei*, Tanaka; and my grandfather and Aunt Mei. As the afternoon faded away and the heat of the day was replaced by the cool of evening, I began to grow worried in the pool. I decided that sitting there would not help. Suddenly Isabel's anxieties did not seem quite so funny.

It was a tender evening: the skies were a soothing palette of vermilion, aubergine, and dark blue, heightened by long trailing wisps of clouds. Crickets sounded to each other in the trees and grass and above us flocks of swallows flew homeward, their tails scissoring them effortlessly through the air. Chinese lanterns were strung out along the trees lining the driveway, looking like a string of gigantic incandescent pearls.

My father and I stood at the top of the portico steps greeting the guests. Unlike most of the Europeans, he refused to wear the standard white dinner jacket; instead he was looking distinguished in his usual black, a lock of hair tickling his left eyebrow.

We could hear the eight-piece orchestra playing an Irving Berlin selection in the gardens. Between shaking hands and welcoming the guests we talked.

"Splendid job you've done," he remarked, humming along to the music.

"After having been to so many parties it's not much to pick it up," I replied.

"Your mother would have been so proud of you," he said, catching me by surprise.

"No. She'd have been proud of us both," I said. "Thank you for that day at the library, for your words."

"I'm proud of you," he said gravely and he took my hand in his. For the first time in my life I felt we were each a living part of the other. And I knew, with the insight that had arisen as a consequence of learning from Endo-san, that he had loved me all along from the moment I was born, even through the years when I distanced myself from him and my family. That was one of the greatest gifts Endo-san had given me—the ability to love and to recognize being loved.

I blinked away the threatening tears quickly and at that moment, precisely on time, the Japanese consul's car entered the portico. I recognized Goro at the wheel but he paid me no heed.

The consul, Shigeru Hiroshi, appeared to be wearing the same jacket he had worn to the Crosses' party. Endo-san introduced me to him, and we both pretended we were meeting for the first time, but I knew it was all an act—a face-saving act. I replied to his queries in Japanese, knowing it would impress my father. Then Hiroshi switched to perfect English again.

"Good evening, Mr. Hutton."

"Evening, Mr. Hiroshi," my father replied.

"This is my deputy consul, Mr. Hayato Endo."

I saw my father look at Endo-san with interest. "We've met before," he said.

"Yes, we have," Endo-san replied. I bowed to him. "Good evening, *sensei.*"

"I can manage on my own," my father said. "Why don't you take our guests in?"

I led them through the house and out into the garden. Hiroshi went on ahead, leaving me with Endo-san. He too looked very good, dressed in his charcoal-gray suit and a maroon tie, which served to accentuate the silver in his hair. I lifted two glasses of champagne from a passing waiter. I lit his cigar and he blew out a ring of smoke into the night.

An Indian waiter walked by; there was something about his appearance that made me think to stop him but then Endo-san said, "How are you? You should not miss your classes any more often than is necessary."

I had informed him that I needed a week off from my lessons to prepare for the party. I had missed him, I told him.

"I have missed you as well."

My father came up to us. Endo-san bowed to him, and my father tilted his head slightly. "How's your island?" he asked.

"Very peaceful," Endo-san replied, casting an ironic glance at me. "I hope you are not thinking of taking it back from me yet."

"No, of course not. I hear you've been traveling a lot."

"Yes, trying to speak to your government officials, to convince them that we are harmless. Meeting company owners to see if we could start some businesses together. Japan is very keen to invest in Malaya."

"I was told about Mr. Saotome's desire to discuss some ventures with me," my father said. "But I'm afraid it was my grandfather's expressed intention that Hutton & Sons must always remain solely in the ownership of the family. We don't have partners and we're not for sale."

"Ah, yes, the principles of the famous Graham Hutton. I shall let Saotome-san know. He will be quite disappointed," Endo-san replied.

"Is Japan thinking of invading Malaya?" my father asked. His voice must have carried in the air, for several heads turned to look at us.

"I do not know. That is up to my government to decide. I'm just a lowly servant of my country," Endo-san said, and I saw the principles of *aikijutsu* at work in his reply.

I laid a gentle hand on my father's arm. He nodded and smiled at me. "For tonight we'll all believe that," he said. His attention was distracted by a group of people coming through the open doors. "I see your grandfather has arrived. Perhaps you should come with me and greet him."

I had often wondered how my father would behave when he faced my grandfather. I watched as the two men, who had caused so much hurt to each other and to the woman they loved, now greeted one another with great civility.

"Mr. Hutton," my grandfather said.

"Mr. Khoo," my father replied, equally bland, aware that he had given and was now receiving great face by issuing the invitation to my grandfather and having him accept. There would never be an open apology from my grandfather and my father now accepted this, changing the tone of his voice the way he often did in his business dealings when things started to go the way he wanted. "I'm very glad you could come."

"I thought it was time I came to see my grandson."

"Yes. It's high time," my father replied, putting his arm around me. Only then did I realize that he was also holding this party for me, hoping that through me the broken bridges could be made whole again.

The two men looked long at each other and I knew they were both thinking of my mother, each with his personal, favorite memories of her.

I stepped in and took my grandfather's arm. "Where's Aunt Mei?"

"She has been arrested," he said.

"What?" my father and I both said.

"Oh, it is nothing." He shrugged in the way I had seen so many times in Ipoh. "She was in the demonstration, protesting with the Aid China Campaign people against the Japanese. The police told them to leave but they went ahead with it anyway. I offered to get her out but she refused. She sends her apologies, by the way. Young people today." He sighed, quite oblivious to the fact that Aunt Mei was already past childbearing age.

I went to look for William and Isabel, who had made me promise I would introduce them to my grandfather. I found them in the kitchen, supervising the servants. Isabel called out to Edward and together they followed me out to where he was standing.

They were nervous of my grandfather and I could understand why. He was dressed in an understated gray Mandarin robe that shimmered as he moved. His sleeves were edged with silver, matching his eyebrows, which he had let grow long, over his cold glinting eyes. He looked tough and compact in his clothes.

There was an awkward silence since none of us knew quite what to say after the introductions had been completed. My grandfather seemed not to know what to think of my siblings. He blinked rapidly with discomfiture, which I found both surprising and endearing.

Isabel saved us all from further embarrassment. "We've all missed Aunt Lian very much ever since she died. She was wonderful to us, and I always thought of her as my mother."

My grandfather inclined his head. "I am happy that she meant so much to you."

"May we call you Grandfather too?" Isabel asked.

My grandfather looked surprised. "You may not," he replied. I felt hurt, and Isabel was taken aback, afraid that she had insulted him.

But I had misjudged the old man. "I would prefer you to call me *Ah Kong*," he said, using the Hokkien term for "Grandfather." Then he smiled, and my hurt turned to admiration and affection. Isabel and William looked relieved. They asked to be excused and returned to the kitchen and I brought my grandfather out to the lawns where we had laid out the tables.

The maids were moving in and out of the kitchen, bringing dishes of food. We had decided to provide a combination of English and Malayan fare, and my father had chosen his usual favorites: Indian fish curry, beef *rendang*, coconut rice, curry *Kapitan, assam laksa*, fried *kuay teow, rojak,* and *mee rebus*. I had hired a few local street hawkers to push their carts into Istana, and they were now cooking on the lawn. I could smell the satay-seller's sticks of skewered chicken and beef as he grilled them over a charcoal fire. Every time he brushed them with a stalk of lemon-grass soaked in peanut oil the flames from the coals erupted, lighting the trees around him and sending a cloud of mouth-watering smells into the night air.

My grandfather took a glass of champagne from a waiter and said, "Where is your Japanese teacher? I would like to meet him."

I searched the terrace for Endo-san, and found him by a group of Japanese businessmen. He saw me and came over.

"We have met before. Mr. Endo, is it not?" my grandfather asked.

Endo-san nodded. At the instant that they shook hands, I sensed something shift, something move out of focus, and then sharpen again. I felt as though I were intoxicated, but I had not yet consumed any wine.

"You are the one who has been teaching my grandson."

"Yes," Endo-san replied. "He is eager to learn, so that makes it more enjoyable. It is quite wonderful that I should find someone such as him. In all my travels I have yet to meet anyone else who has his abilities. He is a quick learner."

"Almost as though he had been taught in another life, hm?"

Endo-san's face lightened in color. "Do you believe in such things, Mr. Khoo?"

"Yes, I do."

"Then you understand that certain things cannot be stopped, that they must be allowed to proceed, regardless of the consequences?"

"I know one cannot escape one's path on the continent of time," Grandfather Khoo said.

A sense of the surreal unsettled me as I followed their bizarre conversation. It was like listening to two monks argue about the existence of nothing. I remembered what Endo-san had said to me at the snake temple; how far away and long ago that all seemed now.

"I have trained and taught your grandson, as best I can, to face the life he has to lead," Endo-san said.

"I understand. But then, as we both know, that is never quite enough, is it? There are so many things one can never be taught to overcome."

"That would depend on the person's strength and fortitude, and the level of desperation he is faced with."

My grandfather did not like that. "That is not fair, Mr. Endo."

"It is out of my hands, Mr. Khoo," Endo-san said, and in his voice I heard an unbearable sorrow.

"What were you two talking about?" I asked him later, when Endo-san had joined another group of people. My grandfather looked distracted and only responded when I touched his arm gently.

"We were talking about fate," he finally said. "How one cannot escape it."

"You seemed to believe him."

"He tells the truth. But it is what he does with it that will make him dangerous."

"You're not making sense, Grandfather."

"Has he ever told you about your earlier lives?"

"Yes, once."

"And?"

"I trust him," I said.

"But you have your doubts."

I did not like the direction of the conversation. On a magnificent night like this I had no inclination to hear about my past, or my future. "Come with me," I said, and pulled at his sleeve.

I led him to the fountain. Lights from the house shone on the frothing water, turning it the color of the champagne being served in the house. He completed a circle around the fountain, as I had done at his house in Ipoh.

"You did not lie to me," he said. "I am unable to tell the difference."

"That was her room, up there." I pointed to the second floor. "She could see the fountain from her windows. Hear it clearly too."

"Will you leave me alone for a while?" he asked, and sat on the edge of the fountain.

"Will you be all right?"

He smiled and then said, "Go and help your father. I will speak to you later."

*

Most of the guests were now arriving all at once and my father looked relieved when he saw me next to him. "The resident councillor and his wife; Monkey Hargreaves, the newspaper editor; and now here comes Towkay Yeap and his son. It's going to be an interesting night."

I was not really listening to him; the words exchanged by Endo-san and my grandfather were bouncing around my mind, trying to piece themselves together to make some sense to me.

Towkay Yeap and Kon stepped out of their car and came up the steps. They shook my father's hand and then Kon said, "We have something urgent to tell you."

I saw the look on their faces and said to my father, "I'll get William and Edward to greet the guests. I'll meet you in the library."

My father was leaning against his mahogany desk by the window when I entered the library and closed the door behind me. "What's wrong?" I asked Kon.

"We received information that the Communists have placed a bomb in your home."

"Where exactly?"

Kon shook his head. "All we know is that it is in retaliation for your use of force against them. They know the party's heavily attended, that everyone they'd like to see dead is here—the resident councillor, the *Tuans*, the press. It'll make for a nice front page."

"Should we tell the guests to leave?" I asked.

"That would cause a panic," my father said.

I did not ask Kon how he and his father had obtained the information. I trusted Kon and to ask would have insulted them. They must have planted members of their society among the Communists.

"Let's think carefully. They would've put the bomb where there would be a large crowd. Check the lawn first. We'll divide into teams and go around the whole house," Noel decided.

"We have some of our men waiting outside your gates. May they enter and assist in the search?" Towkay Yeap asked.

"Of course. And then please ask them to stay for the party." That was my father. A party, once started, had to go on.

Kon followed me outside. The grounds of the house looked festive and full, the guests looking almost like one body in their white and cream dinner jackets and white shirts. Only the women stood out, scattered among the white in their orange and blue and red.

We started under the tables. They were covered in thick, white, starched tablecloths draped with blue bunting, the champagne glasses laid out like frozen crystal flower bulbs in a bed. Kon crawled beneath the first table and came out, dusting his knees. "Nothing," he said.

"Do you even know what it looks like?" I asked, and I was not surprised when he said, "Yes."

"There're eight more of these to do," I said, heading to the next table. We crawled under and examined all the tables, as guests turned and tried to find out what we were doing. "We're looking for my sister's puppy," I said.

"Any luck?" my father asked, when we met in the kitchen.

I shook my head. Something was edging its way into my thoughts. I reached out for it but it was gone. There was no point in chasing after it; I knew if I stilled my mind it would return to me.

"We've checked the grounds, the garage, and the servants' quarters," Towkay Yeap said. "Everything looks normal."

"Maybe it hasn't been put into position yet," Kon said. "They may still be carrying it around, waiting for the right moment and the right place to put it."

Towkay Yeap lit a cigar and said, "We'll have to keep our eyes open." I watched the tip of his cigar and moved subtly to avoid the cloud of smoke. It was then that I recalled my earlier conversation with Endo-san, and the waiter who had distracted me.

"That Indian man on the docks that day," I said to my father, "remember? The one who was shouting and inciting our workers—I saw him tonight. He's one of the waiters."

"Point him out to us," Towkay Yeap said, looking at his son, who followed me as we went out once again into the party.

"Tanaka-san has arrived," I told Kon.

"No time now," he replied, waving to his *sensei* before moving through the crowd. Once or twice I thought I saw the Indian waiter we were trying to find, but in all cases I was mistaken. The music was addictive and I found myself beating time on my leg as we apologized and pushed and shuffled our way through.

"Still looking for that puppy?" a guest asked.

"No, we found him. Looking for a waiter now," I said. We went back into the house, ignoring Isabel, who was waving to us. My grandfather tapped my shoulder. "Something's wrong?" he asked.

"I'll tell you later," I said, before moving on. I caught Kon's eye. "There he is." The waiter was entering the house. We saw his features lit clearly beneath a row of garden lamps, and I knew it was the man at the harbor. We followed him into the house and Kon said, "Go and get our fathers and meet me in the library."

I nodded and ran outside and found them surrounded by their business acquaintances. My father saw me and I indicated to him to follow. They made their excuses and joined me.

"We've found him," I said. We went back into the house and entered the library. The waiter was sitting on a chair; his cheek was swollen, and his black curly hair, so carefully pomaded, now fell across his brows in greasy claws. Kon carried no weapons, and I marveled at the fear he had incited in the waiter, who tried to burrow deeper into the chair as we closed around him.

"Ramanathan here said he didn't know what I was talking about," Kon said. "But he changed his mind. It's still in the back porch. Go and get it before someone picks it up."

"I'll see to that," Towkay Yeap said and left us quietly.

My father leaned closer to the waiter. "Do I treat my workers so badly that you have to kill us?"

"As long as there are workers and owners, then, yes," Ramanathan replied.

"That's your standard reply. I'm more interested in your personal views. Come on, don't you have a mind of your own?" My father threw up his hands. "Bloody Bolsheviks! Traitors, the whole lot of you!"

The waiter, incensed by my father's contempt, let out a curse. "*Puki mak*! Call me a traitor? Look at your mongrel son—that's your traitor!"

Noel hit him, but I caught and held his arm as he raised it again. "What're you talking about?"

Kon stood up and said, "Listen carefully, Ramanathan. You can tell us everything or I can tell them to leave the room and we can go through the same performance once more. The library is quite well muffled against your screams, with the party and the music outside and, as you can see, there's no shortage of sharp objects here . . ." Kon waved his hands carelessly at Noel's collection of *keris*. I heard for the first time how hard and cruel Kon's voice could be, and I remembered how the porridge seller had referred to him as the White Tiger.

"I want money," Ramanathan said. "You have to understand, when they see the bomb didn't explode they'll know I talked. They'll come after me. I want money and a safe passage to Madras."

"Fine," my father said. "I'll pay you. And I'm quite certain Towkay Yeap can ensure a safe journey for you."

"Who ordered the bomb to be placed?" Kon asked.

"Who do you think?" Ramanathan said, pointing a finger at me. "Your friends, your Japanese friends."

I pushed my father aside. "Who? Which friends?" I kept my voice just under control, relieved that it did not show even the faintest quiver.

"You're such fools, all of you." Ramanathan shook his head. "They'll come soon and kick all you Europeans out."

"Surely you don't believe their propaganda? That the Japanese want to expel the colonials and return the countries to their rightful peoples? That they want to create their so-called Asia Co-Prosperity Sphere to share the wealth of the region? They want it all for themselves, not to share power and wealth with the other nations they have brutalized," my father said in a tired voice.

"You're wrong. They'll free us from you Europeans. And they'll kill each and every one of you."

"Who contacted you? What's his name?" I asked.

"I don't know," Ramanathan said, giving me a smug, almost pitying smile. "They're your friends, why don't you ask them?"

This time it was my father who restrained me from hitting the smiling waiter.

Chapter Twenty

William met us as we came out of the library. "Where have you been? Everyone's been looking for you. Isabel wants you to meet someone, Father. You too," he said, catching my arm as I started to move away. We saw Towkay Yeap across the crowd of guests. He nodded his head once, letting us know that the situation had been taken care of. And then Isabel came through the throng of people, and I knew that the man following her was the guest she had asked me to include.

My father's jaw tightened slightly as Peter MacAllister shook his hand. He was tall and broad-chested, with a slight paunch. Beside him Isabel looked like a little girl. She appeared tense and did not look any easier when our father gave her a smile, since we all knew that he would never embarrass his family in public. For the moment he would be perfectly charming to MacAllister. The stern words would come after the party and yet I somehow felt, this time, Isabel would not be intimidated.

I left them. I couldn't help wondering if Endo-san had been involved in the attempt on my father's life. I saw him standing on his own at the edge of the lawn beneath the casuarina tree looking at his island. I refused to believe he had any knowledge of it. It was that simple.

"Your father is a good man," he remarked, as I joined him. We walked to the side of the swimming pool. I had placed hundreds of oil lamps floating on artificial water lilies in it and their combined glow made the water shimmer. All around, candles had been placed on my father's collection of statues and they appeared to move like living things as the flames fought the breeze.

The moon was out, paling the stars into insignificance. The lighthouse a mile from Istana slashed its beam out into the endless sea. I made a decision not to tell Endo-san about Ramanathan's revelations. I used the method of *zazen* to strain out, layer by layer, the noises of the party to pretend that we were the only two people there.

"Philip-san." A voice came from behind us. It was Tanaka, Kon's teacher, and I bowed to him.

"Tanaka-san, *konbanwa*," I said. He returned my greeting and spoke to Endo-san. "How are you? It has been a long time, has it not?"

"I am quite well. Yes, it has been a while. How is Ueshiba-*sensei*?"

"I have no news of him, I am afraid. The last I heard from him was just before he moved to Hokkaido."

"Hokkaido?"

"He wanted to get away from the war, from the generals and the ministers who pestered him daily to teach the army recruits," Tanaka replied. "He had a message for you, should I meet you."

Endo-san sighed, as though he had been expecting it.

"He said he understands your actions now but that does not mean he approves of them. You have your duty to your family but you must not stray from the path he has taught. He also said he would always consider you his pupil."

Endo-san remained expressionless.

"How is your *oto-san*?" Tanaka now went on. I listened carefully, not wishing to miss any part of the exchange of words. Endo-san had never told me a great deal about his father.

"He is recovering from a recent illness. The government treats him well, and provides adequate medicines for him. Thank you for your concern." Endo-san's tone of voice made it clear that the subject matter of his father was closed, but Tanaka ignored it.

"Our emperor should never have listened to the generals," Tanaka said. "Your father was right to stand fast in his beliefs, in spite of the price he has had to pay. So much suffering now. Will the war in China be over soon?"

"I do not know. I hope so."

"You should return home, my old friend," Tanaka said.

"I made an agreement with the government, and I will honor it until my father has been released," Endo-san said. "Tell my family I do not need you to watch over me."

"I'm not doing it merely for their sake. We are all concerned for you, even those who are outside your family."

Endo-san failed to reply and it was clear they had reached the end of the conversation. They bowed and Tanaka walked away, disappearing into the crowd.

"You've never told me much about your father or your family," I said.

"One day I shall," he said, his eyes not moving from Tanaka's figure. He gathered his thoughts, looked at his watch and said, "Hiroshi-san and I will have to leave soon."

"You'll miss my father's speech. You should stay for that; his speeches are famous for their wit," I said, watching his face carefully. I felt nauseous suddenly as, against my will, I wondered again if he knew about the bomb.

He shook his head. "We have an early day tomorrow. But thank you for inviting us," he said.

"I thought Hiroshi-san wouldn't have accepted."

"Oh, why not?"

"I insulted him once," I said, briefly telling him about our conversation at Henry Cross's home.

Endo-san laughed with an almost malicious glee. "That was very wicked of you."

"Will Japan invade Malaya?" It was my turn to ask.

He did not hesitate at all. "Yes."

In one word my world changed. There was no attempt to obfuscate and weave the truth into something palatable like the Asia Co-Prosperity Sphere Ramanathan had believed in. "When?"

"I do not know. But it will be swift." He turned to face the sea. "You need not worry. I will make certain you are safe, and your family as well. But all of you will have to cooperate."

"You knew it all along, didn't you?" I said, trying to wrap my anger within me.

His eyes cut into mine and I took a step away.

"What happened to all the ideals you taught me, the ideals taught by your *sensei*? Love and peace and harmony? What happened to them?"

He had no answer. "Your grandfather . . ." he stopped, then continued, "I told you once before how we've all lived previously. Do you still remember?"

I remembered. After we had returned from the snake temple we took a walk on the beach that had just been washed clean by the receding tide, and as we walked we left behind a trail of footprints in the unblemished sand. He had asked me then, "What did you feel when you met me that first time?"

"As though I'd known you before. I probably recognized you from some social occasion." But I had known that wasn't so. No, the feeling had been different. A telescoping of time.

"Indeed we knew each other a long, long time ago, many lifetimes ago. And we've known each other for many lifetimes."

He had stopped, turned around and pointed to the trail of footprints. "We are standing in the present; those are our lives lived. See how our prints cross each other's at certain places?" He had turned again, and pointed to the vast stretch of unmarred sand. "And there are our lives yet to be lived. And our prints will again cross one another's."

"How do you know; how can you be so sure?"

"It comes to me, when I meditate. Glimpses and flashes, and stabs of feelings, some sharp as a katana, others barely felt."

"How did our lives end?" I had asked, curious in spite of myself.

He had looked out to the sea. A sailing boat was out, balancing on the tightrope of the horizon. "In pain and unfulfilled, without completion. And that is why we are forced to live again and again, to meet, and to resolve our lives."

I had not really believed his words. I found the idea of not being in control of my own life appalling, like being compelled to laboriously copy out a book someone else had already written. Where was the originality, the excitement of turning the next page and filling it in with something new?

The sounds of the party returned me to the present. "What's that got to do with the invasion of Malaya?"

"It means we cannot change anything. Everything has already been set out for us."

"I refuse to believe that," I said.

"Do you think our meeting each other was merely chance and nothing more? Do you seek to trivialize it?"

I shook my head helplessly. "I don't know. All I know is that your country will soon attack mine."

"The invasion of Malaya means we are about to become enemies again. That our cycle of pain and our attempt at redemption will soon begin. That is what your grandfather meant."

He stopped, looking at the guests as they laughed and touched their glasses together. "But I want you to remember one thing, always, even when we appear to be fighting to the death," he said. "Remember always that I love you, and have loved you for a long, long time." He reached out his hand and gently touched my shoulder once. He looked up at the house. "That is your room?" He indicated with a lift of his eyebrow to a set of windows facing us.

"Yes."

"May I see it?"

We left the party behind. This was the first time Endo-San had been given a guided tour of the house but, as we walked through the ground floor rooms and up the stairs, I could tell that he recognized them from my descriptions. We went upstairs into the dimness of my room. I opened the windows, letting the breeze lift up the gauzy curtains. I turned and he was there and the band below began playing "Moonglow." He touched the books on my shelves, and made gentle fun of my attempts at calligraphy. "You are improving," he said, placing the sheets of rice paper back on the desk. He picked up another sheet and laughed and I heard the delight in his voice.

"I see you are trying to copy Musashi's drawing," he said. I looked over his shoulder at the painting of Bodhidharmo, wondering what he meant. He and the forgotten emperor had haunted my dreams ever since I heard my grandfather's story.

"Which Musashi drawing?" I asked.

"The one of Daruma, in my home," he said.

"No," I said. "This is a drawing of a monk from China, Bodhidharmo, who cut his own eyelids off to stay awake. My grandfather told me his story."

"Philip, they are the same person," he said.

In an instant I saw that I *had* unconsciously replicated Musashi's drawing, the drawing that had been copied by Endo-san and for the briefest moment I saw how everything and everyone and every time was connected in some manner. A golden light brighter than the sun filled my room and it was all so very clear, so lucid, that I let out a soft sigh and closed my eyes, hoping to capture it in the memory of my heart. I felt completely at peace, ascending higher and higher in an all-encompassing under-standing. I saw it all, everything, from beginning to end and then to a new beginning again. And after a moment of eternity it was gone, that complete clarity and total contentment and, though I did not know it then, I would search for it for the rest of my life— and fail.

Endo-san stared at me with unmoving eyes. "*Satori*," he whispered.

I did not see Endo-san off, but walked among the guests. As I looked at their laughing faces, their gestures and movements, I felt strange and even cold after my experience in my room. They had not the faintest idea how, very soon and very swiftly, every-thing would change.

Robert Loh, the owner of Lucky Fortune Canning Factory in Butterworth, had become drunk and was now berating Monkey Hargreaves for publishing the signatories of the Chinese Chamber of Commerce's Anti-Japanese petition in his newspaper. Monkey, equally soaked, swung a punch at Robert Loh and the two of them fell to the ground. The other guests opened up for them and I knew they were venting their anger through the two drunken brawlers. I was too exhausted to care.

A Chinese tin trader hit a Japanese photographer who was taking pictures of the fight and the brawl escalated, turning ugly. More Chinese came to the trader's assistance, and the Japanese swarmed in to join the brawl. People started to scream and I was wondering about my own course of action when a single shot rang out.

Everyone stopped, silenced. I followed their glances and turned behind me. On the balcony, lit up by the lights below like a fiery angel, stood Isabel, her white skirts sailing softly in the wind. She held her Winchester rifle in her hands and said, "That's enough. Do you want to wreck my father's party?"

I laughed, all my tension released. A flashbulb went off as someone took a photograph of her. My grandfather started clap-ping and soon everyone joined in. The band picked up their tune and the waiters came in and cleared up the mess.

"Are you drunk?" Kon asked from behind me. "You look disoriented."

"That's how I feel," I said, glad to see him. "Where's your father?"

He pointed to where Towkay Yeap was talking to my grandfather. "Are they friends?" I asked.

"They met in Hong Kong before the Great War."

"So we're almost family," I said, and once again I thought of the moment of revelation and enlightenment in my room, how we were all linked. "Thanks, for warning us about the bomb. You saved my father's life, and probably all of us here. I won't forget it."

"Neither will I," he replied. "My father wanted to tell you we'll keep a watch on Mr. Hutton for some time. Make sure he's safe."

I took a long hard look at him, fearing for his future, for our future. "I was told tonight that the Japanese will soon land in Malaya."

"I know," he said, "which leads me to another thing I would like to ask you." Hearing the brush of heaviness in his voice, I thought, would this party never end?

He made sure we were alone, away from the crowd, before he said, "Have you decided? Edgecumbe's offer?"

I nodded, wondering if we would arrive at the same decision. I had spent the past few weeks thinking of the plan and, once or twice, had been tempted to ask Endo-san for his views. But I knew that would be impossible. I did not want to place him in a quandary. If his government did invade Malaya he would have to choose between betraying his country by not informing them of Force 136, or betraying my trust. Now I laughed bitterly to myself when his words earlier tonight came back to me and I was relieved that I had not confided in him. At the same time it saddened me that I now had secrets from him, when once I told him everything. A change had come and I did not welcome it.

"Do you think we should join?" I asked.

"I'm perfect for it and so are you. We already have the necessary skills to survive."

"How do you feel about going against Tanaka-san's people?"

"I have a lot of respect and affection for my *sensei*, as I know you do for yours. But there *will* be a war and, if the Japanese plan to inflict what they did in China on us here, then I will do anything to protect my home. It's the right thing to do. I know Tanaka-san will understand and nothing has changed between us. He has played no part in the coming war."

I wished I could say the same for Endo-san, that he was innocent, but he had revealed to me tonight his true intentions, his true knowledge.

"I hope you decide to join," Kon said. "We can ask to be assigned to the same group."

"I don't know. I need more time to consider," I said. "I don't think it's a good idea. I have to stay here and take care of my family." As I spoke those words a sudden premonition, perhaps a vestige of the *satori* I had experienced earlier, told me I spoke words of truth, that my family would need me near them.

"All right, I won't contact Edgecumbe yet," he said, and held out his hand. I took it in mine, gripped it firmly, feeling suddenly lost. Somehow he knew my fears and he said, "Be strong, my friend. We'll all have to be, very soon."

I watched him walk away to his father. We were both eighteen years of age.

Noel Hutton went up onto the cramped stage and the band obligingly faded out their last notes. He took the microphone from the singer and said, "Thank you all for coming."

The crowd gradually quieted, then a few of the guests cheered him. "I almost couldn't make this speech tonight, for reasons best kept to myself," he paused. "On your invitations it was stated that this night was to be for my son, William, who has joined the navy. But there's more to it than that. This night is also for all of us, our sons and brothers and fathers and friends and sweethearts, who have decided to join the forces. Some have already been sent to various parts of the world and can't be with us tonight. We send our prayers to them, and pray they will be safe, and return to us soon."

An eruption of agreement rang through the night, and people clapped and tapped their glasses with their knives.

"Tonight is also for those of us who are staying behind, to keep the economy going and our spirits alive, preparing for the day when our loved ones can walk with us again on the streets of Penang, on our plantations and in our homes."

His gaze sought me out in the crowd. He winked at me and said, "And now, a present from Mr. Khoo, a member of my family."

Five flaming spires rose up over us, lighting the darkness above like long sword cuts tearing open the sky to let in the light of the next day. They rose steadily, as if trying to claim their place beside their starry brethren. Finally they could rise no more and at that moment exploded into a series of flaming flowers, each giving creation to the next, as though passing the flame from one to the other, casting their light onto our upturned faces. The crowd cheered and whistled and screamed.

My stomach chose that moment to tell me I had not eaten anything since the evening began. I turned around when I sensed someone come up behind me.

"Time for an old man to go to bed," my grandfather said.

"You didn't tell me about those," I said, pointing to the sky.

"A surprise for you," he said, pleasure creasing his face.

"Thank you," I said, hoping he knew I meant it for more than the fireworks.

He caught the meaning in my words without effort. "Oh, I liked your brothers and your sister. None of that English snobbishness about them. And without lifting a finger I have three new grandchildren."

"Is it so important to have grandchildren?" I knew that the Chinese placed a heavy value on having them, for who else would there be to tend to their graves and place offerings of food and paper money to be consumed in the hereafter? But I was curious to hear his views.

"Would you be able to visit me tomorrow? I am staying at your Aunt Mei's house."

"Yes." I knew not to press him for the answer. He would show me in his own way.

"Come just before noon." With that he turned and went back into the house.

Chapter Twenty-One

The heat of the sun crawled across my bed, into my closed eyes, and the seagulls' cries broke into my sleep. I had no idea when the party ended, only that it was past two in the morning when I went to bed. I looked at the clock in my room. It was already late morning.

I got up and stretched and went out onto the balcony, the patterned Dutch tiles already burning beneath my feet. The lawn was a mess, chairs stacked like abandoned packs of cards on a gaming table, the marquees flapping desolately. The glasses rattled as a breeze shook them. The sea was so bright it was almost without color, just a shifting sheet of light.

In the kitchen Ming was making breakfast and offered to make me some tea.

"It was a wonderful party," she said, passing me a cup. "I've never attended anything like that back home."

"Thank you. You don't have to do that, let the maids do it," I said, as she started to tidy the table. "When is your wedding?"

Her eyes almost disappeared when she gave a smile of love as she thought of her fiancé. "We have not consulted the soothsayer yet. She will give us a date. You will be invited, if you want."

"I want," I said, giving her a grin. "Consult any fortune-teller you like but don't use the one at the snake temple."

She raised an eyebrow. "Why not? She's considered to be the best in Malaya. I know people travel from as far as Siam and Burma to see her."

"Just believe me, and take my word for it."

"All right, I will. I almost forgot, your grandfather said he would send a car to fetch you."

"Then I'd better not keep him waiting," I said, getting up. "Thanks for the tea. I'll be waiting to receive your wedding invitation."

*

The car stopped at the Kuan Yin Teng at the junction of China Street. The granite courtyard of the temple dedicated to the Goddess of Mercy was busy with flocks of purple-gray pigeons, incense sellers, flower stalls, and devotees praying for good fortune. A heavy curtain of incense smoke from the hundreds of burning joss sticks made the temple appear like a fading memory, one moment clear as the wind brought remembrance, and the next forgotten as the smoke reasserted itself. I assumed we were going to enter the smoky interior but my grandfather said, "Let us walk on."

He set a gentle pace, absorbing the atmosphere of the streets as we passed Indian temples, on whose entrance lintels rose layers of stone carvings of gods and immortals, painted in bright colors, the sound of priests ringing little bells floating out to us from within. Hawkers on bicycles pushed their carts past us, shouting out the food they were selling. The streets became smaller, more domesticated, as we entered Campbell Street and then turned into Cannon Street. Children played along the covered passages— what the locals called "five-foot ways"—which fronted the shop-houses and old men and women sat on wooden stools, watching over their grandchildren, watching over the world. Washing hung out on bamboo poles from the first floors, sieving the sunlight, changing it into patches of bright and shadowed hues below where we walked.

"Why do I feel as if we're walking through a maze inside a fortress?" I asked.

"It *is* a fortress, cleverly camouflaged as a warren of streets. There is only one formal entrance here but I have taken you through a side entrance. You are in the streets and lanes of the Khoos."

I had never ever walked into these streets. This was the Chinese heart of the island and it was completely alien to me. I had spent my youth among the Europeans, yet I understood the words shouted by the women in the corner market, and the swearwords shouted by the little boys playing policemen and thieves, words that universally seemed to refer to each other's mothers and their respective private parts. It was an unsettling feeling, as though I had long been asleep and was now awake again, understanding the language, yet not comprehending the patterns of life to which it gave voice.

We entered a passageway covered by the top floor of a wooden shop and came out into the bright sunshine in a granite-cobbled yard. In the center was a building that looked as if it had been transported from the deepest, densest pages of Chinese myth.

"That looks amazing," I told him. "What is it?"

"The Leong San Thong Dragon Mountain Hall Temple, built by the clan association of the Khoo."

He explained to me the significance of a clan association. Each Chinese belonged to a clan, usually either by reason of the village he came from or, more commonly, through his family name. Such associations were common where the Chinese had transplanted themselves, and were formed to provide protection for their members, to resolve disputes, and to act as welfare organizations. The associations also provided education for clan children, arranging medical treatment, and seeing to the funerary arrangement of their members. Each association also played a role in the religious festivals of the lunar calendar and invested heavily in property and businesses, from which it obtained its income to conduct its activities.

"When I arrived in Malaya this was the first place I came to. I sought the advice of the Senate of Elders and accepted their assistance with gratitude. The property surrounding this temple is owned by the temple. The people we walked past just before we entered—we all have the same family name. No one else may live here."

I stroked the two gray stone lions guarding the temple as we went by them.

"Remember the courtyard I told you about, the one my father and I walked across in the Forbidden City? This reminds me of it, but this is very much smaller," my grandfather explained.

The tiered roofs of the temple were turned up at the corners, like the tufts of a Sikh's mustache, and clusters of carvings and statues—dragons, phoenixes, maidens, heroes, gods, goddesses, fairies, sages, animals, trees, palaces—looked over us, delicate, finely featured, like porcelain dolls, all exquisite and detailed down to the eyelashes, to the creases in the robes, to the smallest scales on the dragons.

Under the eaves were more carvings, crawling down the columns that held up the roofs like petrified vegetation. If a building had been immersed for centuries in the deepest oceans like some Eastern Atlantis and then taken out, shimmering with coral and barnacles, it would still pale in comparison. Cylindrical lanterns daubed in red writing hung at intervals across wooden beams blackened by decades of soot from burning incense and candles and by time itself, their tassels quivering gently in the heat.

We walked up the steps and followed the smell of incense into the gloom of the interior. Swallows flew in and out from among the carvings beneath the eaves, as though the stone creatures had been bequeathed life.

We were met by an elderly custodian, his back hunched, his glasses thick and heavy on his wrinkled face. He stared unabashedly at me, wondering what someone like me was doing in the temple. "Ah, Mr. Khoo," he greeted my grandfather, receiving the *ang pow*, a red paper packet of money, with unhidden delight.

"Mr. Khoo," my grandfather greeted him in return.

We stood inside the main hall, beneath the glaring eyes of the gods, their luster covered in the age of smoke from the spirals of incense hanging over us. "This could have been one of the less important rooms in the Forbidden City in my youth," my grandfather said, as I avoided the wrathful eyes and the raised tridents and broadswords.

"It is . . . I have no words."

"According to the older folk this is nothing. The original temple was apparently more incredible still, but it was burned down."

"Who burned it down?"

"Nobody knows, but it was said that the beauty and the opulence of the original building angered the gods and so they struck it down." He walked to the edge of the altar, his hands gently trailing on it, disturbing a fine line of dust, as though his fingers were burning the wooden surface, raising smoke. There seemed not to be a single empty surface, for the walls, the ceiling, the pillars, the lintels, the skirting, and even the windows and doors were bristling with carvings, statues, drawings, and calligraphy.

Another custodian came up to us. "Mr. Khoo," he said to my grandfather.

"Mr. Khoo, please meet my grandson," he said. The man hid his inquisitiveness with greater skill than the first one had done.

This custodian showed us the Hall of Ancestors, the tiers of tablets rising up to the darkened ceiling, generations of our blood, filtered down through my grandfather to me.

Rectangular slabs of marble filled one of the walls in a room next to the hall and on them were columns of names written in Chinese, as well as a surprisingly large number in English, with a brief description of accomplishments. I saw some MDs, many PhDs, quite a few LLBs, and one QC.

"All of the Khoos," my grandfather said. "I have put my name there, look."

I followed his pointing finger. "Next to mine is your grand-mother's, below hers is your aunt's and your mother's. And there, beneath hers, is your name."

He had added a hyphenated Khoo to Hutton, so that my family name now was Khoo-Hutton. I felt a shifting feeling of being brought apart and then placed back together again, all by the single stroke of the hyphen. The hyphen was also similar to the ideogram for "one" in Japanese and, as I discovered, Chinese as well. Once again the feeling of connection and conjunction I had encountered in my room the previous night came over me, fragile and yet evocative as morning mist.

"When you are lost, in this world or on the continent of time itself, remember who you have been and you will know who you are. These people were all you, and you are them. I was you before you were born and you will be me after I am gone. That is the meaning of family."

He took my hands and said, "The story I told you and this temple, these are all I have to teach you."

I bowed my head to him, still overwhelmed by what he had done to my name.

"Mr. Endo is at heart a good man, but he too is lost, confused by all that is happening, by the illusion of the material world. That is why he cannot find his way."

"Where is he going?" I asked.

My grandfather looked sad for a moment. "He wants to go home, like all of us."

My awareness of the world now was sufficient to make me

understand that he did not mean Endo-san's home in the village by the sea in Japan.

"But he is lost and you, young as you are, will have to lead him home."

I often wondered how he knew so much about Endo-san, because he was completely correct. In searching for some form of answer, the totality of which would forever elude my understanding, I returned again and again to the story he had told me, of that time in his life in the timeless palace. The Forbidden City—to what and whom was it forbidden? Did the sentries at the gates raise their gloved palms and stop Time from entering? What had he learned within those walls? What had he seen in rooms forgotten by people, forgotten by the years?

The days after the party seemed to move slowly, without direction. There was a feeling of something coming to a conclusion as William packed his things, his beloved camera and photography equipment, and as we sat in the garden and talked, drinking iced mint tea, or swam in the pool. William had received his call-up papers to serve on HMS *Prince of Wales*, and we waited for the day to come, hoping it would not.

My grandfather, who was staying at Aunt Mei's house, joined us almost daily. He got along well with us all, even Edward, who could not sustain his superior attitude before the older man. Edward believed in the inherent predominance of the Europeans over the locals and it gave me a wicked pleasure to see his lifetime of beliefs weaken. I had lived with such similar misconceptions for so long that to see them proved wrong made me admire my grandfather more. On the one hand I felt sorry for Edward: my grandfather was a stranger to him and therefore Edward owed him nothing. However, a different part of me—the part bequeathed to me by my mother—felt that, by mere virtue of my grandfather's age, respect should have been freely granted.

Always, just before his chauffeur came at the appointed time, my grandfather would ask me to walk with him on the beach, and we would spend a short moment together, something which I soon grew to cherish.

"I shall be returning to Ipoh soon," he said one afternoon as we stood looking out to Endo-san's island. "I would like to spend more time here in future though."

"You're welcome to stay with us if Aunt Mei's house is too cramped."

He shook his head. "A man must always be the master of his own home, especially when he is as difficult as I am. I have considered opening my house on Armenian Street again."

"You have a house there?" I asked. I had never heard my aunt mention anything about it.

"Yes. My first home in Malaya, before we moved to Ipoh to be nearer to my mines. I have never sold it."

"Then my mother forgave you a long time ago, when she chose Arminius as my middle name," I said. I had never liked the name she had given me for I thought it was an absurd choice. But I now thought I understood the message my mother had been trying to convey to her estranged father and it softened the pain of the cruel and constant teasing I had endured from my classmates when I was younger, when they had often called me names like "Verminous Arminius" and thought themselves witty.

"I have never considered it as such but, yes, it could be so," my grandfather said, although he did not sound as convinced as I was.

"Do you still dislike my father? You always leave just before he comes home," I said.

"You are very perceptive. Years of bitterness cannot be swept away so easily. We need time to adjust to each other again. At least we talk when we meet now and do not act like cats that cross each other's paths in an alley."

"He loved her completely, you must believe that," I said. An image of fireflies flashing in the dark came unbidden to my mind.

He appeared old suddenly, on the verge of fading away, and I had to fight the urge to hold him up. "That makes everything that happened—the time I have thrown away, her death and his loss— harder to endure, does it not?" he asked.

There was nothing I could say to comfort him, to refute the truth of his words. I saw the pain he had carried since my mother's death; it was a load that I knew he would never be able to lighten. It frightened me, that a person could be made to bear such a burden, for if what he and Endo-san had said were true—

that these burdens were carried from one lifetime into another—how could one endure the accumulation of grief?

What made it worse was that we could never truly share such burdens with even those closest to us. In the end, the mistakes were our own, the consequences to be borne by us alone.

The day soon arrived when William had to leave us, and it was hard seeing him off. He was already in uniform as we said our farewells under the portico, his large floppy bags around his legs like faithful hounds unwilling to let their master leave. He looked happy, his eyes bright, his hair perfectly oiled to a lacquered glow.

My father clasped him tightly. "You've made me proud, William."

William pulled back from him and looked up at the house, his eyes sweeping from one side to the other and to the rooms upstairs. He turned and gazed at the garden, at my mother's fountain, our father's carp pond, and the flowers that bloomed so full with life under the skies. Perhaps the realization of what he was setting out to do dawned on him then and illuminated the goodness and the richness of his life, for he grew quiet, and his eyes became sad. On an impulse, despite the fact that he was already late, he brought out his camera from his bag and asked Uncle Lim to photograph us all beneath the portico.

My grandfather had asked to be present. He shook William's hand and then decided to hug him. Edward and Isabel too embraced him. My father stood by watching, his eyes so brilliantly blue. I hugged William close when my turn came, the reality of parting unbearable.

"Do your best to take care of the family," he whispered in my ear.

"I will. You be safe."

He handed his camera to me. "Keep it for me. Take some decent snaps and send them to me whenever you can. When I come home again we should plan a trip. Go somewhere. Will you promise me?"

"Yes," I said. "We'll do that."

We watched as Uncle Lim drove the Daimler away with William in it. He turned back in his seat to wave at us. Noel Hutton put his arms around his three children, and we stood like that for a long time.

*

The two-storey townhouse on Armenian Street was high and narrow, with a plain iron gate. It had never been allowed to fall into neglect, even though my grandfather had long ceased to live there. He had the caretaker quickly put it in good order again. We both knew, without words having to be said, that he was doing it to be closer to me and I was grateful to him.

"It's not as grand as your house in Ipoh," I told him the first time I visited him.

"I do not need a big house. The older one gets, the more one wishes to simplify one's life," he said. "This suits me well now." He looked around the small garden. We sat beneath a mango tree whose ripening fruit attracted lines of ants on its branches and scented the air with fresh clean sweetness. "In fact, it feels good to come back here again, to where I started. Your mother loved to play on the lawn here."

It had become a ritual to visit him when I finished work, to sit with him and hear the sounds of the streets quiet, as though they too were adepts of *zazen*, preparing for evening meditation, filtering out the cacophony of the day. I enjoyed feeling the evening fade away into night. On my first visit I had sat across the table from him as etiquette decreed but he had said, very irritably, "No, no. Come and sit next to me." And so after that I always sat by his side without being asked. He would then inquire about the activities of my family, and if I had received any news from William. Then I would pour tea for him. The first time I had done so he had watched me fill the cup, rapping the second joints of the fore and middle fingers of his right hand softly on the table. It happened whenever I served him and eventually I asked him the significance of it.

"That is how we thank the person serving us," he replied. "All Chinese people are familiar with it."

"I'm not aware of it," I said.

"No one knows precisely where and when the practice originated," he explained. "Legend has it that an emperor in China once decided to walk in the streets like a commoner to see how his people lived their daily lives. There was no need to put on a disguise, since none of the common folk had ever seen the emperor. He was accompanied by a faithful courtier and, at a tea house, when their tea came, the emperor said he wished to experience the novelty of serving his courtier."

"Nothing wrong with that," I said, but he wagged a finger at me.

"This was a grave reversal of the heavenly order and the courtier protested strongly. But he was forced to give way to his emperor, who proceeded to pour them tea. Unable to perform the proper manner of obeisance by getting onto his knees, the courtier resorted to bending his two fingers and tapping them on the table to represent the act of kneeling."

I knocked the joints of my two fingers on the table. The folded digits did appear like a man kneeling.

"Or it could also be a convenient way of letting you know that you have poured enough into my cup," my grandfather said.

"Now I don't know whether to believe you or not," I said.

He looked pensive. "On the few occasions when Wen Zu and I stole out of the palace and visited a teahouse, he too asked to serve and this was the way I thanked him. We both used to laugh about how history repeats itself."

We sipped our tea quietly for a while and then he asked, "Do you know the story of the house next door?"

"No," I said. I filled his cup with tea once more. He gave a mischievous laugh and I was glad to see that his somber mood had left him. "It used to be the headquarters of the Malayan branch of Dr. Sun Yat-sen's Chinese Nationalist party, the Tung Ming Hui," he said. I saw the rich irony of the joke history had played on us. There was my grandfather, once a tutor to the heir to the Dragon Throne, living next door to the base of the man who had played a substantial role in destroying it all.

"This was where he planned the Canton Uprising in the spring of 1911. I think that must have been the main reason why I bought this place," he said, breaking into unrestrained laughter now.

"You must invite him over," I said, enjoying his humor. He became serious again.

"I do not know if he is still alive. He returned to China to lead the government. But the country has erupted into civil war, making it so much easier for the Japanese to conquer it."

"Do you miss it, China?"

"Yes. But I miss the old China. The new one will have no place for me. Perhaps I shall pay a visit once the war is over. Would you like to accompany me?"

"Yes. I would also like to visit Japan."

"And how is Mr. Endo these days?"

"I hardly ever see him. He's away very often. And when he's in town, then he's constantly working."

He looked at me with eyes that had seen so much. "And you miss him."

I nodded. "I haven't been taught by him for some time. I think my level of skills is deteriorating. I do practice at the consulate though."

"But it is not the same."

"No."

He shook his head. "What will you do, when the Japanese attack?"

"I don't know," I said. "Maybe it won't happen."

"Since meeting you I have considered you to be a highly intelligent boy. You have to be, since you have all our blood—mine, your mother's, your father's. It would pain me deeply if such a potent combination produced an imbecile. And you have managed to learn a great deal from Mr. Endo, a man whom I respect, whatever his intentions." He leaned closer to me. "So open your eyes now. Open them as wide as the insane monk who cut off his own eyelids. And see, once and for all."

I was taken aback by his vehemence. He had grasped clearly what I had been trying to ignore, that deep inside I knew the Japanese would launch an invasion. All the signs had been there from the first moment I met Endo-san. And I remembered too what Endo-san had said that night when we had sat beneath the vipers at the hotel in Penang Hill: *the great human capacity for choosing not to see.* What made it more painful was Endo-san's admission to me, on the night of the party.

And so, because I respected my grandfather and, more, because I had come to love him, I knew it was time to accept the truth. I told him about Endo-san's revelations about the imminent invasion. However, acknowledging it did not mean I had the solution. "I don't know what to do," I said.

"You will have to make a stand soon. Every person must, at some point in his life. But I truly feel for you," the old man said.

"Why?"

"Whatever choices you make will never be the completely correct ones," he said. "That is your tragedy."

"You're very helpful," I said, hiding my anxiety at his words behind a sardonic tone of voice. It did not deceive him.

"You'll survive," he said. "You've had to all your life. I am certain it has never been easy, growing up as a child of mixed parentage in this place. But that is your strength. Accept the fact that you are different, that you are of two worlds. And I wish you to remember this when you feel you cannot go on: you are used to the duality of life. You have the ability to bring all of life's disparate elements into a cohesive whole. So use it."

I looked at him in wonder. He had explained the circumstances of my entire life in a manner I had never even considered. I thought he had oversimplified many of its aspects but for a moment I felt that the course of my life, my very existence, finally made sense.

"You were of the view that your mother named you after the street she grew up in," he said. "I do not think so. I have always felt there was another reason."

I waited for him to explain.

"After I left China I spent, as I have told you, three years in Hong Kong. I found refuge in a missionary school and there I learned all about the Western God and his son. The son who brought salvation to the world.

"There was a Dutchman there, an old theologian, Father Martinus, who told me about the teachings of another Dutchman called Jacobus Harmensz, who lived in the middle of the sixteenth century.

"Jacobus Harmensz was considered a heretic by the orthodox Christians of his time because he propounded the view that a person's salvation lay in the exercise of his own free will, and not through the grace of God. He was against the idea that man's life, his eternal salvation or damnation, had already been decided before his birth."

I began to shift restlessly in my seat. My grandfather gave me a reproving stare, and then he continued, "I must admit that I never fully understood what the aged theologian was trying to tell me. The concept of free will intrigued me, however, even if I did not believe in Harmensz's theories. The course and the salvation of one's life, I felt, were predestined. I often discussed it with your mother, after I told her of the fortune-teller's words, when she was old enough to understand. She disagreed strongly."

"What has this Harmensz got to do with me?"

"Jacobus Harmensz's name was eventually translated into Latin as Jacobus Arminius. His teachings are now known as Arminianism. Your mother was trying to prove the fortune-teller—and me—wrong, when she chose your name."

"We always have a choice. Nothing is fixed or permanent," I said.

"Those are almost the exact words your mother said to me. The fact that only certain choices are presented to us, does that not indicate that our options have already been limited by some other power?"

"Then what is the point of life itself?" I asked, unable to accept what he was telling me.

"I shall tell you when I find out myself," he said. He took my hand and held it. "Your mother was a remarkable and strong-willed woman. She may have been right. I do feel very certain that she would never have named you after a mere street." He took a last sip of his tea. "I talk too much," he said. "Now I am hungry. Come, I want to eat at the food stalls. It *is* true what they say: Penang has the best hawker food in all of Malaya."

Through our almost daily meetings, we had arrived at a greater familiarity with one another, breaking forever the fetters of formality. I stood up and rubbed his stomach in feigned disgust. "That's getting bigger. That's all you do here—sit, talk, and eat."

"Leave my stomach alone," he said, his voice a low growl but his eyes amused at my impertinence.

It had become our custom to sit at the front of the house and spend some time there before going to bed. It was cooler out on the veranda, which had been built to surround the house and to provide a belt of cool air. The bamboo blinds had been pulled up, like a woman's rolled-up hair, and coils had been lit and placed around our feet to repel the mosquitoes.

It was about three weeks after William's departure. I was leaning against the marble balustrade, listening to Isabel tell us about Peter MacAllister. Our father was reading the newspapers, his attention apparently not on her. I could see she was very much in love with the barrister from Kuala Lumpur. He had taken her dancing the night before at the Penang Swimming Club and had not brought her back until this morning, much to our father's fury. One only had to look at her to know that the beauty of the night still remained in her, fermenting her thoughts and emotions. Noel Hutton remained, like all fathers, unconvinced of the suitability of the man his daughter was seeing.

"Peter says he's going to take me sailing up the coast in his yacht," Isabel said. Beneath her gaiety, I could tell she was worried about what our father would say. "And I intend to go with him."

But before he could reply, we heard Uncle Lim's voice.

"Mr. Hutton?" he said. He stood on the steps and my father invited him in. I could tell Isabel was relieved by the interruption.

"*Saved*," I mouthed silently at her and although she winked at me I sensed an uncharacteristic nervousness in her.

Uncle Lim handed my father an envelope. "It's an invitation to my daughter's wedding on the first day of December. We hope you can honor us by attending."

"All of us?" I asked with a skewed smile. Uncle Lim nodded.

"We'd be honored," my father said, passing the card to me.

Like all Chinese wedding invitations, the card and the envelope were red, the color of joy and luck and fortune. There was a faint smell of sandalwood on the card and my hands became scented when I touched it. So the soothsayer had finally found a date to suit the horoscopes of the engaged couple. I smiled to Uncle Lim, feeling happy for him. "We'll be glad to come," I said.

After he had left I saw Isabel take a deep breath, and I knew what her next words would be.

"Peter wants to marry me."

"He's too old for you," our father replied. "And I've heard of his reputation with women, so you can forget about going sailing with him."

They began to throw words back and forth. I left them and walked down to the beach. On Endo-san's island a small gleam of light broke through the trees. I had not seen him for a while and I felt the sudden urge to spend a moment with him.

I brought my boat out from the boathouse and crossed over to

the island. The sea was thick beneath me, shining with phosphorescence that clung to my oars with each pull. I felt as if I were
rowing on a skin of elastic light.

His house was lit only by a single lamp and the doors were
open. I walked around to the rocky outcrop facing the open sea,
and saw his dark figure standing on the rocks. A light flashed like
a captured star from his hand and, far out to the darkness of the
sea, a flicker of light could be seen in reply.

I crept back to my boat, my need to see him abruptly taken
away.

Chapter Twenty-Two

I sent a note to the Japanese consulate and canceled the classes I had arranged with Endo-san. I could not face him at this moment. I could not deceive myself anymore. It was one thing to hear him admit his knowledge of his country's intention to attack us, but quite another to witness his active role in it. I kept seeing him on that rock again and again, flashing his secret signals out to the waiting sea. I knew for certain now what he was doing, and the role I had played in helping him.

Tanaka, Kon's *sensei*, was the only person who would be able to help me, and I decided to visit him the day before Ming's wedding.

I made my way to his house in Tanjung Tokong and waited in the shade of the veranda. I sounded the wind chime. "Tanaka-san!" I called out.

The door with the mosquito netting opened and he came out. "Ah, good! I have been thinking about you. It is timely that you have come."

Once again we sat on the veranda, but this time there was no tea. "I apologize but I have packed away most of my things," he said.

"You're leaving? Are you going home?"

"No. I have decided to find refuge in a monastery in the hills around Ayer Itam."

"You too think there'll be a war," I said.

"There will always be wars," Tanaka said.

"Stop talking like a novice monk, Tanaka-san," I said and then, shocked at my own rudeness, I apologized.

He leaned closer and studied my face. "What is troubling you?"

I told him everything, about Endo-san's activities and how he had manipulated me. It was an immense relief to finally confide in another person who had known Endo-san, someone who would not condemn me.

Tanaka closed his eyes and appeared to have gone to sleep but he said, "Your duty to your family and home is heavy, as is your obligation to your *sensei*. I know how you feel. Especially about Endo-san."

"How could you, when there is so much enmity between Endo-san and yourself?"

He opened his eyes in surprise. "Enmity? There is none, none at all."

"You barely spoke to each other at the party."

"That doesn't mean we did not communicate. Endo-san has been, and will always be, the greatest friend I'll ever have. In fact, your friendship with Kon reminds me very much of us when we were younger."

"What happened?"

Tanaka listened to the breeze on the bars of the wind chime. It was so quiet I could hear his breathing. I found it hard to believe that an invading army was at that moment preparing to spill over the country like beans poured out from a gunnysack.

Finally he said, "The pacifist views of Endo-san's father were considered not in harmony with the emperor's vision and he was removed from his post as a courtier. The family was disgraced and moved back to Toriijima, where they started a business."

His continued evasiveness exasperated me. I made up my mind that I would obtain the truth during this visit, for another opportunity might not arise. So I said, in a firm and resolute voice, "I've heard all of that before. Why are you actually here? Why of all the places in the world did you choose Penang? You told me once, but I knew you were lying to me."

He flashed his teeth in a quick, guilty smile, but his eyes remained sad. He understood the situation I had been put in and that I could not now accept anything less than the complete truth.

"I apologize for not having been completely frank with you," he said. "As Japan extended her influence further into China, Endo-san's father attacked the government publicly, which in Japan can be seen as a personal attack on the emperor. He was imprisoned and subsequently fell ill and Endo-san's mother retreated into her own world. Endo-san and Umeko, his sister, were the only ones who could take care of their young brothers and sisters."

He stopped, pausing to arrange his words like an *ikebana*

expert with his flowers, shifting, bending, adding, and taking away to achieve the results he desired. "Endo-san was never close to his mother, but even he was affected by her mental state. She would sit in the sun and stare at the lake or watch the farmers planting rice. I visited her often. Sometimes she would sing to me or to her sleeping children."

I heard my own voice reciting the lines of the poem to Endo-san, in exchange for his Nagamitsu sword. I saw now why the poem had touched him so much more than I had anticipated.

"Endo-san's father's health worsened. The government was aware that Endo-san had traveled extensively and so decided to make use of his experience. He was given the choice of working for the government in return for medical treatment and nursing care for his father. When Endo-san was given a position in the consulate here, his father, Aritaki-san, asked for me. I went to the prison to see him and he asked a great favor of me."

"He asked you to look out for his son. And you followed Endo-san all the way here," I said, making a correct assumption.

"I refused at first. Umeko, Endo-san's sister, begged me. And there was a young girl, Michiko, who loved Endo-san so much, and I—" he stopped.

"And you were very much in love with her," I said, finishing it for him.

"I was very much aware that Michiko did not return my feelings. But because I loved her, I promised her that I would look after Endo-san, wherever he went. And also because Endo-san was my friend. Aritaki-san even begged our *sensei*'s help to persuade me. My *sensei* felt that Endo-san required a constant reminder of his teachings. I am that reminder. That is why he dislikes my presence here."

"But you can't leave now. Endo-san will need a friend now more than ever," I said.

"I have seen how he has changed, since he began his work here. We have different beliefs now. I cannot condone this war my country has started. This is the moment when our paths diverge. I will not watch over him anymore. I have tried, but he has closed himself off from all others."

"You're running away," I said in disbelief. "You have put aside your duty." It was a serious accusation to make but the facts were clear and irrefutable. Tanaka did not disagree but sat quietly, his face like a Noh mask, unreadable.

"You cannot outrun a world at war, Tanaka-san."

He looked into my eyes. "And you cannot outrun your fate, my young friend. It is time to say my farewell to you."

"Will we meet again?"

"Definitely. When all this madness is over; when harmony is restored, you and Endo-san will find me here."

"What must I do, Tanaka-san?" I asked.

"What do you think you must do?"

I was unable to reply. He gave me a sad, sympathetic smile. "You already know what you have to do," he said.

I made one final attempt to sway him. "You're his friend; you must stay."

He shook his head. "He doesn't need me anymore. He has you."

We followed the map Uncle Lim had printed on the back of the invitation card. The village was thirty miles away from town, on the southwestern tip of the island, known to the locals as Balik Pulau, Back of the Island. My father drove the Daimler, jaws tight, his expression replicated on Isabel's face. I did not have to be told how the discussions for her engagement to Peter MacAllister had gone in the past two weeks.

I had been too distracted to pay attention to them. Tanaka's disclosure had unveiled another aspect to Endo-san's presence in Penang and amplified the sense of unbalance I was experiencing. It was akin to being thrown continuously by Endo-san at the conclusion of every lesson. I would fall, get up quickly, and be met immediately by another technique until the flow of my blood seemed reversed and I was vertiginous, not knowing where earth and sky stood.

I knew it would make me even more miserable than I felt now but I made a decision to avoid contact with him for the moment, until I was able to overcome my feelings of confusion. I did not know how long that would require and a great heaviness settled itself upon me.

Instead of going through miles of jungle, my father decided to drive around the island, heading to its westernmost tip before turning south. The road rose up on the shoulders of low hills and faithfully followed the curves of the coastline. Below us the thick green of the trees was stitched to the blue of the sea by a seam of white, endless surf. Light splattered like careless paint through the trees above us and the wind through our open windows smelled clean and unblemished, tasting of wet earth, damp leaves, and always, always the sea.

We passed Malay kampongs, slowing down to avoid the naked children playing on the roads. They shouted with excitement when they saw the car. Birds called and flew from tree to tree, disturbed by our passage. Wild orchids clung to the face of the cliff that the road skirted. At Teluk Bahang, the road faded into the jungles and we turned south, passing fruit orchards and durian and coconut plantations. The spiky durian fruit clung like immense burrs on the trees, infusing the air with their pungent, flatulent smell.

Following the little signs planted along the road by the villagers, we went off the main road and entered Kampong Dugong. Banners, all red, fluttered in the air, golden congratulatory words painted on them by a master calligrapher. Uncle Lim met us dressed in formal crimson robes, happy to see us. We were the only Europeans in this village today.

"Please meet Mr. Chua, the groom's father," Uncle Lim said. "He's also the village headman." Chua was in his fifties, a gentle-looking Chinese with a wispy goatee and tough sinewy arms.

My father shook their hands. "May your son's longevity be as the Southern Mountain, his wealth be as the Eastern Sea," he said, the traditional phrases of felicitation in Hokkien.

Chua looked surprised and then he laughed. "Now I know why you have such a formidable reputation, Mr. Hutton."

The village had about five hundred people in it, making their living from the sea and from the surrounding orchards and vegetable farms. There were friendly stares as we walked to the wooden jetty, which appeared to have been constructed whenever an extra plank, an abandoned table or a broken door could be found. It seemed to rock gently as we walked on it, our shadows frightening the translucent shoals of fish in the clear green water.

Isabel refused to set foot on it. "I'm not going on that rickety thing," she said. "I'll go for a stroll in the village with your grandfather."

My father and I walked the twisting jetty to its end. Despite the heat he was formally dressed and he had insisted that I be as well. I took off my hat and leaned against a shaved rubber sapling that had been planted into the seabed to support the walkway. The sky was clear, blue as a dream. All the boats were in and they lined the length of the jetty, swaying and creaking, tied to poles. The smell of salted fish and shrimp drying in the sun brought me back to the village where Endo-san had stopped on our journey to Kuala Lumpur.

"What do you think?" my father asked.

I tried to guess what he was talking about. "About what?"

"Your sister."

I wondered if I could ever tell him about the connection between Endo-san and me. Perhaps Isabel and Peter MacAllister had a past together too. "She loves him, and I think he feels the same for Isabel," I replied.

"That's never enough," his quick reply came.

"Then nothing will ever be enough."

"She needs more time and she's too young."

"She doesn't have more time." I told him then about Endo-san's words to me, about the coming invasion. "MacAllister will either be told to evacuate by the government, or be interned by the Japanese."

"Mr. Endo has no idea what he is talking about," he said, looking hard at the sea. "There'll be no war in Malaya."

I thought again of Endo-san flashing his cryptic light out to sea and felt afraid. The island of Penang was so vulnerable, so easy to pluck, like a child awakened by kidnappers at night from his bed.

"Just speak to MacAllister, find out what he is like. You know how it feels to be the unwelcome man in love with another man's daughter," I said.

"Look," he said, pointing out to sea, apparently not having heard me. A school of dolphins streaked past us, the rambunctious ones leaping out from the sea and then falling in again. We watched as they chased the fish. We could hear their clicks and their strange infantlike cries. "Always loved them," he said. "If I could live again, I would want to be a dolphin, forever swimming the oceans, seeing sights no human eye will ever see." His voice was soft, his eyes softer, their blueness not of light anymore but of a warm, rippling liquid that was depthless.

I was frightened by this glimpse of the dreamer in him, he who had always appeared practical to me, able to solve all problems that came his way. I was afraid for him then, hoping that his practical side would always see him through his life and that his dreams would only come in his sleep, when he was safe from harm.

We heard Isabel calling us and we turned to walk back to the village. "I do know what it feels like to be the unwelcome man in love with another man's daughter," he said.

The wedding was conducted in accordance with Chinese custom. Ming was hidden beneath a layer of red veil and dangling tassels and dressed in a gold and maroon robe. She was taken to the bridegroom's house in a bright red wooden palanquin, where she knelt before the bridegroom's parents and served them tea and promised to obey them. As she passed me her head turned and, knowing she was watching me from beneath her veil, I moved my lips and wished her well. She gave a slight tilt of her head and moved on.

Isabel smiled at me and I said, "It'll be fine." She gave my hand a squeeze.

The wedding luncheon was lavish, as face decreed. We entered the community hall of the village and sat at one of forty tables, wondering what the whole event had cost Uncle Lim. Isabel plucked the menu from the center of the table.

"What does it say?" she asked me.

"Roast suckling pig, sharks' fin soup, steamed ginger fish, abalone, roasted sesame chicken, mandarin orange duck. Almost everything," I said, using my knowledge of Japanese to decipher the Chinese writing. I was distracted by the loud music from the Chinese orchestra and the firecrackers. The last two empty places at our table were filled by Towkay Yeap and Kon. I put down the menu, delighted to see my friend. He too was dressed formally but in his favorite color of white.

The curtains of the wooden stage opened and an opera began. The sounds of the erhu and the peipa, accompanied by clashing cymbals and drums, vied with the singers' high feline voices. My father suppressed a wince as the high notes were clawed for and we all laughed.

"Sorry," he said to Towkay Yeap, his face going red.

"Can I safely say you do not know this opera at all?" Towkay Yeap said, amused. My father shook his head.

"This happens to be one of our most popular ones. 'The Butterfly Lovers.' Very tragic, the story."

Isabel leaned forward and said, "Please tell us about it."

"Once, many dynasties ago in China, a girl, Lady Zhu, wanted to study in a school high in the mountains. Of course, being a girl she was not allowed to study at all. She was supposed to stay at home and take care of her family and later the husband whom her parents would choose for her."

"A tradition worth keeping," I said, giving Isabel a grin.

"*Do* be quiet, Philip," she said.

"Lady Zhu was a headstrong girl, Isabel. Very much like you, or so I have heard," Towkay Yeap said, his eyes narrowing with gentle humor.

"Spot-on, old chap," my father said, crossing his arms at his chest and leaning back into his seat.

Isabel frowned at our father. "Please go on, Towkay Yeap."

"As I said, Lady Zhu knew what she wanted. And so, deceiving her parents and breaking tradition, she put on male clothing and obtained entry into the school. And there she fell in love with a fellow student, Liang, who had no idea at all of her real identity. At the end of the three years of their studies they parted at the Eighteen Mile Pavilion and there Lady Zhu told Liang that she wished him to marry her younger sister. She told Liang to come to her home in a year's time to ask for the girl's hand in marriage. Liang came within the set time and realized there was no such sister, that in fact Lady Zhu had been the one who wanted to marry him. He fell in love with her when she revealed her true self to him. Theirs was a meeting of the souls and Lady Zhu and Liang knew they had each found the one person who would travel with them, even after death, all through their subsequent lives.

"Their parents inevitably discovered Lady Zhu's subterfuge and her family was shamed. The lovers were separated. Lady Zhu and Liang were locked up in their homes. A marriage was hastily arranged for Lady Zhu with a family who did not mind the scandal. Liang pined for her. He fell ill and passed away.

"On the day of her wedding Lady Zhu heard this sad news and

fled to the tomb of Liang, where she cried so hard and so long that even the heavens were moved. The sky churned and grew stormy and dark and the winds began to blow. No one had ever seen such a fierce storm before. Lightning cracked open the tomb of Liang and Lady Zhu threw herself into it, just as her parents and the wedding retinue reached the grave.

"A pair of butterflies fluttered out from the grave. They floated together and rose high into the sky, finally able to be by each other's side, leaving the sorrows of the world behind."

"What an awful story to perform at a wedding," my father said. I caught a glimpse of a crack in his memories, of his abandoned passion for butterflies and what that passion had cost him and my mother and me.

I knew Towkay Yeap had also felt my father's swiftly suppressed sadness. He said quietly, "Ah, but you miss the point, Noel. It is a beautiful tale. What does it tell us? That love will find a way, no matter the obstacles. It tells us that love can transcend time and live on, long after you and I are gone. That is a message most suitable for a wedding; in fact, a most suitable message for life itself, do you not think so?"

Recalling Endo-san's words to me, I agreed wholeheartedly with him.

After the last dish of sweet bean paste in fried dough had been served, Kon and I walked out of the hall. The sun floated above, its rays breaking through gaps in the pinkish cloud bank, like fingers dipping into the sea to feel its waters.

We walked through the dusty streets of the village. There was not a single person outside; everyone was still enjoying the luncheon and the copious amount of alcohol that had to accompany all wedding banquets. The mongrel dogs that had run about us when we arrived, sniffing at our strange smells, were all asleep beneath the porches, their ears twitching at the flies that tried to enter their dreams.

At the water's edge we stopped and enjoyed the wind. We took off our shoes and the coarse sand was like grains of heated rice husks beneath our bare feet. The hall had been too warm inside and I had drunk too many glasses of brandy.

In his completely white attire, Kon had the appearance of

purity, slashed only by his red tie, which reared like an angry serpent as the wind blew. "I've been waiting for your reply," he said, a register of reprimand in his voice. "Have you made up your mind to join Force 136?"

"I'm sorry," I said. "I can't go with you. I have to stay. I have to make sure my family will be safe and only my being here can calm my fears. I'd be worried sick about them if I were stuck in the jungle." I saw the disappointment on his face and felt somehow that I had failed him.

"You went to see Tanaka-san," Kon said. "He told me about your conversation with him."

I made a halfhearted attempt at explaining my situation. He stopped me and said softly, "Don't worry too much about it. I'm sure you're right. Your family would need you here."

I nodded at him, grateful that he understood in spite of his disappointment. That was one of the wonderful things about Kon—he understood so many things without being told.

"You realize that when the Japanese enter Penang my father can't protect Mr. Hutton anymore? That the guards will have to be withdrawn?" Kon said.

"Naturally. They have their own families to protect, after all. That's why I have to stay. I'm certain Endo-san has no knowledge of the attempt on my father's life, but Saotome in Kuala Lumpur—he's been eyeing our company."

We were silent for a while. I enjoyed his presence, glad to have known him, for he was now closer to me than either of my two brothers.

"Will I see you again before you leave?" I asked. It was so peaceful to sit by the sea and I wanted to prolong our time here in this village that lay so far away from the concerns of the world.

"I do not think so," Kon said.

"It'll probably be a breach of your security but will you let me know where you'll be sent to?" I asked.

"I'll find a way," he said and the caveat that I keep his eventual location a secret did not have to be stated out loud. I held out my hand and he took it in his.

"Take care, my brother," he said.

"I will. You watch out for danger," I said, my voice strained. "I'll say some prayers for you at the temple."

He smiled. "You'd better watch out yourself, you are turning Chinese."

Thinking of the duality of life, I asked—more to myself than to anyone else: "That's not such a bad thing, is it?"

Ming had changed into a bright red *cheongsam*, and she and her husband were moving from table to table, thanking the guests for coming. He was made to drink a toast at every table and by the time they came around to ours he was quite drunk.

"This is Ah Hock," Ming said, pulling at her husband's arm, giving a wide smile to Isabel. His name meant "fortunate" and that day, with Ming by his side, I thought he was. He was a squat man with a head of short, uncontrollable spiky hair, his skin dark from his days on the fishing trawler. His long arms were bulbous with muscle and I could picture him on his boat, feet strong on deck, his arms pulling in his catch. He did not look like his father at all.

"Congratulations," my father said, shaking Ah Hock's hand.

"Thank you for your kind wishes," Ming said and then smiled at me. "Everyone here wants to know about you. They ask, 'Who is that unusual-looking boy?'"

"You may tell them who I am," I said. "Only the good things though, mind you."

"I have," she said.

"Well, it's getting late and we have to leave soon," I said. "May you have lots of children and lots of happiness." She gave another smile and moved away to the next table. I never expected to see much of her again. She would have her own life now, in the village that had adopted her.

And once again, in the car as we drove out of the village, I wished them all well in a silent prayer that included everyone I knew, even Endo-san. I prayed so strongly, so earnestly, that I thought when I opened my eyes I would see my entreaties in some physical form, standing guard over us like the gigantic shrine rising from the sea off the coast of Japan. I prayed that the gods that protected the island of Penang and watched over its people should always maintain their unflagging vigilance.

BOOK TWO

Chapter One

My father maintained an old Hutton custom of beginning every Monday with a family breakfast when all of us were required to sit down together for the first meal of the week.

When we came downstairs to the dining room on December 8, 1941, we had no inkling of the events that had unfolded while we were asleep. We sat in appalled silence at the breakfast table as my father read us the news, the tremor in his hands rustling the newspaper. At 12:15 that morning troops from the Japanese Eighteenth Division had landed at Kota Bahru, on the northeastern coast of the Malayan Peninsula, from the Gulf of Siam. Pearl Harbor was attacked an hour later. Until that morning I had never heard of the place.

The expected full-scale assault on Singapore had not materialized. Instead the Japanese had chosen to cut through hundreds of miles of thick, "impenetrable" rainforest and scale the mountain ranges that streaked down the spine of Malaya. I knew who had advised on that tactic. It was a classic *aikijutsu* move: not to meet the forces of Singapore directly but to land obliquely on the east coast, where Endo-san had gone after I had returned from visiting my grandfather in Ipoh.

All that morning the servants moved around the house quietly, their usual soft conversation as they went about their work stilled. I wondered if Endo-san had known and what his reaction would be. Isabel's face told me she was thinking of the same question, and I turned away from her.

I opened the windows in the office and stared at the street below. He had linked me to the war, to Japan's ambitions, and this realization weighed me down as though I had been burdened with another identity, taken deep down to the floor of the ocean. I structured my breathing into the pattern of *zazen* but it was useless.

Admiral Sir Tom Phillips, commander-in-chief of Britain's

Eastern Fleet in Singapore, sent two of his ships to meet the Japanese navy. The HMS *Repulse* and the HMS *Prince of Wales* were two of the best warships the British navy had. William was on the second ship and we stayed close to the radio as news of the battle came to us in spurts and through almost incomprehensible static. Both ships were sunk by Japanese planes and we were informed of it a day later. Over six hundred lives were lost and we had no way of knowing if William was safe.

I heard my father put down the telephone receiver in his office. I went over to his room. One look at his face, contorted with grief, and I knew.

He finally noticed me standing at the door. "That was the Naval Office in Singapore," he said.

"William?" I asked in a subdued voice.

"His ship was completely destroyed by Japanese planes." My father lowered his face into his palms. I hesitated, unsure of what to do. Then I went behind him and placed my hands on his shoulders. Through the open windows the cars went by on the street below. From across Weld Quay a ship's horns sounded as it began its voyage—all the usual noises that had threaded their way through our lives all these years.

I took control without further thought. Brushing aside the staff's questions I informed them that the office would be closed until the situation became clearer to us. They would still be paid their salaries, I assured them. I telephoned Edward in Kuala Lumpur, asking him to return to Penang, and then I took my father home. I caught Uncle Lim looking at me in the mirror as he drove and his daughter's words of warning came to me again— the Japanese would come and cause us suffering. I avoided his eyes and looked out the window.

"What's happened?" Isabel asked, rising from a rattan chair on the veranda. Peter MacAllister was with her, and he too stood up when he saw us.

"William's dead," I said. She listened as I told her what we knew. She did not say anything, but MacAllister sensed her anguish and reached out to hold her.

I went into the house and poured my father a generous measure of whiskey. He took it from me and finished it and then carefully placed the glass on the table. "Your brother's gone. Gone! His ship's gone down in the sea." I thought back to his dreams of being a dolphin, swimming the depths, now searching for his lost son.

Isabel leaned against MacAllister and began to cry quietly. We stood there, that afternoon, the clouds uncaring above, the flowers nodding sagely in the wind, the trees brushing the air, a lock of hair over my father's eyes. My hand moved out and gently pushed it away.

How do you prepare for a funeral when there is no body? There could only be a memorial service, and empty words spoken as sad reminders of a once-full life. That was all we were left with. My father asked me to organize it. "I just can't do it," he said. "I'm sorry to burden you with it."

"I know, Father. It's not a burden."

"I don't want a joint service with the other families," he said. We were not the only family that had suffered a loss, for William had been accompanied by many sons of Penang. A heavy mantle of despair had settled over the island and the streets of Georgetown.

The shop owners where I obtained the necessary items for the service expressed their sorrow to me. "Please tell your father we all grieve for him," more than one said, and I thanked them for their kindness.

The ministry sent William's personal possessions to us. We opened the dented box and found an envelope of the photographs I had taken and sent to him. My father shuffled them, removed one and showed it to us. It was the photograph taken on the day he left Istana for Singapore. We were still smiling then, when Uncle Lim had taken it.

Isabel cried throughout the service at St. George's Church, and I watched MacAllister comfort her. Edward and I flanked our expressionless father. In spite of my decision to stop seeing Endo-san, deep inside I had hoped for his presence. *But you're the enemy now*, I said to him in my mind. *How right you were. The cycle of pain and sorrow has begun.*

The service was short, as we had requested. Through the

crowded pews behind me I saw Endo-san at the back. Our eyes met. I shook my head and closed mine. They were so tired. So tired. I realized I had not slept much since the day we were told the news. I thought of William's final words to me on the day he left his home and of our unfulfilled plans for a trip. The pain of losing him left me feeling weak, ready to fall. I sent my mind out to the faraway place Endo-san had revealed to me but it was done with a sustained effort, as it should never be, and the struggle was exhausting. Somehow I held on and turned the flooding tide of grief. I gripped the pew in front of me and forced myself to take on the unyielding countenances of my father and my remaining brother. I would not be the one who let them down, the one who lost the face held by my family for generations. The load could not be lightened, the burden never shared.

We left the church and returned home. My father wanted the memorial stone to be erected in the eastern corner of Istana, instead of in the church cemetery where previous generations of my family had been buried. I had obtained a wooden box and now asked Isabel, Edward and our father to put something of William's inside it.

A hole had been dug where the stone would be erected. Before I closed the box I put William's Leica camera into it. And then the box, like a baby being put back in the cradle, was gently lowered into the gaping ground, and covered with earth. I said a silent farewell to my brother.

My grandfather approached his son-in-law. The two men faced each other. "Now, finally, I know how you felt when she died," my father said.

"It is not something a father should ever have to go through," the older man answered. He looked at me with concern and I nodded slightly to show him I was holding up. He moved away from my father and said to me, "I have to return to my old house in Ipoh to make preparations, and to ensure that the servants have a safe place to hide."

"How long will you be gone?" I asked.

"I do not know."

"It won't be easy for you to come back here, when the fighting starts," I said. I wanted him close to me here. "You really shouldn't go."

He shook his head. "You know where to find me, if I am not at my house in Ipoh. I will be safe."

I was desperately searching for more reasons for him to remain in Penang but he held up his hand and stopped me. "You must take care of your aunt and your family." He opened his arms to me and I embraced him, trying to extinguish the feeling that I would never see him again.

Above us we heard planes patrolling the skies. Fear had gripped the inhabitants of Penang and an exodus had begun. People were fleeing for the safety and impregnability of Singapore, perhaps sailing even as far as India. But, as I had pointed out to Tanaka, how does one outrun a world war?

After a listless dinner later that evening, my father said, "You should all leave for Singapore. It'll be safer there."

"We have no intention of leaving you behind," Isabel said. Edward and I agreed.

"We should all go," I said.

But my father stubbornly refused. "Someone has to run the company," he said, leaving no room for argument. "This is our home and it's been our home all our lives. The Malays aren't leaving, the Chinese and the Indians aren't running away. I won't desert them. If I did, I would never be able to live here again."

"But we've heard what the Japanese are capable of. The women aren't safe," Edward said, looking at Isabel.

"I'm not leaving, Edward," she said.

"We have to make sure the company's safe, that we're safe," my father said. He turned to me. "Can you find a way to ensure our safety without compromising our integrity? Can you talk to Mr. Endo?"

I wanted to tell him that this was going to be war, so why still be concerned with integrity? Instead I shook my head. "To guarantee our safety we'll have no alternative but to work with the Japanese. They want our company. They want all of Malaya."

"That's quite unacceptable," Edward said immediately, scowling at me. "You are not to make overtures to them."

"They'll take it anyway, eventually, when the troops march into Georgetown," I said.

"Our lads'll turn them around," my father said but he was not as certain now, his emotional balance tilted. I saw my opportunity and moved in firmly, taking control, bringing his balance to mine. "We should take some measures anyway. Just in case."

He leaned back in his chair, and said finally, "Edward, tomorrow, start phoning our plantations and our mines. Tell the managers to destroy all our stocks and equipment. And you," he said to Isabel, "get your hair cut short. You can wear some of William's clothes. But I want you up on Penang Hill until we are certain that it's safe here. If you say even one word, I'll send you to Singapore," he added as Isabel opened her mouth to object.

A sense of relief returned to me. After the last few days of appearing lost, our father was now back on his feet.

I went down to the beach later. It was a timeless moment of the day, the sand still wet and silky from a downpour that had occurred earlier. Dark clouds were racing away inland, leaving the seaward sky clear. The moon was already out, a pale companion to the sun that was setting reluctantly.

Birds flew low along the surface, while some pecked on the beach for the almost invisible baby ghost crabs. I could not see them as they scuttled across the beach, only the tracks they left behind them, marking the sand like writing etched by a ghostly hand.

It was quite chilly, the wind carrying a trace of the rain that now fell almost as unseen as the baby crabs, as though the clouds had been scraped through a fine grater. A solitary figure stood staring out to sea as waves unrolled themselves around his feet like small bundles of silk. I walked up to him, feeling the coldness of the water.

"The sky is on fire," he said.

I looked. It was. The sun lit the sky on the horizon with streaks of red and ocher. Every now and then there appeared bright, silent sparks in the sky.

"What are those?" I asked.

"An air battle. Japanese and British warplanes. A war in Heaven."

I watched without feeling, unable to fathom the aerial struggle. All so senseless it seemed, so distant. Strange that it could have anything to do with this world.

He turned around. Backlit by the sun, his face was shadowed. I had not spoken to him since the night I saw him on his island, signaling out to the darkened ocean.

"Thank you for coming to my brother's memorial service," I said.

He reached out and touched my cheek softly. "Never say things you do not mean. We must always be honest with ourselves. Perhaps you even feel you want to hurt me." He sighed. "I do not blame you."

"But I do blame you. You lied to me. You used me, used my knowledge of the island. You asked me to take you around so you could take photographs of it. And your trip to Kota Bahru last year. Now I know." I moved away from his hand. "And all the other things—all false, aren't they?"

He looked distressed. He lifted his hands, almost as if he thought he could heal me, but when I took a step away they fell back to hang limply by his sides.

"I can't trust you anymore, Endo-san."

"Remember my words to you at the party for William," he began, but stopped, unable to continue.

I thought back to what he had said at the party: that even though we would soon be on opposite sides, I should never forget what he felt for me. I found that to be bare of comfort now.

"Why haven't I been able to do what is right?" I asked, puzzled.

"Oh you will, my poor boy. You will," he said.

And out to sea the sparks grew brighter and more frequent, lighting up the darkening skies like a shower of falling stars.

Chapter Two

As I walked up the road to Towkay Yeap's home, a squadron of planes flew over me and left behind a trail of white petals that floated down gently. Some of these petals fell onto the tops of the trees, where they flapped, puzzling the birds. The rest covered the road and the lawns and I stooped to pick one up.

It was a piece of paper, written in English, Chinese, Malay, and Tamil. It urged us to surrender peacefully, to welcome the Imperial Japanese Army. No one would be harmed if we did so. I folded it neatly and placed it in my pocket.

These papers had been falling from the planes for the past week now, all over the island, as more and more of Malaya surrendered to the Japanese army. The harbor was crowded with passengers boarding ships that would take them to Singapore, impelled by an unspoken but almost palpable sense of hysteria.

I rang the doorbell, but no one came. I pushed the doors open and walked around the house, to where Kon's father was standing, staring at his prizewinning white orchids, lost in thought. He saw me and his eyes cleared.

"You must be looking for my son," he said.

"I was hoping he had told you where he'd be."

He shook his head. "He has left. I have not heard from him and I doubt if I will. Please sit down."

I sat on the edge of a wooden flower box. "He told me he would let me know," I said and the older man nodded.

"Did you try to stop him from joining?" I asked.

"No. Could I? You of all people should know that we all have our own roads to take."

"You're not leaving for somewhere safe?"

He shook his head. "I too have my own path to follow here." He looked, for a moment, much older than his fifty years. "And if I leave, who will be waiting for my son when he returns?"

"Kon looks very much like you," I said, trying to think of something to fill the silence. We had never had much to talk about but now he looked pleased at my comparison. I suppose that was how one made fathers happy. We watched as the planes made another sweep of the skies.

"He is my only son," he said. "I'm sorry about William," he continued. "The gods only know what would happen to me if I lost my boy. I think I would not be able to go on."

"I don't know if all of us can survive this war," I said.

He gave an almost evil smile and raised his eyebrows. "I have no doubts at all that if anyone survives, it will be you," he said. "And I do not mean that based solely on the influence of your teacher. No, I have met Mr. Endo, and it is obvious that he does not choose weaklings to tutor. You are going to surprise all of us, I think."

I got up from the flower box, not liking the way the conversation was heading. His words had bones in them, like the flesh of fish one bites into innocently. "I have to go now. Please let me know when you find out where your son is."

We continued to receive news of massacres perpetrated by the Japanese troops advancing from the north and, although my father kept them to himself, I could see the fears on his face. He had taken out his rifle from the gun cupboard in his study, keeping it fully loaded and within easy reach. His collection of *keris* had also been removed from the library. Our tin mines and plantations in northern Malaya had all been taken over by the Japanese, and it came to me that he would never hand over the family company to them. I began to fear for his safety and the fear grew when, coming home in a humid dusk, we saw a staff car parked in the drive. A white flag with a red circle hung limply above its bonnet.

"Those bastards," my father said, getting out before Uncle Lim had a chance to fully stop our car. I ran after him as he went into the house. We heard voices as soon as we entered the hall and I stopped when I saw Goro, the official from the Japanese consulate, and someone else coming down the stairs. They stopped halfway down when they saw us.

"Get out of my house," my father said.

A Japanese man stood behind Goro and I felt an inexplicable

fear. He had small unblinking eyes and a short moustache and hair cut very short. What terrified me more was not the fact that he had the appearance of a soldier, but that he was not in uniform. I knew instantly that I was facing a man from the Kempeitai, the Japanese secret police that had tortured refugees fleeing from the north of Malaya. I placed my hand on my father to restrain him.

"It will not be yours for much longer," Goro said. "Fujihara-san has taken a strong liking to it."

The man spoke to Goro in Japanese. I understood him clearly, but Goro interpreted. "We will get your company as well, once you all run away."

"We'll never run," my father said.

"What you do is of no concern to us. We will send you all to the camps, or we will kill you." He pointed to me. "Even your half-breed son."

I had to find a way to calm them down. I bowed and began to address them in placatory tones when Isabel came into the hall, pointing our father's rifle at Goro. "My father has asked you to leave. I won't ask again."

"Isabel," I said. "Put it down."

Goro and the man from the Kempeitai did not move fast enough for Isabel's liking. She fired a shot into the wall behind them, dusting them with wood chips and plaster. Goro shielded the other man as they walked down the stairs, their eyes never moving from Isabel's face until they had gone out of the front door. I knew that their sense of honor would demand that they find a way to get back at her.

I turned back to Isabel, who was still holding the rifle in a firing stance. "I could have settled that without antagonizing them," I said.

"You're always trying to defend them," she said, matching my anger.

"I wasn't doing anything of the sort. I was trying to keep you safe," I lashed back at her. "Now you've placed us all in danger."

"Who's been fraternizing with the Japs? You should've heard yourself, in your weak and submissive voice! Groveling to them without shame!"

"That's enough!" my father cut in. "Put that thing away! What are you still doing here? You're supposed to be hiding up on The Hill."

"I stayed to help the servants pack. I've decided to leave with them," she replied.

More than ever now I realized we had to leave Penang, leave Malaya. We had been marked by the Japanese and they would come after us if we stayed.

"We're not safe anymore," I said. "We have to leave for Singapore immediately."

My father remained unyielding. "We won't leave. If you want to you can go ahead," he said flatly. "If you have any understanding of what it means to be part of this family—which you never *did* have—then you'll stand by us!" He stopped and he looked stricken. "I'm sorry. It wasn't supposed to come out like that. I'm sorry."

The longest time seemed to pass before I could speak again. "I'm staying. This is my home too, my only home. I'm staying. But I'll do it on my terms," I said and walked slowly away from them, the choice I had to make now clear to me. In the end it was all so simple and obvious, really.

I cycled to the Japanese consulate. There was a lot of traffic on the roads and many of the cars carried large leather trunks on their roofs, scattering the Japanese propaganda pamphlets on the road as they drove by. An image came to me of a Chinese funeral I had attended once when one of our staff had died. The monk leading the ceremony had scattered sheaves of paper money as he walked and the pieces of paper had floated in the hot afternoon, writhing and twisting like the lost souls they were meant to appease, soundlessly cradling down to earth. Now, as the cars passed, as the words of the Japanese flew up and then swung down again in a pendulous motion, that memory came back to me and I was fearful. I was witnessing the funerary rites of my country, of my home.

I informed the sentry at the entrance of the consulate that I wished to see Endo-san. He opened the gates and I pushed my bicycle through, past the bamboo groves and little pavilions. The rushing sounds of the traffic were absent, denied entry into this place. The Japanese government had purchased the property just before the Great War, when they had been on friendlier terms with Britain. It was not a well-known fact that during the Great War the British and the Japanese had entered into a treaty allowing the Japanese navy to patrol the waters of Malaya, a treaty that seemed to have backfired on Britain, for the Japanese navy had become fully familiar with the coastline.

Considerable effort and expense had been invested to create a dreamlike ideal of Japan in the consulate gardens. I had often cycled past without paying any attention to it, but now its beauty, when so much of the world was being destroyed, made me stop and appreciate it.

A willow drooped over a pond, its surface rippling with the kisses of sparkling carp. A figure crouched at the edge of the pond, feeding them. I leaned my bicycle against a tree and walked down the grassy slope toward him. He smiled when he saw me, scattering the last of the breadcrumbs into the pond, brushing his hands against his trousers.

"What mischief have you been up to now?" he asked.

He used the exact words my father had often spoken to me and William and I had to shake off the sense that every step of my life had been charted long before I was born. It was the war, I thought. It had fractured and dislocated everything I had known.

"I need to see you and Hiroshi-san," I said. Endo-san nodded, and I followed him into the consulate. It was, in comparison with the garden, busy and energetic. Army officers, all in their teal green uniforms, carried documents and walked with brisk purpose. I was led into Hiroshi's office. He looked up and saw Endo-san behind me and I caught a hurriedly hidden look of triumph in his eyes.

"I wish to offer my services to your government," I said. "I believe the ambassador in Kuala Lumpur, Saotome-san, would approve it."

I had rehearsed the words all the way from home, muttering them as I cycled, but still it felt difficult to utter them now. They came out from within me, unwilling to take form in the air, only wishing to melt into my breath. I was choosing a path that had the strongest chance of saving all of us, all of my family, and I would take it. There was a war on and surely no one could blame me—or would even remember, when it was all over.

"We had considered asking you to assist us in the daily affairs of running this island," Hiroshi said, indicating for me to sit down. I remained standing. "You have the language skills and the understanding of our culture to help implement our policies."

"He can assist me," Endo-san said.

"I have one request: let my father continue to run his company after you've taken over Malaya."

"All businesses will be brought under the authority of the Japanese government. But I suppose Mr. Hutton's expertise and experience will be useful," Hiroshi said. "We shall see what sort of role he can still play within your family's company."

He came around his desk and put his hand on my shoulder. "Since you are going to be a member of the consulate, the first thing you should do is to show your respect." He turned me around to the portrait of the emperor that hung on the wall. I knew what was required and so I bowed low and respectfully to it.

Chapter Three

My father had told me to make sure that Isabel changed her appearance as much as possible before traveling up to Penang Hill. I stood over her as one of the maids, who earned a little extra money as hairdresser to the other servants, cut her hair in the courtyard outside the kitchen.

"This is undignified," Isabel complained as she sat on a high stool, a sheet from the *Straits Times* draped around her shoulders.

"Father's orders," I said.

She did not respond. The incident with the two Japanese who had threatened to requisition our home had strained the relationship between us. I still felt the sharpness of her words, how unjustified they were, and found it difficult to forgive her.

"It's for your own good. The more you look like a man, the safer you'll be," I said. "I've laid out William's clothes in your room. You can put them on when you're done."

I left her and went inside the house.

With her shortened hair and wearing his clothes, Isabel could have been William, and for a moment we felt his absence sharply. My father said, "Good Lord!" Even Edward was quiet. Isabel laughed weakly to shake us out of our despondency. Peter MacAllister embraced her and I turned away, feeling an emptiness inside. I was feeling anxious about breaking the news of my association with the Japanese government to my father.

"There're more refugees fleeing the Jap army," MacAllister said. He had been spending more time at Istana, talking to my father, who was slowly coming to accept his presence in our lives. "I met some of them on the quay today. Most had escaped with only a suitcase."

"We can put some of them up here," my father offered.

MacAllister shook his head. "They don't want to be in Penang.

They want to get as far away as possible. In fact, they urged us to leave as well."

We had been receiving almost continuous reports of Japanese victories. The entire east coast had been taken, as had the northern states of Perlis and Kelantan near the border with Thailand. Years from now historians would reveal how unprepared the British government had been, how carelessly it had disregarded Japan's plans for invasion. But for now there was only a flood of fleeing refugees, mostly Europeans who had made their homes in Malaya.

"I'm not leaving, Peter. I've told you that," my father said. He looked at me. "How could I face the people who work for us if we packed up and ran and left them to the Japs?"

I had noticed a change in the way Endo-san's people were now referred to. No longer were they the more polite "Japanese," but "the Japs" or, as was more common now, "the *bloody* Japs."

"Apparently the bloody Japs are traveling all over the country on bicycles," MacAllister told us. I kept silent, recalling a conversation with Endo-san on the train from Kuala Lumpur as the carriage moved through the damp, sparkling jungles.

"Nothing can penetrate this," he had said as the massive columns of trees sped by, wrapped in thick ferns and high vegetation. Many of the fig trees were buttressed at their bases with triangular wedges of roots that grew as thick and high as walls.

"That's not true," I had said. "Many of the locals here either walk or use a bicycle. There are jungle tracks, even though you can't see them. William once told me you can get good maps of them from the Forestry Department."

"Can one obtain those maps easily?"

"I suppose so. I'll ask," I said and a week after I returned from Ipoh I managed to provide Endo-san with the maps.

MacAllister gave Isabel a hug. "I can't see you off tomorrow, darling. Have to go back to K.L. and see to my firm."

"Don't worry," I said. "I'll be with her."

"You must look after your sister," he said. "Can you picture it, a bunch of slit-eyed monkeys on bicycles taking over our country?"

"Well, they're succeeding, aren't they?" my father said.

*

My father had insisted that the female staff at home and at the office hide out at our house on Penang Hill with Isabel. Most, though grateful for the offer, preferred to stay with their families but some had decided to come with us.

"What about Ming?" I asked Uncle Lim as he drove us to the funicular station at the foot of The Hill. My father followed behind us in the Daimler with the maids who had chosen to go up The Hill.

"She will be protected in the village. It is too far out of town for the Japanese to pay attention to it anyway."

"And you?"

"I'll stay with Mr. Hutton of course," he said. His loyalty to Noel was beyond question, but I suspected his real reason for remaining was his obligation to my grandfather, the nature of which he refused ever to tell me despite my most inquisitive efforts.

At the funicular station we joined a long line of people carrying bags and food. It appeared that we were not the only ones who had thought of sending the women up.

"At least this lot haven't run away," Isabel said.

I said nothing, although I felt the pain of the awkwardness that had driven us apart. I realized she was attempting a reconciliation but I felt constrained by the residue of my stubborn anger.

The crowd was made up of English, Chinese, and Malay women. The English women had brought their dogs with them and these barked and pulled at their leashes, adding to the noise of farewells and the tears of the children. My father left us to speak to them.

"How horrible," Isabel said as we watched him reassure the women. "Remind me never to turn into a doting old woman more concerned about her dogs than about people."

"Well, you English all turn out the same eventually anyway," I said without thinking. She punched my arm lightly, as she often did when she feigned disgust at my words and, just like that, I felt a lightening of the resentment against her.

"I'm sorry about the other day," she said, looping her arm to mine and pulling me into an embrace. "You were quite right: we should've talked them into leaving the house."

I waved her apologies away, relieved that the coolness that had developed between us since that day now appeared to be fading. "We were all in a rather emotional state."

"Not you," she said. "I envy you. I don't have the strong control over my emotions that you have. William always said that you were the most detached, the most unflappable of all of us. The most English, as it were."

I was struck silent by what she had said. Was that how I appeared to my family—cold and unemotional, when I had only been trying to hide my uncertainties about my place in the scheme of things? I felt on the point of incredulous, even bitter, laughter.

My father came back to us and embraced Isabel as the line started to move. "Be careful," he said. "Once things have settled down, I think you should marry Peter."

Isabel held him harder. "Thank you, Father."

He pulled away and spoke to the women from our home. "I hope you'll be safe from harm. I'll pray for your safety. God be with you all."

They thanked him and a few wiped away their tears. He turned to me. "Take care of them. I'll send a car to meet you here tomorrow morning." He became quiet. "What I said, the other day . . . when those Japs came into the house . . ." he began.

I stopped him. "You don't have to say anything more."

He looked at me gratefully and then embraced me with an intensity I was surprised to find that I had yearned for from him all my life. "You're a good boy," he said and kissed me quickly on my cheek.

He watched us until we were all packed into the wooden funicular. The doors could not slide shut and one of the women—I recognized her as Mrs. Reilly, a jeweler's wife—had to get off and wait for the next one. The funicular shuddered, slid back down the slope, and then, as the tram at the top of the hill started to move down, the pulleys began spinning and slowly pulled us up. We hung onto the railings; all the seats had been taken by plump middle-aged women who were fanning themselves furiously, like birds flapping their wings in an overcrowded cage. We rattled over the tracks and I felt the heat surrender slowly to the cooler air as we were hauled up by the downward momentum of the descending tram.

At the summit, as we were coming out from the station, a formation of fighter planes flew past and dropped down onto Georgetown. I counted more than fifty of them. The sun caught the crimson circles on their bodies and wings and made them look like open wounds. Their silver, piscine bodies darkened into specks as they lost altitude. A few minutes later we saw smoke puff up from the harbor.

"They're bombing the town," Isabel said. "God damn them!"

The clouds of smoke grew into plumes, black and thick. The planes flew over the town as more bombs were dropped. Out in the harbor the small naval fleet seemed to spin round and round in confused circles, like dizzy ducks in a pond. Some of the ships caught fire, exploded, and began to sink. The women around us became distraught and one of them started to scream, saying she had to go home. "They'll come for us, they'll come for us," she moaned.

"She's right. What if they start bombing The Hill?" Isabel asked.

"They won't," I said, remembering the mock-Tudor house Endo-san had been interested in, the house from which one could see all the oceans that surrounded us, especially when equipped with a powerful set of telescopes.

Isabel heard the certainty in my voice and decided she did not want to argue with me. We made our way to Istana Kechil. After I helped unpack the supplies of food I told her, "I'm going for a walk."

It seemed such a long time since I had been up here with Endo-san, proudly showing him the beauty of The Hill. Now that his actions were clear to me, I felt a hollow sense of loss. Strange that I could feel no trace of anger toward him, only despair. It felt almost as though I had been expecting it. He had betrayed my innocence, but at the same time had replaced it with knowledge and strength and love. I wondered if there was some deficiency in my own being that I could accept his treachery with such calm or whether my training in *zazen* had been more effective than I had thought, rendering me unflappable as Isabel had pointed out.

I went off the road at the junction leading to the mock-Tudor house and made my way carefully down a grassy slope. Even here, I could still see smoke from the harbor and parts of the town and I tried not to worry about my father, hoping he had gone straight home as he had promised. I crawled and half crouched as I came to the back entrance. The gate was rusty and vines had woven their way into the metal fence. I shook it, saw that it would hold, and climbed over.

The house appeared empty but I waited, hidden behind a rose bush, straining to hear the running pads of dogs. After a minute I ran to the wall of the house and leaned against it. I peered into the darkened windows but could not see within. I continued to edge along the wall until I came to the corner, and there I stopped. There was a large metal structure, almost like a tiny crane, on the lawn. A square meshed antenna spun endlessly on it, like an untiring flycatcher. I knew, however, that this thing was not to catch insects and pests but radio signals. Beside the antenna was a pole, from which a flag fluttered, like a fish's tail. The whiteness of the flag only made the red circle on it brighter, more menacing.

The doors to the balcony diagonally above me opened and I heard footsteps, the click of a lighter and then voices. The faint smell of tobacco drifted down to me. From my hiding place I could just see two men; they appeared to be civilians.

"Has the fleet received the message?"

"*Hai*, Colonel Kitayama," a younger man's voice replied.

"The bombing was a success?"

"*Hai*, Colonel Kitayama."

"Inform General Yamashita."

I decided I had heard enough and quietly went out the way I had entered.

I left early before dawn after saying good-bye to Isabel. On the previous evening she and I had sat in the candlelight and talked through the night, something we had never done before.

"What does it feel like to be in love?" I asked her. "You've been in love so many times now, first with that boy from the Straits Trading Company, then with that American writer, and then with that farmer from Australia . . ."

"The list is endless, isn't it?" she gave a wry smile. "What I once felt for them—it's a far cry from what I feel for Peter now," she said. "Peter has a lot of faults—we all do—but love makes you overlook them, and try to see what is good. I couldn't have done that before—at the first sign of weakness I dropped the men

I thought I loved. It's different now. By the way, I should apologize for his remark about slit-eyed monkeys."

I waved it away and poured her another glass of wine. Being Isabel she had ensured there was a generous supply of the good things in life, even while hiding from the Japanese.

"What do you see in someone who is so much older than you?" I asked.

She took some time to craft her reply. I could see the various forms she wanted it to take, before she discarded them and created a new one. "I'm attracted by his wisdom, his sense of already knowing who he is and what he wants from life. I don't want his money, though he's got plenty of that."

"*Love's not love / When it is mingled with regards that stand, / Aloof from th' entire point,*" I said, quoting one of our father's favorite lines.

"At least one of us managed to absorb something during those long evenings when he read *King Lear* to us," she said with a sideways glance.

I made the choice then to tell her about my decision to work for the Japanese, certain she would understand. But she was first aghast—and then furious. "How could you? Knowing what kind of savages they are?"

"I think I can safeguard our family's interests."

She sat quietly for a while and I was afraid that the state of tension which we had resolved at the funicular station had arisen between us again. Then she sighed. "You're a fool, little brother," she said—not unkindly—and I saw pity in her eyes. "I would die before I'd even consider working for them."

We parted the blackout curtains and went out into the garden, our bare feet crushing beads of dew on the lawn, sending up the tangy scent of the night, as though we had walked across a carpet of spices. For one moment I felt as if the war had not begun and that we were here on holiday again.

The lights of the city down below had been extinguished and the only illumination came from the fires which were still ravening. Now and then, as they found a new source of energy to feed on, there would be a surge of flame and the light would reach higher into the sky, tainting it crimson, burning out the clusters of stars.

"I hope they're safe at home," Isabel said. I pulled her shawl around her shoulders. She looked up into my eyes and leaned against me.

"They'll be safe," I said and I repeated the words, as though to reassure myself. "They'll be safe."

My father and I waited a few days before trying to get to the office for we had been warned not to do so until the situation had stabilized. The policemen, dockworkers, and public servants had already disappeared and looting was rife.

It was one thing to see the smoke from The Hill and another to actually see the damage inflicted on the town. The roads into Georgetown had been badly damaged. Rows of shophouses had gone up in flames and fires still burned, for the fire station had been bombed. Bodies were scattered in the streets, many of them people who had come out to see what the noises from the sky were, only to be torn to pieces by machine-gun strafing. Rats ran unhindered, without their usual fear. There was a terrible smell that clung to the air, mixed with the smoke of burning timber and cured rubber that lay thick along the harbor. I was hardly able to endure the stench.

Hutton & Sons' building had not been damaged, although Guthrie's, the Scottish rubber company behind us, had had their roof blown off.

We unlocked the doors and began packing our documents into boxes, destroying any that could assist the Japanese.

"What's wrong?" my father asked when he sensed my hesitation.

I shook my head. "Nothing," I replied, hoping he would not see through my lie. In truth I was feeling as though I had been forced to swallow a cocktail of conflicting emotions. I was officially Endo-san's assistant and, as we tore up reports and files and burned them, I felt I was betraying the Japanese. But by choosing to work for the Japanese, I was also betraying the people of my island. Once again I was caught between two opposing sides, with nowhere to turn. When would I find a sense of my self, integrated, whole, without this constant pulling from all sides, each wanting my complete devotion and loyalty?

"Are you all right?" my father asked again.

"Just thinking of lost days," I said, throwing a sheaf of burning paper into the flames before my hand was burned.

"Things will never go back to being the way they were," he said. "We had some wonderful times, didn't we?"

"We had the best of times," I replied, unknowingly echoing the similar, regretful words many of the fleeing Europeans would voice. "Where's Edward?"

"He went with Peter to K.L. They're destroying all their files as well."

I went to the window. The destruction of Georgetown was heartbreaking. I watched as desperate people headed for the harbor, still trying to find a berth on an evacuating ship.

My father looked at his watch. "Come on, let's go to the quay," he said.

"Whatever for?"

"I want to show you something I hope you'll never see again," he said.

We locked the doors of the office and walked to Weld Quay. I held my head high, my eyes staring ahead, forcing myself to ignore the bodies that lay all around us, my breathing shallow. We pushed through the crowd of locals and found the gates to the quay locked and guarded.

"Noel Hutton and his son," he said to the young British soldier, handing him a piece of paper.

The soldier checked his clipboard and opened the gates. "Where's your luggage, sir?"

"We won't be needing any," my father said.

We entered Swettenham Pier. The harbor had been systematically destroyed by our fleeing soldiers and there were massive piles of rubble everywhere. We could see the remnants of the entire naval fleet of Penang: the tip of a sunken ship's hull, the charred skeletal frames of those vessels that had not gone to the bottom of the sea—many were still burning, sending clouds of smoke to us whenever the wind shifted. There were also bodies and pieces of wreckage floating on the surface of the sea.

A large crowd was heading toward the pier where an old steamer was tied up. There was desperation in the air, voiced by babies' howls and women sobbing. Many of the people carried only a single case, looking over their shoulders all the time. I saw their eyes and they could not meet mine. There seemed to be an equal number of civilians and military personnel. Everyone here was European and I felt out of place.

An elderly couple with four bullmastiffs was stopped by a guard who looked no older than William.

"I'm terribly sorry, sir, but you're not allowed to bring them aboard," he said.

The woman turned to her husband. "Darling, we can't leave them here. We can't leave them to the bloody Japs."

"Look here, can't you just let us board? These dogs are well-trained, they won't be a nuisance," the man said.

The guard shook his head and remained firm, despite threats and pleading from the couple. Finally the man whispered to the woman who clutched his arm but nodded. They spoke to their dogs softly, stroking and nuzzling them. Then the man kissed his wife and watched as she walked up the gangplank. When she was gone from view, he reached into his pocket and took out a revolver. He led the dogs through the masses of people to the far end of the pier. He was alone when he returned to the gangplank a few minutes later, his cheeks damp with tears.

"Why did the man at the gate ask you for our luggage?" I asked my father.

"I was given an order by the military to pack up our belongings and travel passes to board one of the last ships to Singapore," he said. "We were ordered not to tell any of our local staff or friends. The British are leaving the Malayans to the Japs. We are all running away. Just like that. Even Mr. Scott has left. And Henry Cross has sent his sons to Australia." He stood on the edge of the pier, the hull of the Straits Steamship Company's SS *Pangkor* looming over us like a wave about to break. "I can't believe it. Is this how it will end?"

"Are we going too?" I asked, wondering if he had finally seen my side of things.

He shook his head. "No. Not like this. Never like this. We'll stay. We'll keep the flag flying. We'll keep our family name untainted, and we will not lose face."

I wondered if a lifetime spent in Penang had made him think like an Oriental.

"This is the last ship. After she leaves, we'll be on our own," he said.

The crowd pushed and jostled us as they surged toward the gangplank. I felt melancholic as I watched them board. Very soon there was no one left, no one, except the two of us.

He held my arm as the gangplank was raised. I resisted a sudden urge to run to it and shout to the sailors to let me board, let me escape the mess my life had turned into. The steamer sounded its whistle and a low throbbing vibrated the platform as it pulled out. People lined the deck, looking down on us. There were no colorful streamers, no balloons, no laughter. A young boy held his mother's hand and raised his arm and waved a farewell. I took a step away from my father, to the very edge of the pier and returned his wave. It was a farewell not only to a place but to a way of life, a time of life, and I thought the little boy knew even then that the days he had grown up in, the days he had played in, lived in, would never again return.

Although my father had refused secret passage to Singapore, many of the Europeans had accepted it. Overnight the large British civil and military population disappeared, leaving their servants and friends feeling betrayed. The sense of abandonment would never heal and the British lost an incalculable amount of face when they left.

The island became ghostly. Many of the locals headed for the jungles and remote villages in the hills, hoping to escape the Japanese soldiers. Those who remained in town walked about in confusion.

The bombs whistled down onto the streets again in the days that followed, blowing up buildings and killing hundreds of people. I was in the office, attempting to destroy more documents, when I heard and felt the explosions. They rocked through the building even though they seemed a mile away. Going to the window, which was opened to catch the breeze despite the smell from the roads, I saw a bank of smoke rising above the British army barracks. Overhead, squadrons of planes circled like birds of prey. People began screaming in the streets. More explosions followed, rattling the windowpanes, sending jagged fractures through them like forks of frozen lightning. For the first time since the war began a sense of real fear overcame me. Soon the raw, pungent smell of smoke drifted to my nostrils and I shut the window, unable to breathe or think.

The phone rang, startling me. It was such an incongruous sound, the ringing. The town was being destroyed and here was my phone pealing away. I stared at it dumbly. Finally I picked it up.

It was Endo-san. "What are you doing in the office?"

"Just tidying up," I answered weakly.

"Go home. The town is no longer safe. The troops will be coming in soon. Leave now." He hung up.

The troops were coming in. I had been expecting this but still it seemed not possible. We had an army, well equipped and well trained. Surely they were capable of putting up a fight?

Another explosion shook me. This time it was closer. And then another. I had to go home. God only knew if they were bombing Batu Ferringhi. I ran out into the street, and almost decided to return to the office and hide.

The road was pocked with craters. Some cars had gone front first into them, their rears sticking up like the sterns of listing ships I had seen at the harbor. Blood was curdling on the tarmac, thick as engine oil. Windows all around had shattered and shards of glass were sprinkled on the torn bodies like crystallized rain.

There was a sound of rushing wind, a flash of singeing light and a section of the building of Empire Trading was ripped away. I was thrown to the ground, where I did an *ukemi* fall and came up on my feet, the explosion disorienting me, my ears singing like a choir conducted by a madman.

I ran to the shed behind the building where the Punjabi guard usually kept his bicycle. I hoped he had left it there when he had evacuated to the hills. To my relief I found it leaning against the wall. All of his clothes were gone and only his *charpoy*, the canvas folding bed he slept on, had been left behind.

I got onto the bicycle and pedaled home through roads crowded with trishaws and carts as people fled the town. Everyone had the same idea, to get out and hide in the hills or the distant villages. The sun fell like a whip on my shoulders and my shirt began to stick to my skin. I heard a new concatenation of explosions behind me, rippling the ground and the innermost warrens of our hearts.

I did not see a single army official along the way and I wondered where they had gone, whether they had already deserted us. I picked up a straw hat dropped by a woman, glad to have some protection from the noonday sun, my heart aching as I saw the faces of terror around me.

On the Esplanade I stopped, as did many of us. Out on the channel two Brewster Buffalo airplanes—from the airfield in Butterworth, I guessed—were putting up a fight against the Japanese planes, but they were heavily outnumbered. Tracer spat like flashes of light as the Japanese planes pursued the Buffaloes. One of the Buffaloes burst into flames. As it fell the fire became greedy and, like a flaming mouth, swallowed it from tip to tail. It sank into the sea and we could hear the loud splash and the serpentine hissing as the flames were swallowed in turn.

The remaining Buffalo banked and flew away and I let out a moan along with the hundreds who had been cheering them silently in our hearts. Years afterward I learned that they were all that was left of our air defense: two aged Buffaloes against the Japanese air force.

It was only days later that I discovered the British army had already left, had deserted us when it appeared to them that the string of Japanese victories in the northern states would extend all the way south to Johor. They had left behind a mere handful of junior officers; the rest had sailed to Singapore. That was where the final stand would be made. Not here, not in Penang. No stand would be made here at all.

My father was pacing the veranda when I arrived at Istana. "Thank God you're all right," he said. "I tried to telephone you but the line was dead."

"The streets of the town are no longer safe." I described to him the aerial battle I had seen and he shook his head in despair.

"Isabel managed to ring me," he said. "The Hill Station's been bombed."

"That doesn't make sense. The Japanese have a radio station up there."

"How did you know they have a radio station on The Hill?" he asked, his voice sharp.

"I saw it," I said.

"Then they must have been aiming for Bel Retiro," he said, referring to the resident councillor's official residence on The Hill.

"Have the rest of the servants gone home?" I asked.

"No," he said.

"I think they'd be safer here, for now. They can join their families once the air raids have stopped," I said.

He agreed, but when he asked only a handful elected to stay. A few, whom I had known since I was a child, now looked at me with suspicion when I wished them well. My father noticed and said to me when they were gone, "They think you've been helping the Japanese."

"Do you think so too?" I asked.

He kept silent for a while. Then he said, "Yes. Maybe Mr. Endo wanted some information from someone who was familiar with Penang and Malaya. And you provided it."

I dropped into a chair and placed my hands over my face. I supposed this was a good time to let him know. "I'll be working for the Japanese government the day they take over," I said, the words tumbling out despite my resolve to speak slowly, calmly.

My father dipped his head and closed his eyes. His shoulders seemed to collapse in defeat, his disappointment in me twisting like a *keris* in my heart, severing all my breath and flow of blood. He had remained strong all this time and now I saw I had managed what the Japanese had failed to do—I had punctured his spirit, opening a tear that would make him vulnerable.

"Then that is what Mr. Endo has taught you to be. That is what he made of you. So you have betrayed all of us, all the people of Penang," he said. And then he left me and I sat there alone to consider what I had done.

Chapter Four

The Japanese troops met with no resistance when they entered the streets of Georgetown. The British soldiers had already evacuated and in their haste had left the airfields and oil supplies intact, like thoughtful gifts for the new owner of a home.

We had been taking turns at night to keep watch over the house. The electricity supply had been cut off all across the island; my father was certain that the looting would be restricted to the shops in town, but we all felt safer keeping watch.

When morning broke I dressed in formal clothes. The smell of dew on the lawns and on the leaves of the trees and the silence on the roads cleared my mind as I cycled into Georgetown.

The streets were quiet; there were no sounds of hawkers firing up their stoves, no rattle of metal shutters as shops were opened. Even the pariah dogs that roamed the streets seemed cowed. The harbor was silent, lacking the daily shouts of coolies and the noise of sea traffic. Those who were brave or foolish enough came out to watch; I joined a group of people by the roadside.

We heard the faint sound of marching feet. As it grew louder the first lines of Japanese soldiers came out from the road leading to the harbor. A cheer erupted from some of those around me, those who believed the country to be finally freed from colonial authority. The Japanese had, after all, promised to return the country to Malay rule. There was a sudden raising of homemade Japanese flags, many with the central circle of red crudely drawn, thrust up like flowers forced into sudden bloom.

After hearing about them for so long, I finally saw them and, like many others, I thought it inconceivable that this group of ill-dressed, uncouth-looking soldiers had defeated the British.

They came in their baggy trousers, high rubber boots, and loose, mud-stained shirts, their heads covered by cloth caps with dirty neck-flaps, their swords hanging limply, knocking against their

278

dented water canteens. They were only permitted to drink once a day while marching and their clothes were practical for the jungle terrain through which they had to travel.

Endo-san had requested that I be present for the formal surrender of the island at the resident councillor's official home. I left the crowd and made my way to the road leading to the main entrance, as the soldiers marched past the angsana-shaded drive that passed through the gardens where the resident councillor's wife used to give tea parties in support of her favorite charities. In my mind I could hear teaspoons knocking against delicate china, voices rising and swooping, and merry laughter matching the cadences of the water that sprang from the fountain. Now, only the crackle of the leaves in the wind remained from those times.

I took my place next to Endo-san in the garden outside the main doors of the Residence. It was already a beautiful day and the light of the early morning picked up the beads of water on the lawn, letting them sparkle for a brief moment before burning them into steam.

Only a few members of the resident councillor's staff had remained. His family had left Penang with the first wave of evacuees.

"Your father would be ashamed of you," he said when he saw me take my place next to the Japanese.

"He's as ashamed of me as he is of the cowardice of the British army, leaving the island completely vulnerable," I said.

The soldiers halted before Hiroshi and their commanding officer bowed to him. Hiroshi turned to face us and read from a document from General Tomoyuki Yamashita, who was running the war in Asia.

I interpreted the entire proceedings, ignoring the angered looks from the resident councillor and his remaining staff. That was the day I became known as a "running dog," the term used by the locals to refer to a collaborator. There was actually no need for my presence, since Hiroshi, Endo-san, and the military commander all spoke English well; it was a clever move by the Japanese to present me to the English. A military photographer had us pose and took our picture for the newspapers.

We stood on the lawn as the Union Flag and the Straits

Settlements' dark blue flag were taken down without ceremony. The flag of Japan, a drop of blood on a sheet of pure white, floated gently up to the sky as the military band played the *Kimigayo*. I did not sing, although Endo-san had long ago taught me the words. And then I watched without expression as the resident councillor and his people were led off to a prisoner-of-war camp. I never found out what happened to them.

There were immediate reprisals by the Japanese against the looters who had scoured Georgetown. They were identified by informants, then arrested and beheaded. Their severed heads were stuck on poles lining the streets. Quite a few had been innocent, singled out by people who held a grudge against them. Our cook, Ah Jin, who had remained with us, came back from the market and I heard her voice frightening the others in the kitchen.

"The *Jipunakui* caught two young men stealing from a motorcycle shop and cut off their heads in the public square at the police headquarters. You can see them. Their heads are still on those long poles." There were moans of horror and Ah Jin continued, "*Aiyo*, the blood, like pigs being slaughtered in the Pulau Tikus market-*lah*! I tell you, these *Jipunakui* are animals!" She saw me listening by the door and hurriedly took her basket and went out to the yard.

A curfew was imposed and those caught breaking it were shot on sight. Food and supplies were rationed and the firms and trading companies were taken over by the military, although a few—Hutton & Sons among them—were still allowed to be run by their owners. The goods would be shipped to Japan to help with their war effort, much to my father's fury.

We heard nothing from Edward or MacAllister. "I hope they're all right," my father said on our way to a meeting called by Endo-san. The Penang business owners and managers who had not escaped to Singapore had been asked to attend. "You realize you're now working for the second most powerful man in Penang? And probably one of the five most powerful men in Malaya?" he asked. "I suppose I can't hire you back again at your former salary?"

I tried to appreciate his feeble attempt at humor and smiled, hoping he had come to see the sense of my decision.

"I'm sorry. I should have discussed it with you first," I said.

"It's already done. You would've gone and worked for them anyway," he said, and the brief moment of humor and warmth we had tried to achieve was gone, washed away by the bitterness in his voice.

We were shown into the meeting room once used by the resident councillor to run the affairs of the island. Soldiers were moving furniture and boxes, as they shifted the administrative departments of the Japanese consulate to the Residence. Henry Cross, the head of Empire Trading, greeted us. Despite the circumstances he was as well dressed as ever, his height and broad shoulders making him seem the most authoritative man in the room, until Endo-san walked in.

I took my place next to him and looked around the table. There were quite a few faces I recognized, company managers, bankers, factory owners, business leaders; all had at one time or another been invited to parties at Istana and I in turn had been invited to their houses. I gave a slight nod to Towkay Yeap, steeled myself, and looked straight ahead.

"I've been appointed by the Japanese government to assist them in the transition, to interpret and to guide all of us concerning cultural matters," I began. There were the expected murmurs of outrage but I ignored them. "By my side is Mr. Hayato Endo, or as he would prefer to be called, Endo-san. He is the assistant governor. Mr. Shigeru Hiroshi, the new governor of Penang, sends his apologies but he has had to leave for Kuala Lumpur, which, as you may not be aware, has just surrendered yesterday."

There were expressions of shock on their faces and then loud murmurs of disbelief. My father looked at me, stunned and angry. I had not disclosed the news of K.L.'s surrender to him and from the look in his eyes I knew he was thinking of Edward. "You knew this and you didn't tell me? Knowing your brother's there and that I was worried to death about him?" he said.

"He was under my orders not to disclose anything," Endo-san said quietly to him. I stared at the surface of the table, unable to look at either of them.

"We are here to decide on your roles in helping the island's recovery," Endo-san now said in rapid Japanese. I translated slowly, grateful that he had redirected my father's attention. I watched the faces around me, avoiding only his. They covered their unease faultlessly, like good commercial people.

I had asked Endo-san why he required an interpreter and he said, "I wish to hear their replies twice. You would be surprised how much they will say when they think I cannot understand."

It was a convincing reply and there was truth in it. But I was starting to see that my main purpose would be to serve as an instrument of Japanese propaganda.

"General Yamashita's plan was to have members of the military take over the running of your companies and businesses completely. It is my opinion, however, that soldiers make bad businessmen. I suggested to him that we merely place advisors and allow you to assist us in running your businesses."

Henry Cross seemed to speak for them all. "That's quite unacceptable. How much power would the advisors have?"

"Complete authority. You will only remain to ensure that everything is run efficiently."

"What if we refuse?"

"Then your presence here is unnecessary and we shall make arrangements for you to be interned in a prison camp. Conditions may not be as satisfactory as those you enjoy now."

Everything went smoothly after that. "You did admirably," Endo-san said after the meeting. He appeared out of place among the heavy English furniture and I had the dislocating feeling that I was in a dream, seeing this man—the quintessence of all things Japanese—leaning back against a leather Chesterfield and fronted by a slab of oak table. "I know how hard it must be for you. At least those people saw the sense of cooperating."

I wanted to say that it was not cooperation but coercion but that would have been to state the obvious. I saw his rueful smile and so kept my silence.

"Your family will be safe," he said, rubbing his eyes.

"That's all I want."

"Everything will be made good . . . in the end." His eyes now held mine captive. "I hope you do not lose your way."

The Japanese army moved south all the way to the town of Johor Bahru, where they crossed the causeway over the Straits of Johor and marched into Singapore. On February 15, 1942, the news of the official surrender came over the governor's radio and General Arthur Percival was brought before General Yamashita Tomoyuki, the military commander of Malaya.

The photograph of the surrender of Singapore, taken at the Ford factory where the signing of the agreement took place, was sent to newspapers around the world. We stood to attention as once again the Japanese anthem was played. The Japanese Occupation had begun.

"As General Yamashita promised," Hiroshi announced, his voice proud, "Singapore has been delivered as to the Divine Emperor his birthday present!"

Endo-san once described to me how the young Hirohito had spent his summers at the seaside villa owned by Endo-san's family, wading in tidal pools looking for specimens for his collection, for the future emperor was already a keen student of marine biology. I was left to wonder what sort of person the emperor had grown up to be, to want as his birthday present the subjugation of another land.

I had not heard from Aunt Mei and I became worried, wondering whether she had left her home on Bangkok Lane. The roads were busy with Japanese troops as I cycled into town and I was stopped regularly at checkpoints. My identity document issued by Endo-san prevented me from being troubled and I did not have to bow as low as the others. As I was cycling off, I heard a man being clubbed with a rifle when he forgot to bow to the soldier. I forced myself to continue, to ignore the coarse shouts of the Japanese. He'll learn, I thought. He'll learn. We all will.

I knocked on Aunt Mei's door. The windows were shut, the wooden louvers closed. It seemed so different from the old days, when the street was full of sounds and life. Even the suspicious cats were gone.

"Aunt Mei! It's me!" I shouted through the gaps of the door. I had the feeling that the street was not as empty as it seemed and I began to feel curious eyes peering from many of the houses. I knocked again.

The door opened and I was let inside. In the shadows I saw her face, damaged and discolored. I felt a jolt of anger. "The soldiers?" I asked.

She nodded, slowly, because of her bruised face. I sat her down and examined her. "Are you all right? Do you need medicine?"

"No, no. I am fine," she said, her voice squashed by her swollen features.

"What happened?"

"Did not show proper respect to a Japanese soldier."

"Do you have enough food?" I asked.

"Enough."

"You must come and stay with us," I said. "I'll help you pack now."

She shook her head. "I am fine, really. I cannot go with you. I still have certain obligations."

"You should stop worrying about your pupils; I'm sure they are wise enough to go into hiding for a while."

She refused to accept my offer and I stopped insisting. "How's Grandfather? Have you heard anything from him?"

"He is fine. The Japanese have not harmed him. Stays in the house all the time."

"Good. I'll see if I can get a travel permit to visit him."

She looked keenly at me. "I was told you're now working for the Japanese."

"It seemed a good way to save my family. Isn't that what Grandfather said—that the family is all?"

"Be careful. A lot of people wouldn't think so."

"Are you telling me that something will happen to me, to my family?"

She did not reply.

"Tell those people that I joined the Japanese also to prevent more blood being spilled," I said.

"I can tell them, but they are only words."

"Does this mean you won't accept help from me now?"

"I think it is better that you do not come here for a while. The neighbors. They are fearful and they will talk."

I got up from the chair, the feeling of rejection weakening me. "I understand," I said. "I'll see myself out." I took her hand. "You may think I'm doing the wrong thing, but I made a promise to Grandfather to look after you and I won't abandon you."

Chapter Five

Despite my best efforts I could not trace Edward and Peter MacAllister. They had disappeared among the masses of Europeans who had been rounded up into prison camps. Isabel, who had come down from The Hill, was frantic. My father was worried about Edward, I knew, and ate very little. He had lost a great deal of weight since William's death.

"I cannot do anything; Kuala Lumpur is under Saotome-san's command," Endo-san said when I went to him. We heard Hiroshi coughing violently from his office and Endo-san winced.

"May I telephone him?"

"I think it would be more courteous for you to see him in person."

"In that case I'll require a travel pass from you."

"You do not need one. Your document of identification allows you unimpeded travel. Let me have it now."

He removed a wooden case from a drawer and took out a small square block. He inked it in red and carefully placed his seal on the piece of paper. "That is my personal seal. Just produce it whenever you are stopped. You should not encounter any hindrance."

"Thank you, *sensei*."

He ignored the faint hint of sarcasm in my voice. "I hope you can find them. But they are prisoners of war. Remember that."

"I will."

He stopped me as I was leaving. "Please instruct the kitchen staff that all utensils used by Hiroshi-san must now be separated from general use. They must also be thoroughly sterilized."

"Yes. Is it tuberculosis as the doctor suspected?"

"*Hai.*" He appeared regretful. "What we have to suffer in order to obey our country's rulers."

*

285

Since her return from Penang Hill, Isabel had been anxious, walking around the house, unsure and angry. We had forbidden her from going outdoors, even though in her cropped hair and shapeless clothes she would have been almost safe. She insisted on coming with me when she found out that I would be going to Kuala Lumpur.

My father put his foot down, softly, but firmly. "No, you can't go. It's still too dangerous. The soldiers are running wild around the country."

News of rapes and disembowelments reached us almost daily. Families and villagers caught in the path of the troops were raped and bayoneted, sometimes not even in that order.

"I'll do my best to find them," I said, touching her arm. Her other hand came up and stroked my fingers.

The train services had been restored, but obtaining a ticket required going through the military and the Kempeitai would be certain to compile information on all travelers.

The countryside appeared as it had been, unchanged. The train headed into a thunderstorm soon after leaving Butterworth and I put my window up. The leaves of the trees lining the tracks were heavy with droplets of rain, smearing the windows, turning the view outside into a wavering, uncertain landscape.

I slept fitfully, surrounded by Chinese merchants who had managed to obtain travel permits, their voices soft as they discussed the economy. The black market was thriving and the Japanese were already printing money to counter inflation. That was the first time I heard about "banana notes," which were just worthless Japanese money, printed with a picture of a banana tree. "*Aiyah*, can't even buy a banana with it!" these traders complained.

They were curious about me. I heard them whispering in Hokkien as I fell in and out of sleep, trying to determine if I were European or not. I opened my eyes and settled their questions in Hokkien, amused by their mortified faces.

"What are you doing in K.L.?" one asked.

"Going to ask the *Jipunakui* where my brother is."

Their faces turned somber. "You won't find him. The Europeans have been taken to Singapore. Or, even worse, sent to Siam."

"Why Siam? It wasn't invaded by the Japanese."

"Yes, but they signed a treaty to preserve their territories. In return they allow the *Jipunakui* to build a railroad in the north." His voice softened, like the wick of an oil lamp being lowered. "I've heard very terrible things about this railway line. Terrible." He shook his head, glancing around to his companions for agreement.

"Who will you be seeing in K.L.?" another man asked.

"Saotome," I said.

The train entered a tunnel and for minutes I could not see their faces, could not hear them as the roaring passage of the train sang in the tunnel. When we came out into the light again the first man who had spoken to me said, "You must be careful of that man. He's dangerous, with very strange tastes. He is attracted to suffering."

I thought back again to my dinner with Saotome and the girl who had been presented to him. The sweet taste of eel speckled my mouth. "I will," I said, and thanked them.

Endo-san had made an appointment for me, and a military car was waiting to take me to Saotome. Once again I entered the quiet hallways and polished corridors of the embassy. However, this time I was shown into his office, which overlooked a small garden made up entirely of pebbles and rocks. Akasaki Saotome was raking the pebbles, the sound like the mah-jong tiles that one so often heard in the streets of Georgetown as the players mixed the tiles on the tables, "washing" them. A Zen garden, I thought, recalling Endo-san describing to me the one in his home in Japan. The swirls and the patterns created by the sweeping were supposed to still the mind, to appear as the waves on the ocean.

I waited at the doorway leading to the garden. A gust of wind blew and a clutch of leaves spun in the air before settling down on the pebbles, on the circular lines and waves left by the rake.

"Look at that," he said. "Like souls caught in time, *neh*?"

"I prefer to see them as ships trapped in a tide of stones."

"We see what we wish to," he said, hanging the rake on a hook. He skirted the rippling pebbles, his wooden clogs comforting, almost rustic, to hear. Once again I was aware of how handsome he looked, but an image, lying by the banks of my memory like a half-hidden mud-caked crocodile, of him licking his lips, marred his appearance.

"I have examined the records of the prisoners. I did not come across your brother's name, nor of that of Peter MacAllister."

"They were here on the day K.L. surrendered."

"It was a chaotic time; no doubt we may have missed them both. Or they both could have escaped to Singapore."

I shook my head. "I don't think so."

He extended his hand and stroked my face. I shivered at the sudden touch and he smiled. "You must love your brother very much," he said.

I stood very still and he said, "I am very much aware of your abilities. You could probably break my neck easily. But you see," he gave a soft laugh, "I do not need such skills." Again I saw his smile, small as an incision, revealing only a thin red line.

He leaned closer to me and I smelled his scent. It reminded me of smoke from burning leaves, so evocative of dusk at Istana that I found myself savoring it. It was so easy to give in, but I moved my head away and he paused, his hand still on my cheek.

"No?" he asked.

"No."

"I can call the guards, you know."

"You would not do that. You prefer your victims to submit to you of their own accord. So much more enjoyable to control them willingly than to have to take them by force."

His hand left my cheek. "You are shivering. I do not know why you refuse. You think Endo-san is different from me? That just because he is your *sensei* he will watch over you and protect you?" Saotome shook his head. "He and I are more similar than you are aware of. He is myself not so long ago; he will become what I am."

He had clarified the reason I was drawn to him, but I thought of Endo-san, and a surge of strength warmed me, burning away my fascination with Saotome.

"Maybe in another lifetime, Saotome-san," I said.

"Then I shall wait," he said. "Your brother and MacAllister have been sent to Changi prison and there they will stay for the duration of the war. There is nothing you can do for them now."

I bowed formally and left him there in the pebbled garden, among his souls caught in the tides of time.

*

In my heart I knew Saotome had lied to me. Truth was a precious commodity for him; he would not have been generous with it. As I waited at the train station, I changed my ticket and hired a trishaw from a row of them waiting by the road outside.

"Where to?" the trishaw-puller asked, hunched over his bicycle, a stained towel slung over his shoulder.

"Pudu Prison," I replied.

He paled and glanced around him. "That's not a good place to go to."

I offered to double his fare and he accepted, mumbling ominously. The prison was not far from the train station but he took an age to get there. When we reached the gates of the prison he turned his trishaw around. "Wait here until I come out," I said. "I'll pay you more."

He rode off into the shade of a rambutan tree and watched as I knocked on the heavy doors. A hole opened and I said in formal Japanese, "I need to see the chief warden." I held out my identification document. "I am the cultural officer from Penang, authorized by the assistant governor, Endo-san." I held my breath, hoping that like all Japanese subordinates he would not question the ring of authority with which I had alloyed my voice.

The hole closed and the door was opened. I went in and allowed the guard to search me. Another guard came and led me into the prison. I felt claustrophobic immediately, for the place was unearthly with suffering. As we entered, the prisoners, mostly Europeans in filthy loincloths, held onto the bars of a block of cells built over an archway, watching me silently. The prison appeared to be overcrowded with prisoners of war, and their stench made me ill.

I was shown into the chief warden's room. Sunlight came in through a broken glass pane behind him and I blinked as he stood up. I bowed low to him, my head almost touching the top of the table, and introduced myself.

"Endo-san did not inform me of your visit," Chief Warden Matsuda said when I explained the reason for my presence.

"It's my fault. I handle his correspondence and—well, I am still new to my duties. I hope you won't report my lapse," I said.

"You speak very good Japanese," he said.

"Thank you. I was very much interested in Japanese culture from an early age. I find we have much to learn from it."

"That is good, for we are a cultured nation. Now, what were the names you were looking for?"

I told him, adding that they were wanted in Penang for their experience and their knowledge of the tin-smelting industry. He opened a thick ledger and turned the pages. I calmed myself and tried not to appear too impatient. He made a sound and his fingers stopped their tracking across the pages.

"MacAllister, Peter, age forty-seven," he said, taking time to pronounce the name properly, but failing. I had discovered that while the Japanese could roll their *r*'s when they spoke English, they stumbled when they came to the *l*'s, inevitably pronouncing them as *r*'s. And so it was with the chief warden. Curiously enough, with the Chinese the problem was the other way around.

Matsuda glanced up over his glasses. "He was here, but he has been sent to Siam, to the Burmese border." I tried not to show my collapsing heart as his fingers again picked up speed. "Hutton. Is he related to you?"

I shook my head, hoping Matsuda was not familiar with English names. "It is a common name—like Matsuda," I said, thinking quickly.

He laughed. "*Hai.* We have two Matsuda on duty in this prison. You can imagine the confusion. Ah, here it is—Edward Hutton." He read from the ledger. "Sent to the Burmese border two weeks ago, in the same batch as Peter MacAllister."

"What is going on at this border?" I asked.

"We are building a railway to connect China to Malaya. Easier to transport supplies and troops, *neh*?"

"How do I get these two transferred to Penang?"

He scratched his cheek. "You would have to write to Saotome-san's office. Only he has the power to transfer the prisoners. He acts under the authority of General Yamashita." The last glitter of hope fell away. "The two people you were searching for are unfortunate. I have yet to hear of anyone returning alive from the border." Matsuda shook his head. I saw that, despite his duty, he was at heart a decent man and the cruelties of war affected him heavily.

He walked with me from the office to the entrance of the prison. Before the guards closed the massive prison doors he said, "Matsuda is not such a common name. The other Matsuda on duty," and here he looked me in the eye, "the other Matsuda happens to be my younger brother. I am truly sorry that I could not assist you. I would hate to lose my brother."

I bowed to him and said, "*Domo arigato gozaimasu*, Matsuda-san."

He did not bow to me but held out his hand. "If you can learn to bow like us, then maybe I can learn to shake hands like you *gai-jin*?"

I shook his hand.

Isabel ran out to the veranda when I returned. "They've both been sent to work on the railway in Burma. I'm sorry," I said.

She swayed slightly and then found her balance. I held out my arms to her but she never moved. "Your Japanese friends," she said. "What harm could Peter and Edward do to them?" My arms dropped down, empty, and she walked away from me.

"I know you tried your damnedest," my father said when he returned from the office where he had been working with the representatives of the Japanese military. "I only hope she'll forgive you." He stood for a moment, then decided he had nothing more to say to me and went into his room.

I wondered if I really had tried my hardest, and what more was required of me. I decided to visit Endo-san.

He was glad when he saw me dragging my boat up from the eager waves. "I have missed you," he said. "Was Saotome-san of assistance?"

"No, he wasn't." Saotome's words returned to me—*he is myself not so long ago*—as I studied Endo-san's face. Would Endo-san eventually turn into him? Cultured, refined, and yet with a streak of coldness fanning out into tiny veins that would eventually spread though him entirely?

"But still you managed to find out some news. My personal seal was helpful?" he said, knowing me too well.

"Yes. They've been sent to build the railways."

His breath hissed in. "I am sorry."

"You knew about Saotome-san's . . . predilections?"

"Yes."

"You knew, and still sent me there, to him?"

"I know you are strong. That is why I was glad your sister did not go with you. If he could not have you he would have wanted her. And of her strength I know nothing."

"He said he was like you, once. And that you'll be like him, in time."

"And what do you think?"

"I think you want me to prevent that from happening."

"You are growing up at last."

I felt the exhaustion of my journey back from Kuala Lumpur overwhelm me. The memory of the look on my father's face when we spoke was more than I could bear. "May I spend the night here?" I asked.

"Of course. Come, let us go and make dinner. I have much work to do tonight. Hiroshi-san's absences from work have been more frequent."

"How is he?"

"Worsening. I have advised him to request a transfer home but he refuses."

"Perhaps he should recuperate at the house up on Penang Hill," I said, before I could think.

Endo-san looked at me closely. "The house on The Hill? Yes, that is a fine idea."

We walked up the gentle beach toward the light that came from his house through the shifting gaps of the trees as, behind us, the day departed.

Chapter Six

Things soon settled down within a few months of the Japanese victory over Malaya, like sediment sinking to the depths of a pond. We lived in a constant fear that wrapped itself around us, until we became unaware of it. Some days something would happen, like a stick stirring the bottom of the pond and we would again be roused, agitated, the fear sharper for having been blunted for a while.

I traveled to work every day with Endo-san and his military chauffeur. And every day my father watched in grim silence as the black Daimler that was once his came to pick me up. Isabel refused to speak to me and the remaining servants ignored me. Never had I felt so isolated. It was only at the Japanese head-quarters that I felt almost at home. The people there were considerably friendlier than my own family.

I was given a small desk next to Endo-san's office. There were still remnants of the furniture and memorabilia left by the resi-dent councillor. A portrait of Emperor Hirohito stared down at me while I perused documents and reports.

My work was clerical, compiling documents and drafting replies to various military and civil officials around the country. I translated the constant instructions that came from Singapore: schools were to be reopened and all classes conducted in Japanese; everyone had to bow to the Japanese flag and to learn to sing the *Kimigayo* at work and at the schools before the commencement of each day's activities. I had to translate notices of beheadings as well, which angered and distressed me. These notices were posted at various public places in Georgetown. My name appeared at the bottom of all translated documents. I wondered how many were in my position across Malaya, growing notorious as *jau-kow*, running dogs.

After work I trained with Endo-san or, if he was busy, with the military staff. Goro, the officer who had called me a half-breed, avoided me, but in the pine-floored *dojo* I watched him spar with the other officials. He was brutal and quick, his moves vicious and designed to kill. I made a considerable effort not to train at the same time as he did.

Hiroshi, on one of his better days, called for the attendance of the business and community leaders of Penang and informed them that Saotome had sent out an order from Kuala Lumpur that the Chinese businessmen from each state had to provide fifty million Straits dollars to the government.

"But that is ridiculous," Towkay Yeap said. "We do not have that kind of money." There were murmurs of agreement from the rest.

"This is to show your loyalty to the emperor. We still hear reports that there are anti-Japanese elements trying to cause damage to us. Fujihara-san has obtained such information," Hirsohi said, coughing softly, referring to the short, quiet man who headed the Kempeitai. Fujihara was a dour man with sharp eyes and a thin mouth shaded by the one-inch moustache so favored by the Japanese Ultra-Nationalists. I tried to have nothing to do with him, knowing he would not have forgotten the day when Goro brought him to Istana and my sister shot at them. Endo-san had assured me that Istana would not be requisitioned but I did not want to give the Japanese secret police any reason at all to confiscate our home.

The Kempeitai was notorious and I had no wish to know how many innocent people had been dragged from their beds in the night, identified by their masked accusers, never to be seen again by their family. Such were the things that stirred the sediment of our existence.

The Chinese businessmen left the meeting and I felt their loathing of me. In their eyes I was still Chinese enough and I was no better than a stray dog scrounging for scraps.

I became aware of Fujihara's quiet approach to me as I was leaving the meeting room. I felt myself tense up, wondering what he wanted.

"You are a resourceful boy, Philip-san." From the way he said it, I knew he wanted me to be certain that the Kempeitai had a file on me. "I would like you to do something for me."

"I shall be glad to, if it's within my abilities," I said.

"I want a piano for my house. A good one, the best one you can find," he said. "Get it from the people. Inform them that this is an order from me."

He had me write down the address of the house he had requisitioned. I knew it well. It was owned by the Thornton family, and I had heard that they had elected to stay and not evacuate.

"What happened to the people who lived in the house?" I asked.

Fujihara smiled at me and I tried not to shiver. "You and your family are fortunate that I have found another place more to my liking." He walked out of the room and said over his shoulder, "Get me the piano. Goro, my assistant, will help you. You have a week to find it."

I discussed the matter with my father and told Goro that we would be willing to surrender our own piano to Fujihara. The piano in our house was a Schumann, a small grand appropriate for a parlor; it had originally been purchased for Isabel, who had lost interest in playing it years ago. The Schumann was a popular choice in Penang due to its suitability to the climate. My father was initially unwilling to relinquish it—he was still angry at my decision to work for the Japanese—but I knew that his strong sense of doing the right thing would demand that a sacrifice come from our family and not another.

Fujihara, when informed of my offer, declined politely, saying he found that particular make to be of inferior quality. I had no alternative but to recall the names of the families I had known that owned pianos and to send out letters requesting appointments to view them.

Once again I was aware that the intention was to exhibit me to the people, showing them how the Japanese had succeeded in bringing the son of a well-known family over to their side.

Our visits to these homes were understandably much feared and, although I attempted to make them as brief and businesslike as I could, more often than not I failed. I was always accompanied by Goro, who seemed to enjoy the whole proceedings. He surprised me by trying out each piano we saw, performing with a skill that even I could tell was more than competent, a skill greatly belied by the calluses on his hands and the lack of any expression on his face when he played. It made for a grotesque scene, the

Japanese officer playing the piano, with me standing mutely at his side, surrounded by the frightened and resentful members of the household, who were not allowed to sit but instead had been ordered to stand and watch. It made me think of the play I had seen, with my grandfather in the town square of Ipoh, that was performed for the hungry ghosts. I felt that Goro was playing for an audience of unseen visitors whose malign presence I could almost sense.

Goro went through the same routine at all of the houses we visited. He would stride in and demand to be taken to the piano. Then for half an hour he would sit and play the same monotonous pieces over and over again. Finally, at the fourteenth house on my list, I was sufficiently irritated to ask, "Can't you play something else?"

He stopped playing, genuinely affronted. He shifted in his seat and placed his hands on his lap. "Fujihara-san is of the opinion that *Das Wohltemperierte Klavier* consists of some of the greatest pieces of music ever created, and I agree with him. The "Präludium und Fuge"—especially the two pairs from *Book One*, which I always choose to play—are what he likes best and what he often plays. How can I know if this is the best instrument for him if I do not appraise it by using the music he would wish to play?" I was taken aback by his sentiment and his fluent German. "You of all people should know that we are not merely a nation of uncultured savages," he said.

I interpreted Goro's statement about Bach's music to the owner of the house, a middle-aged Chinese man. Although he seemed to be living alone, I could sense within his house the presence of the womenfolk he had undoubtedly hidden when he saw us approaching—I always made a point of announcing our arrival at the various houses as loudly as I could. We were in the sitting room on the ground floor and, as Goro began playing again, I lifted my head casually to the ceiling, which, as in so many of the houses we had seen, was made of wooden planking. My eyes swept the expanse of the ceiling and I thought I saw an eye peering through a knothole. I stared at it for a moment and the owner noticed. He spoke to distract me. "The Japanese officer is wise and correct," he said, his tone ingratiating. "The music of Bach is indeed sublime."

"I did not ask for your opinion," Goro replied in English. He turned back to the piano and played a new piece, only this time he announced fluently in German, as though to emphasize to me once more his people's refinement, "Präludium und Fuge VI d-moll BMV 875."

I ignored him and looked straight ahead, putting my mind in my usual meditative spot, but the drilling of the music made it difficult. There came a startling silence and I brought myself back to the present. I felt the beginning of an intimation of dread, for Goro had never paused halfway through his playing before.

"We shall take this," he said, and stood up. He stroked the piano. "It is the best I have heard." He pointed to me and then to the owner. "Tell him. I do not feel like dirtying my tongue with more English today."

"It's a Bechstein," the owner said when I interpreted Goro's intention to take the instrument. "No one else on this island has one."

"Who has played on it before?" Goro asked.

"My granddaughter. She, too, loved the music of Bach."

"I felt the familiarity of the keys with the great composer's music. It is slightly out of tune, however," Goro said, a frown curving like a sickle on his face. "You have not respected it by giving it proper care."

He hit the hapless old man twice in the chest and I could distinctly hear ribs breaking—two precise, irrevocable cracks. The old man screamed and I ran around from the other side of the piano. He was convulsing with pain as he fell on the carpet, going into shock, and there was nothing I could do except watch. My eyes searched for the knothole in the ceiling and I shook my head slowly, warning whoever was hiding upstairs not to come down.

The only chance the old man had of surviving was for us to get out of the house as quickly as possible so as to allow his family to help him. I restrained myself from attacking Goro and said coldly, "Is that how you prove to me that you are not a nation of uncultured savages?"

He was too taken aback to reply and I used the opportunity to lead his mind.

"I want us to leave. Now. I'll send some people to come and remove the piano," I said and walked out of the house. To my relief I heard Goro following close behind.

I found out later, from the soldiers I sent to collect the piano, that the old man did not survive the assault—Goro's blows had inflicted fatal damage to his heart. I canceled the arrangements I had made to replace the requisitioned piano with our own, for nothing could bring him back to life again.

Fujihara was delighted with the Bechstein and insisted that I visit his home to listen to him play. It was an invitation I could not decline, for to do so would have been an insult to his face. To my dismay I found that Goro had been correct in his judgement of Fujihara's favorite pieces of music when we were selecting the piano. I found it hard to sit through his performance and when he invited me again I made an excuse not to attend, a decision that I knew made him feel he had been insulted.

I had other problems to occupy my mind, however. Isabel still maintained her refusal to speak to me, even when I handed her the letters from MacAllister and Edward.

"These were given to me by Endo-san today," I said.

My father opened Edward's letter and read it quickly. "Nothing much. The censors have blacked out entire lines of writing. He's well, not in Malaya, but then we knew that." He gave the letter to me. It was disjointed, abrupt where the sentences had been censored.

"How's Peter?" he asked Isabel.

"Same news. Not good," she said. "He's in Thailand. Look, he writes, 'Since I Am in Much poor health . . .'"

"Good old Peter," my father said, a brief smile lightening his face. "Thank Mr. Endo, please." Isabel folded her letter and I knew she would read it again in her room, savoring every scarce word.

"And put my name down on the list of people who have to come up with the money," my father added.

"Why?" I could not believe what I was hearing. "That's only for the Chinese."

"Before the Japs came, this was a good place, a place where we all worked together, Europeans, Chinese, Malays, and Indians. I will not let the Japanese break us apart. I'll do my share, even if I'm not a Chinese. If every one of us gives some, the amount can be raised."

"One of the reasons why I'm working for the Japanese is so

that you'll be exempt from such demands," I said, my fingers on my temper loosening one by one. "If you want to be a party to such idiocy, what's the point of my working for them?"

"It only takes one letter of the alphabet to change *reason* to *treason*. You went to work for them of your own accord, so don't ever use us to justify your actions."

"Don't you see, this is the only way of seeing that all of us are safe, to see the family firm is safe!"

"No," my father said.

"The war won't last," Isabel said. "The British army will be back."

I looked at her pityingly. "They've gone, Isabel. They left us, undefended, uninformed. They might mount a counterinvasion but in the meantime we have to play by the rules."

I looked at my father. "You said once that I never considered myself a part of this family. Why do you think I'm doing this now? Do you think I like being thought of as a dog owned by the Japanese? Do you?"

He did not answer. There *was* no answer. He could only hold Edward's letter in his hand, his thumb rubbing it back and forth, back and forth.

Once the former home of the resident councillor had been satisfactorily refurbished to suit the Japanese, I was invited to a dinner. My father was silent, his lips clamped into a thin line as he saw me waiting for the chauffeur under the portico.

The former Residence, now the shared headquarters of the Japanese military and civil administrations, appeared unchanged outside except for a row of banners and Japanese flags. What saddened me was the transformation that had been made inside. I had watched the workers remove William Daniell's oil paintings of scenes of Penang he had executed in the 1880s and replace them with bleak calligraphy scrolls extolling the virtues of the emperor. History had been replaced by propaganda.

I walked around the reception hall and struck up a conversation with the army chief of staff, Colonel Takuma Nishida. In the course of it, I mentioned, "Your plan to land on the northeastern coast of Malaya instead of Singapore was inspired."

He accepted my flattery with grace. "My men were acclimatized to the heat and humidity in Hainan Island and we had excellent sources of information."

I gave a gentle stab. "For that you should thank Hayato Endo-san."

"True. Endo-san selected our landing sites and he advised us to beach in the months between December to February during the monsoon, when the seas would be rough and dangerous. No one would have expected us to launch the attack then."

I felt nauseous, for I remembered telling Endo-san how once in his youth my father had tried to sail the rough seas off Kota Bahru during the monsoon and had almost been swept away forever. The waves had capsized his boat and he had floated for more than a day before he was found. My grandparents had given him up for dead.

Colonel Nishida sipped his glass of wine and added, "If you ask me, if it had not been for Endo-san, General Yamashita would not have conquered your country with such ease. His reputation as the Tiger of Malaya is in part owed to Endo-san. But that is between us, of course."

"Of course," I said.

Now I saw that there had been an unspoken exchange between Endo-san and me. I had accepted the bargain: his protection for my knowledge.

For once meditation did not help. I found my mind hopping from thought to thought, like a monkey swinging from tree to tree; the chattering of my mind would not be stilled. Endo-san had understood when I asked him to take me to Hiroshi. I had not been required to explain to him why I wanted to work for him. Some days I felt that was why he had taught me: in return for betraying me, my home, and my way of life, he had provided me with the ability to keep my family and myself safe. For those reasons alone I felt compelled to remain loyal to him and to the lessons he had imparted.

But now and then, like a weakening flame trying to replenish its heat, a feeling of fury would flare up, burn me up completely, and only my disciplined practice of *zazen* helped me hold on to my respect and love for him.

I knew that there would come a day when even that would fail, and what would happen to us all then?

Chapter Seven

The threats began with the carcass of a slaughtered dog thrown
onto the portico steps. Flies had begun clouding it when the maid
found it and screamed. We came out from our breakfast and I
prodded it with my feet, pushing it to one side to pull out the
blood-soaked note.

" *'Jap dogs—Watch Out for Your Lives!'* " I read, and crumpled it. My father and Isabel watched me, silent. "It's nothing.
Just empty words," I said, forcing my eyes to meet theirs.

"Get rid of the dog," my father said.

Two nights later he shook me awake. "What is it?" I asked.
"What time is it?"

"The house is on fire."

I ran after him down to the drawing room, where, in a corner
near the windows, hungry crackling flames were reaching for the
shelves and the curtains. We doused the fire with water from the
kitchen.

"No need to wake the rest now," he said. He pointed to the
window; pieces of glass lay on the floor like ice in the moonlight.

"I found this," he took out a piece of paper from the pocket of
his dressing gown. " *'We'll get you.'* "

"Keep it," my father said. "And do something. You've no right
to place all our lives in peril."

When morning came, I had made up my mind. I knocked on
the door to Hiroshi's office. "I wish to resign from my position
here."

He looked up from his desk and I covered my shock at how
thin he had become. Of late he had taken to leaving early during
lengthy meetings, sometimes avoiding them altogether. But he was
always aware of the things discussed in those meetings.

"Why?" he asked.

"I've been receiving death threats. My family's lives have been threatened."

"All of us receive threats. That does not mean we should give in to them." He got up and called Endo-san in. "Our young friend here wishes to discontinue his services to our emperor."

"Also, I do not agree with your policies, or your actions so far," I said. "It was not necessary to execute looters. It was not necessary to round up the Chinese and send them to your labor camps."

"Those people were acting against our government, plotting to resist us. They had to be put down. It is always the case, in a period of transition when one authority replaces another, that pockets of resistance appear. Our methods may appear brutal to your young mind, but they are necessary," Hiroshi said.

"I have given you a lot of assistance. All I am requesting is that you release me from service."

Hiroshi took off his glasses and commenced polishing them. "Your family is safe now, even though the Kempeitai inform us that your sister has been spreading inflammatory words among the people of Penang. You are the most famous collaborator on this island. Do you think we will let you leave so easily? It would reflect badly on us. And we will make your life hard. No one would disbelieve us if we let it be known that you personally identified many of the people we have executed. No one at all."

His cold, precise words cut me like the samurai sword resting on a sideboard behind him. I glanced at Endo-san, and he nodded.

I knew when I was defeated. I gave a brief shallow bow and left, almost feeling the smile on Hiroshi's face on my back.

There was only one person I could go to. I headed to a stall at the Pulau Tikus market, where a bucktoothed youth was selling a meager selection of bananas. Food was in short supply and people had resorted to eating broth and harvesting their sweet potatoes and yams. Many had run off to the jungles of Pulau Tikus to avoid the Japanese. The town was quite empty except for a few who had nowhere else to escape to. I brought out a Japanese fifty-dollar note and bought two bananas: buying bananas with banana notes—the sad irony did not escape me.

"I have to see Towkay Yeap today," I said to the youth. "Tell him my name." I whispered it to him; he appeared not to have heard me. "Arrange for a safe place to meet." He ignored me until I laced my fingers together, my thumb pointing outward, my little fingers down, creating the sign of the Dragon Head as Kon had shown me once, a long, long time ago.

The youth sucked his teeth, blew out his breath, eyed me with new respect, and nodded.

On my way home from work I became aware of two men flanking me on bicycles. I slowed down and let them catch up with me. I heard them approach and tensed, wondering if the people sending threats to me were about to keep their word.

"Your request has been heard. Be at the docks on Sunday morning." And then they cycled away, talking to each other as they went.

They took me out on a sampan, the boat as flat as a saucer beneath our weight, the water trying to pour in as we were rowed out on a sea of heaving emerald, the white tops like cream. I could see the blue-violet mountains of Kedah, a thick wet line that washed down into emptiness. We transferred to a filthy trawler reeking of fish guts. On the slimy deck I faced Kon's father. Around us, standing at different parts of the deck, the foot soldiers of the Red Banner Society waited, ready to defend their leader if I made even the slightest move.

"If you needed to see me, you could have just come to my home," he said.

"It was not safe." I outlined my predicament swiftly. "I have a proposition for you. While I work for the Japanese, whatever information I obtain I will pass on to you." From the papers that went through my hands I knew the triads already had the structure and organization to resist the Japanese. They had carried out a few bombings, striking at Japanese ammunition depots, and the Kempeitai were building their files on the triads.

"How can we trust you? You, so well known for helping the Japanese?"

"My family's life. My life. You know where we are. If I betray you, I know we would have nowhere to run. Your son would vouch for me."

He kept silent, looking out to sea, his robe fluttering in the wind. He seemed to have aged a great deal since the last time I saw him. There was a frailty in him, common in much older men, which I had never seen before. It was a form of fading away, as though he had fewer and fewer elements within him for the light to catch and reflect into my vision. I had heard from the Japanese informers that he was still continuing his visits to the opium dens.

"I do not want my family harmed in any way. I want to make it clear to you that I cannot stop working for the Japanese. They have made threats of harm and imprisonment against my family. I also ask that you put the word out to the resistance that the threats to my family and me are to cease."

He nodded in agreement. "Very well. We will order the warnings to stop."

"I'll do my part," I assured him.

"You are too young to be doing this," he said.

"The war does not choose its victims. Kon is doing his part too."

"Yes, he is," the old man said, a sad and distant gaze coming into his eyes. He missed his son so much.

"Have you news of him?"

He seemed unwilling to tell me, wondering if he could trust me. "For myself, I would prefer not to disclose my son's location," he said. "Before he left, however, he insisted I should let you know. He is in a camp just outside Ipoh. The guerrillas have joined forces with the Malayan Communist Party. His group has been successful in disrupting the *Jipunakui* activities." He shook his head. "I hope they do not become too successful, for that is when the *Jipunakui* will really hunt them down."

He walked to the side of the trawler, the water churned to a milky white by the prow. "Please thank your father for his contribution to the fund ordered by the *Jipunakui*," he said. "I know he did not want it made public."

"I was against him paying it," I admitted.

"The fact that he paid is one of the reasons why the threats against you and your family were never seriously carried out. Your father, at least, is a true son of the island."

He beckoned to me to join him at the railing. We gazed down into the water and I pulled back almost involuntarily. The sea was a translucent and enticing green but floating just below the surface was an armada of pale, transparent jellyfish, many of them the size of a small opened umbrella and trailing tentacles almost ten feet long. They appeared at certain times of the month and were one of the hazards of swimming in the waters around the island. I had encountered them many times before, but not in such number—there must have been close to a thousand of them around us. I watched their heads pulsate as they drifted with the currents, remembering the time when I had been stung in my leg while swimming. The pain had been excruciating and I had barely made it back to shore.

"Beautiful, aren't they?" Towkay Yeap said. "A man could survive a sting from one of these but he would never make it through all of them if he fell in."

"There's no reason for anyone to fall in," I said, meeting his eyes.

"Let us hope so," he replied.

I rowed to Endo-san's island beneath the fading sun and the multiplying stars, enjoying the pull and yield of the oars. For once the trip felt unending, as though I were rowing in a viscous dream, all movement slowed. Part of me realized I had entered the deepest state of *zazen* and that I was not holding the oars anymore.

I was kneeling in a field, a field so green, so new with rain that the grass gave off an emerald luminescence. A slight wind bent the tops of the trees, lifting the scent from them, sending it to me. I knew the sea was within reach, for its gentle promise floated on the scent of the trees. And above me I could almost hear the scraping of the clouds' slow movement against the sky. The light was unnaturally bright and the contrasts sharp. A shadow moved into the sun and I lifted my head to look into Endo-san's face. My breathing was stilled, for his face was suffused with both love and sorrow, mingling like the wind and the rain. He was attired in a formal black *men-tsuke* robe, its sleeves and edges lined with a discreet border of muted gold. On his shoulders were his crests and I knew he was one of the Shogun Tokugawa Ieyasu's *daimyo*, a warlord. His hair was white, pulled back into a samurai topknot, and his arms held a *katana* so beautiful it seemed to be alive.

He raised it up in the *happo* stance, both hands going to his right shoulder, his legs bent outward at the knees. A crowd had gathered around the field and banners whipped frantically on the wind: their fluttering sounded like the beating wings of cranes about to take flight to a far-off summer.

He spoke and his voice carried across the field. "For conspiring against Tokugawa-Shogun, you have been sentenced to death. You have been denied the right to *seppukku*. Your family have had their titles and properties confiscated and all have been executed."

But his eyes, oh his eyes! They spoke of other things, of things that had been between us, and things that could now never be. His mouth tightened into a firm, remorseless line, hard as the blade of the sword he now gripped high over his head. But in the depths of his tear-filled eyes I saw his love for me.

I raised my neck, exposing it to the arc of his cut. And then I gathered my trembling voice so I could speak clearly and firmly:

Friends part forever
Wild geese lost in clouds.

It was from a haiku by Matsuo Basho, his favorite poet.

I felt him breathe and then his *katana* seemed to trap a ray of the sun within the blade as it sliced down, and the next moment I was above the field, this timeless field. I saw my body as it collapsed slowly into a curled position and Endo-san crouching over it. Even through the veil that separates life from death I could feel his sorrow. I wanted to console him, to tell him not to feel such sadness, but it was beyond my strength now to reach him.

I sat back in the boat; my hands clenched the oars and a film of sweat chilled my face. I was on the beach of Endo-san's island, unaware of how I had gotten there, every segment of my body shaking as though trying to tear apart from one another. My neck burned with remembered pain and I choked as I tried to breathe.

I opened my eyes and saw him standing beside me, concerned. His hand reached out and gently stroked a line down the side of my neck where in the seventeenth century he had cut me. The skin

306

convulsed when his fingers touched it. Silence, only the sound of the waves and the creak of the boat.

"Are you feeling ill?" he asked.

"Yes," I replied, the word riding on my long exhalation. I knew then, though I found it difficult to accept, that there was more to life than this life. That in all our incarnations I had loved him, and that that love had brought me pain and death: time after time; life after life.

"Now do you see?" he asked me gently.

"Why was I executed? What did I do?"

"You betrayed the Shogun's government by providing information to the rebels."

I did not want to believe what had just happened to me, for to accept it would be to acknowledge that my grandfather had been right when he explained the origin of my name in his house on Armenian Street. But the entire experience had been so real and I was still shaken by the vestigial sorrow within me.

"Through how many lifetimes have we pursued one another? Two? Three?" I asked tentatively.

"Does it matter?"

I shook my head. "All that matters is this life, Endo-san. To have the will to make the right decisions."

He helped me out of the boat. "It is better that you work for us, you know. I can only protect you if you are useful to Hiroshi-san. It is not that I approve of what the army is doing, but Hiroshi-san is correct—all transitional periods are tumultuous and can only be controlled by a show of strength. If we showed weakness, we would never last long."

"Would Ueshiba-sensei approve?" I asked.

He shook his head. "Never."

"Then why are you doing this?"

"It is my duty and my fate. Why, of all the places I have traveled to—China, India, even the foothills of the Himalayas—why did I end up here? Because you are here; because the time has finally come to redress our lives.

"This time," he said, holding my shoulders firmly, "this time there will be balance and harmony. That is why I have been training you so hard, why I have driven you so harshly. So that you may be a match for me."

He let go of me. I took a step back and stumbled on the sand. "I will never raise my hand against you, Endo-san."

"No? Not even if your family is threatened, hurt, even killed? Do not make promises you cannot keep."

That evening he used his *katana* against me in his violent ways and I responded in kind. There was so much anger and so much fear, they fueled our movements and our release. He attacked me again and again, pressing into me, sinking into me with such intensity, as though he wanted to imprint a part of him in me, to leave a portion of his soul in mine. My sword received his force with equal hunger and I opened myself up to him as clouds open up to the sun.

Chapter Eight

It was raining, a soft thrumming on the world. From the window I could see Penang Hill and its lower ranges wreathed in a misty shawl. Dark, heavy clouds rolled over the ridges like surf breaking over sea boulders. The bungalows, which could be seen perched on the Hill on clear days, lay submerged beneath the clouds like shells covered by the tide, as though preferring to cut themselves off from the town below, choosing not to acknowledge the presence of the Japanese who by now had been occupying the country for close to three years. I, however, had no such option.

I was in my office when the file was handed to me by a clerk. I had no idea what the words *Sook Ching* meant. But as I continued reading the report the intent became clear. Hiroshi had received the papers an hour ago. In the background I heard the female clerks talking, and the pecking sounds of typewriters and ringing telephones. Except for the fact that the voices were speaking Japanese, I could have been in the offices of Hutton & Sons, preparing an order for a shipment of rubber.

I felt cold, and it was not due to the endless rain. I read the report again. Under the *Sook Ching* exercise, Chinese businessmen and villagers suspected of being members of anti-Japanese groups were to be rounded up and sent to labor camps. Every state in Malaya had orders to carry out the exercise. It was the retribution of the Japanese against the strong opposition shown by the local Chinese against the war in China.

Hiroshi entered my room. "Have you read the report? Direct orders from General Yamashita."

I nodded. He handed me another sheaf of papers. "These are the first batch of names. Copy them and send them to Fujihara-san, please."

"Yes," I said, but my mind was already searching for a way to save the people on the list.

*

I rushed through the day and as soon as I finished I arranged for another meeting with Towkay Yeap. We met as usual on the trawler, although we had to be wary as Japanese naval boats were patrolling the seas.

"These are the names of people who will be arrested by tomorrow." I recited a list of ten names I had memorized; they were all middle-aged Chinese businessmen. I saw Towkay Yeap recoil at the mention of each one. He was probably on good terms with them. He would wonder when his own turn would arrive, when I would come to him and utter his name.

"All were on the list published by the *Straits Times*—they petitioned against the Japanese invasion of China," he realized immediately.

"You have to get them away," I told him.

"That would put you in danger. Fujihara would know there's a leak."

"I have to run that risk," I said.

"We'll have to hurt you. That's the only way," he said.

I understood. Until now, due to his intervention, I had been relatively safe from assaults and harassment from the anti-Japanese movement. They had orders to stay away from me. That had to change.

"Send your best men," I said. "Only then will it look believable."

"Are you that good?" he asked.

"I beat your son once."

That stopped him short. A look of respect entered his eyes. "Then I shall use my best people. Make sure you do not injure them too seriously."

Fujihara was more cunning than I was. He moved that very night, but Towkay Yeap had managed to warn three of those on the list and they left the island before the Kempeitai came to drag them away. I saw his fury the following morning, when he came into my room.

"Who did you show the list of names to?" he shouted at me.

"Only you. Why?" I asked, hiding my fear, wondering what had happened.

"Someone had informed them. I lost three on the list. They were gone, their houses empty."

"You told me you were only conducting the arrests today," I said.

"Do not ever think you are more intelligent than I am," he said.

He went out, and I let my despair surface. Only three had escaped. I did not want to know what happened to the others but Fujihara made sure I would find out. He came in again just before noon.

"Come with me," he said.

I followed him, keeping my face free of any show of emotion, to the Kempeitai headquarters on Penang Road where the Japanese secret police had taken over the south wing of the former police headquarters. We walked up two flights of stairs. Despite the shortages of war I noticed the corridors along the upper floors had been covered with metal grilles. When he saw me looking at them, Fujihara said, "That is to keep our prisoners from jumping off the building. We alone decide when they are to die."

He led me into a windowless room where there were two Kempeitai officers, both just a few years older than I was, and a man tied to a chair; I recognized him as Wilson Loh, the son of Joseph Loh, a timber merchant and one of the founders of the Aid China Campaign. Wilson Loh had been beaten, his eyes were swollen and blood smeared his mouth and nostrils.

"The prisoner maintains he does not know where his father is," one of the Kempeitai officers said.

"That is fine, because I wish our friend here to see what happens next," Fujihara said, looking at me.

They pulled Wilson Loh up and dragged him outside. We followed them down to a square yard in the center. The sun lit up the poles where prisoners were to be beheaded. The shadows of the poles stretched out behind, like a sundial telling the time. My heart beat faster as I tried to center myself, calming myself with the deep breathing methods I had learned from Endo-san.

They laid Wilson Loh on the ground near a water pipe with a hose connected to it. Forcing his mouth open, they inserted the hose and turned on the tap. Wilson jerked as the rush of water overflowed from his mouth. One of the officers arranged the hose again.

"He was asking for water earlier," Fujihara said.

We watched as his stomach expanded with water. By now Wilson had stopped struggling and he just lay there. I could see his eyes; they were those of an animal in pain.

"Enough," Fujihara said. The tap was turned off and one of the officers placed a foot on Wilson's stomach. He pressed his weight down, and then, holding on to his fellow officer for balance, put his other foot onto Wilson's stomach and started to jump.

I turned away as the sound of Wilson's screams mixed with the gurgle of water gushing out from his throat. I looked up, into the cleansing light of the sun, letting its brightness be the only thing I could see.

I was to discover that Fujihara's ingenuity was endless. He used a variety of methods to torture his prisoners and over the next few months he made sure I was well acquainted with every one. In all those circumstances I held in my anguish, not willing to lose face before him as we stood and witnessed the prolonged deaths. Many of the prisoners were also used as live targets for bayonet practice, Fujihara all the while humming his preferred preludes and fugues under his breath, in his complete enjoyment breaching his own orders to his subordinates for silence. I could even see his fingers twitching as though he were playing his piano. At night the irreplicable sounds of bayonets stabbing into live human flesh, accompanied by his incessant humming, kept me awake. I was unable to close my eyes without seeing the atrocities again.

A week after Wilson Loh's death, Goro came to see me. "Let's go," he said.

"Where to?" I asked. Feeling a rising panic, I had to wipe my hands against my sides. Being summoned by one of the Kempeitai officers was something everyone, even the Japanese staff, avoided.

"Fujihara-san's orders. Don't ask questions."

We drove in a Rolls Royce that had been taken from one of the local Chinese tycoons in exchange for his life. Every now and then Goro would turn around and speak to me. Mostly he ignored me, although he was not impolite. Behind us a military lorry carried twenty soldiers, all armed. We headed past Balik Pulau, the Back of the Island, into the interior, past lush silent forests dripping with early morning rain, as though the trees themselves were weeping. Soon we saw cultivated land. Far ahead I could see the coconut trees of a plantation. And then the belt of green merged with the metallic gray of the rain-beaten sea. From a small hillock we descended into the bowl of the village. A good location for anti-Jap groups, I thought—easy access from the beach, thick jungle all around. There was abundant food here, all grown by the villagers. And then I began to perspire, for the road was familiar; I had traveled on it before. For a few moments I wondered if I were going through a time shift again, such as I had experienced on the boat while rowing to Endo-san's island. But this did not have the same sense of heightened reality about it; this was the present and this was real.

We swung onto a dirt road, past a group of children playing in the shade of a shanty. They peered out as we passed and I saw the wide-open eyes of a little boy, fascinated by the huge vehicles passing by. He waved to me, but I could not wave back. My hand, my entire body, refused to move, for we soon passed under the simple wooden arch that led into Kampong Dugong, where I had attended Ming's wedding.

I got out slowly from the car. A vast silence surrounded us when the engines were turned off. Not even the dogs barked. The villagers looked like everyone else. But what was I expecting to see? Ogres, hatching plots to kill all Japanese? Some were old, some my age; all looked apprehensive at this sudden intrusion into their peaceful lives. They appeared thin and malnourished, but, even before the war I had passed people like them every day in the streets. They were the people of the island of Penang and I was one of them. And they knew that. But what did they think of me, this Japanese collaborator? Did they remember me from the wedding?

Goro ordered the headman to appear. He came out from his hut and saw me. I remembered his name—Chua—although I wished I had forgotten it. Behind me the soldiers got down from their lorry, causing the first ripples of fear.

"Get all your people here, now!" Goro shouted. "Tell them," he said, shoving me forward. I interpreted his orders. Chua bent down to speak to a boy, who ran off. The entire village soon appeared as the soldiers went from house to house, kicking doors open, scattering chickens and dogs. In the crowd I found Ming and she looked disbelieving when she saw me.

Goro began to read from his list in Japanese. I stood, uncertain, until he cleared his throat and looked at me. I repeated after Goro, like a weak echo: "Under orders from General Yamashita, the military commander of Malaya, they are here to arrest those involved in giving assistance to the Malayan People's Anti-Japanese Army, the MPAJA."

A man in nondescript clothes climbed down from the lorry, his face covered by a hood. Only his eyes could be seen, staring out of the holes cut into the hood, darting left and right. Goro ordered him into the crowd. He walked slowly and the people parted before him, unwilling to look at him. He touched a man here, a woman there, and the cries and screams began.

I watched the hooded man move toward Ming and her husband, Ah Hock. I looked into her eyes and her hand went to her mouth as she let out a sob, for Ah Hock had been touched. Children began crying as the troops went among the crowd, dragging the chosen men and women out onto the square. The implication was clear; there was no need for me to translate, no need for me to be here at all.

Chua, when he saw that Ah Hock had been selected, broke away from the crowd and rushed up to me. "We have not aided anyone," he insisted. "Tell them. You cannot take my son away. He has not done anything wrong. No one here has."

I spoke rapidly to Goro, who shrugged.

"Elder Uncle. Please . . ." I pleaded with him. "Give them up, please. You have to protect the rest of your people."

"Why are you doing this?" he asked. "I remember you. You are Mr. Hutton's son. You are one of us."

I found I could not give him an answer.

"What will happen to my son?" Chua asked.

"Prison," I said.

Perhaps he knew the nature of the Japanese, and of men in war, better than I, despite my close contact with them. He looked at me and said, "I pity your belief."

Goro pushed him away but I held his arm. "I'm doing all I can," I said.

He nodded. "Perhaps you are."

He turned to face the crowd and tipped his head heavily. His people had to trust his decision, for was not his son among the prisoners? A moan went through them as the soldiers shoved the thirty men and women touched by the informer into the lorry.

Ming ran forward, screaming. A soldier slapped her twice and, when she still screamed, raised his rifle to club her. I moved in and shielded her from the blow. "I'm sorry," I kept saying. She struggled in my arms as she called out to Ah Hock. I turned to look at him, seeing the confusion and bewilderment on his simple round face. He was innocent, a fisherman trying to survive these times, just a random name plucked out by someone in his village who had wanted to get into the Kempeitai's good books. Ming slapped me and the sting woke me from my stupor. Chua, tears running down his face, came to pull her away but she slapped me once more. I stood there, arms at my sides, as she hit me again and again.

Goro, growing impatient, said, "Take her too."

I had to say something. "No. Let her be."

"Since she wants to join her man so desperately, let her." He gave an order to one of his men.

"You cannot do that. She was not picked out by your man."

"Who are you to tell me what to do?" He pointed his gun at me, jamming it into my cheek.

I pushed it away, moving into him at the same time. The gun discharged into the trees, taking off fragments of bark. I grasped his wrist, molding it into a *kote-gaeshi* lock and pointed the gun back into his face.

"Anyone move and I will take his eye out," I said softly. The Kempeitai officers, who had converged on me, stopped. "Rescind the order," I snapped. "On your family's honor, rescind the order now!"

Goro looked at the troops. "Let her go."

I disarmed him and released him from the wristlock.

"Fujihara-san and Endo-san are going to hear of this," he whispered, rubbing his hand.

I tried to find something to say to Ming, but failed. The tailgate of the lorry was bolted into place and the lorry started with a rumble, breaking the unnatural silence.

A woman howled, the sound sending the dogs into a barking frenzy. She was held back by her friends. An unshaven prisoner shook his head at her. I led Ming to the lorry, where she reached out her hand for her husband's. But the height was too great for them to touch and only their eyes could cross that distance.

I got into the car and followed the lorry out of the village into the gentle rain that was starting to fall. Four miles down the road we swung into a clearing surrounded by a grove of trees.

"What is going on?" I asked Goro.

He looked at me, his eyes shining. "I thought you had read the report."

The guards ordered the prisoners out. One by one they jumped to the ground and I saw their eyes as they passed me. Ah Hock, trying to control his terror, nodded at me in gratitude for saving Ming. A young female prisoner spat at me. When the guards started passing out shovels, I knew what would happen. My legs wanted to give way under me; they felt detached, an unknown part of me.

The prisoners were ordered to dig. Deeper and deeper they went until I could see only the tops of their heads, clods of clay and mud piling up beside them. A few refused to dig further, and were clubbed by the guards. The woman who had spat at me bit her lip and refused to cry out.

Did they know they were digging their own graves? How could they go on? Was it not better to stop and be shot, knowing that a bullet would still end their lives eventually? Was it hope that drove them on, praying that it was just a cruel trick played by the *Jipunakui*? That at some point the guards would have a good laugh, smoke a few cigarettes, and order them up into the lorry again?

There was not even an order to cease digging. Goro gave a hand signal and the guards started shooting. The gunshots exploded like a string of firecrackers set off during the Chinese New Year and the bodies tumbled into the wet, exposed earth. I saw Ah Hock's body jerk as he was hit and I closed my mind and placed it between Heaven and earth, in that elusive spot that would free me from all this.

I forced myself not to show any emotion, not in front of these people. Goro gave me a grin. "Let us go back. I am all wet, and I am hungry." He gave an order to the guards to remain behind and fill up the grave.

In the car, the window half down despite Goro's complaints, I kept hearing the headman's voice. I saw Ming's face and I knew I would never have the courage to face her again. But I had to, there was no other choice for me.

A simmering rage spread through me, squeezing my head in a tight vice. I had believed Endo-san. Believed all his lies. From the first moment he had lied to me. All his philosophizing, teaching me to broaden myself, to learn—for what purpose? To satisfy his pride? So what if I had been linked to him in our past lives? Did I have to be entwined with him in this?

Fujihara wanted me punished but Endo-san intervened. "He is still new to this, let him be. You got the people you wanted. Goro was acting beyond his orders."

Fujihara eyed both of us but remained quiet; Endo-san was, after all, his superior. He put on his hat and walked out. Endo-san came around his desk and put his arm around me. I tried not to flinch. "Are you all right?" he asked.

"You sent me there, didn't you?"

"Yes," he said.

"Why?"

"You have to get to know the cruelties of war." He studied me with concern. "You appear ill. Are you feeling all right?"

I ran to the bathroom and bent over the basin, where I proceeded to vomit whatever was left in me. He came in and handed me a towel. I held it and said, "I don't think I feel up to coming to work tomorrow."

"Go home then. Come in when you feel better," he said.

After he left I opened the tap and cleaned the two fingers I had shoved into my throat to induce my vomiting. I had to deceive him, for I knew now what I had to do.

I described what had happened at Kampong Dugong to Towkay Yeap. I told him everything, from the time I had entered the village, to the final moments. He was horrified and a soft wretched sound leaked out from him.

"It is the Japs' revenge for all the assistance we gave to China during their sweep across the motherland. They are targeting all Chinese, killing them off village by village, town by town."

"I couldn't save them," I said.

"I know Chua. I cannot believe that his son is dead."

"This is just the beginning. I've seen papers. The operations will be widened. Not just here but the whole country. You must do something."

"I don't . . . I don't know what to do." For the first time since I knew him I saw Towkay Yeap at a loss.

And I realized then that there was an emotion worse even than the sharpest fear; it was the dull feeling of hopelessness, the inability to do anything. A lassitude stole over me as though someone had draped a warm shawl over my shoulders. I was so tired that all I wanted was to go to sleep and wake up to find that the war was over or, even better, that all of this had been a nightmare. Towkay Yeap was frightened and lost but I had to go on.

I asked him for a car. "Where are you going? It is already dusk. It is not safe." He raised his hand, his bony fingers pulled into claws by his increasing frailty, as though he had the power to command me to his orders.

"Please tell my father that I'll be home late tonight. I still have something to do."

He understood and his hand dropped back into his lap. "Be careful," he said.

I drove into a clump of high *lalang* and the waving, almost head-high wild grass hid the car from view. At this hour, as the sun set, the frogs were calling out to each other, loving the rain that still fell in soft furry lines, the sort of rain that even a kitten would have loved playing in.

I followed the lights of the village. Somewhere a dog barked. The laterite road sloped down, bumpy with rocks. The sea was sulking at the thick cover of clouds. I went past the gates of the village and felt the ghostly silence of a place still stunned by the morning's events. The doors of the houses were closed, as though to shut out more ill fortune. I heard the wash of waves on the jetty and the creak of boats, like an old man turning over in restless sleep.

I coaxed from memory the location of Ming's house and made my way there. I wondered if Uncle Lim had been told and if he would already be in the village. Except for a light in one window, the wooden house was dark. I went under the porch and knocked on the slatted door, a soft, apologetic knock. Shadows moved in the light and the door opened. She took a step back when she saw me. I was appalled by the vivid bruises on her face. Had the soldier hit her so many times, so hard?

"I was wrong. They never got to the prison." I told her what had happened, feeling the guilt that would walk with me all my life.

"I know," she said.

"I don't understand," I said.

She saw my bewilderment but she shook her head and refused to answer me.

"I must see Chua," I said. She nodded, and together we walked to the headman's home. I tried to think of the appropriate words to say, when we were near the village headman's house. I thought of the pain my father had felt when William died and I knew that there was nothing I could say.

I could only describe what had happened, I thought, knocking on the door. It opened and from the look on Chua's face, I realized that there was not even a need for me to do that.

"We knew when they were taken away that they would never return," Chua said, as we sat down in his simple dining area. A high wooden altar faced the front door and a triad of gods looked down on us, the same Taoist trinity of Prosperity, Happiness, and Longevity which I had seen in my grandfather's home. Chua had lit some joss sticks and the thin white lines of smoke rose high up into the corrugated tin roof. A cream and brown cat with a stubby tail came in, crying. It leaned over and wanted to rub my legs but then stiffened and moved away to a corner.

"I should have known," I said.

"What could you have done? Could you have prevented it? You, a running dog?"

"Has Uncle Lim been told?"

Chua nodded. "He will arrive tomorrow morning to take Ming back to your home. But now there will be a funeral to see to." He sighed and I heard the crack in his voice. "Many funerals."

"Where did my husband die?" Ming asked. She had been crying but now she wiped her eyes. "Can you show us?"

I looked at Chua, and he said, "I would like to see my son too, Ming, but it is not a good idea. We should wait until tomorrow."

"I'd like to go now. Wait for me here, I'll go home and get some warm clothes and a lamp." She closed the door behind her softly and left us sitting before the three gods.

"Is she all right?" I asked.

Chua stared at the closed door. "After you left this morning, that man—the one who had wanted to take Ming as well— returned, together with three soldiers."

Goro had disappeared as soon as he had reported me to Fujihara. I did not want to be told why he had returned to Kampong Dugong. I knew. And the old headman saw that I knew but said it anyway. "He came and they raped her. And then they told her they had shot my son . . . shot them all."

"That's a punishable crime. We must report this. Goro and the others will be disciplined," I said.

He slammed his fist onto the table, his thick fisherman's wrist bending the thin plywood. The sound seemed blasphemous in the silence. "You fool!" he shouted. "Do you still see nothing even after what you took part in today?"

I stared silently at my lap while the gods looked down on us from their altar. The cat sniffed the air and then padded out.

We walked in the twilight, Ming and I, together with the villagers who wished to go to the mass grave of their families. I led the darkened procession with only some hurricane lamps to light our way. Anger and sorrow walked with me, joining hands with guilt—the three walls of my prison.

We came to the clearing and I stopped, trying to get my bearings. A circular break in the clouds allowed the crescent moon to cast its weak light on us. The earth looked freshly turned, as though in preparation for planting. In the spectral light the villagers began to weep.

"Where was Ah Hock?" Ming asked.

I led Chua and her to the eastern edge of the field. "He was standing here," I told her.

She knelt down, and with her bare hands began to dig.

320

"You can't do anything now, it's too dark," I said, but she went on, lifting out handfuls of earth.

Chua gently pulled her up. "We will come in the morning and perform the proper rites for them. We'll get the monks to set their souls at peace."

"I cannot let him lie here alone," she said.

"He's not alone. He has his friends here. Everyone he has known since he was a little boy. Come, my daughter," Chua said and took her hand. He caught my eye. "You cannot go home now. The curfew has begun. I shall prepare a place for you to sleep tonight. I hope the floor won't be too hard for you."

I woke some time before dawn, feeling stiff and cold. Chua's house was silent and a wick in a glass goblet of oil burned on the altar, giving off a warm, liquid golden light like the glow of the Buddha's heart. I had not slept much, keeping my senses open to the possibility of more soldiers returning. I had also caught the sounds of gentle crying coming from Chua's bedroom through the night.

I opened the door and stepped out onto the porch. Puddles of rainwater glowed like the discarded scales of a dragon. The first touches of the sun could be seen at the furthest line of the horizon, and out to sea little points of light from returning fishing boats seemed uncertain, forming and then wavering. The air was chilled by the rain, which had fallen throughout the night. I stepped onto the wet lane that went past Chua's home and walked to Ming's house. The lights were all on and I stood outside, then made up my mind and knocked on the door. There was no reply and, knowing the villagers never locked their doors, I wiped my feet on the mat and pushed the door open.

I stood in the little hall. The floor was covered in linoleum and the furniture was cheap but new. On the altar, all the bowls of oil before the gods had been lit and everything appeared neat and tidy. It was completely different from the night before. Boxes stood by the door to the bedroom, packed with clothes.

I left her house and walked in the direction of the field of bodies and, halfway, I began to run. The laterite was slippery with rain and I fell once, smearing myself with mud. I pushed myself up and ran faster, almost missing the turning into the lane that led to the field. The wind shook the trees and the branches splashed cold drops of water onto me. I came out into the clearing, looking around for her.

The field was empty, smooth except for a mound of earth. I made for it, feeling an unnatural sensation at walking over the bodies beneath me. At the mound I found a hole and inside I found Ming. She had dug up Ah Hock and turned him over, so that his eyes stared through me and beyond to the sky. She lay next to him, her eyes open to the tender rain, her arms around her husband. I could not see her blood, but I smelled it. I went into the hole and grasped her wrists, slippery from her opened veins. She was still breathing, her eyelids flickering once, twice, like a statue that had turned to flesh but was now reverting to stone. I searched in my pockets for a handkerchief to bind her wrists but the cloth blackened immediately. She shook her head. "Stay with me," she whispered. I held her hand and sat down in the cold mud.

Toward dawn her hand tightened on mine and she moved her mouth. I leaned over her and asked, "What is it?"

"Bury us together."

I promised her and, breathing in the terrene smells of the opened earth and raw warm blood and the purifying coolness of the rain, I waited for morning to come.

I never saw any butterflies.

When the villagers pulled me out of the hole Ming had dug with her bare hands, they shrank back at the sight of the blood that had soaked through my clothes.

I looked up into Uncle Lim's eyes and found I could not hold mine against them. He pushed me aside and went to the grave, and I heard his cry, so inhuman, so full of grief and pain. It was a sound only a father could make. Chua stood next to him and the two fathers shook with grief.

I sat on a rock and someone came up to me and offered me a cup of tea. I took it and found my hands were shaking from fatigue.

A group of Taoist monks waited at the edge of the crowd, preparing themselves for the burial rites.

"So soon?" I asked the man who had offered me tea. "Don't the bodies have to lie for a period of time?"

"They are busy," the man said. "They have other fields to attend to." His voice trailed away and I followed it as he turned his head.

My father had come through the crowd. He went past me and embraced Uncle Lim and Chua, gently pulling them away from their children's grave. I wanted to go to him, but in his face I saw that I had lost him.

Chapter Nine

Towkay Yeap was good as his word, for I continued to get threatening messages and a group of thugs attacked me as I was walking in town. I fought them off but sustained a deep cut across my arm. My father was furious. "You have to stop working for the Japs, damn it! What happens if Isabel or any of us get attacked as well? Do you want them to try to burn the house down again?"

The atmosphere at home was stifling. The relationship between my father and me had deteriorated further after the incident at Kampong Dugong and this was not helped by the continued threats, which I alone knew were harmless.

I could only keep silent as he viewed me with deep contempt. How could I tell him about the arrangement I had made with Towkay Yeap? After seeing the appalling acts of Fujihara and the Kempeitai I wanted my father to know as little as possible about my activities. It was a high-pressure game I had placed myself in—on the one hand I appeared to have betrayed my own people, but on the other I was also betraying the Japanese. There was no one I could confide in, and more than ever I wished Kon were here with me instead of in some wet and impenetrable jungle.

Sometimes I felt as though I no longer had any control over the turns and tangles of my life. What a mess I had made of everything, I thought; what a terrible mess. Where had I gone wrong?

A month after Ming's death, I received a message from Towkay Yeap, asking to meet me at Tanaka's old house in Tanjung Tokong. I considered the possibility of it being a trap, set as a retribution for my complicity in the massacre at Ming's village, and so made my way there an hour earlier, before the sun set. Being early would give me a tactical advantage.

The bungalow was empty, the expanse of the sea making it even more desolate. Evidently Tanaka had carried out his intention to hide away in the Black Water Hills. He had not removed the wind chime though and its little brass rods spun in the wind. The sun's setting glare set fire to it, seeming to animate it to greater movement, as though it were turning into an instrument that transformed light into music. I blinked as my eyes caught its reflections.

The lawn was overgrown and I lay low in the grass watching the house, trying to sense any activity with my *ki* energy. I did not hear the rustle behind me but I sensed the stealthy approach of another person. I rose up to meet my assailant only to find it was my friend Kon.

"You'll never be good enough to sneak up on me," I said.

"I knew you would come before the appointed time," he said. He was undernourished, his head shaven bald and only his smile had remained the same. He scratched absently at his scalp, saw my glance and said, "Sorry. Lice. That's why I had to cut it off."

"You won't get into the E & O looking like that," I said, not hiding my pleasure in seeing him. I still could not believe that it was actually him, in the flesh. "What are you doing here? I thought I was meeting your father."

"I asked him to arrange this meeting."

"What's wrong?"

"Too many things," he replied. He extended his hand in the direction of Tanaka's house. "May I offer you some tea?"

There was a figure at the doorway when we took the steps onto the veranda. A young woman came out of the gloom of the house and stepped into a square of light left by the receding sun. Even her shabbiness could not hide her unusual beauty. Her eyes, large and black, lifted her face to greater character. She was not completely Chinese but was of mixed parentage, like myself.

"Su Yen, this is the friend I told you so much about," Kon said. He introduced us quickly and we went inside, closing the door behind us. It took me a while to accustom myself to the darkness. Still, Kon went around the windows, making sure the curtains met. He lit a candle and we sat down on the floor.

"Su Yen's a guerrilla from the Malayan Communist Party. Force 136 and the MCP have made a pact to work together against the Japanese," Kon said.

"I know," I said. "I've read the reports by the Japanese spies."

Information on Force 136 was sparse, but Japanese intelligence reported that it had been formed by the British just before the war and that the recruits came from all walks of life. Bakers, tinkers, teachers, businessmen, anyone who had any form of expertise that could be exploited, all were sent to a military training base in Singapore to be trained extensively in jungle guerrilla warfare. It was a new form of combat, almost revolutionary. These recruits were later inserted into pockets of resistance in the jungles across Malaya.

I knew the scant facts and now Kon told me in greater detail. The British government had made a deal with the leaders of the MCP—ammunition would be supplied to them if they worked in tandem with Force 136 to carry out attacks against the Japanese.

War, I suppose, made strange bedfellows of former enemies. The Malayan Communist Party, known by the abbreviation-mad British as the MCP, had been active in the late 1920s, spreading its doctrine among the plantation workers and tin miners. There had been extensive strikes which had been put down brutally by the government. Driven underground, the MCP had taken to the jungle, vowing to take over the country.

Their success rate had been impressive, Kon said. Military bases, prisons, government offices, and the homes of high-ranking officials had been attacked, bombed, or successfully destroyed. Occasionally a village on the outer fringes of smaller towns would supply Force 136 with food and medicine. However, reprisals by the Kempeitai against these villagers were swift and fatal.

"I know that too well," I said. I told him about Ming's village, and countless others that I had visited with Goro. "The cleansing campaign, as the Kempeitai call it, is still going on."

"Do you know where Tanaka-*sensei* has gone to?" Kon asked. "Did he go into the mountains as he had planned?"

"I don't know. I suppose so."

"And your *sensei*?"

"He's second in command of Penang."

Kon widened his eyes and I decided to tell him everything.

He laughed bitterly when I finished. "Tanaka-*sensei* and I often wondered what he was doing with you. Now we know. All those times you took him around the island . . ." He shook his head. "So it's true that you're working for them. We heard that you were helping them. But I'd always dismissed it." The word "Kempeitai" was unspoken but it hung between us like a bad smell.

"Do you think I was wrong to do so?"

He shook his head. "I'm sure you have your reasons."

I glanced at Su Yen quickly, but decided to ask Kon anyway. "Is it wise, working together with the MCP?"

"As wise as working for the Japanese," Su Yen said.

"I suppose I deserved that," I said. "But why are you here? It isn't safe for you."

"Five of us have come out of the jungle. We're all in Penang but we have no idea of each other's precise whereabouts. We're to meet in two days' time at an appointed location to carry out our assignment."

"And you need my help."

"We have to destroy the military's main radar and radio station in the north. You've told me before that it's on The Hill. We need to know exactly where it is."

I got to my feet and walked to the window, peeping out through the slit in the curtains. It was already dark and the sea was indistinguishable from the land, except for a strip of gleaming foam where the ocean surrendered to the earth, again and again.

"I can't tell you that," I said.

"It's important. We have to blind the Japanese so our ships and planes can come in undetected. They have to drop supplies to us and we have to open a safe lane for the eventual assault."

"I can't allow you to bomb the station. Do you know what will happen if you succeed? The retribution against the people of Penang will be horrific. Innocent people will suffer. And the Kempeitai will hunt you down and kill you."

"That is the price of winning the war," Kon said. "We have no choice."

"Of course you have. Forget your assignment."

"The MCP leaders will kill him if he fails," Su Yen said.

"Then hide here, in Penang."

"I can't," Kon said gently. "I took on a duty and I have to complete it."

I squeezed my temples. "Too many people have died already."

"Do it, Philip. For me," Kon said. "Tell me where the station is."

He did not have to mention the debt I owed him for saving my father's life. So I told him the location of the house on Penang Hill, which I had pointed out to Endo-san and which, in effect, I had recommended to the Imperial Japanese Army.

"You can't go up by the funicular. The station was damaged by the Japanese bombing and there are now guards watching it," I warned him.

"How, then?"

"You hike up, through Moon Gate." I explained to him where that was. "Keep your eyes open for army patrols."

"That was the way you showed your *sensei*," he guessed.

I nodded. "I have to go."

Kon walked me out to the road in the dark. "We shouldn't meet here again," he said.

I felt compelled to ask, "What happened in the days before Penang was lost? I went to look for you but your father said you had left."

He told me. After the day of Ming's wedding he had made his way to Singapore to meet Edgecumbe at the headquarters of the Special Operations Executive, under which Force 136 operated. He was put through some quick general training, along with police inspectors, planters, miners, schoolteachers, anyone who knew the country and could speak its varied languages.

"It was exactly as Edgecumbe had described. We parachuted into a landing zone in the jungle on the day Kuala Lumpur fell. An earlier team of guerrillas met us. It was a strange group—pale, weak-looking English, surly Chinese communists, and friendly Gurkhas and Temiar aborigines.

"The first few weeks were good and everything was new and exciting; we all thought it was an adventure. But then the monotony set in and we were constantly on the move, always on our guard. Food became scarce and I wondered how a handful of us could make any difference to the war.

"But the worst times were during the monsoon. The rain often fell for weeks without stopping and we had to sit under a leaky, overpatched tent for days and days. And when we were on patrol we would sit huddled beneath our oilskins, or under the giant ferns, in constant misery. I almost gave up. Quite a few went mad." He paused for a long moment. "They became safety risks and I had to shoot them.

"Things began to improve when Chin Peng, the head of the MCP, ordered us to team up with Yong Kwan. We made our way to his hideout, which has been our base for—what is today's date?"

I told him and he became silent. He crouched down and scratched at the ground with a stick. "October 1944," he said, his voice sounding lost. "So I've been away for three years." When he looked up I saw fatigue in his eyes.

"It'll be over soon," I said, but the words rang with hollowness. Yong Kwan had taken an instant dislike to Kon. The Communists had a history of enmity with the triads. "The men in the group realized I was a better tactician and fighter than Yong Kwan. We made so many successful raids and attacks on the Japs that we had to lie low for months. We managed to hit quite a few important targets. And we took food and medicines from the camps we had attacked. I fed my team well. Things became worse when I met Su Yen. We became friends and, because we were young and lonely, we became lovers."

"Yong Kwan's woman?"

"Yes."

"You're insane. Why is she here with you?"

"She is carrying a child."

"Yours?"

"We don't know. But we have to abort it. We don't know how much longer the war will drag on. She can't give birth in the jungle."

"Let her stay here. You can't make her get rid of her child."

"I'm not making her do anything. She insisted on it." He saw the look on my face. "That's not your worry. I can deal with it myself. I know people in town. Thank you for giving us the information we needed. You and I are even now."

"Yes, we are."

"Come with me," he said. "You know it's the right thing to do."

"I don't know anymore, Kon."

I did not know when I would see him again, if ever at all. I was torn between wishing him success in his mission and hoping he would not carry it out. In the end I decided not to say anything and bowed to him.

The radar station was destroyed three days later. It happened at midday and the explosion could be heard and seen from Georgetown. Part of me exulted, and hoped Kon had managed to get away. But I was also fearful. The Japanese responded decisively and indiscriminately and I was called on to read out more names in town and in the outlying villages. I knew the people they dragged out were blameless but there was nothing I could do. I felt angry with Kon because he did not have to live with the consequences.

A deep fear, so constant now in my life, was like a growth in me. When did I let it enter, steal silently in, and latch on to me? There were days when I could hardly breathe, as though my blood, coagulated by fear, could not flow.

Each day I accompanied Goro to the *Sook Ching* exercises and he would return from them triumphant. I felt the rage in me burn stronger and I wanted to kill him.

I knew I had saved countless lives through the information I had been supplying to Towkay Yeap. But I could not save all of them. Enough had to go into the fire in order for me to stay unblemished in the eyes of Fujihara and the Kempeitai. The secret police had taken to following me and made no effort to hide themselves. I made a bitter complaint to Endo-san.

"It is for your safety. You are a target for the anti-Japanese groups, you realize that? And besides, you have nothing to hide from me, have you?"

I nodded my head but averted my eyes from his. Did he know of my collusion with the triads? Was he aware of the role I had played in the destruction of the radar station on The Hill? There was no way in which I could elicit anything from him. He was too canny, with the cunning and maturity of a man three times my age. I was outclassed and I realized, too late, that it had been like that from the very first day.

Walking on the beach with him after work, a mile away from Istana, I asked, "You must be aware of what Fujihara-san is doing."

"Yes, I am."

"And yet you feel nothing?"

"I feel a great shame and pain. But I have my obligations. And this is war. This is part of the journey we have to travel. And, yes, it is a hard road."

A squadron of Zeroes flew over us, tiny as mosquitoes above the land they were patrolling.

"When I am gone, what will you most remember of me?" Endo-san asked, his eyes on the planes as they faded into the distance.

I pondered the question. "I don't know. I don't even know what to think of you now; how can I even contemplate what to recall of you?"

The island settled down after the first burst of arrests, watching, waiting. I had become very much feared through accompanying Goro and I felt the hatred of the people as I went about my work.

The streets remained relatively empty as most people were in the jungle or in the countryside, where contact with the Japanese was minimal. In Georgetown entire streets of houses stood empty, their inhabitants either in hiding or taken away by the Kempeitai. Food supplies were hard to obtain and prices on the black market were astronomical. People resorted to planting sweet potatoes and yams in their gardens. Inflation went unchecked and more and more banana notes were printed. I stopped bringing food and supplies home from work, even though I was entitled to, because my father and Isabel refused to touch any of it. That angered me and left me with a growing sense of helplessness. If they did not want to accept my assistance, what was the reason for my involvement with our new masters? I sat mutely as they consumed watery yam broth cooked with the leaves of the sweet potato trees the servants had planted in the vegetable yard at the back of the house. Eventually I spent most evenings at Endo-san's island. More and more I depended on him for support and I would sit in silence with him, staving off the sense of loneliness and rage. It was ironic, as he was their cause.

"Tell me it will all be fine one day," I said to him as I cleared away our meal.

"It will be. But to get there you will have to travel across the landscape of memories, across the continent of time," he answered softly.

"As long as you are there to guide me."

"Only sometimes. Like now for instance. Sometimes you will be alone; sometimes you will be with others. But I will be there at the end, waiting for you. Never forget that."

"What if I forget you?"

"You have not so far. You cannot forget what is within you. And I am within you. Look into yourself when you feel lost and you will find me there."

"I'm so afraid, Endo-san. So very frightened. I'm not strong enough for this," I said, and he came and hugged me. I listened to the inner sounds of his body, the beating of his heart, the exchange of breaths in his lungs, the roar of blood rushing through his veins. A universe was in there, dying and being renewed every second.

His short burst of laughter was weighed down with irony. "I am afraid too."

He pushed me away gently and gave me a letter. "I received this today," he said. "I am sorry."

I read the letter from Edward. "No," I said. I felt fatigued, sick with the war. "I'll have to tell them."

"I do not envy the burden you have to carry."

"Some of the burdens came from you, Endo-san. You and your people." I went outside to the strengthening stars. "I have to go home now."

"Of course you must."

I sat at the breakfast table and waited for my father and Isabel. They saw my face and sat down. I handed the letter to my father. He read it, folded it and said, "Peter's dead. He was killed trying to escape. Edward thinks he can't go on any longer. He's suffering from dysentery and starvation. There is no medicine for them."

Isabel gripped her fork tightly, pushing it into the surface of the table. I reached out to hold her wrist but she turned the fork and stabbed it into my hand. "Don't touch me!" she said as I suppressed a cry of pain.

"You can't blame him, Isabel," my father said, but the words had a tone that came from duty and obligation, not belief.

"Edward's dying, and he continues to help those killers, those

332

monsters who've killed Peter." She pushed her chair away. "Get out. Get out of this house. You don't belong here anymore."

"Maybe you should stay away for a while," my father said. "Until you decide where your loyalties lie."

I watched as the four points of blood from the tines of the fork erupted from my skin, my wounded hand growing cold as though the chill of the air had found an opening to penetrate me. I knew my father's heart was breaking and, because I loved him, I agreed. "Yes, perhaps that would be better," I said. I folded my napkin properly, placed it back on the table and left the dining room.

People refused to let their rooms to me. Hotels and guesthouses told me they were full. And after walking the streets of Georgetown I knew I could not stay there, even if I had been able to find a place. I was too hated by now and the townspeople did not encourage me to linger. Even Towkay Yeap refused me lodgings when I showed up at his gates, saying he did not want it to be known that he was sheltering me. "That is the price of playing both sides. Eventually all sides mistrust you."

"But you trust me, don't you?"

He merely looked at me, then closed his door.

I made my way to Aunt Mei's home and, like the other time I visited her, she came to the door reluctantly and closed it quickly behind us. "I told you not to come here until everything was safe," she said, not hiding her anger. I felt something was wrong for she looked as though she was hiding something. I opened my senses, sending my *ki* outward, and sensed she had a visitor.

"I cannot give you a place to stay," she said.

"How did you know I wanted a place to stay?" I asked.

"I—I heard word on the streets, that's all," she said. "Now you must go. Your presence here is not good."

As I left her I glanced up and saw a figure hiding in the shade of the veranda upstairs. Isabel. I stood under the sun, willing her to come out. The figure moved and she looked down at me. We stood that way for a long time. I lifted up my hand in a half wave. She closed her eyes and returned to the darkness of the house.

I walked to the end of the road and summoned a trishaw. I

would ask Endo-san for shelter. It was the first place I should have gone to.

Endo-san had never named his island and I asked him the reason for that lapse.

"I never wanted to give a name to this island," he said. "Look around you. What name can you give to something like this?"

We had been swimming in the sea after my lesson with him and were now resting under the shade of the curving coconut tree, its spiky leaves rustling like a thousand beetles as the wind shook it. We sat in a shared silence for some time, watching the cormorants dive for fish.

My hands touched the rock on which I had, a long, long time ago, carved my name. I found it difficult to fathom the swiftness of time, to accept that it was already two months into 1945. The Japanese had been in Malaya for four years; I had known Endo-san for almost six. He and I had drifted into a comfortable routine, although I remained worried that I would give away my role as Towkay Yeap's informer.

I thought of Kon for a moment and said a prayer that he would be safe. I wondered where Tanaka was and, thinking of him, I recalled him telling me how he had followed Endo-san to Penang.

"Tell me why you came here," I now said to Endo-san. "I've asked you once and you never answered. Let me know now, please."

He shook his head. "Some other time, when this is all over."

My disappointment showed and he said, "I promise you I will tell you, when the time is right."

I thought of that moment on the ledge, of letting go, trusting him. That feeling would always be there, giving me strength again and again, whenever his actions affected me.

"I will hold you to your word," I said.

But he was looking at the cormorants and appeared not to have heard me.

Chapter Ten

Something in the air had changed, something indefinable, as though a new element had been dipped into it, slowly spreading like the coming of a different season. We received radio reports relayed from India and Australia and we knew that Japan was suffering badly in its engagements against the United States in the Pacific Ocean. When I walked to town to make purchases, people's faces were lighter, stronger. Shopkeepers began to sound defiant to me.

Attacks on the Japanese increased, driving Fujihara into a frenzied rage. He would go on daily raids, hunting down the hidden radios and transmitters that relayed fragments of news. Even so, a network of anti-Japanese groups existed in Penang, passing news and information across the country, providing accurate details to the guerrillas in the jungle. Most of that information had been provided by Towkay Yeap, who had obtained it from me, but I was sure he would have other informants, all working in different areas of the government.

On the days of the arrests Fujihara would come back to our office expressionless if he found a forbidden transmitter set, or in a vile mood if his searches had failed to produce anything. But, whether he found any or not, he would often have a group of prisoners and then he would disappear for a few days to the square in the police headquarters. Goro would accompany him and return looking like a contented tiger.

"You should join us," he said. "Sometimes I use them for practice." He made punching motions in the air. "Nothing so real and satisfying as hitting a live person."

I read the documents that came over daily on the telex and a single name began to recur like a hardy weed. It became clear that amongst the scattered groups of resistance fighters, one calling itself the White Tiger had the highest success rate. Eventually

General Yamashita made it known that this particular group had to be stopped.

I knew it had to be Kon's group. I sat in my little cubicle and wondered if I had made a terrible mistake, if in fact the path of my life should have been with Force 136. Then my father and Isabel and everyone else on the island would not have seen me as a traitor.

I missed them, and I missed Istana. They occupied my mind during all the minutes and hours of my days. I tried not to show it to Endo-san and pretended all was well. Every evening I stood on the landward side of his island, gazing at the imposing structure that had once been my home, at the solitary casuarina tree planted when I was born that stood out from the bluff, so alone. Sometimes, when the gods of light decided to favor me, I would see a figure moving about on the lawns and know it was my father, and a deep chasm of loss would open up inside me.

Fujihara came into my office and Uncle Lim followed behind. I felt fearful immediately. He had aged so much. His hair was almost completely white and his clothes hung loose as withered leaves. I felt the guilt of Ming's death, fresh as though it had been the day before.

"Is this not your driver? He says he has some useful information for us," Fujihara said, the anticipation of a prey's fresh blood making him vibrate with excitement.

"Uncle Lim, whatever you are going to say, I hope you've thought carefully of the consequences," I said, trying hard to remain calm.

He did not answer me, but in a firm, steady voice that only shook once before he controlled it again he said, "There's a radio transmitter in Istana. I believe the daughter of the house has been using it to pass information to certain people on the mainland."

"He's lying," I said quickly. "He's been affected by his daughter's death."

"Let us see, then," Fujihara said. "I think you should come with us."

Fujihara left to round up his men and I went into Endo-san's office and told him of the Kempeitai chief's intentions.

"He is acting within his powers; you cannot expect me to intervene," Endo-san said.

336

"You can prevent any mistreatment of my sister," I said. He knew of the exchange between Fujihara and Isabel at Istana before the surrender but I reminded him of it again.

He shook his head. "Fujihara-san's mandate comes from the emperor's representative in Malaya and that person is—"

"Saotome," I said.

"Who has taken a personal interest in this matter," Fujihara said, entering the room. "I have spoken to him now. He has requested to be present when we interrogate this Hutton woman." He gave me a smile, the first time I had seen him do so. "Your sister. Ready to go?"

I pleaded to Endo-san with my mind, reaching out to him with unspoken thoughts—*come with me, at least come with me, and give me strength*.

"I think I would like to join you as well, Fujihara-san," Endo-san said.

The head of the Kempeitai, triumph in his nostrils, agreed readily. "You are most welcome, Endo-san. I shall wait for you outside."

"Get me my coat," Endo-san said. I went out to the cloakroom and paused, listening. When I was certain that I was alone I telephoned Towkay Yeap. "Tell my sister to destroy everything she has. The Kempeitai are coming."

It was all a mistake, I thought. Surely Isabel could not have been in league with any anti-Japanese groups? She would not have known anyone who was involved and she would never have been so foolish as to place herself and her family in such danger. As I hurried out to the car I tried to convince myself of this but all my efforts were useless against an overpowering feeling of dread.

All the way to Istana I could see only the fluttering flag on the bonnet of the car. The two cars entered the driveway, through the stone pillars that gaped now like a toothless mouth. All the iron fittings and decorations in the country had been taken down by the Japanese, smelted down and sent back to Japan. I was saddened by the derelict condition of the gardens, the trees growing wild, the grass uncut and scattered with leaves. My father had taken such great pride in his garden before the war.

The windows of the house were closed and only a single shutter was open, a thin wisp of curtain curling in and out like a lolling tongue, as though mocking me.

I stood by the car, unsure if this were still my home, unsure if the house would recognize me.

Two Kempeitai officers walked up the steps and knocked on the door. Uncle Lim stared ahead, perhaps remembering the first time he had entered by these doors, to see the master of the house. He refused to look at me.

My father opened the door, saw me and his shoulders slumped. I hoped desperately that Towkay Yeap had managed to warn him.

Fujihara pushed himself in. "We are here to search your house. This man here," he pointed to Uncle Lim, "is certain that your daughter has been passing information to people sympathetic to the enemy."

The officers went upstairs. "Make sure the servants are all kept in the house," Fujihara said to them. I attempted to follow but Endo-san held me back with a soft touch on my shoulder.

My father's glance went to Uncle Lim and back to me but his blue eyes betrayed nothing. There was nothing to say. I could feel the heavy silence of the house, disturbed only by the sounds of doors being opened and closed upstairs. We heard the breaking of glass and splintering wood in the library as my father's collection of butterflies was destroyed by the officers but he remained expressionless.

The officers came down again. "There is no one. We found nothing."

"The boathouse," Uncle Lim said.

We made our way down to the beach, and the sea winds, so reminiscent of the lazy, happy days of my childhood, were unnatural companions to our business. We approached the boathouse. It was just a wooden hut, large enough to store my boat and the small sailing boat my father had long since stopped using. They found the box in the cupboard where we kept our fishing lines and rods. They also found Isabel hidden in the cabin of my father's sailing boat.

She kicked and fought them as they dragged her out. Fujihara reached over and, faster than I could stop him, slapped her twice and pushed her onto the sand.

"Where's your rifle now?" he asked and kicked her in the face. I anchored my father, restraining him from going to Isabel.

The box was opened and I cursed silently. A small transmitter set fell out, then a headset and a small microphone. A pile of papers took flight in the gusting wind and the Kempeitai officers chased after them, like boys on a beach.

"No," my father whispered. "Lim, what have you done? Why?"

"Your son led Ming to her death, Mr. Hutton," Uncle Lim said. "This is justice."

"That's not how it happened," I said, but nobody was listening to me.

"We now have incontrovertible evidence," Fujihara said. "Thank you, Mr. Lim."

"Isabel . . ." I said. I took her hand and lifted her to her feet. "Why? Why did you have to risk your life like this?"

She looked at me with such hatred that I flinched from the physical force of it. "William and Peter are dead, Edward is dying day by day in the prison camps and Father is working himself sick trying to keep our company and our workers alive. Everyone is playing their part in fighting these animals. Everyone except you. You chose the easy way: to work for the Japs. I feel sorry for you because when the British come back and kick your friends out, this house, this island, this country, will never be home for you again. You'll remember too much. And too many people will never forget what you did."

I thought of Saotome and Fujihara, waiting, ready to participate in her interrogation. "Don't you know what's going to happen to you? Did you ever consider the consequences?" I asked.

"Remember what I said to you, such a short time ago, the night we spent on The Hill?"

I knew, I remembered. But still she said it again, as though to ensure I would never forget. "*I would die before I would even consider working for them.*"

Endo-san pulled her roughly and said, "Come, enough of this nonsense. Fujihara-san, gather the radio and whatever else you require and let us return. The sun is too hot."

Isabel pulled free and hugged my father. "I'm so sorry," she whispered.

My father rubbed her head, smelled her hair. "You did the right thing. We'll find a way to get you out of this."

I stood alone, outside them, knowing I had no right to be with them now.

Fujihara lifted a camera from his case and walked around the boathouse taking photographs, humming all the while. Endo-san said to Isabel, so softly I thought it was just a stream of wind. "You must not escape."

My father looked up sharply. Endo-san repeated his words. "You must not escape." He patted his coat pocket once, as though to feel his heart. I did not understand, but Isabel did.

She pulled away from my father as he was wiping the tears from her face. Isabel nodded slowly at Endo-san. Then her eyes met mine.

"Forgive me," I whispered, as a horrible comprehension awoke inside me. She held out her hand and I took it, it seemed, for the longest time. I was unwilling to release her, but she pulled her fingers away and turned and ran along the waterline, her shining figure reflected on the wet smooth sand, leaving behind a trail of footprints. The waves came in and rubbed them away and still she ran, creating new ones, running forever, in eternal motion. The world in my head was silenced. All I seemed to hear was her breathing—or maybe it was hers and mine. We breathed together and I felt her exertion, her fear, and her exhilaration. She had an unnatural lightness, moving so easily her feet seemed to glance across the wet sand, her weight never once falling entirely onto it.

Endo-san shouted a warning to Fujihara then reached into his coat pocket and brought out a pistol. He lifted it in the calm, natural motion he had once taught me in the jungle near Kampong Pangkor. He took aim before Fujihara could drop his camera and stop him.

He fired only one shot. It brought her down slowly, her body still moving as if she were sinking into the sand as she ran. My feet could finally move and I sped toward her as the waves came in and washed her, waving her arms and her hair gently, moving her as though she were still alive. But I knew she was dead the moment Endo-san shot her. He never missed.

I lifted my sister out of the water, feeling it stream over me. So precise was Endo-san's aim that I almost missed the wound in her back that had struck her heart. And so skillful had he been that the bullet appeared to have plugged the wound, for the blood had already stopped flowing. Only a bright circle of crimson stained the water where I stood until it broke apart and the waves carried it out to sea. Isabel appeared unblemished, her eyes gently closed, drops of seawater pierced by her lashes, her lips half open to the air that she would never taste again.

I kissed her forehead and laid her down on the sand above the reach of the sea. In the seconds before the rest of the Japanese officers reached us I opened myself up to my anguish, knowing I was responsible for driving my sister to the acts that had finally come to this. A constricted sensation gathered deep within me, seeking to release itself. My mouth opened but no sound emerged. It was a silent lament that only I, and perhaps Isabel, could hear.

No one, I told myself, could ever understand how much I had suffered and to witness such sorrow without comprehending would be to cast dishonor upon it. So the hurt would be lodged inside, like the bullet within Isabel. I placed a heavy seal over my wound. No trace of my blood would ever show.

I stood up slowly, straightened my wet clothes and turned to face the Kempeitai officers. They took a step back, frightened by the intensity in my eyes. There was a moment of total silence. No one knew what to do next. Even Fujihara was quiet. I sought out my father but his face was as rigid and blank as mine. I was brought back to myself by Fujihara's voice.

"You let her go! How dare you shoot her! Saotome-san will be informed when he arrives!" he shouted. It was the first time I had seen an eruption of emotion from him and it assuaged me, however slightly, that Isabel had been the cause of it, had broken his self-control.

"Your prisoner was escaping and I shot her to prevent that. Please do inform Saotome-san," Endo-san said, as unruffled as a courtier. "I shall, of course, prepare a written report for him as well, telling him how you let the girl escape."

Fujihara kicked the radio, breaking its shell. "Get the body! She will not be properly buried. I want her thrown onto a heap."

I protested, but Endo-san said, "Be quiet. There is nothing more to be done. And what is a body anyway? Your sister is gone."

So she was. They lifted her body and took her up the steps. We followed behind and I had to hold my father up, for he could not walk. But when we reached the top he broke away from me, stopped Endo-san, and bowed to him, before turning his back on us.

The Kempeitai could find nothing of any use in the papers Isabel had not managed to destroy but Uncle Lim gave them the names of two of her contacts. Fujihara took out his frustration and fury on them. One of the names was my Aunt Mei's and he forced me to sit and watch as they tortured her. She only screamed toward the end and she never revealed anything of use to them.

I sat with her as she began dying, her nose broken, one eye blinded. I held her and warmed her, feeding her water from a teaspoon.

"You must forgive your sister," she whispered.

I shook my head, puzzled, and she said, "That day, when you came to seek shelter with me, it was not Isabel who told me to chase you away. No, she never wanted that. She was there to find a way to help in the war." She stopped, taking a deep breath. "She said she had to do something, anything. And so she came to her old aunt, her old teacher . . ."

"To balance the harm I was doing, to restore the family name," I said, feeling numb.

"Yes. I was the one who said she could hide the radio for us and transmit the news we heard from Madras to Singapore. Lim knew about it from the start."

She let out a cry of pain as she tried to shift her body. "The war will be over soon," she said. "We've been getting news every day. Japan is finished."

The door opened and Fujihara's shadow darkened the cramped cell. I sat there on the rough stone floor as they took her out into the square. Her trailing hand brushed mine softly as she was taken away.

Uncle Lim had obtained the vengeance he wanted for Ming's death and we never saw him again. Some said he was murdered and some said he ran to avoid retribution from my grandfather. But sometimes I think he returned to China and I pray that he found some happiness there in his fading days.

My father was detained for over a week. I visited him in the Fort Cornwallis jail every afternoon but we seldom talked. Endo-san had used all his force of character to prevent Fujihara from employing his extreme methods on my father.

The cell was damp and hot, the walls scrawled with names and the final messages of the men before they were taken out to die. I placed the tiffin carrier of soup on the floor and knelt in front of him. A sparrow hopped onto the sill, stood between the bars, cocked its head at us, and then flew away.

"They'll let you leave soon. Fujihara just wants to play with us. You didn't know about the radio, nor about what Isabel was doing," I said.

"That old woman was right," he said. "She spoke the truth." He laughed softly. I held my breath, hoping he was not going mad. "You're the one who will bring us all to an end," he said.

My grandfather's words—and those irresponsible words of the soothsayer at the snake temple—returned to me. I cursed her then for determining my life with her careless utterances. I cursed my fate, all written even before I had a chance to have any say in it. And I cursed the day I met Endo-san.

My father grasped my hands. "My poor boy," he said.

Chapter Eleven

Akasaki Saotome arrived in Butterworth and I met him on the island side as the ferry came over. The season of the monsoon surrounded us again and the skies were dark with energy. Lightning stabbed out of and into the clouds and the wind picked up the scraps of rubbish on the pavements. Saotome strode down the gangplank, as filled with power as the skies over us.

We bowed, and he said, "You are still considered a loyal member of our government. I am sorry about your sister. But traitors must never be tolerated."

"I'm sorry too. She was shot while trying to escape."

He stopped. "Fujihara-san did not mention that to me."

"It happened just a few days ago." I could see his disappointment and a wave of disgust came over me. "You have wasted your trip, I am afraid," I said.

"Now what has Fujihara-san been telling you, hm? I am here to catch a tiger." He recovered from his disappointment and laughed. "Come, let us go before we are drenched. How I loathe this country and its endless seasons of rain."

The briefing was held in the main meeting room, which was furnished only with an *ikebana* flower arrangement created by Hiroshi. It was a lush, almost monstrous design, unlike the spare, stark forms that Saotome favored. All the flowers were indigenous to Malaya and the combination of hibiscus and ferns and orchids was quite unrefined.

Hiroshi was rearranging it with great fuss when we entered, his coughs shaking his entire body. They racked him frequently: only a few of us had been informed that he was afflicted with tuberculosis, but there would have been talk among the staff as well, of that I was certain. He had lost so much weight we could almost see how his ribs rattled when he coughed. There were days when he could not get out of bed and Endo-san had taken over the majority of his responsibilities.

Saotome sat down and said, "Hiroshi-san, please excuse us. I do not wish to breathe your air."

There was a long silence, Fujihara not even bothering to hide his amusement. I looked down onto the table, feeling embarrassed for Hiroshi. Such a public humiliation was quite unwarranted. He pushed back his chair, arranged his notes on the table, bowed, and closed the door after he left.

"Good," Saotome said. "We are here today to shut down the activities of a group of irritants once and for all. The group calls itself the White Tiger and it is one of the cell organizations of Force 136 and the MPAJA which has been inflicting serious damage on us. I have reports confirming it was responsible for the loss of our radar station here. We have a well-placed source within it."

Saotome passed a brown file around to Endo-san and Fujihara. He waved for me to leave them. "I've always attended the meetings," I protested. I had to find out more, find out what they had in mind for my friend Kon.

"Not today," Saotome said.

I closed the door behind me, passing Goro, who was standing outside the room. I walked down the corridor, sat in my office and began to think calmly. In the next room I heard Hiroshi coughing wetly and I decided to see if he was feeling all right. As I placed my hand on the slightly open door of his room I paused, wondering if I was hearing voices. I was confused, for Saotome's voice seemed to come from behind Hiroshi's door. I could hear, though with some difficulty, Saotome say: . . . *act as the bait, and our man will let them know that the second highest ranking Japanese is passing through their territory. Once they attempt to capture me our troops will come out and seize them. We will cut them open and hang them in the Padang in Kuala Lumpur, make them an example to the other groups who dare fight us. That will show them we intend to remain masters of this country, however much we are losing battles. I want that White Tiger's head.*

I heard Fujihara laugh, and from behind the door a cough rippled through Hiroshi. I realized this was how he kept his finger on the affairs of his staff. Cunning little bastard, to place a microphone in the meeting room. I smiled when I realized the device had been hidden in the *ikebana*.

The past days had been typical of the monsoon weather, balmy days turning to heavy rains in the early afternoon. It was sticky and hot. I left work early before they came out from the meeting, so as to avoid the rain. My mind was in turmoil as I cycled out of the army headquarters, past the saluting sentries. How to warn Kon's team that it was about to be ambushed? And who was the man working for the Japanese in their group?

I cycled into town and parked my bicycle near the steps of Empire Trading. The windows of Hutton & Sons were shuttered and the office had been closed until my father could return. The staff would be waiting for him, for without his presence throughout the Occupation the Japanese would have sent them to the prison camps. Walking across the back lanes I made a few evasive turns. I stopped at a battered shophouse and knocked rapidly on the door. After a few long minutes it was opened and I was ushered into the gloomy interior. I was immediately lifted by the fragrance of burning opium, sweet and cloying, the scent of too-ripe fruit. I felt giddy, and had to take a few deep, deliberate breaths. A harridan led me up a flight of creaky stairs, past yellowing calendars showing girls in *cheongsam* selling beer and whiskey, their tight dresses slit up to their hips. I came to a landing divided into separate cubicles by wooden screens. A shaft of sunlight sprayed in from a cracked shutter. Outside, the flutter of pigeons on the gutters added to the oppressive silence within. The sound of breaths, inhalations and drawn out exhalations, were like spectral whispers, as though the walls were murmuring to each other across the space. Dark figures lying on wooden divans shifted as smoke curled up from their pipes. Soft moans and softer cries floated from them. All the normal sounds of an opium den, I supposed. I tried to shut them out.

Towkay Yeap lay on an opium bed facing me, a look of repose on his face as his cheeks collapsed to haul in another drug-saturated breath. A young girl, no more than twelve, tiny-waisted and looking ancient in her face paint, knelt before him, rolling pinches of the dark, sticky opium into balls. As he finished the pipe she took it from him and lit another opium ball, her movement expert and her face quite bored. The air burned with the heated opium as she passed the pipe back to him. His wisps of hair trembled slightly as the fans above us spun lazily, too slow to cool the air. They seemed to turn without purpose, like flowers spinning on the wind.

He offered me the pipe, but I declined. He gave me an evil, contented smile. "What news do you have for me today?"

"Your son will soon die," I said softly.

I thought he had not heard, for he seemed preoccupied with his ivory pipe. He opened his eyes again as I started to speak. "My son is invincible."

I gave a snort. "You've been at the pipe for far too long."

He eyed me lazily. Putting aside his pipe he swung off the bed and led me into a room further into the darkness. He closed the door behind us and sat down. "You have not lied to me yet," he said. "How is my son in danger?"

Swiftly I told him of the ambush and the hidden soldiers. "You have to send some of your people in to warn them," I said.

"My men . . . what remain of them . . . they are all old men now . . . the young have died, or have joined rival triads. They have left me, they say I am weak, and useless. As you can see . . ."

"It's your son, Towkay Yeap," I said, impatient. He was as lost as wind-spiraled leaves and I feared he would not last out the war.

He put his arms on my shoulders. "Then I have a favor to ask of you."

I knew what he wanted, but I shook my head. "No. I cannot save him. I have neither the skills nor the abilities. Once the Japanese discover I'm gone, what do you think will happen to my family?"

"I will find you a guide. Someone from the jungle tribes, perhaps."

"No."

I got up to leave but he said, "You are his friend. You have no choice. No one else can do it."

I sat next to Endo-san on a stone bench on the North Coastal Road while he worked through a bundle of documents from his office. The atmosphere in the administrative headquarters had been oppressive and I was glad to accompany him here when he asked me.

I considered the problems of a rescue attempt on Kon. I was not trained to fight in the jungle, although I knew that what I had been taught by Endo-san would stand me in good stead. But if I disappeared completely for weeks what would happen to my father? Should I fail, I too would have to take to the jungle and that certainly did not appeal to me.

The sea had almost been drained by the tide and flocks of seagulls and crows flapped down to the mud, searching for clams and mussels and sea snails. Men and women in rubber boots up to their knees and with rattan baskets on their arms sank with each step into the mud as, with similar intent, they joined the birds. Clouds began piling up, high and unconquerable, like medieval towers and bastions.

"You seem preoccupied," Endo-san said.

"Just thinking of my life since you appeared."

"Has it been a good one?"

"Yes. Some days, yes," I said softly, my hand reaching out to touch his palm when he put aside his documents. "Other days, not so good."

"Look," he said. Across the channel in Butterworth the rain had begun, rubbing out the coastline like a dissatisfied artist. We watched as the waterless bed of the sea became spotted with a million drops of rain.

"We should go," he said, rising to his feet. "We will get wet."

"No." I held his arm and he sat down again. We opened our umbrellas as the rain came, sheets of it, as steady as glass yet as giving as strips of cloth. The men and women on the muddy beach were lost to us and the birds took flight while, behind us, the hawkers shouted out warnings and closed their stalls. The heat faded perceptibly, chased off by the wind. The rain fell on us, around us, dripping down our umbrellas onto our laps and thighs. For those few minutes we were surrounded by water and he and I were the only people in the world.

"What would you do, if you had a friend in danger?" he asked and the question sent my heart drumming.

"It would depend on the strength of the friendship, but if the bonds were strong, that friend must be saved," I replied, wondering what he was trying to tell me.

"Regardless of the danger?"

"Yes, regardless. Isn't that what your *sensei* Ueshiba would have said?"

"*Hai*," he replied.

Through it all we never looked at each other. We sat in a companionable silence, finding a rare moment when we could just enjoy each other's presence as though all the war years had been wiped away by the falling rain and we were again merely a master and his pupil, and nothing more.

And then, just as swiftly as it came, the afternoon shower moved inland and it was over. People came running out from beneath the shelters of the shops and the water streamed off the pavements into the monsoon drains, the roads giving off steam.

In that brief period of beauty and love, of water and silence, in that moment as we waited there on the bench, shielded from the world by the palace of the rain, I finally found a sense of purpose. I made up my mind to warn Kon. I decided that I would no longer hide under the protection of Endo-san but play my part as Isabel had done. The time had come when I had to do what was right and I would not allow myself to be deceived again by fear, by confusion, or even by love. I saw then that, for me, the teachings of Endo-san, his belief in the universal forces of harmony and balance, these had failed. I had to stop believing in them now and as soon as I came to that decision I saw the simplicity of it all. It was as though the heavy rain had washed my mind clean and left behind a new certainty.

I realized this would mean the end of what Endo-san and I had shared, for with the abandonment of the principles that had governed his life I was betraying him and everything that he had tried to teach me. And if I were captured there would be nothing he could do for me. Nothing at all. But I had to cut us free from the eternal knot in which we had been entangled; that was the only way forward.

Were those droplets of rain that strayed from my eyes, or were they the tears of an adult relinquishment of something that had become so essential in my life? I truly did not wish to know.

Endo-san got up from his seat and said without looking at me, "You should stay here for a while longer. I have to go back to work."

The unusual tone in his voice made me agree. I leaned back and watched him walk away to his waiting car, watching until he was driven away.

I looked down at the bench and saw the brown file he had left behind, spotted with raindrops, looking like the hide of an animal. I glanced around behind me and, after making sure no one was interested in me, I opened it. He had removed most of the documents, for it was much thinner than the one Saotome had handed out in their meeting.

I read through the few pieces of paper. All had been pressed with the red seal of Saotome, like welts on skin. They confirmed what I had heard outside Hiroshi's office but they told me more.

Fearing that Kon would not take the bait, Saotome had also captured Kon's *sensei*, Tanaka. The convoy carrying Saotome back to Kuala Lumpur would also be carrying Tanaka to his execution for not reporting to them when they took over the country, and for working against the Japanese. It was a baseless charge, trumped up by Saotome, serving only to lure Kon out into the open to rescue his *sensei*—Tanaka, who had traveled so far from Japan because someone had asked him to look after Endo-san and because once, in their childhood, they had been friends.

That evening I took my boat out onto the ocean, watching the fishermen's lights on their trawlers as they went out to sea. I let my thoughts drift like the nets they cast out, dragging in whatever was in their way.

I thought of my two brothers and of Isabel and knew that Edward's suffering in the camps and William's and Isabel's deaths were in some way due to me and my association with the Japanese. I considered whether things would have been different had I not met Endo-san but I could find no answers there.

The events of the past weeks, against which I thought I had constructed an unbreakable barrier, now found their way in. I was exhausted and I knew it was time to stop fighting and so I surrendered myself fully to sorrow. At that moment I saw with perfect clarity what my future would hold for me, that however many lives I had saved and however hard I tried to redeem myself in the time to come, it would never be sufficient to restore my peace of mind. Isabel had spoken the truth: I would never be able to forget.

I spent that night on the beach on Endo-san's island, unable to go in and face him. The house was silent when I entered at dawn. I called out his name but he had already left in his own boat. I felt a keen sense of loss but I pushed it aside. I rolled up my futon mattress which had not been slept on and placed it back in the cupboard. I looked around the house after packing all my clothes. The Nagamitsu sword Endo-san had given me was missing, but his own sword resting on its stand halted me. I looked at it, wondering how a work of such beauty could also bring about death so efficiently.

I walked quickly to the beach and got into my boat. The sun had risen from the sea to be absorbed into the heavy clouds that hung unmoving in the sky. The sea was unfriendly, drowning whatever faint light was shed onto its surface.

When I neared the shore I pointed the bow to Istana and allowed the waves and the will of the ocean to guide me home. I looked back at Endo-san's island as I was taken farther away and I wondered if I would ever return to it again.

The boat sawed into the sand just a footstep away from where Isabel had fallen. I stopped there and said a quiet prayer for her. I looked up to the tree and saw my father against it, the tree and its planter. I went up the narrow steps and approached him, not bothering to conceal my shock. He looked so much older, his hair lifeless as discarded threads, his eyes a vortex surrounded by lines, sinking into his skull. My entire resolve seemed to collapse and I had to gather it whole again with an effort.

"I have to go away for a while," I said. "To see Grandfather—and to set things right."

"I know. Sooner or later everyone has to do that," he said. "And I'm sorry."

I told him I did not understand what he was trying to tell me.

"I promised to take you to the river, where your mother and I found the fireflies. And I never did."

"It doesn't matter. We can go after the war and you can show me then," I said. "But now you must come with me. I can find a safe place for you to hide."

He shook his head. "Do what must be done and come back. I'll be here, waiting for you. And together we'll go to the river."

He bent down and I saw he had the cases of his butterfly

collection, stacked on top of each other, all badly broken and cracked by Fujihara's men. He had cleared away the broken glass covers and now scooped out a handful of desiccated wings.

"Time I set them free," he said. He waited, studying the tops of the trees for the passage of wind. At the moment he judged correct he flung his arm out and the wind caught the weightless butterflies, lifting them in a stream up to the sky, where the early rays of the sun gave them color and life again, so they looked as though they were fluttering their delicate wings in search of the elusive scents of flowers.

I bent down with him and we both took out another handful, and another, and another, until there were none left and we watched as the ribbon of wings was pulled farther and farther out to sea by the wind until it faded from sight. In my heart I said a prayer that they would go on flying forever.

"One more left," he said. In his palm lay the Rajah Brooke Birdwing, the butterfly he had been hunting just before my mother became ill. Bits of broken glass had shredded the edges of its immense black wings, but it still looked sleek and powerful, ready to soar again.

He opened my hand and placed it in my palm. "Do what you wish with it."

I stroked its wings, which still felt smooth and silky. From the look in my father's eyes, I knew what had to be done. So I launched it into the unseen currents of the air, where it seemed to stretch its long-unused wings with a yearning pleasure that was almost tangible. I felt my father's hand on my shoulder as we tracked its resurrected flight. It rose higher and higher until it was lost in the brightness of the new day.

I had bribed the man in charge of the incinerators to cremate Aunt Mei separately, instead of collectively with the bodies of the other prisoners the Japanese regularly killed. It angered me that I could not have done the same for Isabel; her body had disappeared.

I entered Endo-san's office and informed him that I was duty-bound to let my grandfather know of Aunt Mei's death and to return her ashes to him for the proper rites to be performed.

"I understand," he said. "Once again, I am sorry you have to go through this. It is an unbearable burden."

The light of the morning entered his office from the garden, illuminating the flag of his homeland that hung behind him. I shivered, for he stood just off center from the red circle in the flag and I had the impression that blood was seeping out from him, pooling on the white sheet.

He placed his hands by his sides and gave a slow bow. I hesitated, and then bowed to him. As he stood straight again, the sun lingered on the incipient tears in his eyes and somehow we knew that the next time we met everything would be changed. These old days would have disappeared forever.

"I wish you good fortune on your journey," he said. "May you accomplish what you set out to do."

In the steadiest voice I could maintain I said, "Please take care of my father."

"I will," he answered.

We both stood for a moment, unable to move. I knew what I was waiting for, although it shamed me to admit it. If, at that very moment, he had asked me not to go, I would have obeyed him. He was about to speak, but then decided against it and so said nothing. I shook my head at my own weakness and turned to leave.

"Wait," he said.

He went to a sideboard and said, "I almost forgot this."

He took Kumo, my sword, out in the traditional manner, its length floating on air, with only the tip and the hilt supported on his open palms. "I sent it to be polished and oiled. You as the owner should actually do all of that but . . . think of it as a parting gift from me."

I could do nothing else but receive it from him. "Thank you," I said.

"Take it with you. It might come in useful. I've amended your travel documents so you now have the right to carry it. Like the old warriors of Japan," he said slowly, the possibility of the sword's usefulness hard for him to accept, he who had lived and taught me the ways of harmony.

"I shall keep it safe," I said.

"I will not cease from mental fight; Nor shall my sword sleep in my hand," he whispered.

I could never hide anything from him. He knew he had failed me and that I had chosen to make my own way, free from the lessons that had been bequeathed to him by his *sensei* and then passed on to me.

I held the sword up in a salutatory form of farewell, nodded once and then left him.

Chapter Twelve

Michiko and I sat on a bench along Gurney Drive, which had once been the North Coastal Road, facing the narrow sea, doing what most people do along here, *makan angin*—eating the breeze. The promenade was a popular place. Young lovers were out taking their evening stroll. Hawkers lined the side of the road selling Indian *rojak*, fried noodles, rice, and sugar cane juice. Almost everyone who walked by was eating something or holding a packet of food.

We sat for a long time without speaking; we knew each other well enough for that by now.

Then Michiko said, "You do not use your grandfather's family name, the one he combined with yours at the clan temple? Nor the name Arminius, which your mother gave you?"

"No, I've never used them. It seemed wrong to do so. They identified a person I felt I didn't know," I answered—and stopped, as a new thought occurred to me. "No, each name in its own way wanted to decree a future for me, a future in which I would have had no say."

"But your mother's wish was for you to live your own life."

"Yet even in having such wishes, she was already imposing on me her idea of how I should live that life," I said.

I had made a conscious decision when the war ended to slough off the two names, as though that act in itself could provide me with a different identity, and grant me freedom from both my mother's dreams and from the life my grandfather was certain had been intended for me. I explained all this to Michiko.

"You've lived almost all your life without them now," she said. "Do you think it has made any difference?"

"I don't know," I said.

"Yes, you do." She pointed to my heart. "There is an emptiness here, am I right? As though something is lacking."

I shifted on the bench, uncomfortable with her assessment of me. No one paid any attention to us; we were just two old people sitting on a bench, dreaming of our youth, sending away and greeting in turn the few days that were left to us.

"This is the exact spot where Endo-san and I sat, on the day I made up my mind to save Kon," I said.

"How could you continue to live here, when so much of the island reminds you of the war?"

"Where else can I go? At least here I have these memories to keep me company. When it gets too much I can always go away and come back feeling better. Better this than to have your entire home wiped away, isn't it?"

"Yes, that is true," she said, and then became quiet.

"I'm sorry," I said. "That was cruel of me."

"I cannot remember my home at all. There are days when I think the war not only reduced my home to ashes, but also all my memories of it. All turned to ashes now."

The tide was coming in and curls of white streaked the flat, muddy surface as the wavelets folded upon themselves as they neared the shore. The shoreline reflected itself on the smooth, wet surface of the beach. Cries of the Indian mynahs and crows in the trees competed with the hawkers' shouts. Michiko was drinking the juice from a large, young coconut and it lay heavily on her lap. Like a severed head, I thought, and then pushed that image away. She was growing weaker by the day and I was worried.

She stroked my hand gently. I liked the warmth of her touch. The wind played with her hair and she brushed it away from her face.

I twisted around and pointed to the row of bungalows fronting the road. "That house used to be owned by the Cheah family," I said, directing her gaze to a run-down mansion fenced in with wire. "Their family owned the largest biscuit factory in Penang. And that other house has stood for a hundred and ten years. In a week's time it will be torn down to make way for a twenty-storey apartment block." I could not keep the bitterness in my voice from rising. "And that one too," I said, pointing to another home, "My father's friend lived there. His family owned a bank."

The road was lined with magnificent homes dating back to the

1920s. Many had been demolished, but in the geography of my memory I saw them every day, entire, complete, standing proudly in a row. And in my memory I recalled the people who had lived there, who had passed through those homes; the scandals and the tragedies of their lives.

All gone. Even I could not buy up all these buildings. Now the homes had become wine bars, coffee shops, eating places, seafood restaurants charging exorbitant prices, and shopping malls.

"You love this island intensely," she said.

"I used to love this place. Now, I feel disconnected from it," I said. "It's another world now. We have to make room for the young. Maybe that's why I've spent so much of my money and time buying old houses and restoring them. I want to delay the inevitable."

We got up, walked back to the car, and drove to the center of town, crossing Kimberley Street and its many shops selling joss sticks and Teo-Chew food, into Chulia Street and then heading into narrower and smaller streets. Between Campbell and Cintra Streets was the section once known as *Jipun-kay*, Japan Street. I was moving back in time as we parked and walked, for it was here that Endo-san first took me to lunch, I told Michiko. There were, before the war, geisha-houses in the area, as well as an unusual profusion of camera shops, which had made the locals suspect that they were fronts for spying activities.

My words to Endo-san in the early days of our acquaintance come back to haunt me every day: *I want to remember it all.* And I have done so, as Isabel had foreseen. I've been blessed with the gift of memory. It has helped that the island has not changed much, not in this part of town anyway. Some days I walk along these streets and lanes, hear the sounds, taste the smells, and feel the heat of the sun, and when I turn to tell Endo-san something, I realize with a shock that I'm not in the past anymore. The owners of the shops—the narrow Indian stores selling used books supplied by backpackers returning home, the budget hotels and Internet cafés, the rattan store where I bought my walking stick, the owner thoughtfully sawing off the end to fit my stride—all recognize me.

I have become a fixture. I'm often surprised that the guide-books don't list me as one of the features of these streets and alleys—an old man, hair all white, walking up and down these aged and ageless streets, searching, searching, looking for something that can never be found again.

We came out from La Maison Bleu, the former mansion of Cheong Fatt Tze, and thanked the caretaker for giving us a tour inside. The sun bleached the indigo walls, turning them powder-dusty. "That's Towkay Yeap's house," I said, pointing down the street to show her. I took her arm and led her there.

"I bought it a few years ago and since then have attempted to do what the people of La Maison Bleu have done. You saw how they've made the old house look as though Cheong Fatt Tze would hold parties there again and maybe even take his ninth or tenth wife? Well, that's my intention for Towkay Yeap's house."

Penelope Cheah was waiting for us. I introduced her to Michiko. I stood quietly as the restoration architect opened the latticed doors. I did not know what to expect. But then the doors were pushed open and I was back—back to the day when I first visited Kon. Everything was as it had been. The architect had delved into the depths of my recollection to recreate the house and I knew she had also scoured the records of the Penang Museum and the Chinese Chamber of Commerce for photographs and paintings to guide her. On the wall by the doors an incense holder held a joss stick, the smoke sending a curling message to the God of Heaven.

I stood on the threshold, suddenly afraid. Michiko took my hand and said, "Go in, it has been waiting for you."

I held on to Michiko's hand and stepped inside and stopped in the Hall of Guests. A large wooden screen, carved with a thousand detailed figures and leafed in gold, barred all outsiders from the house within. Red lanterns hung from the eaves of the ceiling and square wooden pedestals inlaid with mother-of-pearl supported vases and jade figurines. The tiles felt cold under my bare feet when I removed my shoes and I began to cool down from the heat outside.

On one side hung Towkay Yeap's portrait and even as I turned my heart knew what I would see. Kon's picture faced his father's and once again I saw him, with his youthful smile, his black shining eyes, dressed all in white with his favorite red tie.

"Where did you find that?" I asked.

"In one of the vaults at the Chinese Chamber of Commerce," Penelope Cheah said. "Placed there by his father."

"Is that your friend, Kon?" Michiko asked, moving forward.

"That's him."

"He looks very familiar," she said.

"Probably because you've been hearing so much about him," I said.

I went into the courtyard where the sun came in and stood by the spiral staircase. The wrought-iron railings were new, but almost like the ones Towkay Yeap had used. I heard the female voices of his household, the *amahs* chattering in the kitchen, the sound of the steel cleaver on the chopping block as lunch was prepared, and I caught the smell of glutinous rice steaming as a soft wind blew through the house. A dog barked at my presence, and a male voice scolded it: "*Diamlah!*"

I went up the stairs, into Kon's room.

Sorry about the mess. I have a large collection of books of Chinese history and art.

I turned suddenly and furrowed my brow. "What is it?" Penelope Cheah asked from behind me. I held up my hand to silence her.

Do you think my meeting him, and our meeting, all of it was by chance?

I waited for his reply.

Some mistakes can be so great, so grievous, that we end up paying for them again and again, all our lives until eventually we forget why we began paying in the first place.

And then, like a kind god completing my spell, a peddler cycled by outside, and once more I heard the cries of the hawker and the knocking of his wooden clappers as he pedaled his pushcart past the house, selling wonton noodles.

I have missed you, my friend.

As I have you.

In a well-known Nyonya restaurant we sat down for an early dinner. The food, like the Chinese immigrants who had come to Malaya in the days of British rule and who had assimilated the ways and customs of the Malays, was a mixture of Malay and

359

Chinese cuisine. The Nyonya Chinese had a reputation for creating excellent dishes and I have never tasted anything resembling them anywhere in the world. I watched in anticipation as Michiko's face expressed amazement, delight, wonder, and enjoyment as she tasted the Curry Kapitan Chicken, with its light coconut-milk gravy, as she nibbled at *otak-otak* and *jeu-hoo-char*—all washed down with hot jasmine tea. She tasted all of the dishes but I noticed that she had only taken small portions onto her plate; I hoped the day had not been tiring for her.

"I really cannot eat much since I fell ill. But this food is delicious," she said. "No wonder I've been told that the most popular pastime here is eating."

"Another reason why I am tied to this place," I said and smiled at her.

"You should smile more. You look much, much younger."

The restaurant was run by three ladies, and Mary Chong, the youngest among them, stopped to talk to us when she brought us our pot of tea. She, too, knew me from a long time ago. But Cecilia, the older partner, scowled when she saw me, and went into the kitchen.

"How's business?" I asked the usual question. The place looked dingy and well-worn. I remembered when they opened, almost twenty years ago. Wherever I traveled to, the first stop I made when I returned was at this restaurant.

"Not so good," she sighed. "All those new American coffee places attract the youngsters. We get the usual crowd, mostly. You we have not seen in some time, although we have heard things about you."

"Yes, Mary. The rumors are true. I'm gradually drinking myself to death."

"Then you should just eat yourself to death in our restaurant. I'm sure the food here tastes better than your sauvignon blanc."

I raised an eyebrow. They got that part correct. Michiko laughed.

Mary continued in a more somber tone to Michiko, "You're a Japanese, aren't you? Did Philip tell you he saved my husband's life in the war?"

"Damn it all, Mary," I said.

"You're not going to stop me," Mary said. "I tell it to everyone I know, to all the tourists who come in here. Many people think he was a Japanese collaborator in the war, but he saved my husband's life, as well as many of my neighbors."

"Not many people think like you do," I said. "And they have good reason. You know why Cecilia refuses to serve me." Michiko, I knew, had noticed Cecilia's exit. "I was with the Japanese when they pulled her father out and killed him. I had to read out the names of the condemned."

"They don't know you," Mary's reply came quick and certain.

"This is the last time I'm coming here to eat," I said.

"Ha! You always say that, but you won't find another place like mine and you know it," Mary said and, knowing she had had the last word, returned to the kitchen.

"Sorry about that," I said to Michiko.

She shrugged her thin shoulders, not bothering to hide her amusement. "How did you save her husband?"

"It doesn't matter," I said. I had no wish to talk about it. It was warm in the restaurant, and I was starting to perspire from the tea.

"Now you know what happened to my father's butterflies," I said. "But I never discovered what happened to his collection of *keris* blades. He hid them too well before our house was ransacked by the Kempeitai."

"Have you searched the house for them?"

"Every inch of it, without any success. Maybe they were taken away by the Kempeitai after all. Ownership of weapons was prohibited during the Occupation. Like feudal Japan."

There was a distant look on Michiko's face, which made me concerned. "What's the matter, are you ill?"

She shook her head. "I think I know where your father concealed the blades."

I did not believe her at all but sought to humor her. "Where? Tell me?"

"I will not. But I will show you," she replied. She refused to reveal anything further and, after a while, she requested that I continue with my tale.

Chapter Thirteen

The journey from Butterworth to Ipoh took three hours, as we stopped frequently for checks of the rails. The MPAJA's favorite targets had been railway lines and major roads, as well as army camps and mines. Anything to disrupt the Japanese, I thought.

I was tight with fear. As tiny Malay villages and one-street towns dropped behind me, I questioned my courage. Which of us was the stronger? Kon, who had given up everything he had ever known to fight the Japanese, suffering untold hardship and the possibility of death every day? Or myself, who had accepted the Japanese, their conquest and rule, and who tried to live day-to-day in safety? Who had made the correct decisions?

More and more often now it occurred to me that Kon was living the life I should have lived, making the choices I should have made. He had taken the proper turnings, made the appropriate stand, while I had done otherwise. He would return from the war a hero, welcomed by everyone—and what would they say of me?

The railway station in Ipoh, a large cream building flanked by towers topped with Moorish minarets and cupolas, was quiet. A small group of Indian men sat reading newspapers in their white *dhoti* and vests, as doves floated to the steel crossbeams and shadowed alcoves. The town however was busy with trishaws and bicycles. I paid for a room at the station hotel and hired a trishaw to my grandfather's home.

After knocking on the doors for some time, I realized the house was empty. I walked around to the back but found only a tool shed and the servants' rooms. I stood in the sunshine, wondering what to do next. I opened the tool shed, hoping to find what I needed. There was a bicycle leaning against the wall, rusty, heavy, and high. I adjusted the seat, and cycled out into the limestone hills of Ipoh.

I hid the bicycle and walked up the slope, trying to recollect the path my grandfather had shown me. At the top I almost missed the temple, for the walls had begun to merge into the color of the cliffs. I waited outside and shouted for him. After a while, when no one appeared, I pushed aside the guava tree, now grown big enough to make the effort difficult, and entered the abandoned temple. A squirrel paused in washing its face, glared at me for daring to disturb it and ran up the walls into a crack. I walked into the passageway and came out into the enclosed circle and there he waited, his familiar roguish smile causing me anguish.

"I have missed you," he said and the sound of his voice and the twinkle in his eyes made me realize I had missed him greatly as well. I approached him and found I could not meet his gaze.

"What has happened?" he asked.

I described to him everything that had happened since William's funeral. Then I told him how Aunt Mei had been executed by the Japanese and he sat down on a little clump of stone. I handed him the dented Huntley & Palmer's biscuit tin which held Aunt Mei's ashes. It was the only container I could find at short notice. He received it and cradled it in his arms, as he had his daughter once when she was still an infant.

"I appreciate you delivering this to me," he said and I stroked his head softly. His hand came up and held mine. It felt so cool and soft; surely it was never the hand of a tin miner.

"It was Lim who betrayed her, wasn't it?" he asked.

I nodded. "Because of me and what happened to his daughter. I'm so sorry," I said, hating the vacuity of those words, knowing that they would never be sufficient to extinguish the pain of his loss.

And so I crumpled the fore and middle fingers of my hand onto the surface of the biscuit box, pressed them into the kneeling position and tapped them softly against the lid, wordlessly asking him for forgiveness.

He stared at the crooked fingers and then he reached over and covered my hand with both his own. He brought my hand up to his forehead and accepted my meager offering.

"Your aunt chose the manner of her life. There is nothing that could have been done." He said this in a distracted manner and I saw the effort it took for him to keep from breaking down. I had loaded another weight onto his suffering and it hurt me to understand that while one person can never really share the pain of another, they can so easily and so heedlessly add to it. Whatever my grandfather had said about Aunt Mei's choices, I was the link that had resulted in her death.

"You should not blame yourself," my grandfather went on. "I told you once before, you have the ability to bring all of life's disparate elements into a cohesive whole. Do you remember? At this moment, however, you must reject the heritage of your father's people. Guilt is an invention of the Westerners and their religion."

I shook my head. "Guilt is a human attribute."

"We Chinese are more pragmatic. It was your aunt's and your sister's fate. Nothing more," he said with great firmness.

I could have told him it was guilt that had made him reach out to me and invite me to his home for the first time. That and regret—which, after all, is another aspect of guilt. But what could I have achieved by arguing him around to my point of view? His belief gave him comfort and if I could not alleviate his burden then at least I would do nothing to intensify it now.

I said instead, "I went to your house but it was empty and locked up. Are you living here now, in this cave?"

"Yes. It reminds me of my youth in the monastery. There is magic here, as you may well be aware. Some nights I have visitors," he said.

My skin crawled and the hairs on it stood on end; I hoped he was not growing senile.

He gave a snort. "Do not look at me as though I had taken leave of my senses. The spirits of the ancient sages and hermits visit me sometimes and we talk. Look, I found this because one of them showed it to me."

I followed him to a rock face that appeared to have been recently chiseled away. Lines of writing, recognizably Chinese, were carved on it in a square of four characters by four. "I was told to remove the outer layer and this was what lay beneath," he said.

He read and translated the sixteen ideograms to me:

I have journeyed the limits of this world,
Seen magical things

And met many people,
And I find that across the Four Oceans
All men are brothers.

"I know that. It's well-known, isn't it?" I said.

"Yes."

"It must have been written before the poet realized what cruelties we can inflict on one another," I said. The optimism of the poem seemed so incongruous now.

"It was written in one of the most turbulent periods of China's history, thousands of years before Jesus Christ delivered almost the same message."

"What are you trying to tell me, Grandfather?"

"Do not let hatred control your life. However hard the circumstances are now, do not turn into someone like Lim, or the Japanese. I can see it rising to the surface in you, ready to lash out."

"But what can I do?"

"You had become lost but I think you are beginning to see the correct way again. You must be strong now, for your greatest trials are still ahead." Somehow or other I knew those words were not his own, but transmitted through him from another source. I shivered, but his arms held me. I felt the strength of his age and wisdom reach out to find a home within myself and my fears subsided.

"There is nothing more I can tell you. And now you must go, off to what duty dictates. The bonds of friendship call to you," he said.

"Are you certain that you are my grandfather and not one of the timeless sages roaming these hills?" I asked.

"Now wouldn't that be a most wonderful fate? Walking these beautiful hills, free as time itself?"

"It would be," I said.

He took out his jade pin, the pin that had once saved his life. "I want you to have this."

I shook my head. "No. You must keep it, to test all the tea you'll drink with me, when the war is over."

The moment I spoke, I realized that he had stopped doing that ever since the night I had first met him and that, in all the time we had spent together, on every occasion when I had served him tea,

I had never once seen him use the pin. He had always been certain of me.

"I have no further use for it," he said. He placed the jade pin in my palm and folded my fingers over it.

I embraced him tightly, unwilling to let him go, and remembered the days we had spent in his house on Armenian Street. I rubbed his paunch. "You must eat properly. This is shrinking."

"Leave my stomach alone," he said sternly, and for one short moment we almost succeeded in smiling at each other.

I never saw him again, not even after the war when I searched all over Ipoh for him. The townsfolk heard that he had been captured by the Japanese in the final days of the war, so they informed me, for he had been an active supporter of anti-Japanese activities.

"My brother told me his only grandson betrayed him to the Japanese," a pomelo merchant said to me with complete assurance.

But I felt sure, when I hiked those ageless hills, calling out his name, that the Japanese never found him. No, he had found something here and he had accepted it. And the strangest thing was that, in spite of the older monks in the various monasteries in the vicinity agreeing to its existence when I questioned them, I could never find my grandfather's temple again.

Chapter Fourteen

I returned to the station hotel and went into the bar. Doors opened out onto a ten-foot-wide veranda that ran around the front of the station. Sunlight was kept to a minimum by large bamboo shades, and dusty ceiling fans spun around and around, casting shadows on the checkered tile floors. Low, cushioned rattan chairs surrounded the bar at the end of the veranda, where groups of Japanese soldiers were drinking, singing, and terrifying the waiters. Across the station, people were going in and out of the Ipoh municipal offices. It was windless, and the red sun flag of Nippon lay wrapped around the flagpole.

Kon's father had instructed me to go down and walk around. I bundled my sword in a cloth and went across the main road and entered the busy streets. Heat and smells welcomed me. Stalls were selling the fried yams and taro which had become the staple food for so many of us. Most of the shoppers carried stacks of money in baskets just to make the smallest purchases. Like the women in Penang, the women here had made no effort to look attractive, a deliberate tactic in order not to catch the eyes of the *Jipunakui*. A girl stared deliberately into my eyes, turned around, and walked away.

I followed her. She walked on without increasing her pace. We turned around corners and into alleyways until I was lost and the sounds of the streets were reduced to a soft hum. The girl knocked on the wooden door of a shop, which was made of interconnecting panels of wood. A small rectangle was taken out and she stepped over and inside. I followed her in.

The wooden slat was slammed back into place and hands, several pairs of them, gripped me hard and pushed me around. I suppressed my natural instinct to fight back. We entered another room, then a hallway, until I was confused by the turns. We came out in a courtyard and I blinked at the sharp sunlight, my annoyance increasing.

A man my age sat on a wooden bench, picking his nose. My fists linked and formed the triad hand signal Towkay Yeap had shown me. I was pushed down onto the cemented floor.

"So it's a half-breed," he sneered, "come to warn us against the *Jipunakui*."

From the movements behind me I guessed there were three more I could not see. The nose-picker now came forward. "Tell us then."

I shook my head. I had made it clear to Towkay Yeap that I would only tell it to Kon directly. There was no way of knowing who Saotome's mole was. I sensed the sudden movement behind me and turned to block the blow, but for once I was too slow. It caught me at the side of my head—there was a loud explosion within my brain—and then the explosion turned to darkness.

A mosquito woke me. I opened my eyes and slapped it away. The air was humid and laden with unseen moisture and I felt I was drowning. I found I was being carried on a stretcher and I turned over and dropped onto wet earth. Pushing myself up, I faced four strangers, all Chinese, with that particular appearance of toughness which spoke of life on the streets. Their hands held rusted Sten guns and they waved them at me to continue on the almost invisible path we were taking. The nose-picker was holding on to my sword and I vowed I would get it back from him, even if I had to kill him.

We walked on in silence. The forest was quiet, broken only by the drilling of woodpeckers and the calling of birds. Shafts of sunlight—was it still the same day?—mottled the leaves and branches; I had never seen so many shades of green and brown. We pushed through spotted ferns taller than any of us, their stems swinging back to hide our passage. The ground was covered with leaves as large as dinner plates, which crunched under our feet.

We walked until the light in the trees weakened into late afternoon. The pain in my head where I had been clubbed began to lessen and I felt less dizzy. We had to stop every time the scout ahead put up his hand. Once we ducked into the wet undergrowth as a patrol of Japanese troops moved through the jungle. I was certain we were heading toward the drier limestone cliffs, for the growth began to thin and the ground started to rise. I was soaking wet and my breathing was ragged. We must have been walking for three hours, though I was by no means certain.

The path rose steeply and then dipped into a vale. Above us the interlacing branches of trees acted as a natural canopy and we were safely out of sight of the planes flying above. Our lead scout pursed his lips and a bird-cry fluttered out. We waited in the clearing as, all around us, guerrillas rose out from the bushes. We had arrived at the outer fringes of the White Tiger camp.

With the guerrillas escorting us, the going became faster. We dropped into the vale and then the ground started to rise again, taking us to the cliffs, where we reached the end of the path. "What now?" I muttered, swatting at the flies around my face.

Kon appeared out of solid stone. The cave's entrance was concealed by a fold of rock, curved like the shell of a sea snail. He smiled when he saw me but, as I began to bow, he shook his head quickly.

"Don't act like a Japanese here," he warned me, his lips moving near my ear. My sword was returned to me and Kon grinned when he saw it. "You've come prepared."

According to the intelligence reports I had read, the White Tiger camp had originally been led by Yong Kwan, but it had gained its fame due to Kon's impressive guerrilla skills.

"Why did the camp adopt your name?" I asked.

He shrugged his shoulders and it pained me to see how bony they had become. "It was after one of the early raids. We'd burned down a military base and we had to run through the entire night. By dawn we were on the brink of collapse and we dug a hollow to hide. And then a tiger came, an albino. It was the most astonishing sight; none of us had ever dreamt such a thing existed. It just stood and looked at us before vanishing into the trees like a ghost. One of the men here had heard of my nickname and told the others. They took it as a good omen and, since then, the group has been called the White Tiger."

We entered the cave. It was cold inside and the walls were damp. The sound of dripping water added depth to the darkness. A narrow passageway opened up and inside the cliff was a small circular opening which let the sky in, similar to my grandfather's cave but smaller. "We cook whatever food we can find inside so the smoke doesn't escape through this opening," Kon said.

Sunlight spilled through the opening in the branches overhead and, as faces turned to watch us walk into the circle, I felt as though I was walking on stage, accompanied by the loyal light. In addition to the smell of food cooking there was a strong smell of bat droppings. Clumps of bats hung high up in the shadows, looking like some strange hairy moving fruit. Now and then one fell away to swoop down and up again, squeaking, before flapping away into the opening above.

I estimated the number of guerrillas to be around thirty, but the cave was quiet. No one seemed to speak. There were an equal number of Chinese men and women—the women often looking as tough as the men—and a small number of Indians and Malays.

"Where's Yong Kwan?"

"Out killing Japanese. We'll see him tonight."

"Is there a place to wash myself?" I asked.

Kon led me out of the cave to a spot where a bend in the stream had gouged out a shallow pool. I sank into it with pleasure.

"Your father sent me," I said to him.

He nodded. "I guessed that. How is he?"

"Quite well," I lied.

He raised an eyebrow at me in disbelief. I felt a sadness at the paths along which our lives had led us. Kon's father was right; we were both too young. I wondered how we would ever recondition ourselves once the war was over. Had our experiences damaged us for the rest of our lives?

"What are you doing here, really?" Kon asked.

"The Japs have laid bait to lure you out into the open. Have you heard of Saotome?"

He held up a hand to halt me. "Tell it to Yong Kwan tonight."

"What's he like?"

"He used to teach mathematics at a Chinese school. Probably trained by the Chinese. It wouldn't surprise me if he had tried to indoctrinate his students as well."

Strange how we referred to our own people in a manner set to distinguish them from us. After all, weren't Kon and I Chinese? Yet throughout our conversation we had spoken only in English.

"He's also a total bastard. Very cunning and ruthless. I have a feeling he's in this for something else, not just for the glory of Communism."

I ducked my head into the water and came out feeling better, cleaner. I climbed out of the river, dried myself and put on my clothes.

"How's Penang?" Kon asked.

"The Japanese executed hundreds of people after you blew up the radar station," I said, wanting him to know the price that had been paid on his behalf. But as soon as the words came out I was sorry. I was not completely free from blemish either. "That was uncalled for," I said. "I apologize."

He shook his head. "I deserved it. You didn't have to come. I told you, we're even now."

"There should never be talk of debts and payments between friends." I told him of Tanaka and his part in the trap Saotome had planned. "He's the bait Saotome is using to lure you out."

The expression on his face tightened.

"I didn't tell you the last time we met—William's dead; he went down with his ship. Edward is in a slave camp, and Isabel . . ." With halting words I spoke about Isabel, and he was silent.

"Your aunt was correct, you know. The British are making plans to take back Malaya," he said. "We've been working with soldiers who are being parachuted in. Everything is in place for the assault."

"You still trust the British, after the way they betrayed us, abandoning us to the Japanese? I read many of the documents they left behind in their haste to evacuate. The whole defense of the country was a mess. There were even orders to the European community to leave secretly in the night, to board ships and sail away," I said.

"Who else do we have?" he asked, his voice bitter.

We heard movement behind us and turned, Kon's hand going for his knife.

I recognized Su Yen, the female guerrilla I had met at Tanaka's house. "I've been looking for you," she said to Kon.

"We could have killed you," Kon said.

She went to him and kissed him. He pushed her away and said, "Come on, we decided it's too dangerous to do that any-more."

She shrugged and said, "Yong Kwan won't be back until tonight and your friend can always find something else to amuse him." She looked at me briefly, and in her eyes I saw a warning to me not to stand in her way.

But Kon was firm, and sent her off.

"The baby?" I asked.

He nodded slightly. "She bled all the way back here. And she's changed after the experience. She hates everything and everyone now. I think Su Yen lost more than the baby when the midwife worked on her."

I really did not want to hear any more. I wanted desperately to get out of the forest. It frightened me, this vast, endless yet confined landscape without landmarks I could recognize. I would not have survived for long here and my respect for Kon grew stronger.

We heard voices and laughter. "That must be Yong Kwan returning. Come on, let's go back," Kon said. He touched me on my shoulder and stopped me. "Don't let anyone know Tanaka-san is my *sensei*. Yong Kwan will use it against me."

"I won't."

Yong Kwan was a balding man in his late thirties, stocky, with hard eyes. Like almost everyone there, his MPAJA uniform had seen better days.

I told him in detail about the ambush. "Saotome will be driven along the trunk road between Ipoh and Cameron Highlands, followed some distance behind by his troops. His intention is to lure you out and he especially wants Kon." Here I saw Yong Kwan look displeased that Saotome did not consider him important enough to capture.

"You'll probably be informed as to when Saotome will arrive by his mole here. You have a traitor in your midst and you can only catch him when he brings you the news," I said, as I concluded. "Now I must return to Penang. Please get one of your men to take me back."

He shook his head and pointed to two of his guerrillas. They came behind me and held my arms. One strung out a coiled rope and tied my hands together.

"You're a well-known collaborator. We're not letting you leave until we're certain of the truth of your claims."

I swore at him. He stepped up and swung his palm against my face. I spun from the force of the blow and dropped to the ground.

"Stop it!" Kon snapped. "He was sent by my father."

"Your father," Yong Kwan sneered. "An old, powerless man, addicted to opium, a brothel keeper? Sending him to inform us? I have the security of the entire camp on my hands. He stays tied up until we get Saotome." He kicked me when I attempted to rise to my feet.

Kon made a move toward Yong Kwan, but I said softly in Japanese, "Let him be. I'm telling the truth."

The words, meaningless to Yong Kwan, infuriated him. "What is that Japanese spy telling you now? And you, are you also the Japs' dog?" he asked Kon.

Kon looked deliberately at every one of the men surrounding Yong Kwan and walked out of the cave.

I lay trussed up on the ground the entire night. By dawn the next day I was cold and stiff. My bound wrists were sore and my ankles, where they had tethered me during the night, had started to bleed, staining the ropes. I was desperate to get away. I could not stay, for Yong Kwan would kill me. If I returned, Fujihara would kill me. I had been away from Penang for too long now and my absence would be noticed.

I lay and thought about the consequences of my association with Endo-san. And I had not a shred of doubt that if death was to be my fate then I would rather that Endo-san end my life.

Kon brought me a bowl of hot gruel, squatting down next to me as he fed me. He sent the sentry away. "We've received news. The contingent will be on the road in tomorrow at noon. Yong Kwan is holding the man who brought the information."

"Who is he?"

"A rice farmer from a small village a mile from here. The village has been providing us with food and medical supplies. He's admitted that he's working for the Japs for the money." He opened his knife and cut my ropes. "We'll need as much help as we can get. You've seen Saotome up close, so you'll have to identify him for us."

I got up, stretching my sore body. The sun was high as we made our way to the cave. A group of guerrillas surrounded Yong Kwan, who was pointing to a map. He saw us, but went on with his instructions. I saw that most of them deferred to Kon, glancing at him to see if he approved of Yong Kwan's plan. But I thought it was simple and effective and so did Kon.

"We divide into two groups," Yong Kwan said. "One group takes out the car carrying Saotome and the other will deal with the truck carrying the troops. And you," he pointed to me, "you'll be in the team attacking Saotome. I want him alive."

"What about the soldiers guarding Saotome?" Kon asked.

"The soldiers?" Yong Kwan laughed. "No need to bother bringing them back here."

"I'll be in that team as well," Kon said, his voice firm. We had both agreed that Saotome would probably place Tanaka in the same vehicle as himself.

There were four people in each of the two teams. Yong Kwan led the first, with Kon and me and another guerrilla following behind him. The second team, which broke away from us after an hour's trek, had three Chinese MPAJA guerrillas and a Malay. They would be stationed farther up the trunk road.

We trekked through the jungle, our passage made difficult by the complete absence of tracks or paths. There was just thick, soggy undergrowth. Sweat soaked my shirt and the rifle sling. I had left my sword behind, which made the going easier. The mosquitoes enjoyed dancing around our faces, tormenting us. Once we disturbed a hornbill and it cried out, annoyed as it flew off, its massive wings sounding like a woman slapping wet clothes on river rocks. Soon the black-tarred road could be glimpsed through the low-hanging branches as we emerged from the jungle.

Before the war, this road had been popular with people going up Cameron Highlands for their holidays. Yong Kwan had chosen to lay the ambush at the junction of the road to the Highlands. Cars always stopped here before turning. My father loved it up there, for it gave a welcome respite from the endless heat, and Isabel used to enjoy walking in the strawberry farms, the vegetable gardens and the misty, undulating tea plantations. I knew that around the bend was a hidden spot where a waterfall collected in a rock pool. We had had many a picnic there, swimming in the cold clear water, picking leeches off our bodies after the swim and chasing insects and butterflies. A feeling of loss lowered my spirits and Kon asked, "What's wrong?"

"Nothing, just lost memories."

He understood. "The road to Cameron Highlands. You British had some good years here," he said in an ironic voice.

We slithered down onto the road and ran to the ditch on the opposite side. I checked my watch. It was half past eleven. We had assumed that Saotome would leave Ipoh in a few minutes and that it would take him three-quarters of an hour to reach the junction.

We sat in the shade of the *lalang*, listening for the approach of the cars. Twice we heard the sounds of vehicles but they were small lorries, carrying only a few soldiers. I shook my head at Yong Kwan after checking them. There was a soft rumble and I lifted my head, but it was only thunderclouds in the sky.

"Let's hope it doesn't rain. It's the time of the monsoon again," Kon said, studying the sky.

"You said yesterday the war would soon be over?" I asked, feeling hopeful yet apprehensive as to what the end of the war would bring.

"I think so. We have other teams meeting British troops coming ashore from submarines off the Straits of Malacca. Arms and ammunition were stockpiled in the jungles by a few far-sighted men before the Japanese took over. How do you think we've managed to fight for so long? We'll lead the British to these weapons and when we receive the order from Malaya Command in India, we'll destroy every major Japanese installation and military facility."

I looked at my watch. It was noon and I was hungry. I was about to open my water bottle when I heard the whine of engines coming up the steep incline of the road.

Saotome had made sure the guerrillas would not miss his importance, for the car was decorated with two flags proclaiming the status of its passengers within. As the vehicle slowed down at the junction I gave a signal to Yong Kwan and we rose up from the ditch, pointing our guns at the car, surrounding it.

Saotome opened the door and got out, looking distinguished in his formal uniform. His sword leaned against his thigh and his boots had been polished. He looked surprised when he saw me. "Well, young Philip. Imagine meeting you here."

He was unconcerned, knowing he had reinforcements behind him. At that moment we heard gunshots and he turned to look back along the road. We waited, then the first of the Chinese guerrillas appeared, lifting his fist into the air. Saotome understood what had happened and his hand went to his sword. Kon pointed his rifle at him and said in Japanese, "Don't move."

"The White Tiger. Look what I have for you inside."

"Come out please, Tanaka-*sensei*," Kon said. The door on the other side opened and I saw the shaven head of Tanaka-san. I did not bow to him and neither did Kon.

The unexpected sound of lorries coming up the road stopped us. "More vehicles?" Kon said. Saotome smiled. And then the road was overrun with Japanese soldiers, and in the lead I saw Goro, charging toward me. Saotome had anticipated our plan.

I fired a shot at Goro, but missed. Saotome reached again for his sword and I kicked him in the shin. He stumbled back, which gave me the opportunity to pull out his sword. I turned and faced Goro. Yong Kwan shot three soldiers and the Chinese guerrillas, hearing the gunshots, came running from behind us. Everyone began shooting. Kon moved next to me and said, "Take Saotome and Tanaka-*sensei* back to camp. Move!"

I pointed the tip of Saotome's sword into his throat. "Let's go." Tanaka was already climbing up the embankment into the jungle. I pushed Saotome up the same way and we stumbled into the slippery undergrowth. I lost my grip on the sword, and Saotome kicked it away. He opened his buttoned holster and lifted out his pistol but, at that moment, Tanaka pinched a nerve in Saotome's neck. I saw his eyes roll up, and the lids come down, and he was unconscious. I picked up Saotome's sword and tried to determine which way we should go. We lifted Saotome and made our way into the jungle. Behind us the shots had died off and it was suddenly quiet, the birds and the monkeys frightened away.

"Do you know which direction we should follow?" Tanaka asked.

"Not at all," I said, trying to find some landmarks I could remember.

I jumped when Kon touched me from behind. "I've wounded the officer but we've got to move faster. There were more soldiers coming up the road," he said.

"His name's Goro and he knows me."

"Then you can't go back to Penang," Kon said.

"I must," I said. "My father's all alone there."

They had lost two guerrillas but Yong Kwan was beaming widely. Capturing Saotome had given him an immense amount of face.

We entered the camp and everyone hurried into hiding, knowing from past experience that the Japanese troops would soon start searching the area.

"They won't find this place," Kon assured me.

"What about their spy, the rice farmer?"

"He's dead. Yong Kwan killed him before we left."

As Saotome came to consciousness, Yong Kwan hit him across the face. Saotome rocked on his seat, his bound hands unable to rub the pain away from his cheek. He looked around and saw me. "It appears that Goro-san is not with us. Unless he is dead, your position would be very tenuous now."

I did not reply but walked to the entrance of the cave. "Where's Tanaka-san?" I asked Kon. He looked around us and then said, "Come with me."

I followed him out into the clearing, where a small, heavily patched tent had been erected. Kon waved to the guard, opened the flap and we ducked inside. Tanaka, like Saotome, had been bound to a chair that had been crudely hammered together from a few pieces of planking.

"*Sensei,*" Kon said.

"Tanaka-san," I greeted him.

We untied his hands and he flexed them as he thanked us. He appeared not to have changed at all in the past few years, unlike Endo-san. I wondered what had happened to him, for I had not heard from him since our parting.

"Did you go up into the Black Water Hills as you said you would?" I asked him.

He nodded to me. "I went up into the hills and stayed there with the monks. I would not have come out again until all this insanity was over. But Saotome-san found me. How I do not know."

"It was my fault. I told Endo-san where you had gone," I said.

"No matter," he replied.

"Yet Endo-san wanted me to warn Kon and to rescue you. I don't understand."

A look of forgotten happiness visited Tanaka's face for a moment and I knew he was recalling the days of his youth spent with Endo-san. "After so many years, you should know your *sensei* by now," he said.

"He feels bound by the duty of his position," I said, thinking carefully about what Tanaka said. "But the duty of friendship and the principles of his teacher also pull at him."

"And so, through you, he has found a way to harmonize the conflicts in his life," Tanaka said. "When you see him again, tell him I have missed him. I have missed our evenings spent drinking and talking. When the war is over," here he looked wistful, "when the war is over, we must all meet again, and talk, and drink as though we were young again."

"I'll tell him, Tanaka-san."

He smiled an old man's smile at Kon. "And how are you? I see you have done what you told me you would do. That is good. On behalf of my people, I apologize to you for the terrible things done here." He bowed with difficulty.

"*Sensei*, please," Kon said, distressed.

Tanaka let out a sigh and asked, "What is going to happen to me now?"

"I'll speak to the leader of the camp and get you released," Kon said. Tanaka looked at him with concern. "Do not be too sure. In times like these, everyone wants us dead."

"You have my word I'll get you away from here," Kon said. I wondered what he had in mind. For as long as I had known him he had never made promises easily.

An argument arose between Kon and Yong Kwan later that evening after the Japanese spotter planes had patrolled above us for an hour. The monsoon season chose to begin that night and the rain started to fall, gently at first and then heavier, until it was impossible to see into the darkness ahead. Through the violence of the storm we heard their voices. The guerrillas looked at each other uneasily and I remembered a Malay proverb taught to me by my father: *When elephants in the jungle fight, the mouse deer suffers.*

Kon came out of Yong Kwan's sleeping quarters. I put on a tattered raincoat that let in more water than it kept out and ran to meet him. "What's wrong?"

"Yong Kwan wants them questioned tonight," Kon said.

"Even Tanaka-san? But didn't you tell him he is innocent?"

"He doesn't care. Yong Kwan is very much like the Japanese he loves to hunt. He's also found out about my connection with

Tanaka-san from Su Yen." He paused for a moment and I saw that he was gathering strength to ask something of me.

I stopped him before he spoke. "You don't have to ask. I'll do it. I'll take Tanaka-san with me when I leave."

"Then I shall be in your debt. You don't know how much Yong Kwan enjoys playing with his victims. I refuse to allow Tanaka-san to suffer. Take him back to Penang when you return. Hide him in the hills."

We sat around a cold dinner of yams and stringy wild-boar meat. There were a few British soldiers in the camp now, part of the advance team that had been recently deposited by submarine along the Straits of Malacca. Their sunburned skins marked them as new arrivals; the older European guerrillas all had a luminous pallor, like spirits of the jungle, the result of too much time spent in the half-light of the trees.

"I have to leave as soon as possible," I said to Kon. I was worried about my father. The fact that Goro had escaped meant he was already on his way back to Penang. He had seen me, and both Hiroshi and Fujihara would use him in any way they could to punish me.

"Then let's go now and prepare Tanaka-san. I will show you the way to the main road," Kon whispered in Japanese.

We made our way to the tent where Tanaka had been kept. The ground was beginning to flood, turning into mud. The guard was not there and the tent was empty. We were too late.

We ran back to the cave, Kon pushing his way roughly into the throng. At the entrance to a passageway one of the guerrillas stopped us. "You cannot enter. Commander Yong's orders." He raised a rifle at us. We waited, wincing at the screams that echoed through the cave. An hour later the prisoners were brought out, Saotome bleeding from his nose and mouth, his jaw broken. He was still conscious, and so was Tanaka, who could not walk, his legs broken by Yong Kwan. They were taken out into the rain and tied to a sapling. The rain fell harder, washing away their blood.

"Keep them here for the night," Yong Kwan said. "We will continue tomorrow."

We stayed in the rain as he returned to the cave. Kon took off his raincoat and placed it over Tanaka. "It will not be long now, *sensei*. Please have strength." He walked slowly back to his tent and started packing.

"What are you doing?" I asked.

"You have seen his condition. He cannot make it out of here with only you to help him," he said. "I think it is time I returned to Penang. I have been dreaming of home for some time now. I long to walk in my father's gardens again, to walk in the streets of Georgetown." There was a wistful tone in his voice, like a little boy who missed his bed and his home greatly. "I just want to go home. And anyway," he looked up into the slopes of the tent, "I am fed up with this constant rain."

We waited the entire night but the rain never abated. Toward dawn he said, "Time to leave." He found another piece of canvas and turned it into a coat. We went back into the rain, Saotome's sword in Kon's hand. I cut away Tanaka's ropes with my sword and we lifted him up gently. I saw that he was bleeding badly from a stab wound which I had not noticed earlier. I tore off my shirt sleeve and tried to stop the flow of blood. He opened his eyes, and gave a weak nod.

"What about him?" I asked Kon, pointing to Saotome.

"Leave him to Yong Kwan," he said.

But Tanaka whispered, "No." He touched my hand and said, "You know what has to be done."

I shook my head. "He is only getting what he has inflicted so often."

"That is not the Way," Tanaka said. "You are an *aikijutsu* student now and there are obligations. Be merciful."

I looked deep into Saotome's eyes but I saw Isabel, running across the endless beach. I saw Peter MacAllister and I could see Edward, and I knew then that my brother would not be coming home to Penang ever again. Saotome could not move his jaw but I knew what he wanted from me.

"No, I won't do it." I sheathed my own sword and he shut his eyes, defeated.

"Where are we going?" I asked.

"We'll head for the river and follow it to Ipoh. It's not far," Kon said. We both carried Tanaka and headed out of the camp. Despite his terrible injuries, Tanaka did not cry out. We were almost at the river when I realized we were being followed.

"Stop," I said. "Listen."

The river was in full flood and we had difficulty hearing. "I'll go back and check," Kon said. "Keep heading for the river."

I let Tanaka cling to me and we made our way down to the river's edge, a natural levee that fell away abruptly. The churning water almost ten feet below had breached the banks, carrying fallen tree trunks from the highlands, their branches rising out of the unforgiving water like the hands of drowning men. The river was loud, thrusting and twisting, an endless surge of pure power. I heard a rustling behind us and tried to turn, but Tanaka's weight on me made it difficult to move.

"It's me," Kon said. "You were right. Yong Kwan is behind us with Su Yen and some of the others. They are very close. I think Saotome may have raised the alarm."

"Let me down," Tanaka said. I dropped him gently to the ground and he held back a grunt of pain. "I cannot go on. You two must leave. Especially you," he said to me. "You must return to your father."

"We cannot leave you here," Kon said. "Yong Kwan will make you suffer for as long as possible."

There was a moment of complete understanding between master and pupil, and finally Kon nodded and said, "I will do it, *sensei*."

Tanaka lifted a circular amulet from around his neck. It was a *mon*, his family crest. "This is for you," he said. Kon held out his hand and I could see a faint tremor as he closed his palm around the gift. He took out Saotome's sword and drops of rain instantly made the shiny steel surface look like bubbling molten metal, as though the blade itself was heating up.

Tanaka, with Kon's assistance, got himself into a kneeling position. I was horrified at the agony he must be suffering and yet he managed to keep himself upright and rigid.

"You cannot go through with this," I said to Kon, my voice clogged by anger and grief. "We still have a good chance of getting away. Don't be a fool!"

Tanaka shook his head. "I want him to do it," he said to me. "Do not judge your friend harshly. Someday, perhaps, you will understand how grateful I am to him."

There was nothing more I could say, and so I bowed and whispered, "*Sayonara*, Tanaka-san. I am honored to have known you."

He managed a wry smile. "Who knows, maybe we will meet again?"

"I hope so," I said. I backed away and allowed Kon to stand over Tanaka.

"Is your stance correct?" Tanaka asked.

"Yes, *sensei*," Kon replied, and I heard how his voice was just as choked as mine had been.

"Place your weight a bit more on your right leg," Tanaka said. "Control your breathing. Loosen your grip on the handle—yes, well done."

I watched Kon compose himself, his eyes closed in concentration as he carried out Tanaka's instructions precisely. At this moment nothing mattered but performing his task. It was a final gesture of indebtedness to Tanaka and he was determined to do it well. He lifted his sword into the cutting position.

There was a rustle of foliage behind me. I wiped the water from my eyes and saw Su Yen appear from the jungle. She pointed a pistol at Kon.

"I do not think Yong Kwan would like that, Kon," she said, her voice hoarse. "So you are running away and leaving me here, without even telling me or asking me to follow?"

Kon lowered his sword and I saw the pain in his eyes. But I thought I saw also an element of shameful relief, as though he were glad he had been interrupted.

"Are you going to shoot me?" he mocked. Su Yen hesitated, her expression uncertain.

Again Kon raised the sword high but a shot sent him stumbling back to the river's edge. Yong Kwan had stepped out from behind the trees and now he moved toward Kon. I was furious at my own momentary lack of awareness, for not having felt Yong Kwan's presence.

"Stop him!" I said to Su Yen. "Use your gun!" But the girl just stared dumbly. In a swift, unstoppable motion I had my own blade out. It bridged the distance like a whip of light, the tip wedging softly into the side of Yong Kwan's neck, ready to cut it open.

"Put the gun down," I said through the rain. I gave the sword a gentle nudge, drawing a driblet of blood. He winced and obeyed me.

I kept all my attention on him and shouted to Kon, "Are you all right?"

"I'm fine," he said, using his sword to push himself up onto his feet. Tanaka had remained unmoving all this while, as though completely certain of the outcome.

From the corner of my eye I watched Kon gather all his will, a resolve which I doubted I would ever possess. Once again he lifted his sword to the sky, his stance correct. Blood from the gunshot wound soaked through his shirt, to be washed away instantly by the rain, as though the sight of it offended the gods.

He swung the sword down in a movement so perfect Tanaka would have commended it. I saw the *sensei* smile, his eyes closing just before the last moment, and I had a feeling that he approved. His body fell over and I let out a breath and closed my own eyes. I did not see Su Yen raise her pistol again. She fired twice and Kon staggered, spun around and fell off the edge of the levee into the river. By the time I reached the edge he was gone, swept away by the torrent.

Yong Kwan was grinning with satisfaction. "The girl knows who is going to take care of her. Don't you, Su Yen?" He held out his hand to her and after a moment of hesitation she went to him.

A shaft of immense pain opened up and an overpowering rage, as turbulent as the river, shook me. I smashed Yong Kwan's face with the hilt of my sword, knocking him unconscious. I faced Su Yen. "I should kill you, you little whore," I said coldly.

She was expressionless, her hair in strands over her face. In the rain I could not be certain whether she was crying, as I walked away.

I searched the stretch of river for my friend, shouting his name. But there were only spinning tree trunks and fallen branches riding the current. It was useless. I turned back to the jungle and made my way home to my father.

It took me three days to find Ipoh again. I repeated Kon's instructions in my head, sometimes hearing his voice and thinking I had gone mad, possessed by the jungle spirits that my *amah* used to tell me often played tricks on people who had gotten lost, making them walk in circles for days, distracting them with false sounds and laughter. There were times when the rain would stop suddenly, leaving the leaves dripping like taps that had not been turned off properly. Then the sun would raise steam from the undergrowth, creating a perverse kind of fog that was not cold but hot and heavy, impossible to breathe in.

I was aware that I was lost, and I sat on a root, unable to move, immobilized by despair. The rainforest refused to release me, and all around me the straight columniation of trees, thousands of years old, continued their reach to the sun. I grieved for my friend, but there was no one to bring me comfort.

I talked to Endo-san and asked for his help, knowing I was on the edge of succumbing to defeat. But the thought of my father made me get back on my feet and I walked on, trying to use the sun to give me direction. After a short distance I found shelter in the hollow of a fig tree. I sat down, slowed my breathing, and began to meditate.

I did not know how long I sat there, but the noise of aircraft brought me back. I opened my eyes, looked up through the canopy of leaves, and saw two of the largest planes I had ever seen roar past. I made note of the direction they were flying in, feeling a jolt of hope as I followed them through the trees. Within an hour I heard explosions, and knew that the British had returned, this time to complete the work they had abandoned. I followed the twisting spires of thick black smoke that braided upward into the skies and knew Ipoh was within reach.

The planes—I was told later that they were Lancasters and Halifaxes, capable of great distances and used for bombing missions—circled Ipoh, dropping their bombs on Japanese-occupied buildings. I said a prayer of gratitude to Isabel and her friends who had supplied precise information to the British. I came over a rise and Ipoh lay before me, its hills dulled by the rising gray clouds. Fires were burning and, on the wind, I heard the faint sounds of sirens, like the cries of an awakened baby.

I sat and waited until the planes circled one last time and flew away to the west, back to India. I walked into the town of Ipoh, passing little kampongs where I met smiling children and old men, waving to me. They knew that the Japanese were finished.

In the center of town, in front of the padang, I entered the railway station and went to my hotel. The hall porter's desk was surrounded by hysterical Japanese women and I pushed them away and asked for my key. The Indian hall porter held on to the key, and looked at me steadily. "Maybe you should not go back to your room," he said.

I held out my hand for the key and thanked him. "I have to."

They were waiting for me, Goro and the officers from the Kempeitai. He grinned and ordered an officer to handcuff me. "Endo-san informed us that you would come back for your father," Goro said. "You will be charged with spying, with assisting the MPAJA and with the murder of Saotome-san. If found guilty, you and your family will be publicly beheaded." His smile turned into a sneer. "You *will* be found guilty, I can assure you. And I will be your executioner."

Chapter Fifteen

I was taken in a military lorry to Butterworth, where Goro ordered me onto a boat. I felt only a strange sense of serenity as we crossed the channel into Penang. My heart was calm, as was the sea, and it seemed as though we moved across a surface of glass. Even the jellyfish floating in the deep green waters seemed to hang suspended in stillness. I neither felt the wind, nor saw the clouds resting on the peak of Penang Hill, where the tiny houses shone and glittered in the sun.

I felt the sound first, a deep, almost inaudible hum, vibrating through the membranes of the air as the Halifaxes came over, flying unnecessarily low, certain of their invincibility. I saw their shadows move over our boat, then over the surface of the sea as though some immense creatures were moving beneath us. In their wake air and water were disturbed and sea spray blew into my face. Goro ran out from below deck and watched the planes as they headed for the docks. He jumped below again, where I heard him attempting to frantically radio the air force.

The first Halifax reached the docks. Seconds later explosions rocked the harbor. We were so close I felt the singeing heat from the blast. The other two planes flew on into town. As clouds of smoke curled up into the sky my heart ached at the destruction. In their indiscriminate bombings in Europe the Allied Forces had killed thousands of civilians. Now as I watched I realized that this time, as in Ipoh, their selection of strategic locations was unerring, the targets of their bombing precise. The Japanese naval base was completely destroyed and the air above the army barracks around Fort Cornwallis shimmered from the flames burning up the military camps. The Fort itself, which housed those prisoners of war who had not been sent to the Death Railway, remained miraculously undamaged. This show of precision lit a bright flare of hope within me. I felt that Isabel and Auntie Mei and their friends had somehow played an effective part, that their deaths had not been fruitless. In the wind, Isabel's laughter, the laughter I had known all my life, came to me. It sounded so rich and filled with joy, with all the wondrous things of life, that I felt a lightness of heart within myself.

There was no harbor left when we arrived. The boat swayed in the shallows and a sampan came out to carry us in to land. Debris and wreckage knocked against the hull as we neared the shore. The stench of burning buildings choked us and the air was dark with thick columns of smoke. Embers, some still curling with fire, floated away with the wind. I heard cries and screams. A corner of Hutton & Sons had been shorn away, exposing the offices on the top floor.

I was pushed up the stone steps from the water's edge. I stood on the pier, trying to absorb and comprehend the extent of the destruction. Everything seemed to be charred. The roads had caved in completely, and vehicles had been thrown around by the explosions; some lay on their roofs, wheels sticking into the air, while others had been crushed into unrecognizable shapes.

The Halifaxes had turned around and were coming our way again. We saw their black eggs drop from their bellies, accompanied by a thin whistling sound. The first one hit the arms depot, and we were thrown off our feet by the resulting chain of explosions as the ammunition ignited.

A Japanese guard was holding onto a railing. The next moment he let out a cry; a wicked looking piece of shrapnel, two feet long, sprouted from his chest. Blood spurted from his mouth as he pirouetted and collapsed. There was a clatter almost like rain on a tin roof as the row of godowns behind us was hit by flying debris. The thin corrugated metal walls folded under the assault and, as they crumpled, they brought down the roof. I heard the sounds of a hundred glass windows breaking into clouds of fine, powdery fragments, filling the air like dust from a vigorously beaten carpet.

I dropped flat onto the ground, between two overturned drums of oil. The planes flew past, the ground trembling. And then they were gone.

The persistent ringing in my ears faded. I heard my breathing first, then the erratic beating of my heart. My legs felt rubbery as

I rose to my feet. Goro managed to look dignified even as he struggled upright. In his eyes I saw something that until now I had never seen in any Japanese: defeat.

He gathered his people and together we made our laborious crossing over the burning roads. He stopped the first car we encountered, hauled out the hapless Malay driver and drove to government headquarters. Along the way I noticed the faces of the people of Penang. Hope had erased some of the weariness of the Japanese Occupation. Their shoulders seemed straighter, their chins higher. I was glad of this subtle transformation.

In the headquarters everything was calm. It was as though they were not aware of the bombing; perhaps they equated it with the earlier sporadic bombings carried out so halfheartedly.

I was taken into Endo-san's office. He was staring out of the high glass windows, looking at the lawns and the bougainvillea. A macaque sat on the glistening grass, eating a rambutan, its tail beating the ground gently. Probably from the colony in the Botanical Gardens, I thought with detachment.

Endo-san's hair, I noticed, shone brighter than ever. He was dressed in his gray *yukata*, trimmed with subtle threads of gold, and a black *hakama*.

"Get out," he ordered Goro and then sat down behind his desk. I stood my ground.

"Tanaka-san, your childhood friend, is dead," I said. I saw him flinch before covering his emotions.

"How?" he asked.

I took him from the events that had led to so many wasted lives to the final words of Tanaka before his death. Endo-san looked down at his hands lying on the table. Finally he said, "You should not have let Goro escape. He made his report not to me, but to Saotome-san's office. We could have avoided all this."

"Everything was done in vain, then," I said.

"You know why you were arrested," he said softly.

I nodded. "How is my father?"

"He is in jail."

"You said you'd watch over him," I said, and the rising anger in my voice could not be controlled. "Let me see him!"

He picked up a document. "You have been accused of passing military and government secrets to the triads. Do you admit this?"

I made no reply, thinking only of my father.

"Which triad? Towkay Yeap's?"

"It doesn't matter, Endo-san. The war is lost. It's time you went home."

He looked tired suddenly. "I hope so. I want to go home. Once the war is over at least my duty is done." His voice turned soft and his face followed. "I wish to see Miyajima Island again. I want to walk through the fields where I grew up, the streets where I played, and talk to the people of my village. I just want to go home."

I felt a sharp stab of sorrow, for his words had struck a soft resonance, like an aged monk gently sounding a bell in a temple far away as I recalled what Kon had said. He too had only wanted to see his home again.

"Let me see my father," I said, feeling exhausted.

He came closer to me and held out his hand. I hesitated, and then took it. He brought me to him and gently he put his arms around me. I put my face into his chest, and for a few minutes we pretended things were as they had been, before the war.

"My dearest boy," he whispered.

I pushed myself away from him. "Do your duty. Do it and go home."

I was taken to Fort Cornwallis, just a short walk away from the offices of Hutton & Sons. In the sort of twist so beloved of history, the Fort, once built to house the British garrison, was now used to imprison the remaining British soldiers and civilians who had not been sent to the Death Railway. The prisoners, thin to the bone, wearing only tattered clothes, watched from the depths of their cells as I was led into the darkness of the Fort.

I called out to my father, I called to the prisoners on either side of my cell, but they had not heard of Noel Hutton. It was only on the day they took me to face the Tribunal set up to hear my crimes that I saw him.

I was grieved by his appearance. He walked like an old man, with small, tentative steps, no longer sure of his path. But when he was placed next to me, he gave a shadow of his old smile and asked, "You did what had to be done?"

"Yes, Father. Did they hurt you?"

He shook his head. "They treated me with great civility. Largely, I think, due to Mr. Endo's intervention."

The Japanese never did things in half measures. Throughout my association with them I had seen the lengths they would go to just to prove their point. So it was with my punishment.

Hiroshi decreed that the evidence against me, which consisted mainly of Goro's testimony, was overwhelming. I had passed information to the enemy and I had played a part in the murder of Saotome, whose body had been thrown into the entrance of the Kempeitai headquarters in Ipoh even while I had been wandering around lost in the jungle. I was to be executed in the field outside the Fort. Noel Hutton was to be imprisoned for harboring me, for being the father of a traitor.

I steeled myself to receive the expected judgement with equanimity for my father's sake. When I turned to look at him he nodded once to himself and I saw in his face the same expression he always had whenever his commercial negotiations reached an impasse. During those negotiations he would often find a solution, but not now. There was none.

"I'll find a way to get you out," he said.

I wondered if his mind had been affected. His eyes were extraordinarily bright, shining with a certainty I felt was misplaced. He spoke to Endo-san. "You know the war is as good as over, yet still you persist in carrying out this travesty—this perversion."

"My duty continues right to the end of the war," Endo-san replied, before we were led out into the sun and taken back into the lightless world of the Fort.

Endo-san visited me daily. I asked to be allowed to see my father but I was refused. On the last evening of the day before I was to be executed, I knew the restraints I had bound over my emotions would soon break. I felt time draining away and there was nothing I could do to halt it.

Endo-san came later than usual that day. The lock rattled and the door was opened. I stood up from the wooden pallet that was my bed as Endo-san entered.

"Let me see him," I said.

"You will see him tomorrow," he said. "Do not worry about

your father. He is well. I have been spea   .m these past few days. I have just come from his cell."

"What did he say? Did he have a message for me?"

Endo-san shook his head.

In spite of myself I had been hoping that my father could somehow put everything right again, as he had done when I was a child. But I was on my own now.

"Will you make sure he is safe? That no harm comes to him?" I asked.

"I will ensure that he has what he requires," Endo-san said.

"I do not want to see him tomorrow," I said. "I do not want him to be there. Can you at least see to that?"

"I will try," he said. "I have also requested the return of your sword to me."

"I never used it to kill," I said. I should have, I thought. I should have sliced Yong Kwan's throat. Perhaps then Kon would still be alive.

"That is good," Endo-san said.

"So it is ending the way it always has," I said. "In a way, you will be killing me again." I had to fight with all my strength not to collapse under my fears but he saw my struggle.

"Would you like me to stay here with you tonight?"

"Yes," I said. "I would."

Chapter Sixteen

News travels fast in a small place like Penang. I remember how everyone used to be related, or connected, or knew each other. Somehow we always knew if a man was having an affair or if a woman loved her drink too much. Once I played truant and spent the day in the streets of Georgetown. When I returned home that evening my father was waiting for me. I had been seen and the news was passed to someone who then felt bound to let him know.

I was certain the *Jipunakui* had also helped in letting the people know of the fates of the last of the Huttons. On the day I was brought to the field outside Fort Cornwallis a crowd had already gathered, restless and eager. My father was there, and my heart sank. So Endo-san had failed me in spite of my pleas.

The crowd's reactions were mixed. Many perceived me as a traitor who had collaborated with the Japanese. These jeered and threw stones at me and were immediately dragged out by the Japanese soldiers and beaten. Once again, I thought, how could we ever understand these savage, cultured, brutal, yet refined people?

There were some in the crowd whom I had helped and they stood in silence. In the mass of faces I thought I saw Towkay Yeap's and I wished I could tell him about Kon, how he had longed to come home.

I shifted between times, seeing my mother as she lay dying beneath her sheets, seeing Aunt Mei smile at me as we sat in her house. I saw Endo-san the day he took me to his island but we rowed on and on and then he was gone, and I was left alone on my boat, the oars somehow in my hands. I closed my eyes and attempted to harness whatever strength remained in me.

When it was read out that I had passed information to the secret societies the jeers were silenced and, like the whisper of a breeze the crowd started chanting our family name. The sound swelled and filled the sky, strong as the monsoon winds. Goro fired a few shots into the air but the sullen silence that descended was even more powerful than the chanting.

The once immaculate padang where people had played cricket was littered with stones and bald patches of sand showed through the dry grass. In the middle of it was a square of blinding-white sand, perfectly raked. A wooden post had been planted in its center, jutting out like a desiccated tree trunk in the desert. I was made to kneel on the sand and Goro tied me to the post. I held my father's eyes in mine and whispered, "Forgive me. You shouldn't be here."

He shook his head gently. "You did what you had to do, what you could do."

"I'm so, so sorry." I felt the closeness of tears behind my eyes and I resolved not to let anyone see them.

Endo-san walked up to me. Time seemed to turn around again, for was he not in the very same clothes I had seen him wearing, when I was deep in *zazen*, as he prepared to cut me centuries ago? The black robes with the beautiful gold trimmings looked similar; only this time his hair was short, he did not have a top-knot, and in his hand he held his Nagamitsu sword.

He stood before me. It was true. It was happening, time was running backward. There on his face was the same expression I had seen then. I felt faint, yet there was no fear, only a recognition that he had been right all along. He said to me: "Your father will die. But you will live."

"No! That was not what I asked of you!"

He turned to look at my father. I saw them exchange glances and I knew that another agreement had been made, one that had excluded me. They brought my father next to me and he knelt heavily; I could even hear the popping of his joints. I pulled at my ropes and screamed at Endo-san.

"It's no use shouting. There's nothing you can do to change this," my father said softly. "Show some dignity before the people of Penang."

I stopped my struggle. "Why?"

He gave me his beautiful smile but he chose not to reply. Instead he asked, in an almost childlike voice, "Will it hurt?"

"No," I said. From the depths of my knowledge, of my lives lived, I could say to him, "It won't hurt. They'll do it properly."

And then the crowd began to whisper our name again, like a wave beginning far out at sea, growing in strength as it surged toward the shore. Endo-san gave a warning to Goro and the Japanese soldiers not to fire their weapons. The chanting *"Hutton! Hutton!"* rolled on, increasing in volume and emotion.

"Listen to that!" my father said. "Make our name live on. Let it always have those qualities associated with it. Only the good."

Endo-san removed my father's chains and made him comfortable. Goro, feeling cheated, protested but Endo-san said, "He dies a free man."

My father squeezed his wrists and then placed them behind his back. How often had I seen him walk, enjoying his garden, with his hands clasped behind him? He straightened his back and lifted his chin.

Endo-san stood up, bowed his head for a moment and unsheathed his *katana*. It came out silently, like a ray of sunlight piercing through a bank of rain-cloud and just as brilliant. He bowed low to my father. "I would be honored if you would allow me to complete this."

My father dipped his head in assent and then opened his eyes, which blazed brighter than I had ever seen them. He looked up to the sun, now rising rapidly, feeling its warmth for the last time. The clock tower struck half past nine as the morning wind cooled our burning faces and lifted his hair.

He reached across and stroked my head. "Never forget you are a Hutton. Never forget you are my son."

Endo-san bowed again and raised his sword. I recognized that stance. *Happo.* Both hands brought to the right shoulder, feet planted firmly on the ground, the sword raised like the purest voice to Heaven. The chanting of the crowd quickened and I found my lips moving along to the cadence of our name.

I forced myself to watch. I told myself that I would not turn away, that I would be with my father to the end. Endo-san took a breath in and brought the blade down. The crowd was silenced. High up in the sky, unseen, a squadron of Halifaxes could be heard on their daily run.

*

Endo-san arranged for my father to be buried in the grounds in Istana, next to William's memorial stone, and not displayed publicly as Hiroshi and Fujihara had wanted. Days after his death I was led out of Fort Cornwallis, weak and half blinded by the light reflecting off the walls, the godly light of Penang that I loved so much. I had not eaten anything and the water left daily by Endo-san had stagnated as I lay curled in a corner. I did not speak to Endo-san during his visits and left his questions unanswered.

I was released and placed under house arrest, which meant I was restricted to Istana and in Endo-san's custody.

"Did Hiroshi order my release?"

"Hiroshi-san is dying. I issued the order."

As we drove to Istana I wound down the windows and, for the first time in days, I breathed clean, true air. I still could not feel anything of the layers of events piling upon each other.

I had slept badly in my cell, pursued by vivid dreams and memories. Now, as we drove along the winding coastal road I felt my wounds being soothed by my old friend, the sea. How many times had I made this journey with my father? He was often a source of the most bizarre information—"There's that tree where the branch fell on the resident councillor's car and broke his wrists"—"That house there has an underground secret passageway leading to the beach"—"That stall serves the best *assam laksa* money can buy."

Everything I knew of my home I had learned from my father.

And I would never see him again.

Endo-san put his hands on my shoulders and turned me around. I tried not to flinch, but he saw my swiftly hidden expression and let go of me. I went out to the balcony outside my room, its tiles still hot from the day, pleasurable under my feet. The sea was turning red as the sun dropped and his island lay innocent, fired by the light like a pot placed in a kiln. Clouds of birds circled it, flying in from the corners of the sky. Brahminy kites floated on the heated air. Reluctant to return home, they soared endlessly like mythical creatures that never needed to touch the earth, not even once in all their lives.

"Thank you for arranging the funeral," I said in a formal tone, and bowed to Endo-san. In my mind I still saw those kites in the sky and I envied them.

From within his *yukata* he removed an envelope. "Your father requested writing materials the last time I visited him."

I received the envelope with both hands. He continued, "You are of course still under house arrest. You are not allowed to leave Istana without my authority. I have your sword in my care. You are not allowed to carry it. Please see to it that you obey these orders. I would find it difficult to intercede on your behalf again."

He put his arms around me once more and held me in a strong embrace. And then he left me there on the balcony, alone except for a scattering of evening stars.

He appeared on the beach moments later, walking stiffly, leaving smudges on the sand behind him. He pulled his boat down to the water, climbed in, and rowed across to his home.

I opened the envelope and read the shaky writing and the unwavering words.

Fort Cornwallis Prison
Penang
31st July, 1945

My dearest son,

There are so many things unspoken between us and now time has decreed that we shall never have the moment to voice them.

I was initially distraught at your relationship with Mr. Endo and with the Japanese. They are a cruel people—perhaps no more cruel than the English or the Chinese, some would argue—but I will never fully comprehend them or their unnecessary savagery. My distress at your closeness with Mr. Endo was somewhat lessened by the influence he has had on you: learn from him, for he has much to impart, but make your own decisions. Do not let your ties to the past—or fear of the future—direct the course of your life, because, however many lives we have ahead of us to redeem and repair our failings, I feel we have a God-given duty to live this life as best we can.

I have known for some time of some of your humanitarian activities—the father of your friend often kept me informed of the good you have achieved while working for Mr. Endo. Thus, on the day of my death, I can walk out with my head held high, secure in the knowledge that none of my children—not one—ever took the easy road; that they strove to keep sanity, reason, and compassion alive and burning in these tragic times.

Mr. Endo and I have spoken much during these last days. I have finally gained a sense of who and what he is and was and I feel I can trust him with my life. Such different beliefs we have! But having spent all my life out here in the East, I sense more than a grain of truth in his.

I have made a pact with him. He has informed me that he is only able to give one of us a reprieve, because apparently you did strike a terrible blow against the Japanese. I am aware of your repeated requests to see me, but I have asked Mr. Endo not to allow it, for I fear you will sense my eventual intention.

So, time runs on. Already I can hear the crowd outside. I know that in time they too will know the extent of our sacrifice and forgive us our ties with the Japanese. I have never regretted staying behind to defend our home. We have done the right thing and I know that History will judge us fairly and kindly.

My son, grieve if you must but not for too long. I fear for you and the burdens imposed on you by your duty. In the last fragments of my life I truly wish, in spite of my Christian faith, to believe that we will all live again and again so that I may be blessed, perhaps in some future life on the far side of a new morning, to meet you again and to tell you how much I love you.

With the greatest of love,
Your father

I heard his voice clearly, so full of the love he had felt for me, for all his children. I leaned against the balcony railings, all my strength snuffed out as suddenly as a candle flame. The hollowness in me expanded; I shivered all over and clenched my fists as I finally let myself grieve.

Chapter Seventeen

I had to wait a few days after our dinner at the restaurant before Michiko felt strong enough to show me where my father had hidden his collection of *keris*. She now spent all of her days in my house and I had taken to shortening my hours at the office to have more time with her.

"It was cruel of me to show Endo-san's sword to you. I did not know he had used it to execute your father," she said one evening after I had finished telling her of Noel's death. Both of us were in a somber mood. I had not thought about it in such a long time, yet every detail remained so clear.

"I never saw it again after that. I never knew what he had done with it. To hold it in my hand again, after all this time, was a shock to me. I wanted you to leave immediately."

"And what changed your mind?" she asked.

I took a long time to find a reply that made sense. "I felt that there must have been a reason why you showed up here. And to turn you away seemed a grave disrespect to Endo-san's memory."

There was also something else that I had wanted to ask her, and now I felt we knew each other sufficiently well for me to do so. "The bags that you arrived with, they are all that you have left?"

"Yes. I have tidied up all my affairs. My husband's company is in good hands."

"It must have been difficult to let it all go." I was thinking of the time when I too would have to do the same. I had been making the requisite arrangements to trim away the unnecessary strands of my life but I was faltering, not yet ready to take the final step.

"It was necessary," she replied. "That is what growing old consists of, mostly. One starts giving away items and belongings until only the memories are left. In the end, what else do we really require?"

I examined her words carefully, and the answer came slowly but without any equivocation. "Someone to share those memories with," I said finally, surprising myself. I had never actually made the decision not to discuss my activities during the Japanese Occupation. The stagnation of my memories and my unwillingness to voice them had happened naturally, coagulated over the years by a combination of guilt, loss, a sense of failure, and the certain knowledge that no one could ever understand what I had gone through.

And at that moment I realized that the corollary to that state of affairs was the loss of my ability to trust, the very cornerstone of aikido. When training as a student in Tokyo I insisted as often as I could on being the *nage*, the one receiving the attack and the one controlling the outcome. This contravened the etiquette of all *dojo*, which requires the equal sharing of opposing roles. It made me unpopular with my fellow pupils, although I viewed my preference as being only the extension of a strong personality, something in which I took pride. When I became an instructor I never ceded the role of *nage* to anyone and I was never again the *uke*, the one who was thrown, where once I had reveled in flight.

This knowledge, like all great and worthwhile enlightenment relating to the human condition, was bittersweet and came too late.

"I appreciate what you are doing. I know it is hard for you," Michiko said, her gentle tone breaking into my thoughts like the passage of a bird's low flight across the face of a pond.

I swept her words away with my hand. "It took great courage and strength for you to make the journey here too. I'm glad you came."

"I took a long time to decide. It was not an act of impulse to come and upset the tranquillity of your life here." She asked me to help her to her feet. "I shall show you where your father concealed his blades tomorrow morning."

She was waiting for me when I finished my morning practice session, her Panama hat shading her face, holding a spade in her hand. I had asked her to train with me daily, and at first she had, but as her strength began to wane she preferred to walk on the beach instead and watch each day arrive.

She took me to the river where we had watched the fireflies, using the spade as a walking stick. Although the sun was shaded by the clouds and we walked beneath the shadows of the overhanging trees, it was a warm morning. Only as we approached the river did the air become cooler. At the frangipani tree my mother had planted she stopped. "Dig around here," she said.

"How can you be so certain?" I was doubtful, but willing to indulge her.

"The clues were all in what you have been telling me."

I dug deep into the ground around the tree, taking care not to damage its roots. About four feet down I hit something that sounded metallic. I dropped the spade and scrabbled with my hands and finally loosened a rusted box from the grip of the earth.

It was heavy and it took all my strength to prise the lid open. Inside, wrapped in layers of stiffened oilcloth, were the eight *keris* my father had collected. They were all in good condition, except for a light dusting of rust on their blades. I picked up the *keris* that Noel had purchased from the deposed sultan and dipped it into a bar of sunlight. The diamonds on the hilt fractured the light into the trees and it was as though fireflies were moving through them, competing with the glare of the day. One scale of light danced on Michiko's cheek.

"I can understand your father's interest in them," she said. "They are magnificent. What are you going to do with them?"

I shook my head. "I don't know." I shoveled the mound of earth back into the hole. My arms were aching by the time I finished. We sat on the banks, the box between us. There grew in me an inexplicable sadness, which she sensed.

Michiko's arrival with Endo-san's *katana* that I had long thought lost, the discovery of my father's *keris*, all these seemed only to underline to me the inescapable fact that I had never had any choice in the direction of my life. Everything had already been planned for me, long before I was born. My mother's hopes for me, in her choice of my abandoned name, had not been borne out.

I told Michiko all this and she said, "If it is true, then you are a very blessed man."

She saw that I did not understand her and she tried to clarify. "To have the awareness that there is a greater power directing our destinies must give great comfort. It would give a sense of meaning to our lives, knowing that we are not running around vainly like mice in a maze. It would soothe me to know that all these," she tapped her chest, "my illness, my pain and loss, and yes, my meeting you, all have a reason."

She saw the stubborn set of my face. "I've never felt blessed," I said. "There must be free will to choose. Do you know the poem about the two roads, and the one not taken?"

"Yes. That has always amused me, because who created the two roads in the first place?"

It was a question I had never considered.

Chapter Eighteen

Endo-san once said, "All fights revolve around the interplay of forces," and these words, I began to realize, could also be applied to wars. The balance had shifted and the Allied forces, wearied but stubborn, were advancing steadily against the Japanese. The Halifaxes now visited us daily, alternating bombs with pamphlets that told us of Allied victories. We heard about the kamikaze pilots, warriors of the Divine Wind, but even they could not stop the Allies. Although isolated in Istana, I still caught snippets of news. I could tell how the war was going just by the faces of the servants.

I entered the kitchen and spoke to Ah Jin, the cook. "Go into town and get me a few cans of paint on the black market," I said, handing her a basket of banana notes and telling her which colors I wanted.

She returned a few hours later. "*Aiyah,* sir, the town going crazy, everyone spend, spend, spend. Fifty thousand Japanese dollars for a loaf of stale bread." She handed me six tins of paint but I told her to leave them on the landing beneath the attic stairs, along with some brushes.

"Everyone's getting rid of their banana notes," I said. "Do you know what that means?"

She looked out of the kitchen windows to where Endo-san, who had moved into Istana, stood peering through a pair of binoculars, sweeping the sky and the sea.

"*Ya-lah,* the *Jipunakui* will be chased out very soon," she said.

I went into the study and returned with more banana notes. "Take this and give it to the others. Spend it all, as fast as you wish." She beamed and went to the kitchen, where I soon heard her excited voice calling the rest of the servants.

Early the next morning I left my room and checked that Endo-san was still sleeping. I carried the six cans of paint up into the attic, moving carefully through the unused furniture and wrinkled leather trunks, many still bearing P&O Liner labels, all large enough for me to lie inside. My footfalls raised only silent dust. I opened a small window and climbed out onto the ledge. The wind breathed softly and the sun seemed undecided about rising.

I crawled up the steep clay tiles of the roof. My fear of heights was gone. I had learned that there were other, greater things to fear. I opened one of the cans and dipped my brush in it.

I had to make many trips and each time the climb made me breathless. As the sun floated up I started to perspire. By the time I was finished I had cracked eighteen of the tiles with my weight. But at last I stood on the ledge, satisfied with my efforts.

On the sloping roof, facing the sea, facing the direction from which the planes often flew in, a rather rudimentary Union Jack, with its rough red, blue and white lines, shone bright and welcoming in the rising sun.

There was nothing much for me to do now. I could not leave Istana and so I spent my days on the beach, staring out to sea. An eerie sense of anticipation hovered like a hungry ghost in the air and, although people would later say it was a figment of my imagination, I was certain of what I saw that day.

The light in the eastern sky throbbed, intensified, as though the wick of an oil lamp had been suddenly turned up. It burned with a terrible sheen of pure brightness and pulsed into red, violet, and shades never seen before. On Endo-san's island, birds in the trees clattered out in a panic-stricken flapping of wings. A numbing coldness spread out from the very center of my being; I had to choke for air, as I had not breathed in those seconds. A silence so oppressive halted the world that even the waves seemed to pause in their march to the shore.

The moment lengthened and then passed, and left me quiet. The world sounded different, less sure of itself.

News of the Hiroshima bombing reached us that evening. I was certain the servants had a radio hidden in the house, for the mood in Istana changed subtly, and the dark moods of the previous weeks perceptibly lifted.

I waited for Endo-san on the lawn and we drank his bitter tea as he told me the full extent of the destruction to that city. His entire home on the outskirts of Hiroshima was gone. "It is as though my family had never existed, as though *I* had never existed. You are talking to a ghost. There is no past now, no living ties left." He had been written out of history.

I tried to imagine Penang obliterated, its roads and buildings turned to sand, the sand melted to glass, then dissolved further by the heat, and finally scattered by the terrible wind, a wind that was not divine, the toxic air killing me with every shallow breath.

"We have our Divine Wind, and now the Americans have theirs," he said. The war was over that day and we both knew it.

This time it was I who went to him, I who held him as he wept. How strangely comforting it was to feel his tears. My thumb wiped them gently from his eyes, yet still they came. A lifetime's sorrow flowed from him that day. I licked my thumb and tasted his tears, and I was not at all surprised to discover that there was nothing unfamiliar about them. I had tasted them before, a long, long time ago.

Endo-san accepted the subsequent bombing of Nagasaki without emotion. I knew he slept with difficulty. I saw him often on the balcony, looking homeward like a yearning sailor. I did not have to wonder what weighed down his thoughts and kept him from rest.

The emperor of Japan, once a boy who crouched over a tidal pool near Endo-san's father's estate, fishing for samples for his marine biology collection, surrendered three days later.

I held the scroll in my hands and unrolled it. It had only been recently written and I could trace the smell of ink. It came from Fujihara, and my first impulse was to tear it up and burn it. Instead I let one edge of it curl back tightly to meet its opposite end.

I had not heard from him since leaving Penang to warn Kon. He had not been at my sentencing and I could not recall if he was present when my father had been executed. Now he was asking a favor of me and I felt a bright burst of rage. But I opened the scroll again and tried to think.

I was at his house in Scott Road at the time he had requested.

Through the open windows I heard him playing one of his habitual Bach pieces on the piano, the Bechstein piano that I had been ordered to obtain for him. The music was full of horror, part of the terrible things I had been forced to witness, and I wanted to turn around and leave. But I knew I could not weaken now. I called out to him from the veranda.

"Come in," he said without stopping his playing.

I entered and found him in the drawing room, bare of all furniture except the piano. To one side was a reed mat, and two swords, one short and one long, lay on the mat like fish caught on a line.

He finished the piece and a serene look came over his face. He lifted his hands from the keys and closed the piano softly. "Thank you for coming," he said.

He was dressed in a white cotton robe and as he knelt on the mat I asked, "Why have you chosen me to assist you in your suicide?"

"I wanted someone who would be willing to see me die. And you are Endo-san's pupil, so your abilities must be formidable."

I moved toward him and picked up the two swords. He would use the shorter one to pierce his abdomen and then slice it open while I would stand behind him with the long sword, ready to finish the ritual if he wavered, or lost his resolve.

He smiled at me. "Now is your opportunity to appease the spirits of your sister and your aunt." He opened his palm for the short sword.

I held the swords in my hand and said, "I am not going to assist you. Outside are a group of men from the anti-Japanese societies. *They* will make sure that each and every spirit you have made suffer will be appeased."

He backed away from me, stunned, his eyes taking in the men who now appeared behind me. "You lost the war, Fujihara. But what was worse, you lost your humanity. I will not let your death be an honorable one." I placed the swords on the piano and said to the leader of the group, "Do what you like with him."

The men set about tying up Fujihara and I knew, from their grim but delighted faces that he would suffer much and suffer long.

I paused in the doorway as I left—there was something else. "Burn the piano when you are done," I said to the leader. I knew then that I could never listen to the music of Bach again.

*

It was bedlam in the consulate offices. I felt only pity as the staff ran about destroying letters, documents, and all incriminating evidence. Endo-san stood away from it all and Hiroshi snapped at him, "What are you doing, standing around? Help us burn these papers."

"What will damn us will not be papers, but the memories of men, Hiroshi-san. And those you can never destroy," Endo-san told him.

Hiroshi, his face made lifeless by his illness, coughed and sat down. "This is all a waste of time, is it not? Is this what we have become, a nation of paper destroyers?"

He got up and leaned heavily on the desk. He opened his drawer and Endo-san said, "Hiroshi-san, you still have your duty. We all have."

But Hiroshi ignored him and put his gun to his temple. The clerks stopped their work. A typist dropped a bundle of documents, which scattered, lining the floor with tiles of arcane patterns.

I turned away and so did not see what happened, but the report of the shot cracked inside my skull and the unexpected smell of blood and death thickened the air in the room.

That night many of the staff followed Hiroshi's example. The rest waited to surrender themselves to the British.

"Do not follow Hiroshi," I said to Endo-san. "Don't do it, please." In his eyes I could see that he wished to, but his strong sense of duty, the necessity of completing his task by handing over the administration of Penang to the returning British, restrained him. But once that was done, what then? What then?

Once again my abilities were required, when the time came to return Penang to the British. The roads were festooned with whatever scraps of decoration the people of Penang could find, and banners trailed from lampposts and street signs. All the trappings of the Japanese Occupation were taken down, burned in pyres that scorched the roads, heat shimmering in the air like departing spirits. The British troops returned to Georgetown and were greeted with shouts of gladness and affection.

I was at the door of the former home of the resident councillor when a small army convoy, three trucks, and what I later learned was a jeep, rumbled up the driveway. A red-faced, hawk-nosed officer jumped out of the jeep and looked at me with suspicion.

"Who the hell are you?" he asked. I did not reply but led him to Endo-san. As we stepped up to the veranda I heard the slam of tailgates and the crunching of boots on gravel. I turned to see a company of British soldiers, bayonets fixed, spilling around the sides of the trucks and then forming into lines on the lawn. These were not at all like the men who had abandoned Penang four years earlier. They wore neat new olive uniforms tailored for the jungle and wide brimmed hats topped with red and white-feathered hackles. Something else was different about them too, and it was not just that they looked fit and healthy and were grinning in triumph. Then it struck me: most of them were younger than I was. I suddenly felt the loss of those four years more keenly than ever before.

"Lieutenant-Colonel Milburn. Fourth Battalion. Royal Northumberland Fusiliers," the officer introduced himself. "We're here to make sure you don't kill the remaining prisoners in your care. General Erskine will sail into Penang harbor in two days' time. You will then formally surrender to him. In the meantime, a guard will stand watch to make sure you don't escape."

"We have no intention of it," Endo-san said in English. "Would you like some tea?"

On the appointed day we waited at the harbor. I looked at the people crowding around us, their faces sapped by the war. A few smiled at me. I felt a lightening gladness and wished my father could have been here.

General Arthur Erskine stepped onto the wooden platform built by the army to replace the destroyed jetty. I studied his well-fed body, his healthy hair and skin, and wondered what he must make of this group of scrawny Japanese who had overrun a British colony.

Endo-san walked up to him and, speaking through me for the benefit of the other Japanese, said, "On behalf of the Emperor of Japan I, Hayato Endo, surrender myself, my people, and the island of Penang to you. And I also hereby release a prisoner of Japan, Mr. Philip Hutton."

I was interpreting his words when I saw Goro push out from the crowd of Japanese. He moved toward us calmly as Endo-san leaned over and signed the document of surrender. I saw him raise his gun and aim it at Endo-san.

"You have brought disgrace to us by surrendering," he said, his small eyes narrowed in rage, almost disappearing into his face.

I leaped toward Goro as he fired and I saw the shots puncture the ground, sending up little puffs of dust. One shot hit Endo-san in his thigh and he grunted in pain. I slammed into Goro and twisted his arm away, but he was faster. He dropped the gun and pulled a knife from his boot. He came in with quick slashing motions and I felt a light sting on my stomach. My shirt had been opened and my skin bled a delicate line.

General Erskine pushed away the troops who had converged to shield him. Lifting a restraining palm, I said, "Please tell your men not to fire."

The next stab happened before I could finish speaking. But I was ready: I allowed the blade to enter my circle and, using my hands in a shearing move, I hit the nerves on the sides of Goro's wrist. His hand went numb and the blade fell away like a rotten twig from a tree. I kicked it out of his reach and grasped Goro's wrist, ready to break it in a *kote-gaeshi* lock. He kicked out sideways and caught me on the hip. I gritted my teeth and battened down the pain. My hands traveled up his arms like a snake after its prey on a branch and wrenched his elbow, bringing him forward to drive my knee into his face.

He broke away and punched me, catching me twice. The earth spun for a few precious seconds and I staggered drunkenly. I knew I could not afford to let him touch me again but he was relentless. Dust rose up around us as we shuffled our feet, changing stances, adjusting balance, shifting, constantly moving. Out of the corner of my eye I saw Endo-san close his eyes and realized what he was trying to impart to me.

I ceased all movement abruptly, placing myself in the spot where the sea touches the sky. I became the center. I opened up myself. Goro saw the opportunity and swung a hard unstoppable punch into my chest that would certainly have ruptured my heart. But he would never know.

When Goro punched I was already entering to his side and my

palm slammed upward into his face and broke his nose. He stumbled to his knees and I circled my arms around his neck, cutting off the flow of air. A deliberate fury overtook me, sharpening my senses, so that I could feel each frantic throb of the pulse in his neck. I wanted to tighten my hold on him, to squeeze until not even a single atom of oxygen could penetrate him. I increased the strength of the lock on his neck and his body jerked with dying spasms, his arms flailing wildly and impotently behind him.

I heard my grandfather's voice saying, as he had the last time I saw him, *Do not let hatred control your life*. But the pull of my rage was as strong as the treacherous currents of the sea, taking me out further into the deep. I began to add pressure to my grip. I decided then that Goro would die.

At that moment Endo-san spoke and his voice brought me back to the shore. "Let him go."

I released Goro and he folded like a piece of cloth to the ground, his eyes fluttering as the air rushed into the vacuum in his lungs. I breathed with difficulty, my entire body shaking, my vision askew. I felt Endo-san put his arms on my shoulders and the disjointed world focused itself again.

He was bleeding but, for a fleeting moment, his smile made him look young again. "That took too long," he said.

"I shall strive to be quicker the next time," I answered, and for those few moments we were once more merely a *sensei* and his pupil.

Chapter Nineteen

Endo-san was taken to the General Hospital where an army doctor removed the bullet from his leg. He slept deeply for the first time in a long while, assisted by ample doses of morphine. I sat by him every day and, to pass the time, I would look at the flowers in the garden of the hospital from the window. Some days it rained and my attention would be mesmerized by the droplets of water trailing down the glass panes.

One evening, when the lights on Penang Hill were beginning to show themselves, General Erskine visited us. He was a stocky man, hair cut short, his face indicative of getting his own way. I heard the creak of boots on the tiles and the guard by the door stood to attention and saluted him.

"We still can't decide whether to arrest you as well or not," he said. "We've received so many conflicting reports. Some say you aided in mass murders, others say you saved entire villages."

"When you make up your mind, I'll be here. I won't be going anywhere," I said in a tired voice. I was uncertain what to feel. The years Endo-san and I had shared seemed like they had been a whole lifetime. I could not believe it would all be over soon.

General Erskine indicated the sleeping figure of Endo-san. "Who is he to you?"

"My teacher and my friend," I said.

"He taught you how to fight like you did at the harbor the other day?"

"Yes," I said.

"Dangerous chap. We're going to make sure he and all his men pay. A War Crimes Tribunal has been set up. He'll be charged as a war criminal," he said.

"I owe him a great deal," I said, looking out through the window as though I had not heard him, which annoyed him.

"He and his kind killed your entire family," he said, then his voice became quiet, but not soft. "I absolutely loathe them. My brother was in Changi Prison. They came up with all sorts of amusing games to torture their prisoners. Now I'm informed that you worked for them. Disgraceful."

"Will you send him back to Tokyo?" I asked.

General Erskine shook his head. "He's not too important in the scheme of things. The tribunal will be convened here."

"Who will be in charge of it? You?"

He nodded with satisfaction. When I looked into his eyes I knew what the outcome would be.

I unlocked the door and let myself into the offices of Hutton & Sons. The damage suffered in the bombings had not been repaired and the entire place had been vandalized by the Japanese staff— chairs broken, paintings slashed. Filing cabinets lay overturned, spilling paper onto the floor. I entered the room where my father had always sat, which was now mine. I found comfort in the little things he had left behind that had not been stolen or destroyed: his letter opener, the spare Trinity College tie he kept in his drawer, the notebook in which he had scribbled down his ideas. I removed all signs of the Japanese administrator and tidied the room as best I could.

The bell rang and I went downstairs and opened the door. A young girl stood on the steps, pale and uncertain. She gathered her courage and her words and spoke in a rush. "I'm looking for work. I'm hardworking and I know how to type—a bit."

"What's your name?"

"Adele."

"Can you start now?"

She smiled with relief as I made my first decision as the owner of my father's company.

I spread the word and, gradually, the old staff returned, bringing with them relatives or friends who were also looking for employment. My past role in the war was never raised openly, but I knew the people of Penang would never forget. Some saw me as a courageous person who had resisted the Japanese as much as he could. To my surprise, I found that this view had a large element of truth to it. Others thought of me with contempt and hatred, telling people of the deaths I had caused. This too had the resounding ring of veracity and I never refuted it.

I worked myself to exhaustion, making hazardous journeys to our plantations and mines. Standing in the sandy, pitted landscape of the tin mines outside Ipoh, I realized I could not fully regenerate my business yet. There was another storm coming. And so when the Communist terrorists started their guerrilla war against the British government we were not unduly affected. We had enough to keep the business afloat, but not so much as to suffer great losses whenever the Communists attacked our mines and rubber plantations. I recalled Kon warning me that these terrorists, who during the war had been allies of the British, would eventually seek the death of every Englishman in Malaya. It was also ironic that the terrorists now adopted the term "running dogs" to refer to the local inhabitants who refused to aid them, who chose instead to assist the British.

I missed Kon. One evening after work I made a visit to his home. I knocked at the gates but no one came to open the doors. I climbed up the outer wall and sat on the top, looking down at my friend's home. It was empty, no lights shone and the great lanterns remained unlit, even though twilight had come. Towkay Yeap had disappeared. I sat on the high walls until the streetlights came on and cast my shadow into the neglected garden, onto the pure white orchids of Towkay Yeap. I took one last look and then jumped down onto the road and made my way home.

I had visited Endo-san regularly over the previous weeks. He was still detained in the General Hospital although his leg was healing well. He continued to bear himself with great dignity. Sometimes we would talk as I wheeled him around the gardens, and sometimes we sat in stillness, watching the movement of the world, listening to the unspoken words between us and finding comfort in them.

One evening he said, "I promised you once that I would tell you everything, why I did all those things."

I held my fingers to my lips and let him know there was no need. "I understand now why you had to work for your country," I said. "You did it because of your father, and your family. Because you loved them."

"As did you," he said.

"It doesn't make it easier."

"No, it does not. But still the attempt must be made."

"Yes. There is no other way. There never has been."

"Are you still practicing?"

"No," I said.

"You must not be lazy."

"I'm waiting to train with you again."

"Then you had better maintain your standards and not waste my time."

He asked me to wheel him to a grove of hibiscus trees. "It is good to be outside, even in this weather," he said. "I could never stay cooped up within walls. You understand that?"

I placed my hand on his shoulder. It seemed a long, long while before I could speak again.

"Yes, I understand," I finally said, wiping a drop of rain from my eye.

"Good. Now, while we are out here every day your lessons shall continue. Go through your footwork exercises and show me how far you have deteriorated."

On the day of Endo-san's judgement I made a ritual of putting on my clothes, feeling the quietness of the house as I left. I drove slowly in the cool dawn, enjoying the light fragrant smell of the dew on the trees that grew along the Tanjung Bungah Road. I parked behind Hutton & Sons and walked to the Esplanade, sitting on the stone breakwater, my legs dangling over the rocks and the sea. Fat, gray pigeons waddled up and down the pavements, pecking for food. Some stalked up to me and when I waved my hands at them they hopped away on a clatter of wings as if affronted by my rudeness.

Just before the clock struck I walked to the courthouse. Although the War Crimes Tribunal was headed by the military, General Erskine had decided to hold the hearing in the High Court building, probably to give a cloak of justice to the proceedings.

A crowd of people had already gathered and they became silent as I passed them. From the first day of the hearing the court clerk had, for a discreet payment, kept me a seat near the front. There I sat, conscious of the eyes upon me. I had no doubt that Endo-san would be found guilty, for there had been no lack of witnesses; even my own testimony had been torn apart and I had been left looking like a war criminal myself.

The crowd in the public gallery wanted to taste blood and they jeered as Endo-san was brought in. At a quarter past nine, led by General Erskine, the members of the Tribunal appeared and the spectators were silenced.

I could only see the back of Endo-san's head as General Erskine read out the judgement. Endo-san was found guilty of the massacre of civilians and soldiers during the course of the war and was sentenced to imprisonment for the rest of his life. He would never see Japan again.

The crowd burst into cheers, shouting and stamping as Endo-san was led out. Our eyes met, and I nodded. I was soon forgotten as the crowd left the building. I sat alone, until the court clerk informed me in soft whispers that he was sorry, but he had to lock up the courtroom.

Three days later I found General Erskine waiting for me at Istana, sitting on my rattan chair on the patio, his jaw tight with anger. Out of the corner of my eye I noted his men moving through the grounds and the house.

"What are you doing in my house?" I asked.

"Where is Mr. Endo?"

"I suppose he is no longer in your custody, if you are asking me that," I said.

"He escaped while being escorted from the hospital to the jail. Knocked five of my guards unconscious. It seems likely that he would come to you for shelter."

"No, he hasn't come to me."

"Where did he stay during the war?"

"At the Japanese consulate," I said, certain that he was unaware of Endo-san's island.

He removed a creased photograph from his wallet and showed it to me. It was an aerial shot of Istana and there, prominent and visible on the roof, were the stripes of the Union Jack I had painted.

"I couldn't believe my eyes when I saw that on your roof today. A pilot who flew one of the Halifaxes took this. He's made a barrow-load of money selling it to every British soldier out in the East. They say it reminds them of what they've been fighting for. It probably saved your house from being bombed." The general shook his head in wonder. "Strange, sometimes, what wonderful things can emerge from a war like this."

"Yes, strange things we have seen," I said, my mind on Endo-san.

"Did you paint it?" General Erskine asked.

I brought my attention back to him and nodded.

"Must've been bloody dangerous to climb up there. What possessed you?"

I thought for a moment of those last days of the war. "It was a tribute to my father." As I spoke I felt that, somewhere, my father had heard and that he was smiling at me.

Chapter Twenty

Michiko's condition was deteriorating and, although she attempted to conceal it from me, I knew. I heard her pain in the quiet of the night when she thought I was asleep. As I sat up in my bed, a memory of the time when my mother lay suffering returned and I saw what was required of me. This time I did not run away and hide.

I went into Michiko's room and sat next to her bed. There would be no sleep for us tonight.

"Where were you when the bomb fell?" I asked, taking her hand in mine. It was clammy and rigid with pain and I stroked it gently as I spoke.

"Far enough away not to die immediately. But now I think, not far enough," she said, allowing me to assist her into a sitting position against the headboard. "I thought I had escaped the worst of it, but my doctors have told me that they have seen cases like mine. The body only shows the damage when it wants to, even if it is years later. At least, that was their conclusion, since they could find no other reason."

"And your family?"

She closed her eyes and wiped her mouth with a silk handkerchief. "I lost everyone of my family. My brothers and sisters, my father and my mother. Endo-san's family and everyone who had stayed in Toriijima were all killed."

"I'm sorry."

"So am I. I did not love Tanaka-san, yet I used his feelings for me and asked him to follow Endo-san here. And now you have told me that I caused his death."

"He would have died as a soldier in the war or when your village was destroyed," I said.

She shook her head. "I was selfish."

I handed her the pills that she continued to take out of habit, even though they had long ceased to make a difference.

"I blamed Endo-san for agreeing to work for the government in exchange for his father's freedom. After the war I waited for him to come home. But he never did, and no one ever knew what had happened to him. But I never stopped thinking of him." She winced with pain.

"He only did what duty demanded," I said, holding her hand more tightly. "He tried to bring a sense of harmony to all the conflicting elements of his life."

I could not bear to see her suffering. And I felt a selfish fear that I would not be able to tell her everything. I had waited so long for all of it to come out: the guilt, the regrets, the darkness that had filled my days for such an eternity. There was nobody else I could ever have spoken to about the mistakes of my life and to have found her, someone who had known and even loved Endo-san, was something I had never dared or hoped to ask for.

"I do not have much time left to me," she said.

"We will go to Endo-san's island when morning comes," I said to give her something to focus on, to look forward to. My initial reluctance to show her Endo-san's island was gone, now that I had come to know her better. It would be cruel not to take her there.

"Yes," she said. "I want so much to see it." She coughed and then said, "May I live there, until . . ."

"Of course," I said quickly, not wanting her to finish what she was trying to say.

"Are we going in your little boat?" she asked. "I would like that very much."

I shook my head, and told her about my boat, the boat that had taken me so many times across the sea to Endo-san's island. The wood was rotten and falling to pieces and it had sprung an irreparable leak. The last time I would ever use it, I took it out to sea at sunrise. I rowed to a position just off Endo-san's island and waited with it as it slowly filled with water, stroking its peeling sides and cracked wood, talking softly to it. The sea came in with respect, a little at a time, and I felt the water rise up my feet, then my shins, and then my knees. All the while I watched the light of a new day touch the trees of the island, until a strong wave came, leaving me to float on the surface. I held my breath in the water and watched as the boat of my childhood dropped soundlessly away, raising silent clouds of sand when it hit the bottom of the sea. Like the lonely casuarina tree it was as old as I, and I never regretted not giving it a name. It had been my boat, and that was enough for me.

There was nothing much to pack. She had left all her clothes in her valises and Maria helped me carry them. I held Michiko's arm as we made our way carefully down the steps to the boathouse. She was dressed warmly. A storm had come in the early hours before dawn and the air was still cold. We had sat watching the lightning from her room, wondering what the day would bring.

The journey across to Endo-san's island, which I had made so often and so easily in my youth, tired me now. "It seems such a distance away," she spoke, shading her eyes with her hand.

"We will be there soon. These old bones of mine are making the trip seem long, that's all."

"I am glad I came here, and I am glad I met you. Thank you, for last night."

I grunted as drops of perspiration stung my eyes. She reached across and dabbed them away with the edge of her sleeve. We passed the rocks that had once appeared so much like a row of rotting teeth to me but which I discovered later on in my life looked beautiful, like ancient markers warning people to stay away from the place they guarded.

I pulled the boat high above the waterline and helped her step out. Her eyes went immediately to the landmarks I had described. "Here is the rock where you wrote your name!" she said, running her fingers over my scratching. "It is real," she whispered, wonder in her voice. "It is all real."

I led her into the bamboo trees. The gardeners of Istana had done their weekly duties and the place was well kept and lush. We came to the house and she let out a soft cry. "It looks exactly like the guest cottage on his father's estate," she said. She stopped to take in the house. "You have taken care of it well."

I helped her into the house. I had left everything almost as it had been. The old and torn tatami mats had been replaced, but Endo-san's ink drawing of Daruma, the monk with the lidless eyes, hung in the same alcove as it had when Endo-san was alive.

I found a futon mattress in a cupboard and unrolled it for Michiko to lie on. Her breathing was worse and I tried not to show my worry.

"Are you all right?" she asked.

"I am afraid," I said. It had been so long since I felt such intense emotion that I stopped to consider it, to *feel* it. "I'm frightened to tell you the rest of what happened. I want, I need to tell you, yet I am so afraid."

She saw my bewilderment and the tender compassion in her expression made me believe what she said next. "I am not here to judge you. I am not here to condemn you, or to forgive you. I have no such right. No one has."

It was now her turn to hold my hand. "I am here because I once loved a man, and I never stopped loving him, that is all," she said.

She squeezed my hand harder and a smile appeared on her face, and I knew I need have no fear. She alone, of all the people in the world, would understand.

"Tell me," she said.

Chapter Twenty-One

The monsoon returned like a family guest, to be tolerated by some, hated by others, loved by one or two, and the brilliant sunshine of our days became a clouded memory again as fleets of storm clouds sailed in and anchored themselves in the sky.

I ran on the beach before sunrise every day, through the morning drizzle, always keenly aware of the island on the edge of my vision. Once I saw a small sampan heading for it and my heart quickened. But as it broke though the veil of rain I saw it was only a fisherman braving the choppy waters, his cormorant sitting on the prow. He waved to me and I returned his greeting, wishing him a good catch.

It was less than a week since General Erskine's visit and Endo-san still had not been found. I was not unduly worried: Endo-san was capable of taking care of himself, and would probably have a safe place in which to shelter. I would wait for him, however long it took.

"May I speak to the master of the house?"

I gave a tiny start. It was already dusk and a soft rain was falling. I was sitting on the terrace beneath an umbrella, holding the letter informing me of Edward's death four months earlier, and staring at the sky, looking at the overburdened clouds that were trying to bend the line of the horizon. The words, although spoken softly, jolted me out of my thoughts.

I placed the letter on the table and looked up to see Endo-san.

So time—mischievous time, cruel time, forgiving time—plays tricks on us again and again.

"I would like to borrow a boat from you," he said.

He held out his hand and I reached across the table, reached across time, and gripped it as hard as I could. He pulled me to him and embraced me. Then he stood back a little and reached out to touch the top of my head.

420

"You have grown so much since the day I first saw you," he said. "You looked so sad, that day, sitting here, unmoving, your eyes on the sea."

"You were right, you know, when you told me we would have to endure terrible things," I said. "There were times during those years I hated you and could have killed you. I had to remind myself of my true path. Some days I failed. I failed everyone."

He could not argue with the truth of what I said and so he merely asked, "What are you going to do now?"

I shook my head. "I'm not certain. I suppose I'll rebuild the company, rebuild my life." I paused, then I said, "It all depends on you."

"I cannot be with you now. This is where we set out on different roads."

"I can walk the same road as you."

He shook his head. "That would be to delay our fates." He turned to me and held my hands, his eyes studying my fingers, my palms. "We must achieve harmony now, find an equilibrium, so that the next time I see you, the sand will have been wiped smooth. And then we can walk, on and on, toward the horizon of an endless beach."

It was difficult to accept his point, yet somehow it was as clear as a bird in the sky to me.

The clouds had moved away and we went out through the garden of statues. At my father's grave, Endo-san bowed, his heart speaking words I could hear so clearly, resonating like echoes across a canyon.

We took shelter under the casuarina tree, the lonely tree that still looked so steadfastly toward Endo-san's island. Water dripped down on us, carrying with it the essence of the leaves.

"You have the most beautiful home in the world," he said.

I was breathing heavily, my breath choppy as the wind-tousled sea.

"Are you ready to go?" he asked.

I gripped the wet bark of the tree as though trying to cling to it, to fasten myself to its unmoving presence so that I did not have to take another step. But I saw the pain in Endo-san's expression and I could not deny him his wish.

There was nothing to pack except my white *gi* and black

hakama—both had been gifts from Endo-san. I rowed once more across the water, and he sat facing me, facing his island, his expression unchanging as the boat navigated the confluence of currents that ran hidden beneath us. And I felt, too, the confluence of time. The oars vibrated and seemed to sing with each pull and dip. I saw, from a great height above, our little vessel, two figures in it that I knew were us. We looked so small as the boat stitched the fabric of the sea like a needle, leaving a flowing white thread behind. And I saw the green island in the immense sea, the borders of the sea curling with a lining of light, like a vast piece of rice paper, its edges alive with weals of red embers, ready to burst into flame.

From the sky I fell back into myself in the boat. I felt the spray as the swells rose up like hands to push us back. Still he looked to the open sea, his eyes open but unseeing.

Silence closed in from the edges of the sky; the wind became a memory and the persistent swells melted into flatness. But I continued to row; there was no drag as we moved closer and closer to the island. We left no wake, no curls of water spreading out in a silky *V* as the boat slid forward. The confluence of time shifted and entwined, merged and diverged, but did not separate. I knew Endo-san and I were partially responsible for this psychic tear.

Then I heard a wave spread itself out on the sand in the immense cathedral silence and time resumed again. We had rowed past the line of protruding rocks and were now being gently pushed in by the waves. The boat slid into the sand with a rasp, like a knife cutting into soapstone. I got out and pulled it high up on the beach. Endo-san stepped out onto the soft sand.

We walked up the little pebbled path that wound around the grove of bamboo. Birds sang in the chorus of the leaves. He stopped. "Listen to that," he said softly. "How I have missed them!"

I wanted to ask him what had happened on the boat, that inexplicable silence, and how he had managed it. He raised his fingers and stopped me before I could say a word. "I do not know," he said. "Accept that there are things in this world we can never explain and life will be understandable. That is the irony of life. It is also the beauty of it."

We approached his house and again I admired its simple elegance. Endo-san had once told me that it had been built like an *aikijutsu* movement, and only now could I truly understand what he had meant. A strong base, effective, lyrical, in total harmony with the world.

We slid open the door, exposing the musty smells and dampness within. A light layer of dust lay on every surface. I was relieved that General Erskine and his men had not discovered the place. Endo-san moved to the alcove, knelt, and bowed to it. Reverently he opened his hands as though in supplication and gently lifted my Nagamitsu sword from its cradle. It was the only weapon there and I wondered what he had done with his own.

He opened the *katana* a notch and I thought I heard a sigh, an exhalation of breath coming from it. Even in the dimness of the house it seemed to snatch a sliver of sunlight from outside and throw it into the room, lighting it with disdain. He sheathed it and placed it on the mat before me.

We changed into our cotton *gi* and black *hakama* and we went through the ritual of tying the cords around our waists, each stroke, each insertion and pull and knot signifying the movements of the universe. The back piece of the *hakama* pushed into the small of my back, forcing me to stand up straight.

I picked up my sword, my Nagamitsu sword, brother to Endo-san's, crafted by the same swordsmith. It had a comforting weight. I slid the blade open an inch, as Endo-san had done. There was now a point of light in the shadowed room, the sole star in a universe of darkness. I pushed the sword back into its scabbard and it went in without a sound.

We went out into the sandy enclosure where my physical lessons had always been conducted, the lessons that had given me so much, but had demanded so much more in payment. As my bare feet touched the cool, damp sand, the memory of those lost days surrounded me and the enormity of what I had to do hit me like a blow.

"I cannot do this," I said.

He lost his temper. "Do not be a child! You ceased to be one the day you became my pupil." A sigh leaked out from him, tired and despairing. "If you fail to complete what is necessary, we shall have to go through all the pain and suffering again. You will have failed me." He knelt on the sand and, for the first time since I had known him, he appeared defeated.

I held the sword in my hand and stood there without moving for a long time. I remembered that day on the ledge up on Penang Hill, and I had to accept that he was correct, finally, at this point. I had to extend my trust in him another step forward, into another life.

I went into the house and came out with a towel. I knelt before him and gently cleaned his face; he sat there, turning his face this way and that to facilitate me. The sun had found a hole in the clouds and the sand gleamed brightly, white as angel bones.

He lifted a fistful of sand and let the breeze carry it away. "*Shirasu*," he whispered, as though giving voice to the slipstream of escaping sand.

When I had finished he reached out and touched my face.

"So much to tell you," I began to say, but he silenced me.

"Do you think we still need words, after all this time?" he asked.

I shook my head. He pulled me to him and held me tightly. Then he kissed my cheek, his hand stroking my head. I wanted to capture every element of him, every scent, every feel. And I tried to, but it was so hard. I infused my lungs with his smell, trying to lock it there. I opened every nerve in me to feel him, to imprint the sensations within me forever. But of course it was futile.

He pushed me away gently as I struggled to hold on to him. "Let go," he said. "Let me go."

I knew he was right, so I released him. I picked up my sword and went into the ancient *happo* stance. He closed his eyes and said into the wind,

"Friends part forever
Wild geese lost in clouds."

My hands stopped trembling and I felt him steadying me, guiding me. The purest, clearest emotion I would ever experience filled me. A golden light sang within me and I felt it all the way to the tip of the sword. I closed my eyes and absorbed the beauty of the moment. Then I opened them again, saw his gentle smile and met his eyes for the last time.

Endo-san was right. In the end, we fellow travelers across the continent of time, across the landscape of memory, we did not need words.

Chapter Twenty-Two

It was done, this tale of mine. I stood up heavily. I was sore: my body, my bones, my heart.

"You did not fail him," Michiko said. Tears glazed her cheeks.

I could not find the answer to that. As I wiped my sword clean, sheathed it, and knelt beside his body, I felt very certain that I had not disappointed Endo-san. After all, I had risen to the occasion, as he had demanded, as he had prepared me to. Yet as the years passed, a sense of failure had gradually corroded that feeling of certainty.

"Will you do the same for me?" she asked when I did not speak.

I had not anticipated that, and I moved away from her, pretending to polish my empty cup with a cloth. "I will not."

She was surprised. "Why?"

I was suddenly angry with her for placing me in a quandary. "Has my telling you of Endo-san's life not indicated anything to you?"

"It has shown me that you are willing to perform the ultimate duty for a friend, for someone who holds your highest affections."

I shook my head. "I would never again do what was asked of me. Not a day goes by when I do not in some way regret my actions."

"You had no choice. It was all determined a long time ago. Accept that. Endo-san did. So did your grandfather."

"I cannot accept it. It is too easy. We all have the power to choose. I made a series of wrong choices and it all culminated here, on this island, with Endo-san kneeling before me."

"You had two roads to walk on and they had been created before you set foot on them. Does not the Christian God say, *There is none like me, declaring the end from the beginning, and from ancient times the things that are not yet done?*"

"Never heard of it," I said.

425

"Isaiah, Chapter Forty-six, verse Ten," she replied, quick and sure. "It goes on: *My counsel shall stand, and I will do all my pleasure . . . I have spoken it, I will also bring it to pass; I have purposed it, I will also do it.*"

I went to a chest carved from Paulownia wood and opened its lid. I lifted out a bundle wrapped in cloth and untied the cords around it. My own Nagamitsu sword lay inside, snug as though it had been sleeping all this time. It appeared as priceless as it actually was. I brought it to Michiko and knelt before her.

"I have not used this since that day," I said. "And yet every day I'm aware of its presence. There were some days when I wanted so badly to row out to sea and drop it into the depths."

"Why have you held on to it then?"

"Because I was frightened," I said, and stopped. I forced myself to continue. "What if I forgot him, forgot everything that had happened?" I felt I was not explaining myself with sufficient clarity and I clenched my fist in frustration.

She nodded her head gently and I saw that she understood what I was trying to say. "You will not forget. He gave you the greatest gift he could. He taught you everything he knew and it has kept you strong and safe and unafraid all your life. All your life," her voice became firmer, emphasizing the words.

I stroked the hilt of the sword, absorbing what she was telling me.

"Remember what he said when he first showed you how to do an *ukemi*?" she continued. "He said that if he failed you, then at the very least you would be in a position to protect yourself, to fall safely and to stand up again."

In spite of the circumstances I was impressed with the strength of her memory. She seemed to be able to recall everything I had told her.

"That is his legacy to you. Not your guilt and pain and sorrow," she said and I knew that she was telling me the truth. I had not seen it all this time, but now my eyes were open again.

She took my hands in hers. "Do you not recall what you told your sister? The mind forgets, but the heart will always remember. And what is the heart's memory but love itself?"

At first I did not know what it was, this flow of damp heat that seethed in my eyes yet cooled the skin around them. And when I

426

realized it was tears, a lifetime of habit and discipline made me attempt to stop them, to hold them on the rim of my eyes and refuse them release.

Michiko saw my struggle and with both her hands reached out for my face. Using her thumbs she ruptured the trembling skin of my tears and I welcomed them. Finally, they came.

I made no sound, but stood there like a statue in Istana's garden, feeling the accumulation of grief flow out of me, accompanied by a rush of images that could have been forgotten memories or remembered dreams. I felt myself lifting up, on the arches of my feet, then on my toes. Michiko reached up from where she lay on her mattress and grasped my hand.

I was wrong; the burden could be lightened, the weight could be lessened. I closed my eyes once, for a long time, knowing the tears would never return.

She made herself stand up with some difficulty. She had been— and still was—a woman of great beauty, but illness had imprinted its mark upon her. Hard as she had tried to fight it, I could feel her weariness of the battle.

She brought out Endo-san's own katana and set it next to mine. "These should always remain together." She managed a rueful smile. "It is their fate."

She was right. I saw now what I had been waiting for, the true reason why I had kept my own sword all these years. I pushed them closer together, almost touching: Cloud and Illumination, shadow and light.

She placed Endo-san's letter, the letter that had brought her to me, on the tatami mat. "You have not read this."

My eyes stayed on it for a long time, until the weave of the tatami began to move like waves in my unblinking vision. I looked away and said finally, "I do not think I wish to now. I think it is time I let him go."

I helped Michiko to the door and she leaned against its frame. I pointed out to her the ground beneath the tree where I had buried Endo-san. "I left no marker, no gravestone. Once I am gone no one will ever know where he lies."

She turned her attention to the unmarked grave and, for a moment, swift as a stone skipping across the smooth surface of a lake before it sank, I saw the memory of her love for Endo-san.

I held her as she wept. We felt Endo-san's presence, felt his arms encircle us, and for the first time since the end of the war, half a century before, I knew we were all finally at peace. Nothing could harm us now.

Chapter Twenty-Three

I accepted the Penang Historical Society's invitation to attend the party for the fiftieth anniversary of the end of the Japanese Occupation, to be held at the residence of the governor of Penang. Since Independence in 1957 a succession of Malay and Chinese appointees has held the post. The days of the British live now only in fond memories.

A few days before the event, the secretary of the society called me and asked if I could donate a souvenir from the war and I replied that I would see if I could oblige her.

I informed Adele and the staff of Hutton & Sons that I had found a suitable buyer for my family's company and that their positions would remain secure, as one of the expressed conditions of the terms of sale. Ronald Cross, who now ran Empire Trading, having returned from Australia after the war to succeed Henry Cross, was keen to expand his family business for his grandchildren. I was certain that Ronald, having lived in Penang all his life, would honor the memory of all the Huttons who had been linked to my great-grandfather's dream.

After my announcement Adele came into my office and embraced me. "I'm going to miss you terribly," she said.

"You should retire," I said. She was not much younger than me, I recalled.

"And do what? Sit at home and take care of my grandchildren?" She shuddered at the thought and I laughed.

"It'll take months to finalize the sale. I'll still be in Penang, you know that. I'll never leave," I said. "You can come and visit me any time at Istana."

She pulled back from me. "In all these years, this is the first time you've asked me to come to your house."

"I should have done it a long time ago," I said.

*

Everyone who had fought in the war, those who still lived, came to the anniversary party. It was a strange crowd, mostly of very old people meeting their friends again, knowing it might be for the last time. And so, when they spoke fondly of the antics and quirks of dead friends and lost lovers, the voices were louder, the laughter richer, and the tears heavier yet gladder than in previous years. I walked around the glass cases exhibiting my father's collection of *keris*, which I had donated to the Penang Historical Society in his name. There was also an exhibition of memorabilia and documents relating to the war and I came to a frame where a faded photograph caught my attention.

It showed a young European man—not much more than a boy, I thought—standing in a row of stern-faced Japanese officials, watching as the Japanese flag was raised. He appeared lost, out of place among that crowd, but there was a strong and determined expression on his face. It took me a few seconds to come to the realization that I was that young man. I searched for Endo-san but he had been cropped out of the photograph a long time ago.

The president of the Penang Historical Society, in his rather lengthy speech thanked Mr. Philip Arminius Khoo-Hutton for his efforts in protecting the heritage of Penang and for his generosity in donating a pair of invaluable weapons to the society. It was the first time ever that I had requested the use of my full name and I experienced a moment of wonder, almost turning to see who was being spoken of, before I walked to the podium and handed the Nagamitsu swords to the president. They appeared almost unremarkable under the spotlights. Flashbulbs went off and as I let the swords go I said a silent farewell to them.

When I arrived home I did not go to bed but went and stood by my lonely casuarina tree. I took out my grandfather's jade pin, which I had worn from the moment he gave it to me. It felt cool and weightless, nestled there in the cryptic creases of my palm, and I thought of my life, of everything that had happened and everyone I had known.

There had been many at the party tonight who still considered me a friend of the Japanese in the war, as many as those who knew of the innumerable lives I had helped save. But in the end, did all of that matter? All those people would soon, like me, be ground into the ashes of memory, to rise into the sky and leave the world.

The fortune-teller, long since dead, had said I was born with the gift of rain. I know now what she meant. Her words had not been a curse; nor had they been words of blessing. Like the rain, I had brought tragedy into many people's lives but, more often than not, rain also brings relief, clarity, and renewal. It washes away our pain and prepares us for another day, and even another life. Now that I am old I find that the rains follow me and give me comfort, like the spirits of all the people I have ever known and loved.

When I had heard my name—my complete, dear name, given to me by both my parents and by my grandfather—used for the first time earlier this evening, I experienced a feeling of integration and fulfillment that had eluded me for all of my life. With the delicacy of a butterfly entering the reveries of the venerable Chinese philosopher, as though alighting on the most fragile of petals, that feeling sought and found a permanent abode within me and stilled forever the empty echoes of my dreaming heart.

The night was so full of stars and the sea so dark, I could not tell where the ocean clasped the sky. Endo-san's island looked so peaceful, waiting for me as it had been doing even before the day I was born. I knew the time had come for me to spend the rest of my days there. I looked forward to it.

I would like to borrow a boat from you.

I thought again of the first moment we had met in this world. I could not blame him for coming into my life. And I could not blame him for leaving it, leaving me on my own to face the consequences of my choices and my actions in the war.

My grandfather had tried to show me the truth of this when he told me the story of the forgotten emperor: even with all the warnings we had, still our lives followed the direction that had already been inscribed and nothing could have changed it.

Since Michiko's death, I have thought over my grandfather's words and I have come to the conclusion that he was not entirely correct when it comes to the inevitability of a person's destiny. While I now accept that the course of our lives has been set down long before our births, I feel that the inscriptions that dictate the directions of our lives merely write out what is already in our hearts; they can do nothing more. And we, Endo-san, Tanaka, Michiko, Kon, myself, and all the lost members of my family, we were beings capable mainly of love and memory. These capabilities are the greatest gifts given to us, and we can do nothing else but live out the remembered desires and memories of our hearts.

And that is the point of life itself, I whisper into the night, hoping my grandfather has heard me.

A breath of wind brings the scent of the fragrant tree to me and, as I curl my fingers gently around my grandfather's pin, a growing lightness lifts my heart to a place it has never been before. I know this feeling will never leave me again.

Author's Note

All characters who play active roles in the novel are fictional and bear no resemblance to any person living or dead.

All military and government personnel depicted in the story are fictional, with the exceptions of Admiral Sir Tom Phillips, General Yamashita Tomoyuki, General Arthur Percival, and Sir Francis Light, founder of Penang, who are mentioned as part of the historical background.

Historians however will quickly recognize that I have taken certain liberties with events. There was, for example, no ceremony on the surrender of the island of Penang to the Imperial Japanese Army and the occasion depicted herein is based on the actual surrender in Singapore.

Also, while the Emperor Kuang Hsu and the Dowager Empress Tzu Xsi were actual historical figures, the "Forgotten Emperor," Wen Zu, is entirely my own invention. The reform movement under the Ching Dynasty occurred only once, in 1898, and my description of its recurrence in a weakened form eight years later is merely dramatic license.

Morihei Ueshiba was the founder of modern-day Ueshiba-ryu aikido. But I should make it clear that the consequences of the use of his techniques in this story in no way reflect his philosophy.

La Maison Bleu, Cheong Fatt Tze's mansion where Philip's parents met, still stands. I urge all visitors to Penang to go and see it and to admire the impressive work of restoration that has been done.

Acknowledgments

My grateful thanks to my agent, Jane Gregory, and to Mary Sandys and Broo Doherty for their unwavering faith and support.

I would also like to thank the following people for their kindness, hospitality, and friendship: Professor Jan Botha, Louise Botha, Mr. Justice Edwin Cameron, Natie and Sonya Ress, Ian Hamilton, Wade van der Merwe, Professor Dr. A. Archer, Paul van Herreweghe, Professor John McRae, Ferdi and Elsa van Gass, Coba Diederiks, Dawid Klopper, and Teo Bong Kwang.

Tan Twan Eng was born in Penang and lived in various regions of Malaysia as a child. He studied law at the University of London, and later worked as an advocate and solicitor in one of Kuala Lumpur's most respected law firms. He divides his time between Kuala Lumpur and Cape Town and has a first-dan ranking in aikido.